G000099278

Confessions of a Dutch Reading Club

Confessions of a Dutch Reading Club

Patricia van Stratum

Copyright © 2011 Patricia van Stratum

The moral right of the author has been asserted.

Apart from any fair dealing for the purposes of research or private study,
or criticism or review, as permitted under the Copyright, Designs and Patents
Act 1988, this publication may only be reproduced, stored or transmitted, in
any form or by any means, with the prior permission in writing of the
publishers, or in the case of reprographic reproduction in accordance with
the terms of licences issued by the Copyright Licensing Agency. Enquiries
concerning reproduction outside those terms should be sent to the publishers.

Matador
5 Weir Road
Kibworth Beauchamp
Leicester LE8 0LQ, UK
Tel: (+44) 116 279 2299
Fax: (+44) 116 279 2277
Email: books@troubador.co.uk
Web: www.troubador.co.uk/matador

ISBN 978 1848765 290

British Library Cataloguing in Publication Data.
A catalogue record for this book is available from the British Library.

Typeset in 10.5pt Book Antiqua by Troubador Publishing Ltd, Leicester, UK

Matador is an imprint of Troubador Publishing Ltd

Printed in Great Britain by the MPG Books Group, Bodmin and King's Lynn

For

Dr. Jean Casper Maria van Stratum,

Anna, Tom, Max, Tim, Jess,

the maker of the coat of many colours and the utopian socialist

CHARACTERS

The members of the Dutch Reading Club

Dr. Titus Dekker	General Practitioner
Joost Kuijpers	Artist
Huub Schevers	Antiques shop owner
Paul Bazelman	Civil servant, Ministry of Education
Hans van den Elsen	Business consultant
Bert de Lange	Wine and spirits shop owner
Piet van Rijn	Manager of the *Kringloopwinkel*
Milo Jansen	Community worker and musician

Others

Father Dr. Antonius van Aken	Author of the book 'Priests Dying'
Dr. Thomas van Aken	Editor
Bob van Dillen	Taxi driver
Mrs. Mieke van Dillen	Wife of the taxi driver
Mrs. Dekker	Wife of Titus Dekker
Mrs. Venus Bazelman	Wife of Paul Bazelman
Mrs. Cia van den Elsen	Wife of Hans van den Elsen

Prologue

Somewhere in the middle of perhaps the flattest country in the world, tucked up against the side of a wide river, is a small prosperous town. In medieval times, it was a well-fortified city with a double moat and a defensive wall; some parts of which remain, together with examples of fine buildings dating from the sixteenth century. Beyond these old boundaries are more recent developments: new houses and numerous businesses. In the surrounding countryside there are vast areas of greenhouses specialising in flower and fruit growing; many sheds for cultivating mushrooms and acres and acres of miniature high-yielding apple trees. This is not a poor town in terms of wealth or culture. It has a thriving theatre, a large library, a well-used book shop, a number of good quality restaurants, a café with a spacious terrace, several antiques shops; in addition a small marina, some good hotels, a once Catholic but now Protestant Cathedral, a museum with an onion tower, a railway station, a busy taxi company, a number of art galleries – and its own occasional unpredictable distinctive smell, which can sometimes spoil the impression of this otherwise pleasant and respectable place, in the heart of The Netherlands.

Once a month, the town's Reading Club meets to discuss a book; usually a novel suggested by one of its eight male members. This is the story of how the club prepared for and celebrated its tenth anniversary.

CHAPTER 1

The Taxi Driver

The humidity inside the bathroom was often high, causing condensation to make crazy the back of the mirror and distort reflections. Unless the window was ajar, water vapour turned into droplets which beaded the slightly rusting window frame and made frosty the ten bottles of men's toiletries and the single jar of hand cream. And on very cold days, tell-tale puddles formed beneath the underbelly of the bath. Today it had been raining and now there was an east wind. The taxi driver, having just showered, was pristine pink, but in a fog of steam. He opened the window and immediately the unpleasant town aroma entered his not-big-enough bathroom and went up his nose. He had heard various explanations for what seemed to him like a concoction of horse manure, wine vinegar and infant vomit. Was this unpleasant air made by the local farmers illegally spraying their fields with liquid fertilizers? Was it from the pollution which emanated from German factories and floated down the nearby river, or the stench of some dubious growing medium used in the darkened mushroom sheds? Was it, perhaps, the pong from the animal feed factory behind the Jaguar car

1

showrooms or simply a by-product from the sewage works in the east of the town? An estate agent told the taxi driver that no-one ever bought a property in town on a 'bad odour' day. He did not know which story to believe.

Wrapped in a too-tight towelling robe, the taxi driver walked into the narrow kitchen-dining-living space where his wife was sitting with her feet up on a stool, rubbing hand cream into her legs. He wanted to quiz her again about that smell.

'What do you think it is?'

'A mixture of human smells,' she replied.

'Humans don't smell like that.' He looked annoyed.

'Some of the members of your Reading Club do.'

'Don't be so silly. And they're not my Reading Club. I'm not a member, not yet.'

'You want to join.'

'Yes I do. Don't make rude remarks about them.'

The taxi driver's wife stood up, placed both of her always-red hands on her hips and set her head to one side like a defiant child endeavouring to win an adult argument. 'I've worked for some of those men. Others I've come across in town. They're not quite as sweet smelling as you think.'

'What do you mean?'

His wife continued, 'Piet van Rijn smells as if he keeps a dead rat in his pocket. That Dr. Titus Dekker suffers from a foot fungus, equal to any 'baby's bottom' French cheese. '

'I've never noticed.'

'Huub Schever's house smells of hard-boiled eggs and sprouts. Paul Bazelman, that pompous teacher...'

'No, ex-teacher,' the driver interrupted, 'he works for the Ministry of Education now.'

'Alright ex-teacher – his smoking makes everything in his house stink of cigars – including that glamorous wife of his. My cousin, Bert de Lange, smells of sour wine from his shop.'

The driver grinned. 'I know you have a great sense of smell, but this is ridiculous.'

'No, they all smell,' she continued. 'Joost Kuijpers, the

miserable artist, smells of garlic and oil paint. Hans van den Elsen, that slick, so-called business consultant, he pongs – too much expensive French cologne. Even our dear friend, Milo Jansen, smells of cold wax and incense.'

The taxi driver laughed and his wife smiled.

'You think I'm joking,' she said, changing the angle of her head. 'Everyone smells, including you.' She dropped her hands from her hips, went across to her husband, and brushed away an invisible hair from his shoulder. 'I don't want you to be hurt again. They won't have you in their club. These men are not as respectable as you think.'

'It's time for me to get ready for work.'

The driver returned to the bathroom to mop his still-damp forehead. He leaned out of the window and took a deep breath of the evening air. Usually the town's pungent vapours induced in him a slight feeling of nausea. Tonight, however, he translated this sensation as a sign that the wind of fortune was gusting in his direction and, later, he would smell the sweetness of a long-awaited success. He was going to be a member of the Reading Club. In the bedroom he dressed for the evening's driving.

For several years, the taxi driver wanted to join the club.

'Why?' his wife asked, as he stood ready to leave for work

'Why do you keep asking the same question?' He sighed. 'I've told you. I'd get more enjoyment from reading.'

'Really!'

'I'd be introduced to books which I might not have discovered myself.'

'Go to the library. Ask the librarian for suggestions.'

'I'd hear different opinions.'

'OK. But you know other readers who can give you theirs. You don't have to join a club.'

'I'd enjoy meeting with an interesting group of men, each month. It would be intellectually challenging.'

'Intellectually challenging,' she repeated the words slowly.

She knew exactly what voice to use if she wanted to torment her husband.

'Don't you believe me?' he said.

'I think you're fooling yourself.'

'Stop teasing me about wanting to become a member.'

'I don't want you to be upset, if you're not accepted.'

'But I will be accepted.'

'You're putting too much importance on joining. It won't solve our problems. You'll still be a taxi driver and bankrupt businessman and I will still be a cleaner and an out-of-work shop assistant with a fine arts degree. Other people can't make you feel better.'

'When I become a member tonight, I'll feel good.'

'If you become a member.'

'Piet is arranging it all.'

'Piet! Don't rely on that man.'

'I'm quite optimistic.'

'You've more chance of becoming the Queen of the Netherlands. Tell me what's stopping you from knocking at the door of wherever the Reading Club are meeting tonight and telling them yourself that you want to join?'

'A stupid idea!'

'What are you so afraid of? These guys are not so special. I should know, I clean some of their houses. You don't even like some of them.'

'Not true. I don't like the way a few have behaved towards me, in the past,' the driver said, as he straightened his tie and smoothed down his freshly-ironed white shirt. He ran his thumbs under his wide braces, looked in the mirror and remembered the time when he had told one of the members that he had read all the books they had reviewed. He had expected an immediate invitation to join the club. Instead, the guy laughed, as if he did not believe the driver capable of appreciating the club's choice of literature.

'What happens if the library can't get you the book of the month? Do you want to buy books you don't enjoy reading? Can we afford that?' his wife said.

'I'm not worried about the books; I can always borrow them from Piet, as I do now.'

The driver thought for a moment about Piet – likeable although somewhat unreliable Piet – who was his envoy at the Reading Club tonight. He was relying on Piet for his membership. Maybe this time he will be more successful. Last year he failed in his attempt to get the driver into the club. Tonight Piet will be reading out a book review written by the driver. Hopefully, the members will appreciate it and agree that he is an intelligent reader capable of making an invaluable contribution, and want him to join immediately. Perhaps they will install him in the Reading Club this evening.

His wife continued, 'What happens when it's your turn to entertain the Reading Club in our flat? We don't have room for eight men; there will be nine if you join.'

'No problem!'

'I work for some of those men, vacuum their carpets, dust their shelves and clean their lavatories. There are several I don't like very much. I don't want them coming into our lives; seeing how we live in only three rooms.'

'Piet said, there are several members who don't have space in their homes to invite the club. No-one seems to mind very much.'

'Piet, Piet, Piet! Don't trust him. He'll let you down, I know he will.'

The taxi driver's wife adjusted the back of her husband's jacket. She ran her hand over the material – that expensive material. Her hand lingered in the small of his back. This suit had cost almost a month's wages. Since he had gained a few extra kilos, his jacket sometimes did not hang well. She smelt his freshly-showered body and patted his shoulder.

'Why do you persist, when you've been turned down in the past?' she said quietly.

'It'll be different this time.'

Back in the bathroom, the driver rinsed his mouth with a blue mint-flavoured solution. He wiped the condensation from the mirror and took one final look at his teeth to make sure that no food particles were left in the gaps. Then he stroked his hair, shook a few drops of face balm onto his hands and patted his cheeks.

From her armchair, the driver's wife called to her husband, 'How many more times do you have to go to the bathroom? You'll be late.'

'I've never been late. Stop fussing. I'm on my way.'

He was ready for his evening shift. There was a passenger to collect from the station at 6.30, followed by his regular customer Piet van Rijn, for the monthly Reading Club meeting. After several other trips, he would return towards the end of the meeting to collect this passenger and hopefully to hear that he was to be offered membership of this elite club. Piet suggested that the driver arrive half an hour early, in case the club wanted to meet him tonight.

Dressed for work, the taxi driver looked like a corpulent bishop in a suit. In front of him he carried a hard globe of a belly. His sympathetic, but expensive tailor made him dark blue double-breasted jackets, which fastened across his equator so that the material in his southern hemisphere hung like a curtain, cleverly minimising the true circumference of his girth. Although there were other taxi drivers in town, none were as smart as Bob van Dillen and he became known as 'The Taxi Driver'. People rarely used his name. Because of his spruce appearance, many folks asked to be driven by him in preference to the more experienced guys who paid less attention to their appearance. Bob was a fastidious man, showering before and after work, changing all his clothes at the end of a day's driving and hanging his suit near an open window to air and rest for a day; while another suit did the driving. His limo was immaculate and even under the seats was dust-free; the chrome shone and the glove compartment contained nothing more than his licence, his insurance documents, a pen, note-pad, and usually the latest Reading Club novel. The combination of Bob's perfumed face balm together with the upholstery polish, which he applied each week to the interior surfaces, gave the inside of the taxi a unique fragrant atmosphere; a few of his passengers described it as overpowering.

Even on very hot summer days, Bob did not remove his jacket. He drove a Lexus limousine, a discreet yet expensive car with air conditioning. He worked in a constant temperature throughout the year, only leaving his cab briefly in order to open doors for passengers or to place their luggage in the boot. He spoke several languages including excellent English and this facility made him well placed at the town's modern hotel to be at the disposal of business clients. Like other taxi drivers, he had an intuition for assessing his passengers' nationality and the nature of their work. This, together with his intelligent conversation, helpfulness and elegant appearance often earned him good tips; mostly from foreign visitors rather than from his countrymen and women who tended to be more frugal with their appreciation.

Although he had the outlook of an upright holy man, Bob's exterior belied the turmoil of his inner world. In reality, he was a frustrated taxi driver, a failed entrepreneur, the non-academic only son of a professor of social and economic history and, up until now, an unsuccessful applicant for the Reading Club. Bob disliked moments in his day when he had to wait a long time for his passengers. It was during these empty periods that his mind took itself back down a spiral of self-pity, self-doubt and self-criticism, down a shaft and into the pits of his bad luck, his failures, his near bankruptcy and his firm belief that he was not a good enough son. He frequently described his dark thoughts and nightmares to his friend and counsellor.

'My father's at the bottom of this shaft – wearing his professor's robes. He's got that superior distant look on his face. I can see he's disappointed in me.'

'Anybody else there?'

'There's my sister, not even looking at me, and that awful brother-in-law, who's also a doctor. All three of them have their faces tilted up with academic pride.'

'You feel a bit inferior?'

'Yes.'

'What happens then?'

'They ignore me – the unqualified, undignified, unintelligent, cab-driving member of the family – they ignore me. They make me feel like shit.'

Sadly, the brilliance of Bob's father had passed him by. A small consolation was that Bob's son had inherited the grandfather's academic intelligence. However, five years ago the boy took his fine mind to Boston USA where, together with his Indonesian wife, he now worked at the university.

Bob was always early for his appointments and he appreciated when his passengers were punctual. Out of all his clients, Piet van Rijn was the one who kept him waiting the longest. He was always the last to leave the home of whoever was hosting the monthly Reading Club meeting. It was as if Piet could not bear to waste any opportunity for a conversation. Sometimes he appeared half an hour after everyone else had left. The driver liked Piet – who didn't? – but, he also felt some resentment for this fellow who was a bad timekeeper and who rarely finished any of the Reading Club's chosen books. Mostly Piet relied on others for his comments. In contrast the driver was an avid reader, always had a book beside his chair at home, another next to his bed and a third in the limo. Except tonight, he had left his book behind.

There were plenty of opportunities for reading at home. It was an easy decision between the driver and his wife, not to have a television. She was brought up in a strict Protestant community. When she was a child, the church elders discouraged the congregation from owning TV sets because of their potentially corrupting images. She became accustomed to living in a household without one; where instead, the Bible was read, women sewed and men smoked their pipes whilst perusing the local religious papers. Like many people of their age, the driver and his wife did not agree with this outdated attitude towards the television. It was for her more out of habit and for him more the delights of a quiet house where he could read, that they made their decision. They both wrote regularly; his wife kept a diary in which she recorded the events of her days. In a box containing small cards, the driver kept a record of all of the books he had ever read. He borrowed many from the local library and he owned a few, which he had bought or were given. On his cards, he recorded the books' details, the essence of the contents, together with quotations he liked. He had read all of the Reading Club's books, including some in English. He had considered following an internet course in literature, but his wife wondered what use that would be to a taxi driver.

It was during these waiting times that the driver was careful not to become depressed. His good friend and counsellor assured him that he was not going mad, but was recovering from the trauma of losing his business.

'I get in a bad state. Start thinking I'm a failure, I'm useless as a husband, a father and as a son.'

'That sounds bad.'

'I know it doesn't make sense. My life is not all rotten. There are many who do worse jobs than me, and some people, I know, can't work. Some don't have the opportunity.'

'That's right.'

'I know what I should be thinking. We've talked about that many times.'

'We have.'

'My life is not all bad. I keep telling myself this. I know what I should be feeling. But it's a fight. This voice inside my head shouts when I am waiting around.'

'I thought it helped if you read while you were waiting.'

'Yes…yes it mostly does. But sometimes nothing works. Time gets…stretched out. Minutes seem like hours.'

'I'll pray for you,' the counsellor said, indicating the end of his attention giving.

Tonight Piet asked the taxi driver to return early and wait outside the doctor's house. He did not know that the driver, whilst waiting, could get into an unstable frame of mind. There was only one man in the Reading Club who could be trusted with that information and it was not Piet van Rijn.

The club meeting was nearing its end when the driver arrived outside the home of Dr. Titus Dekker in the Thorbecke Straat. He was forty-five minutes early. From inside his parked limo, he could see several bicycles, which were propped up against the wall of the doctor's late 17th century house. Bert de Lange had arrived on his wife's heavy upright bike, with its willow basket on the front for shopping and for carrying their white Highland Terrier. The taxi driver was not a dog lover, which was untypical, since so many of his fellow countrywomen and men have canine pets. He thought that there were sufficient problems fitting all the sixteen million inhabitants into the Netherlands without an additional population of dogs. Bob might be happier about these animals, if their owners were more careful about where they took their pets to defecate. His neighbour allowed his beast to foul the side of the road every day, even though there was a canine lavatory nearby. On several occasions, a few of Bob's passengers had accidentally carried traces of excrement on the soles of their shoes. The smell in the cab lingered for days.

Milo Jansen was the driver's trusted friend and counsellor. Earlier that day, Bob had seen him riding along the dyke road in the rain with his long grey coat flapping. With one hand he held the handlebar and in the other an opened but lopsided umbrella. His bike was now in front of the doctor's house. Also parked there were two more bicycles, which had no front lights. However, there was no guarantee that the lights on any of the other bikes worked. Most Dutch people are not worried about this little breach of the law. In the event of an accident, the cyclist is always favoured. But for a professional driver like Bob van Dillen those without-lights bicycles can be a real hazard along unlit roads leading out of town.

Piet van Rijn was the only member to travel to and from the Reading Club meetings by taxi. He claimed that on his way home from a previous meeting, he was pushed off his bike by a group of local Moroccan youths who were congregating in the centre of town. Apparently, they accused Piet of riding into them. Piet had drunk a lot on that evening, so he did not feel very confident in blaming his assailants. His wife was angry and said that he should have gone to the police. But Piet, who liked to appear easy going, said that it was probably his fault and going to the police would not help community relationships. He did not tell his wife that he was later breathalysed, cautioned and told to apologise to the youths for the accident.

Having been parked outside the doctor's house for fifteen minutes, the driver was tired of waiting. He levered himself out of his car, adjusted his jacket and straightened his tie. Now he had a good view on a row of eighteenth century, narrow, step-gabled, carefully pointed, inner city houses. These professionally renovated dwellings belonged to rich people. Once he had visions of living within the city walls himself, but he knew that he would never realize this dream since his business failed.

Most of these houses have internal shutters fixed on the windows of the rooms which look out to the street. Some people close these at night so as not to be seen by the outside world. However many Dutch people, including those who live in new houses, prefer to keep their shutters and curtains open and the lights on. It is as if they invite people to look inside their homes and admire the interiors. The driver was pleased that his wife and he agreed that they do not want anyone to see into the windows of their flat. Their blinds are closed when the lights go on. They value their privacy. This is how it is with moderate people.

This evening the doctor is using the large dining-room at the front of his house for the Reading Club meeting; the shutters are open. Perhaps he feels proud to be a founder member of the club and wants passers-by to notice this group of respectable fellows in his home. The taxi driver wondered if the members had been discussing him. He felt nervous. What had they talked about?

Now the driver had been waiting twenty minutes. No-one

had come out of the meeting to invite him inside. He looked along the street. It was empty. He walked over to the window where, on tiptoes and by clinging onto the windowsill, he was able to peer into the room. Around a large antique oval table sat the eight members. Everyone was engrossed in the meeting and did not notice him looking in. Seeing the empty glasses he knew they had been drinking. He had already decided that he would not drink alcohol at these meetings; he wanted the members to know he was a safe driver and a sober reader.

Bob could see that in front of each man was a copy of the book which they had been reviewing, 'Priests Dying', by Father Antonius van Aken. A few had notebooks. It looked as if they had nearly finished the meeting. Perhaps they were deciding which books they would read during the coming months. The driver wondered if they had made their decision about his membership. On the other hand, they could be debating Piet's suggestion of inviting this Father Antonius to talk at their forthcoming tenth anniversary meeting. Piet had told the driver about his plan.

'At the right moment I will suggest that we invite Father Antonius to be our guest at the anniversary meeting.'

'Sounds like a good idea. I'd like to meet him,' the driver said.

'Not sure what they'll think.'

'Why wouldn't they agree?'

'I'm a new member. I've seen how newcomers get ignored.'

'Really?'

'There's a sort of pecking order. These things happen in groups.'

'Is that so, Piet?' the driver said, overlaying his words with sarcasm.

'Yes,' said Piet, missing the tone of the reply.

Piet held a degree in sociology which, according to the driver, was of little use in his current position of managing the local *Kringloopwinkel*, a barn of a place, where people take their unwanted possessions for others to buy. The profits go to needy folks in other parts of the world. The taxi driver told his wife that any fool could run a charity shop; a degree was not required, just a good deal of common sense. Although, he sometimes wondered if Piet ever had any sense about anything.

Last year, Piet asked the driver if he would like to become a member of the Reading Club.

'Shall I ask the club if you can join?'

'I'd like that. Will they think I'm good enough?'

'Of course, you read all our books.'

'I know my family would be impressed. Both my father and my sister belong to university reading groups.'

Unfortunately, after that meeting in which the proposal was promised, Piet reported that he failed to get the consent of the other members. He said he was shocked by some of their responses, but would not tell the driver the details. Bob had felt angry at Piet's newly acquired loyalty towards the members of the club. He was talking as if he was sworn to secrecy or was bound by some agreement on confidentiality. Bob might have been more convinced about Piet's choice of non-disclosure had he experienced him as a discreet man. On the contrary, after each Reading Club gathering, Piet, intoxicated by beverages and brotherhood, provided the driver with an account of the meeting, including the book bits, the non-book bits and any other bits which he thought might enhance his tale. Piet behaved as if the information being withheld was of great significance to the continued existence of the club. Had the driver not been so affected by the group's decision, he might have found Piet's loyalty laughable. Instead, he found it aggravating. At the time, Bob's instinct was to keep quiet about his inner feelings. Perhaps that was wise, because Piet said he remained optimistic about membership and promised to try again later. Bob felt miserable and it took him some time to get over the rejection. However, that was now in the past, tonight would be Piet's second attempt at securing the driver's membership of the Reading Club.

Bob peered into the doctor's window for several minutes. It was a wonder that no-one saw him. His feet and hands grew numb and his belly was hurting from been squashed against the wall. He needed to move or cramp would spasm his vulnerable calf muscles. In transferring his weight he missed his footing. He was falling. He grabbed at the ornate cast-iron railing on the windowsill. Too delicate to endure his weight, the metal structure began to bend. It squeaked, like a reluctant tooth being uprooted. He let go. Simultaneously, his other arm missed grabbing the far end of the railing. It flung itself bang against the window.

Everyone around the oval table turned in the direction of the sound. Bob, huge and uncomfortable, was backside down on the pavement. There he remained for a few moments hoping that no-one had seen him. His ankle hurt, was it broken or just numb? He could not immediately get to his feet. Everything was hurting and his cheeks were flushed. 'Oh my God!' he groaned, 'I'm stuck.'

Two faces appeared at the window, quickly followed by the doctor who was gesturing and mouthing words which, Bob thought, meant that he was wanted at the front door. He smiled as a light anaesthetic of success moved through his body.

'They want me to go inside. I've been accepted,' he said aloud in the empty street. He rolled over onto his side, got onto his hands and knees, then with difficulty stood up. He pulled down that expensive double-breasted jacket, ignored the pain in his backside, the tear in his trousers, and limped to the front door.

Inside the doctor's house, just before the driver's fall, the Reading Club had been enjoying some lively discussions about Father Antonius's book. Huub Schevers suggested that they should be considering the next month's book, so the doctor was drawing the discussion to a close.

'Does anyone want to say anything more about 'Priests Dying'?' he asked.

'I'd never have chosen that book for myself. I am pleased I read it,' Joost Kuijpers said.

'I was impressed with you Piet – writing down all those comments. Don't expect me to write like that. I haven't got time. But it was interesting,' Bert de Lange smiled.

Piet, an ex-seminary boy, had read out as his own work most of what the driver had written in his lengthy book review. As a Catholic, albeit a lapsed one, he thought he had been careful to omit the Protestant references which the driver had made.

'Yes, I agree, well done, Piet. Shall we decide on next month's book? Any suggestions?' Titus asked.

'Before we do that, I'd like to make a suggestion about our forthcoming tenth anniversary,' Piet said.

'OK.'

Piet gave a slight cough and waited for the rest to be quiet. He looked nervous.

'What's this great idea?' Hans van den Elsen said, then laughed as if he had made a joke.

'Since we've all enjoyed Antonius's book and he was teacher to three of us – me included – and he helped us to love literature – I wonder – would it be a good idea to invite him to our anniversary night? I know he gives talks about his book.'

'Sounds like a good idea to me,' said Titus.

'Fine by me,' Joost nodded.

'He was my teacher and he was always very long-winded,' said Paul Bazelman

'You obviously take after him?' said Hans.

'I'm alright with that,' said another.

'That's agreed,' Titus said. 'Could we ask you, Piet, to contact Father Antonius and invite him to the tenth anniversary meeting?'

'Yep, I'll do that.'

'Now to choose next month's...'

Titus was interrupted by a bang against the glass and everyone looked around.

'Someone's at the window.'

'Who's that?'

Two of the members sitting near the window got up and looked outside.

'It's that bloody taxi driver. He's sitting on the pavement,' one of them said. 'What does he want?'

'He's always asking about this club. He's a nuisance.'

'I think he wants to join.'

Huub immediately said, 'The club's full with eight members. I can't get more than eight people around my table.'

'The size of your table is a strange way to limit the size of the club,' Hans said.

'The inside of the taxi driver's cab smells like a brothel,' Paul said.

Huub asked, 'Are you familiar with such places?'

Everyone laughed and Paul blushed.

'It would be difficult to have the taxi driver in the club because his wife works for some of us,' Titus said.

'Since when are we judged by what our wives do to earn their livings?' Hans said.

'What do you think, Milo?'

'I think the taxi driver and his wife are good people who have had hard times, but I am not sure it would be a good idea for him to join us at this time.' Milo was about to say more but Titus interrupted him and turned to Piet.

'What about you, Piet? You know him well. Do you think the taxi driver wants to join and do you think we should consider him?'

'He's very interested in reading.' Piet hesitated, 'I'm not sure he would make a suitable member.'

'What's he doing outside?' Titus asked.

'Sorry. He's waiting for me. He's a bit early. I'll tell him to wait in the cab,' Piet said as he stood up.

'Stay where you are. I'll tell him to piss off,' said Titus as he went over to the window and saw the driver on his bottom on the pavement. The members were unaccustomed to Titus swearing. He was always so controlled and serious. He banged on the window and gestured to the taxi driver to go to the front door. 'GO TO THE DOOR,' Titus shouted, as if the taxi driver could hear through the double glazed window.

When Titus opened the front door, the taxi driver was smiling and was about to step inside when Titus put up his hand to stop him entering his house.

'We're still having our meeting.'

'That's alright. I'll come in and listen.'

'No you won't. Mr van Rijn will be a little longer yet. He said you could wait in the cab.'

'Oh, I thought you were inviting me in.'

'Please stay in your cab.' Titus did not wait for the driver to move back. Had the driver not stepped back quickly, the ornate doorknocker in the shape of a peacock would have banged his nose. Having shut the door firmly, Titus went back to the meeting.

'Any suggestions for next month's book?'

'Nothing too thick, this time,' said Huub.

'Huub, you always moan, whatever book we choose.'

Hans said. 'What about 'Animal Farm'?'

'Hasn't everyone read it?' asked Bert.

'No, I don't think so.'

Titus concluded. 'We'll read 'Animal Farm'. George Orwell, British writer, for those who don't know.'

'Not another English book! Can't we read something by a Dutch author?' Bert said.

'It's got to be better than that bloody awful book you recommended about addiction!'

'OK, Gentlemen. That's decided. Who'd like to host next month's meeting?'

'I will,' offered Piet, 'in the *Kringloopwinkel*. Of course it is not as grand as this house. No fine paintings or antique furniture. Probably you will think most of what we sell is junk. But you could find something to buy for your wives. Sorry Huub, I forget you're not married.'

'Don't worry Piet, I am very pleased that I'm single.'

'We can have the meeting in my office, then after you can

17

have a look around to see if you would like to buy something. Everything is sold for charity. I would like you to see the place where I work.'

'Fine. We'll meet at Piet's workplace next month – having *all* read Animal Farm'. Piet, who was so pleased that his two suggestions had been accepted, did not notice that the doctor was sending him a warning. But Joost understood what Titus meant and he looked at his friend and shrugged his shoulders.

The driver, confused and bruised had returned to his car and got inside. Several parts of his body were stinging. He looked down at his knees to see the small tear in his trousers. Maybe there were other damages – he'd look later. He grabbed the steering wheel and held onto it tightly. His face creased as if he was in agony and he screwed his eyes tight shut. He was on the verge of crying.

'Damn that doctor! Damn Piet! Damn the whole bloody Reading Club! Damn, damn, damn!'

He let go his grip and punched the steering wheel several times, then held it again firmly, and stayed fixed in this position for a minute or two. Then his face began to unfold itself and as the creases lessened, he sighed. Eventually his hands let go their tight hold and they slid off the steering wheel, limp onto his lap. He opened his eyes. He felt tired. His earlier confidence had disappeared and there was about him an air of weary resignation. He sighed again, and then looked up. Through the doctor's windows he could see that the readers were standing up and directing themselves towards the host. Perhaps he should wait to hear what Piet said about the evening. It could be that the members had not had time to discuss his membership or that they might have agreed that he could join at the next meeting. Maybe he had got into a state for nothing. He searched for excuses. Anything rather than believe that they did not want him in their midst.

In turn, the members thanked their host and one by one left the house. Piet lingered first by the table, where he emptied the remains of all the wine bottles into his glass and drank the dregs in two swallows. Then he loitered in the room-sized hall, probably talking to the doctor and his wife and finally, after being seen off, he stopped on the half-moon doorstep, which had enough space for all the Reading Club to stand upon. There he took out a small packet of tobacco and papers and started to roll himself a thin lumpy cigarette. He was swaying slightly. Piet was drunk again. The taxi driver wondered how much longer he would have to wait.

Piet gestured to him, 'Would you like a smoke?'

The driver shook his head.

In a loud whisper the driver said, 'Never mind a bloody smoke, I want to know what they said about me joining. What did they think about my review?' Of course Piet did not hear. He was not meant to.

The driver shook his head again. He had given up the habit years ago and the desire to have a cigarette was long gone. He thought he saw Piet add a little extra ingredient to his roll-up. Perhaps it was cannabis. Piet claimed that he had a sleeping disorder and the drug helped him to manage his symptoms. The taxi driver wondered what the host, the reputable Dr. Titus Dekker, would think when the drug's sickly smell seeped under the front door of his grand house. He knew, by the questions from his foreign passengers, that many people had the idea that cannabis was legal in The Netherlands. He always said that was untrue – selling and buying marijuana was illegal. He understood that it was tolerated in certain controlled areas, but this town, *his* town, was certainly not one of them. He did not tell his passengers that it was possible to buy certain drugs in the coffee shops in a nearby city. But feeling some embarrassment at his country's bad fame regarding drugs, he would always conclude his information by quoting the Dutch saying –'letting a little evil in can keep the big devil out'.

'And they have you in their club and don't want me,' the driver said aloud, but not loud enough for Piet to hear.

'Can't hear you,' Piet called from the other side of the street.

The driver signalled, 'Doesn't matter'.

Piet remained for a few minutes on the doctor's doorstep, his tall, lean body casting a long, thin shadow across the street to the grand house opposite. For a sixty-year-old, he had a generous head of light brown curly hair, which was partly escaping from under an ancient trilby hat. The driver often wondered if some of Piet's clothes had not come from the charity shop which he managed. Tonight's ensemble was particularly tatty. His grubby creased raincoat was several sizes too big; it was tied at the back with its own belt in the way that was fashionable in the 1970s. The back hem had come undone – it had been like that for several months. Piet savoured the last part of his narrow cigarette, then propelled the butt through the air with a flick of his forefinger against his thumb. It bounced off a car roof and wedged itself between the cracks of the cobblestones. Bob watched his passenger cross the road without looking up and down the street for sudden cyclists.

Piet was in good spirits. 'We had some great talks about 'Dying Priests'. They've agreed to my suggestion of inviting Antonius to the tenth anniversary of our club, which is in ten months time. They want me to write to him.'

'Oh really.'

'Do you know this is the first time they've listened to me. They're all right these guys. There could be a job in it for you. Antonius lives in Belgium and will need picking up and taking back. Fancy doing that?'

'I'd be honoured to collect the priest. I'd like to hear what he has to say about his book. Perhaps by that time I might be a member of the club myself.'

Piet kept referring to the book as 'Dying Priests', but the driver knew it was called 'Priests Dying' because he had read it about six weeks before. Bob had been impressed and moved by the story, but shocked at the treatment of the young boys who were training to be priests. Privately he considered they had been brainwashed and emotionally abused, but he did not say that to Piet, who had been to a seminary himself. Bob could never have imagined sending his own son away from home at the age of twelve.

Piet claimed that he had scanned the book. The driver concluded that this probably meant he had glanced at the introduction and flicked through the other pages. Three days before the meeting, Piet, on the pretext of 'running out of time', had asked the driver to jot down a few comments about the book. The driver saw this as a golden opportunity to demonstrate his ability as a reviewer. He understood that Piet would inform the club that he, the taxi driver, was the true author of the review. After this, an unconditional invitation for membership would follow. The driver asked if he should make a copy of his book review for each member, but Piet had said that would not be necessary.

A Review of 'Priests Dying' by Father Antonius
by Bob van Dillen

I have read a few books written by Church leaders but this was my first by a Catholic priest. I did not think I would appreciate it because I am a Protestant, but I found it was written with great sensitivity and courage. I learned a lot about another faith and of the struggle of a man whose thoughts and feelings often went against the teachings of his Church. For the material for his autobiography, the author looked back at the journals, which he kept since he first attended a minor seminary in 1940 at the age of twelve, through the years, up to 2003 when he began his book. I felt inspired to start keeping a journal myself and I was envious that he had done that since he was a boy.

Frequently he used original texts; quoting his simple boyhood words, recalling events from his years of studying and development, revealing his doubts and disappointments regarding his faith and his Church and finally sharing his reflections on the decline of the Dutch priesthood and his feelings about old age and death. I was shocked when I read that he doubted the Catholic understanding of heaven.

He wrote about his appetite. As a boy he was often cold and hungry. Later he talked about his inability to feel warmth for others and his loss of appetite for spiritual nourishment. This is not a book preaching at the reader, glorifying suffering, or justifying the past. I have read a few Protestant books written with this theme. Instead, it is the story of a humble life of one who was often lonely, occasionally angered, sometimes frustrated, and frequently disappointed by the behaviour of people in his community. He comes across as a real man, not as one of those cold, marble saints.

He wrote about feelings, which I would not dream of confessing myself; fantasies which most men pretend they do not have. He revealed vengeful and spiteful thoughts. He described his desires, grievances, even feelings of hate; many things we would not expect a man of God to hold. At times he was a most tormented man. At times it felt as if he was expressing my own thoughts.

The author does not always describe the Catholic Church very favourably. This is quite a bold thing for a priest to do. I am not sure that I would have the courage to criticise my Church in the same way. Some of his community will have been annoyed and shocked by certain aspects of this book. He is very careful not to name or blame individuals when he describes the characters in the Abbey School, such as the strict teacher-priests, the kind brothers who cleaned his curtained cell, or the boys smoking. He is, however, quite critical about abbots who had the best opportunity to change things but who often repeated the mistakes of their predecessors. This is a story about the day-to-day life of an abbey as seen through the eyes of an outspoken and not too popular priest.

Whilst Father Antonius praised aspects of his education; the music, the literature and the languages – he eventually gained a doctorate in history – he criticised the absence of science. His mathematics never went beyond the simple arithmetic sufficient to keep parish accounts.

He was unhappy about the solitariness, which influenced his relationships for the rest of his life and kept him at a distance from others. When anyone came close to him, he felt awkward. It was difficult to make friends in or outside the abbey. Even when he met people he liked, he was confused as how best to go along with them; especially the women. He wrote openly about his vow of chastity. Surely that is a taboo subject for priests. Once he described wanting to be an ordinary man with a wife and family. He wrote about the very pleasing sensation he had experienced when a female acquaintance had allowed her glance to linger on him. Another time a woman had brushed up against his robe and a special feeling had shot through his body. He thought that the Church should change its attitude towards women and encourage priests to have close friendships with them. Not sexual; he was pleased that he had been celibate. He wanted to see women in higher places in the Catholic Church. However, he thought that a step too far in his lifetime.

During his priesthood, he lost his belief in the Bible and his trust in the Church. He became confused. Secretly he read literature, which was banned by his Church. He studied the Old Testament completely from beginning to end (I have never done that). He was shocked by the way God was depicted. He was unconvinced by the explanation of the Creation and unsettled by the story of Abraham and his willingness to sacrifice his only son. Despite this leaning away from his Church, there was something unexplainable, which kept him tied to God during these uncertain times, and he developed a personal belief of his own. Privately he rejected many of the teachings of the Catholic Church, while still keeping his belief in Jesus Christ. Despite his sadness and anger, he remained loyal to his Order, continued to participate in the prayers and services, and took seriously his responsibilities as a priest and a teacher. He had made a promise to his parents and the Church and he did not want to break it. His internal debates make interesting reading. I have experienced some of his dilemmas myself.

Father Antonius considered leaving his Order a few times and he described his fear of going into the outside world without the security and familiarity of his abbey and the shame of embarrassing his family if he left. That was very honest. He hoped he could help improve the Church from inside rather than leave. He regretted that he had not achieved this ambition. Although I am of a different faith, I could identify with the priest's feeling of failure and his uncertain connection to his Church. I have had doubts myself.

He remained critical about how people in the abbey were managed and of the arrogance of priests who looked down on the congregation and expected that their privileged position would continue forever. It is quite different in my Church. We would not tolerate such behaviour from our Church Elders. He saw that society was changing, people were beginning to question their beliefs, science was bringing forth additional evidence concerning the beginnings of the world and people were becoming more materialistic and less faithful. The days when the priest could tell people what to do, had gone. There was a decline in Christian beliefs and Church congregations became smaller. He could see the signs, but as he said, the Catholic Church in the Netherlands failed to recognise what was happening. He offered some solutions to his abbey as to how to change, but these were ignored. He knew he was considered a revolutionary, but he stayed. As he predicted, the number of young men coming forward for the priesthood quickly declined after the 1960s and then more slowly from then onwards. Hence, the title of the book 'Priests Dying' refers to this disappearing group.

He maintained that the traditional Catholic confession had been a damaging experience, for him and many of his seminary pupils, especially the very young. The ritual gave them an unnecessary burden and left a lot confused. He claimed his own method of writing, of reflecting without the judgement of another, was more beneficial. He had done it for years and encouraged others to follow his example. He wrote 'EVERYONE SHOULD KEEP A JOURNAL'. He believed that writing worked at a different level to speaking. 'It's good for the mind and spirit,' he wrote. 'It encourages the development of thought and understanding.' He concluded that without regular access to his secret journal, he would not have survived as a seminarian or a priest.

One literary critic wrote that many people would identify with the dilemmas, which the priest described when his faith was challenged. It was one of the best books I have ever read.

Signed Bob van Dillen

Piet was in a daze of pleasure as he sat in the passenger seat of the limo. Although the taxi driver was anxious to hear what the Reading Club thought about his book review and membership, he waited for his passenger to settle. The driver had taken over ten hours to write his comments; he used the computer in the taxi office to type the report, his wife read it and made some suggestions, he bought several sheets of the best quality paper on which to print it and he enclosed his review in a new blue soft sided file. He reread the final draft many times and was very proud of his achievement.

'How was your evening?'

'Fine,' said Piet, fumbling for the seat belt but not managing to do it up.

'So they've agreed to your suggestion?'

'Yes,' said Piet after he finally clicked the seat belt closed.

The driver wondered whether he would get more than just one word answers. He caught a whiff of Piet's breath and could not decide if it was the alcohol, the cannabis or a mixture of both that he smelt.

'We've chosen to read 'Animal Farm', by George Orwell, next month.'

'I've read it,' the driver said sharply, 'who suggested that?'

'Hans van den Elsen. He said the animals in the book remind him of some people he knows.'

'Members of the Reading Club, perhaps?'

'He didn't say.'

Piet continued, 'For the following month we have chosen 'The Power and the Glory', by Graham Greene.'

'Is that because Father Antonius mentioned it in his book?'

'Did he? I don't know. Titus suggested it,' Piet said, sounding slightly confused.

Then, unable to hold back the question which was foremost in his mind, Bob asked, 'Did they like my review?'

Piet paused, grinned and then he said, 'I think they were

impressed by what I said about Antonius's book.'

The driver took a deep breath and held it for a moment before exhaling it in a sigh. 'What exactly do you mean? Did you tell them that I had written the review?'

'No,' said Piet, smiling faintly and speaking with a slight slur. 'I didn't tell them that you made a few notes; a brief summary of the book.'

Instant rage exploded inside the driver's body and a host of grievances against Piet filled his mind. With great effort he resisted expressing his feelings. He held tightly on to the steering wheel. His skin tingled as the nerve endings made ready to gear his muscles for a fight. His nose became alert and Bob was aware of a pungent smell. Was it from the town or could his wife be right when she suggested that Piet had a dead rat in the pocket of that awful raincoat? Whatever the source, he felt faint and nauseous. Keep calm, he told himself. Don't jump to conclusions before you find out exactly what happened. Keep calm, he repeated.

Eventually he said, 'I wrote more than a few notes. Mine was a comprehensive review. You said that they would be impressed. You said you were sure they'd ask me to join the club, after they'd read what I'd written.'

'I can't remember what I said to you, but I wouldn't have promised that I was going to ask the club about your membership.'

The driver paused. He knew that was not true. Piet had definitely said he would ask about his membership. Piet had misled him. Piet had lied to him. And now Piet was attempting to pacify him.

'There'll be other opportunities, stay cool,' was all his passenger said through his grin.

The driver said nothing, but Piet could see he was angry, especially at the last remark. Perhaps 'stay cool' had not been the best thing to say.

'Will you take me home now? 'Piet said with a half smile.

CHAPTER 2

Piet van Rijn

The driver started his cab and turned into a one-way street in which an assortment of smaller, narrow houses appeared to be squashed together. Some buildings had been there for 400 years, others were more recent additions, appearing during the eighteenth and nineteenth centuries; a few were built in the 1930s. Several had lost some of their charm, thanks to 'modern' extensions and alteration. Long, narrow windows with stained-glass fan-lights had been levered out, and out-of-proportion wider replacements put in. A number of old dwellings had been converted into shops. A few had long histories of different inhabitants: traders, merchants, spinners, weavers, artists, bakers. Even the smallest was once home to several families living together. Frequently a tiny dwelling would house as many as twelve people. Today a couple would complain that a place of this size is too small.

Parked at the end of the street was a large removal van which they could not pass.

'Sorry, we won't be long.' Two students were unloading boxes and furniture.

'It's OK; my passenger has all the time in the world.' Bob put the cab into neutral.

Although Piet was in a soft yet confident mood, he was aware of the driver's expression and could sense his disgruntled feelings. The evening's cocktail of chemical and emotional experiences had created within Piet a euphoria which he was reluctant to disturb. He was enjoying the balm of his intoxication and felt slightly annoyed that the driver was in another mood.

'Why are you so upset? The Reading Club made a good decision to invite Antonius to the anniversary meeting. You know I didn't make any agreement that I would ask the club about you becoming a member – not tonight. I never said that. I think you're being unfair – it's such a pleasant evening. Don't you agree, it's a very smooth night? You should feel honoured that they want you to go to Belgium and collect Antonius. Relax man!'

'Antonius? I think it is more respectful to call him Father Antonius. Piet you're drunk.'

'No, I'm not.'

'Let's say you are intoxicated by a few things tonight, including having your idea accepted in the club. We'll talk about the membership, which you promised me, when you have sobered up. You've let me down.'

'That's stupid; no-one's let you down. For God's sake let's change the subject. I promise to talk to you about your membership the next time we meet. Alright?'

There was a long silence. The taxi driver nodded his head slowly as if he was not in complete agreement and turned off the engine. This street was too long for him to back up the limo. The students were now struggling to remove a heavy sofa from their vehicle when an obnoxious smell assaulted Piet's nose.

'What's that stink?' he said.

'Your coat's got a few stains on it. That could be the reason.'

'Don't be ridiculous. It's really bad.'

The driver ignored him. He did not want to talk about smells. If he was going to collect the priest he wanted to know more about him. 'Did you ever meet Father Antonius?' he asked.

'Yep, he was my teacher,' said Piet pinching the end of his nose. He seemed unperturbed at having to wait behind the removal van as it was being unloaded.

When he was twelve years old, Piet was taken by his parents to the seminary school which was attached to the abbey. His mother employed their local baker to take them there in his three-wheeler van. Since she was a big woman and the organizer of the trip, she sat in front with the baker. Together they talked throughout the journey about local people, completely ignoring Piet and his father who were squeezed in the back, either side of a small trunk holding all Piet's things, which included an awful suit which his mother had made out of workmen's corduroy. She had the future in mind when she sewed this garment. Not only was it an awful colour, the fabric was harsh and the suit several sizes too big. It had a peculiar smell, which it retained for all of its life. Piet was given a large wooden crucifix and his mother had allowed him to take his collection of empty matchboxes. He was to be a boarder at the school and he had the same ambition as the other thirty boys who arrived on that day: they all wanted to become priests.

'Was he a good man?' The driver asked, remembering some of the unpleasant characters Father Antonius described in his book.

'Yep,' said Piet who had given up holding his nose, 'I liked him. I can remember my first day at the seminary. I arrived in a baker's van. That's when I met him.'

Piet recalled that the little van smelt of freshly baked bread and he felt hungry. A slight haze of flour dust hung in the back of the vehicle. By the end of the journey, some of it settled on top of the trunk, on their Sunday best suits and on his father's very bushy eyebrows. After one and a half hour's travelling, the van stopped in the driveway of the Abbey School and the baker went smartly around to the passenger seat to open the door for Piet's mother and to ease her out of the small passenger seat and onto her feet.

Piet and his father waited patiently whilst the baker lit himself a cigar before he went to the back of the van. First, he pulled the trunk out; then he helped Piet's father who was stiff after the journey. Piet slid out unaided. It was very busy in the school drive; there were a few grand cars, some smaller vehicles, together with one or two horse-drawn carts. Other boys arrived by bus and the local boys walked.

'You arrived in a baker's van!'

'Yes, it was the quickest and cheapest way. We couldn't take the trunk on a bus.'

Piet remembered that when his father got out of the van, he was not able to straighten himself immediately and began complaining about a pain in his back. His wife shot him one of her looks which implied, 'Oh shut up, Pa!' Then she told him to brush himself down and to wipe his eyebrows. She noticed immediately that there was some flour dust on Piet's Sunday suit. She had only bought it a few months previously for his confirmation. To his embarrassment, she started to remove the flour from the back of the suit. She was vigorous and in her enthusiasm, it felt to Piet as if he was being spanked rather than being brushed. He let out a cry; she was hurting him. It was at that moment that Father Antonius passed by. He smiled at Piet's mother, but not at Piet; probably because he thought that the boy had committed some offence and was being rightly chastised.

Piet watched as Father Antonius walked quickly across the drive; his long off-white robe level with the bottom of his trousers, revealing proper black shiny shoes and plain black socks. The robe swished out at the front and back as he walked. His red stole flapped in the breeze and round his waist was a sash. Piet remembered thinking that he wanted to wear a long white garment and to walk like a priest.

In the one-way street, the sofa seemed to be jammed in the back of the removal van. One of the students called out an apology and the driver gestured that there was no rush and jerked his thumb towards his passenger as if to say, 'I don't mind waiting. He's paying'. Bob rested his hands on the lower part of the steering wheel and asked, 'Why did your parents send you to a seminary?'

'They wanted me to be a priest. I was the second son. That's how it was in those days. Priests were a part of our lives. My uncle was a priest.'

Ever since Piet could remember, there were priests in his house. They called in for a coffee and for one of his father's cigars. He remembered how his mother was much at ease with these men. Her brother was a canon regular; most of his life he worked in a mission area. Piet only met this uncle a few times and he wanted to be like him, his boyhood hero.

When Piet was nine, he assisted with the communion wine at Mass. He thought that a great opportunity because often a little was left over and, when he thought no-one was looking, he poured the remainder into his cupped hand and drank it. One day a woman of the church saw him doing this. She informed the priest who told Piet's mother who confronted him with the truth. Piet denied he had drunk the wine and accused the onlooker of lying. For this double sin he got two slaps around the head, one from his mother and the other from the parish priest.

The taxi driver moved his hands up to the middle of the wheel and pulled on it to adjust his position so that he was half facing Piet. He continued:

'But did you want to be a priest?'

'I used to play priests with my sister. At first, I made my own robe from an old dust sheet, which my mother kept for covering furniture when my father was decorating. It stank of turpentine. Then for a birthday present, I was given some miniature garments especially designed for minor would-be priests. My sister assisted me at the altar, which was a plank of wood resting on the wall in our back garden. Believe me; I was hooked on the idea of being a priest.'

'You played at being a priest?'

'Sure. I made a censer out of a rusty kitchen sieve and garden wire. I screwed up newspaper and sprinkled it with a mixture of water, earth and some brown liquid which I found in the garden shed and I pretended it was incense.'

The driver repositioned himself, straightened his tie and adjusted his jacket.

Piet continued. 'Sometimes the paper lit and smouldered; other times it wouldn't light. Once when my sister was swinging the censer vigorously, the paper ignited and she burnt her arm. She was really mad at me.'

'Not surprised.'

'When my mother was not looking, I would take the brush used for cleaning our outside lavatory, rinse it in rainwater and then pretend I was conducting a funeral by sprinkling a make-believe coffin and the imaginary congregation with my 'holy water'. My sister usually refused to join in this part of the ceremony, claiming that my holy brush stunk and that she would catch some awful disease if any of the water landed on her.'

'Was it difficult to live away from home?' the taxi driver asked, as he ran his fingers down his lapels to ensure that his collar was in place. He then sat up straight so that he could see his own reflection in the rear view mirror. He stroked his head. Disappointment about the club membership was still lingering, but he decided to talk to Piet another day. It was time to take his passenger home. He hooted to alert the driver of the van and revved up the engine of the cab.

Piet continued, 'Yes, I didn't like it. Then I got used to it. It was very difficult on the first day. It was all new and strange.'

Piet remembered how all the new boys and their parents were ushered into the abbey church by the school principal. All were in their Sunday-best clothes. Mothers wore dresses and hats, fathers wore suits, and several had their caps in hands. Some clothes had not travelled too well. They had started the journey neatly pressed and ended up rather creased. One woman had become so hot that her dress had stuck in between her legs and two boys were jeering at the view of her backside. The teaching staff of the school were seated in the choir stalls of the abbey church. Piet had spotted Father Antonius sitting there; a small man with an abundance of wavy brown hair. He had a presence – an aura about him.

Father Principal welcomed them. He had a big belly, curly hair and a hooked nose, which was a rarity on a Dutch face. He possessed a loud voice and was surrounded by the fragrance of cologne. This was very unusual, as Piet would learn, since most of the priests and brothers smelt of relit cigars, over-percolated coffee and clothes worn day and night for several weeks. However the principal's robe was a lighter shade of off-white, suggesting that he made special arrangements to have his garments regularly laundered. The garments buttoned down the front and not quite up to the neck to give a glimpse of a dog collar for the priests and a plain shirt for the brothers. All the priests wore red stoles, the abbot had a blue one and the brothers were without. If a brother was undertaking a dirty job, he would wear a long apron, which covered the front of his robe. Only when the confrères were off duty did they wear ordinary clothes.

The taxi driver remembered reading about the sleeping arrangement for the young boys in the seminary. He wanted to hear Piet's impression. 'What was it like sleeping in a cell?' he asked.

'Strange at first, because I could hear the boys around me. I can remember a priest addressing parents and explaining that boys were not permitted in each other's cells. Right from the beginning they were worried about us becoming homosexuals.'

'Surely not.'

'It's true. There would always be someone on duty throughout the night to ensure that everyone had a good night's sleep and no-one broke the rules; lights were switched off at 9.30 and on again at 6.15.'

'What were the cells like?' The taxi driver remembered Father Antonius's description. He thought it a bleak arrangement.

Piet sank back into remembering. 'The dormitory was a very large room divided into sixty wooden cubicles, each closed by its own curtain. Imagine all those boys in one room! These cells were arranged in groups; six lines of ten – most in the middle of the room, backing onto other cells.'

'Lots of kids together. Wouldn't be allowed these days,' the driver said.

'The central cells had no windows; they were darker; less cold in the winter, but warmer in the summer than the outside ones. Between the rows were narrow passageways. Each cell measured two metres by one metre eighty.'

'Not very big.'

'Enough space for a bed, a cupboard, a small sink with a cold water tap and a metal chair for storing clothes and for kneeling against during early morning prayers. Bloody sparse!'

'Did you come from a large family?' asked the taxi driver, probably wondering how parents could send their twelve-year-old son away for six years, only seeing him three times a year during holidays.

'For a Catholic family we were small – only four children survived. The twins died before birth and two others died at a few days old.'

His father's job with the civil authorities entitled his family to a house, which was large enough for Piet and his brother to have their own bedrooms and for his two sisters to share one. He had taken this privacy for granted.

'Could you take any of your own things?'

'Only a few. When we found my cubicle there was not room for all of us. My mother sent my father to have a cigar in the courtyard. Then she made my bed and put away my few possessions. All my stuff was marked with 96. I kept that number until I left the seminary. She fixed my crucifix on the wall and found a space for my collection of empty matchboxes. When I started to cry, she told me to be brave – like my Uncle Jacobus, the missionary. Then they left.'

'What did you do then?' the taxi driver asked. He was beginning to feel some sympathy for the little boy Piet was describing.

'I cheered up a bit. I looked around at some of the boys and decided they would make good friends.'

Piet remembered that when all parents had left, the dormitory priest continued the tour of the school with the boys. First into the recreation hall where everyone was given a locker; Piet's was number 33. Then to see the billiard tables; the better one was for the older boys and the battered one for the younger ones. There were two table tennis tables to share amongst 130 boys. Next, they were shown the outdoor lavatories – eight urinals and eight closets. There was a large gap above and beneath each small door so it was always possible to look underneath or over the top to see if there was an occupant. These buildings were part of a recent extension. To visit the lavatories, it was necessary to go out of the main building. In winter, it could be extremely cold.

'You should write all that down, Piet.'
'What for?'
'Make a book about your schooldays. It's interesting. Give it to your grandchildren to read.'

'I'm not too keen on writing. I prefer to tell stories.'

'Have you seen Father Antonius since you left the seminary?' the driver asked.

'No, not for forty years,' Piet said. 'Now my old teacher is a famous author and I'll invite him to attend a meeting of the tenth anniversary of our Reading Club. I haven't seen him since I left the seminary school and went to university. I wanted to be a social worker and not a priest.'

The taxi driver wondered if Piet considered his present job as social work, but he decided against asking him.

Piet continued, 'He lives in a Belgian abbey since his book was published. I think he used information from his journals, which he kept since he first entered the seminary at the age of twelve.'

'Yes Piet, I know all about that,' the driver said, 'I wonder if Father Antonius has a record of your first day at school? Perhaps you are mentioned somewhere in his journals.'

Piet ignored the suggestion and continued with his calculations about when Antonius began his writing:

'That must have been at the start of the Second World War. According to one reviewer he is still writing his journal on a regular basis,' Piet said with some authority.

'Yes Piet, I know that, I'm the one who told you. I wrote that in my review. Remember?' Bob said, as the students' van began to move away and he followed.

As they were nearing his home Piet said again, 'There's an awful smell in town tonight. What is it?'

'There are lots of theories about that. My wife has an interesting explanation. You should ask her the next time you see her.'

'I look forward to hearing her idea,' said Piet, as he fumbled for money in his wallet to give the driver the fare. The wait had cost him an extra fourteen euros.

Later, Bob returned home, not with the sweet smell of success but with the bitter taste of rejection. His wife knew from his footsteps on the stairs and the slow turn of the key in the lock that her husband was unhappy. He did not have to say a word because she could tell by the edges of his mouth, the droop of his shoulders, and the texture of his skin that the Reading Club had turned him down. She could smell defeat on him. He tried to cover his disappointment by telling her that Piet had had no opportunity to talk to his colleagues about membership. He claimed that they spent too much time discussing the invitation of Father Antonius to their tenth anniversary celebration. Bob had lied when he said he did not mind that he still had not achieved membership. Quickly he turned the conversation around to the suggestion that he would drive to Belgium to collect the priest. He did not want his wife to know that he felt let down and humiliated by Piet.

Bob lowered himself into the armchair with the sunken seat. He unconsciously rearranged his ample bottom to avoid getting pinched by a wayward spring and carefully placed his hand over the tear in his trousers. His wife sat in her chair, angled halfway between being opposite and alongside her husband's. She put down her writing and picked up the jar of hand cream on her side table.

'Did Piet use your review?'

'I think he used it to supplement his own ideas.'

'Did he tell them that you'd gone to a lot of trouble to write it?' She creamed her hands.

'No, he didn't. That wouldn't have been appropriate.' Bob took up the evening paper as if to indicate that he did not want to continue talking about this subject. However, his wife had not completed her enquiries.

'Have you given up the idea of becoming a member?'

'Only for the time being,' he said without looking up.

'I hope you'll not go to the trouble of reading books and writing reviews on Piet's behalf again.'

The driver put down his paper and looked at her. 'I enjoyed writing about 'Priests Dying'. I'll continue to read what the club chooses. Usually Piet gives me a copy, in case he's not able to read the book himself.'

'Please yourself!' She picked up the notebook in which she recorded her experiences of the day. 'Has he told you what the next month's book is?'

'Yes, it's 'Animal Farm'.'

'That's an old one,' she said.

'The club doesn't always read the latest fiction. The following month they have chosen, 'The Power and the Glory', by Graham Greene, which was published in 1940. Father Antonius wrote that he was influenced by it when he was a young man.'

'I thought you'd read 'Animal Farm'.'

'Yes, I did, in Dutch, many years ago. This time I'll read the English version.'

The driver had already decided that he would re-read 'Priests Dying' in preparation for his journey with the priest. Hopefully he could impress the author with his knowledge. Perhaps Father Antonius could provide an entrance into the Reading Club for him. He was not giving up on his dream of membership. One day he would achieve that. He continued, 'Piet was asking about the smell in town tonight. It was quite strong outside the doctor's house. I told him he should speak to you about your theory.'

She grimaced. On hearing only Piet's name she could conjure up his smell within her nostrils.

'I smell a rat!' she said, and they both laughed. Although she noticed the tear in Bob's trousers she chose not to say anything.

CHAPTER 3

Father Antonius

In the early 1800s an abbot of a lesser-known Catholic order decided that his residence in Belgium was inadequate for himself and his ten confrères. With funds donated by a wealthy patron, he purchased an elegant country house, in a village on the Dutch side of the Belgian border, with the idea of developing it into an abbey. On the day of the move to the new premises, the confrères walked alongside the abbatial carriage. With his talkative parrot, Guido, perched on one arm, the abbot waved to the villagers with the other hand, and the small procession entered the grounds of the new abbey site. The village brass band played some triumphal marches, the mayor gave a welcoming speech, while the parrot squawked a Gregorian chant.

This religious community grew. In the 1880s the abbey founded its own minor seminary offering an education towards the priesthood for boys between twelve and eighteen and a major seminary for the formation of priests prior to their ordination. Up until the late 1980s, priests staffed both establishments. The Order specialised in the formation of canons rather than monks, that is, priests who performed the choral prayers, who ran the local parish churches, taught in the abbey schools and worked in social care. Over the years an assortment of buildings of varying architectural merit were added to the country house: a church, some extensive living quarters for the confrères, a minor and major seminary, a library, a farm, a brewery, a printing works, a bookshop, a community hall and a wing for the elderly, sick and dying priests.

Father Antonius was educated at the minor seminary, received his formation at the major seminary, took his vows in the abbey, worked as a parish priest in a nearby church and was a reluctant teacher in the junior seminary up until its closure. Three members of the Reading Club had been boarders at the minor seminary at different times between 1956 and 1966.

Antonius was the monastic name later given to Jean-Pierre van Aken who was born in 1928, the third son of a Dutch Catholic family. In 1890, Jean-Pierre's grandfather was thirty when he married a French Protestant woman who was eighteen years old. Together they built up a successful business producing high quality linens for which there was a great demand. By the time Jean-Pierre's grandmother was 47, she was a rich woman, but widowed. His parents moved into her fifteen-roomed house which had a small drive, tall iron gates and a huge garden. There was sufficient accommodation for all the family; his grandmother had her separate ground floor apartment. His father inherited the family mill.

From his mother's twelve pregnancies, only eight went full term; two children died before they were a year old. Up until he was eleven, Jean-Pierre was the third eldest. It was often the custom in Catholic families for the first son to take over his father's business or trade, while the second one was dedicated to the Church to become a priest. Unfortunately, the brother above him drowned and that changed Jean-Pierre's position in the family. He became the second son. Instead of heading for an academic career – his primary school teacher told his parents he was the most intelligent child she had ever met in her thirty years of teaching –

he was redirected to become the family's gift to God.

Up until this point in his life, Jean-Pierre gave little thought to the Almighty. Yes, he went to church – there was no other option – but once there he usually took the opportunity to do some daydreaming rather than listen to the sermons, which seemed to him to be so unfriendly. It was his elder brother who was the altar boy, not he. Now he felt both excited and nervous at the prospect of his future life. In between the time of his brother's death and going to the seminary, his home life changed. His mother began treating him more kindly, serving him special food, which she did not give to anyone else, and his father cautioned his siblings when they started to tease their brother about becoming a priest.

Jean-Pierre thought that he could probably get along very well with God and he began extending his prayers and feeling his beliefs a little more deeply. God took on a new persona, more like an imaginary friend, rather than the Almighty Creator. There were many aspects about the Church which Jean-Pierre did not understand, but he trusted that all would be made clear to him before he had to give sermons or to hear confessions. He could certainly imagine himself dressed in a priest's attire: the long off-white robe, not quite reaching the ground to show off a shiny pair of shoes. His father told him that clean shoes indicated an honest heart. He heard that the Abbey School gave the best education and he was looking forward to learning new subjects such as Greek, Latin, and music – especially music. Maybe they would give him lessons so he could play the abbey's famous grand organ. He could see himself breaking the host and blessing the communion wine. He was looking forward to making some new friends because, apart from one or two, he did not like the majority of the local boys.

In 1940, Jean-Pierre was twelve when he entered the seminary. That year The Netherlands was occupied by Germany, the universities were closed and school life for the boarders became erratic. Sometimes the junior seminarians were in school, other times they were sent home because the abbey did not have sufficient food to feed them. Or, as happened on a few occasions, their dormitories were temporarily occupied by a platoon of German soldiers. Neither his mother nor his father welcomed their son's return home. They knew that his school and its abbey had no strategic importance to the occupying forces and it was therefore a much safer place for Jean-Pierre to be lodged. However, in those days parents did not explain adult concerns to their children, who were expected to do what they were told. In one of the first entries in his journal, in 1940, Jean-Pierre recorded a feeling of hurt and rejection because of his parents' coldness and silence when he returned home for a week:

No one is happy to see me. No one is talking to me. What have I done to make them so unkind?

Even his grandmother was not pleased to see him. It was she who gave him a small exercise book and suggested that he write down his thoughts, when he had no-one to talk to. This he did, at first imagining that he was having a conversation with her. At the time, he did not appreciate his parents' concern. It was only much later in the 1960s, when rebuilding The Netherlands was almost finished, that people had time and distance to reflect on how the population behaved under occupation. Then he began to understand what his father had done in order to protect his family and the workers in his linen factory, and why this was never spoken about during the war or once it had ended.

Partly cut off from his country's occupation in a seminary, and only glimpsing it briefly on his visits home, Jean-Pierre experienced the war as a collection of uncomfortable, unrelated, and sometimes frightening experiences. Many things were never explained to him by the adults. He recorded his observations in his journal.

1940

Boots hitting the cobblestones made a lot of noise. The sound banged in my ears and on my chest. They carried rifles. Papa said the material for their uniforms had been made in our town.

Grand-mère shouted something in French. She would not tell me what it meant. My elder brother made the German salute and strutted around the room in goose-step fashion. He got a slap around his head. My three little sisters hid underneath the bed. My other brother sat on the floor playing with his toy soldiers.

Jean-Pierre heard a neighbour talk about the Mayor of the town, his father's old school friend, who was taken away to a concentration camp, never to return. He did not understand then what was meant by the allegation that this man was fronting an organisation of mayors to form a resistance group against the Germans. From an uncle he heard the criticism about the Dutch royal family who left the country – Queen Wilhelmina went to England and her daughter, Juliana, fled to Canada. Prince Bernard became a fighter pilot in the RAF. Jean-Pierre had no understanding of politics but he recorded that the prime minister – a useless aristocrat, his grandmother called him – was sacked by the Queen because he was advising the nation to co-operate and not resist the Germans. His grandmother told him that she had listened to *Radio Oranje* in a neighbour's house, but his father warned him not to talk about that to anyone. He recalled hearing his parents laughing at the anger expressed by his grandmother when she observed that more and more people were colluding with the occupiers. She told several people, 'If I was twenty years younger, I would be resisting the bastards like a crazy man.'

Away from his home, Jean-Pierre wrote (as if addressing his grandmother) about his experiences in the seminary: his class-mates, his teachers, the abbot, the priests, the brothers, his struggle with the early morning prayers and his different lessons. He described how he missed his parents, his brothers, sisters and especially his grandmother.

1941

Ma cherie Grand-mère

I got top marks in Latin and we had pea soup, nothing like Mama makes, this was thin. No specks of bacon and it had a funny smell. My feet get very cold in the night and I got a slap around the head for talking on the way to Mass. I miss you and everyone else. Now I am here I do not think I want to be a priest. They talk about sins; I do not understand what they mean. I am trying hard to be good. I want all of you to feel proud of me. I have not made any friends yet.

As he grew into adolescence, he made less reference in his journal to his family but he wrote more about his changing mind and body. He recorded the issues, which he took to confession. Sometimes he worried about what to confess, or that he did not have as much to tell the priest as his other class-mates. Several times, he wrote about his wavering faith, which a few days later was followed by a surge of belief. On one occasion, he revealed to a priest that he saw a vision of Holy Mary at the end of his bed. He was told he was probably suffering from indigestion and that praying to the Holy Virgin would diminish his hallucinations. His adolescent adoration for the young professor who taught him Latin was recorded in his journal.

1943

I do not think he likes me. I am not good enough. He always chooses the boys who are the best footballers to read out their Latin and he never picks me. I asked him if I could have extra lessons, but he laughed at me. He said that I knew enough. I feel very nervous when I'm near him and I am afraid of my own feelings. My underbelly comes to life and I feel sick when I see him. Have I committed a sin?

All of his entries were written in small writing; he used abbreviations and his personal hieroglyphics so that, if discovered, his journals could almost not be deciphered. His grandmother assured him that it was permitted to keep his writing private. She said that he did not have to tell anyone.

The boys in the seminary were always hungry. No-one wasted a crumb. Jean-Pierre wrote frequently about this feeling. Later in life, he developed a mild obsession for receiving his meals on time and always eating everything on his plate. His capacity to savour delicate flavours and different textures of food was diminished by the seminary table rule. No boy received a second helping until the first was finished. Consequently, nearly all ate quickly, ramming large portions into their mouths in order to be ready for any extras. When he ate like that at home, his grandmother reprimanded him. He wrote:

1943

On my first day home from school, Grand-mère was very angry with me. She said that she would rather share the table with a pig. Never before had she seen a person eat so quickly. She said that the Catholic priests were turning me into an animal.

Food was scarce, especially in what was to become known as the 'Famine Winter' of 1944-45. To keep alive, people ate rats and tulip bulbs. Thousands died. Jean-Pierre's grandmother told him how the rich people from Amsterdam, who were starving, took their riches – their gold, silver and sometimes their furs – and went on their bikes into the countryside in an attempt to buy food. On the subject of her bicycle, the old woman could become hysterical. Although she never relinquished her French spirit, she had adopted a lot of Dutch ways, including riding her beloved bicycle. The Germans had confiscated it, and for this crime alone she never forgave them. Her son found a replacement, but this had bone-shaking wooden wheels, because all rubber tyres had been seized. A number of years after the war, when she was in her mid-seventies and becoming senile, she would call after people if she thought they were German. 'Return our bikes,' she shouted in French. Her daughter-in-law looked on embarrassed, but the rest of the family laughed.

Much of what Jean-Pierre wrote about the war came from conversations with his grandmother and not from what his parents told him on his visits home. Mostly she got her information from neighbours of similar age who had less to fear from the occupiers than the younger generation. She talked about, and later Jean-Pierre recorded, how in 1941 the Jews were taken to Germany to be killed. Many Dutch public servants helped with this and she said it was those people with rubber tyres on their bicycles. While she was adamant that if she was younger she would be a member of the Dutch Resistance, Jean-Pierre was not sure that, had he been older, he would have joined her. He looked to the example of his father who closed down most of his factory, sacked his workers and sold his machinery, so that he could not be expected to produce material for the German uniforms. Later, the boy found out that his father used the family capital to help support his ex-workers. Some of the other mill owners came in a position where either they complied and produced material to clothe the German forces or, if they resisted, they were sent to prison camps.

In 1944, when the allies freed the southern part of The Netherlands from German occupation, Jean-Pierre remembered getting a glimpse of Montgomery, the famous British soldier whose temporary headquarters were in the town. He wrote in his journal:

Many people came to see the English soldiers in the street in front of the church today. Mama said that she never thought that she would be pleased to hear the sound of tanks rumbling through our town. Now the Germans have gone, Grand-mère hopes that the allies will give her some new tyres for her bicycle. I think that she is too old to ride a bike, but she is positive that she is not. I suggested to Papa that I stop my studies at the seminary and come back home to help him start up the factory again. He smiled and said that he wanted me to complete my education and become a priest.

The following year Jean-Pierre saw Churchill when he came to visit Montgomery. He thought the British Prime Minister looked like a big toad in uniform. In the years after the war, he recorded what his grandmother called 'an excess of Dutch heroes'. Collaboration was reframed or denied. Many people who kept a low profile during the war asserted themselves as working for the resistance. The French grandmother, who would have resisted had she been younger, became critical of those Dutch inhabitants who had faced the worst decision of their lives – to comply or be executed. Jean-Pierre who embraced his father's way of dealing with the occupation, thought that his grandmother was harsh in her criticism. As an older person, she was little threat to the occupiers who could not be bothered by her opinion.

By the time Jean-Pierre was thirty, the Dutch Government commissioned a history of the war. The chosen author took fifteen years to complete his numerous volumes. Surprisingly, the historian adopted the same attitude as Jean-Pierre's grandmother, which was to judge many people as cowards and traitors. He diminished the myth of a glut of heroes and increased the numbers of those folks who willingly collaborated. Like the French woman, the writer had the advantage of not having the threat of a bayonet at his back or a jackboot at his throat.

Considering the country was at war, the seminary provided a good education. Jean-Pierre excelled in all of his subjects, especially the classical languages and in music, where his talents in playing the violin, not the organ, were nurtured. He became enveloped in the daily ritual and cloaked in his own beliefs. He participated in the early morning prayers and grew accustomed to being alone, although part of a group. At eighteen, he entered the abbey as a novice and was given the monastic name of Antonius. He wanted Bernard, but the abbot said that he had given that name to someone else. It was probably this request for another name that set Antonius apart from the other novices who obediently accepted the directions of their superior. A tiny seed of doubt was sown in the mind of the abbot who wondered whether this young man, with his blue questioning eyes, was capable of keeping the vow of obedience. Later, other abbots held this same concern, as if in succession each one inherited this uncertainty about Antonius from his predecessor.

It took Father Antonius six years to complete his formation. During the first twelve months, he demonstrated his obedience and his capacity for subservient work by being very thorough in the menial domestic chores which he and the other novices were given. In the years following, he was encouraged to use his mind in Philosophy, Church law and Church history. In Eloquence, he practised using his voice in church and compiling sermons. Moral Theology taught him how to represent the views of the Church in special cases. For example, what to do if a man said he wanted a divorce because he was going crazy living with his wife; what to do if a woman said that she did not want to bear any more children; how to respond to confessions of adultery, imagined or real – in fact what to say to the confessions of the sins against the ten commandments. He learned the structure of the response in the confessional stalls. The supplicant would begin, 'Father I have sinned...' The priest would respond with a sermon. There should be repentance, followed by penitence.

For the majority of confrères, their six years of formation were completely absorbing, but for Antonius it was different. He questioned what he was being taught and this often left him feeling doubtful and confused. In particular, the biblical version of the Creation troubled him. He came to hear of other explanations; ideas put forward by scientists and atheists regarding the beginnings of life. Intellectually he thought their theories more convincing than any religious story. However, when he examined his feelings, he knew that God existed and created the world. He believed, because in his inner core that was the feeling in the marrow of his bones. He was a Catholic because out of all the other religions he heard about, this was the one he knew by heart, in his heart. As a genetically programmed dot, he had been a Catholic in the womb. It was his language, his mother tongue, his nature and natural to him.

Before senility took over his grandmother's mind, Antonius talked to her about the persecution of the Huguenots. Perhaps it was in hearing her Protestant views that he developed his sensitivity towards the diverse ways that various Christian faiths have evolved. He was concerned by inter-faith prejudice and he felt ashamed of the atrocities committed in the name of religion, including by his own Church. He loathed the descriptions of the torturous deaths of martyrs and the act of crucifixion. Sometimes he would try to reconcile past events by reminding himself that each act of grace or disgrace should be viewed in its own context; but his wretched feelings quickly returned when he visualised acts of violence which Christians wrought upon believers of other religions, even upon fellow Christians. Finally, he calculated that his inner conviction about the existence of God was much stronger than the total of his doubts. He went forward to his ordination feeling confident that his uncertainties would disappear with time. He wrote:

1952

My Ordination

Inside the abbey church it smelt of hot wax and mothballs from Sunday-best clothes. The congregation arrived early to get a good view and the first four front pews were reserved for my family and neighbours. My grandmother needed a lot of persuasion to attend the service. I knew that her reasons for doubting my commitment had to do with her negative view of the Catholic Church and not because she did not care about me. Last week, at a family supper, she handed me a letter and asked that I read it when I returned to the abbey. In it, she said that I should not feel obligated to become ordained. It was not too late to say no. I was not too old to go to university and become a professor of history.

I had no intention of changing my mind. I knew that she had written the letter with my wellbeing in her heart.

Some church women had been out early gathering wild flowers, which now adorned the altar. The privet was in bloom and this, together with the burning wax, created a heady perfume. As soon as we processed into the church, I smelt it. The pastel colours of the stained glass were vibrant and the sunlight illuminated the statues of Saint Timothy and Saint Therese. The confrères stood in the choir stalls. Beneath their robes their arms were folded across their bellies. The bells chimed, clanging together to make their familiar discordant sound. Organ music filled the air and stirred my internal world. I was overwhelmed by the interior of the church, which seemed much higher than usual as if making room for a spiritual presence.

I had read the service several times and I practised it one evening with the abbot after he gave me the final talk about my forthcoming commitment to God. The Bishop conducted the ordination and, although I enjoyed hearing the words, he said them rather mechanically. When I came to prostrate myself on the floor before the altar, a great feeling of elation stirred inside me. I accredited this to the love of God. I felt something similar, but not so strong, a number of times when alone in my room. At the conclusion of my ordination, I went around the circle of priests and they in turn blessed me. I had a strong feeling of fellowship and my eyes moistened.

After the service, many confrères congratulated my family, including my atheist brother Thomas. Coffee and cakes were served in the dining-room. I feel like a changed person; confident that my uncertainties will disappear now that I am a holy father.

However, Antonius's changed status did not bring him that spiritual reassurance. One main challenge came from Thomas, his younger brother, who declared himself an atheist when he was fourteen. Going to university to study literature only served to increase Thomas's non-belief. Regularly he confronted Antonius with alternative views and information, which questioned many aspects of his faith. Thomas gave his brother a copy of Graham Greene's book, 'The Power and the Glory'. This was banned by the Church, but not before it shocked and offended the Catholic community. Antonius found himself identifying with the whiskey drinking, fornicating priest, who wrestled with the dilemma of whether to give himself up to the anti-clerical government agents or to remain in hiding. He considered some aspects of this character more believable, even more appealing than the image of the priest as a superior man, above temptation and just below heaven. He wrote in his journal:

1956

I do not understand why the Church has banned this book when it portrays the dilemmas of many men who choose the difficult path of ordination. I wonder whether we are all destined to suffer like Christ or Father José, the unfortunate priest in the book. I pray I will be spared a difficult death.

In the late 1950s, Antonius read about the Theology of Liberation, which began in Latin America. There the priests made a choice to stand alongside the poorest people instead of clinging to the better classes. Antonius was reminded of how his father discreetly supported his workers during the war years. Later he heard about the 'Labourer Priests' in France and was impressed that these fellows put aside their priestly garments to work together with those who toiled at rough jobs. For a while, he thought seriously about leaving the Order and joining the workers, but he realised that he could never be good at practical activities because when he was younger he had sustained an injury, which left him with a damaged spine.

Finally in the 1960s and 1970s emerged the so-called 'Critical Priests' who challenged the beliefs of the Church in respect of many issues, such as abortion, euthanasia, divorce and the position of women in the Church. Antonius felt inspired by this group but decided not to leave his Order; instead he planned to apply their ways of thinking to the situation in his abbey.

His first challenge arose out of a concern that the number of young men coming forward for priesthood was declining. He decided to address the abbot and used his journal to prepare what he would say:

1975

Since the war the attitude of Dutch Catholic society towards religion has changed and the elevated, authoritarian position of the clergy in the community came to an end. The days when a priest made annual visits to families to enquire whether there was a baby in the cradle or one in the womb, have gone. People no longer want to have large families nor do they wish to send one of their sons to work for God in archaic religious communities. The majority of the population will not tolerate being told how to behave. They have tasted individualism and perhaps the lean years of the war gave them a craving for a freer and more materialistic life. The number of young men coming forward for priesthood is declining. They do not want what we offer. There is no status, no job satisfaction, no prospects, and no pleasure in becoming a priest. In fact, any young man thinking about such a commitment might be considered weird, sad, weak or merely seeking special relationships with other men.

I believe, out there in society, there are young Catholic men with religious convictions who would like to find a means of giving their lives to God, in ways which respect and utilise their skills and abilities, at the same time allowing them to further their careers and to live a spiritual life in a religious community. Insisting that every applicant for the priesthood has to relinquish his academic ambitions and acquire a degree in theology is not only a deterrent but it is a waste of skills, which could otherwise benefit the Order and society. Surely, it should be possible to support youngsters through their studies and then allow them to follow their careers. Their work for God would be in serving the community and in being exemplary employees. It might be necessary to create a new category of community priests for those who were not interested in becoming full priests. After a day's work and at the weekends they could be involved in supporting the religious life of the abbey.

Antonius rehearsed what he would say before speaking to the abbot. He even discussed it with his brother who, for a change, did not disagree with him.

Thomas smiled and said, 'If those changes are introduced then you could find that you are permitted, if not encouraged, to lecture at the university. It's about time that the abbey made use of your skills as a historian. You are wasted teaching eleven and twelve-year-olds in the seminary. I know you hate this work.'

However, when the abbot eventually agreed to listen to Antonius's ideas, he soon became very angry. He resented being given what he considered to be a directive by one of his priests and he was particularly upset at the mention of 'special friendships between the confrères', which he concluded referred to homosexuality. The suggestion that this existed in the abbey was vehemently rejected and Antonius was reminded of the vow of chastity, which he and other confrères had taken. The idea of the community priests was dismissed and not to be mentioned again. Antonius was reminded of his vow of obedience which included not dictating what the abbot should do. At this point Antonius lost his temper and said a few harsh things, which he later regretted. For his part, the abbot avoided talking to Antonius for several months and denied his request to move him from his teaching post in the seminary to become the abbey archivist and historian.

In his free time, Antonius had studied for a doctorate. It was hard work because his research was undertaken when all his other duties were completed. He worked late into the night and became accustomed to living with little sleep. For many years, after he became a doctor of history, he had a recurring nightmare which he described a number of times in his journal:

1995

Again, I was woken by that recurring bad dream. It is 1967 and I am in the quarters of the abbot. He is smoking a thick cigar and sitting relaxed behind his huge mahogany desk. I asked to see him in order to talk about my doctorate. At that time I had a full time teaching commitment at the abbey school and I wanted to request two days leave from my duties in order to prepare for the public defence of my dissertation. My thesis, a substantial volume of 350 pages, was published and I had a copy to show to the abbot. For some moments he looked at it, thumbing through the pages, perhaps to see which illustrations I had included, or maybe looking for a picture of himself.

'A nice booklet,' was his first comment, on a book which took me seven years to write in my spare time. 'A nice booklet,' he repeated.

His remark felt like a slap in the face.

He continued, 'I hope that you will be modest about this work and not feel yourself better than your confrères.'

He never once gave me any words of praise, or small acknowledgement for the sacrifice this achievement was for me. When I sought his permission to begin this work, he had sighed and asked:

'For what reason do you want to do this? Our abbey has no need for erudite people but for good priests who are willing to deny their own needs and desires and to sacrifice themselves for the good of the faithful. Be careful that you do not become too proud of yourself.'

Soon after this, he ordered the principal of the abbey school to increase the number of my teaching periods. The abbot never asked me once, in my eight years of research and study, how I was progressing. Now I stood in front of him again, hoping for a sympathetic response to my request for leave.

But he laughed at me and barked, 'I had not expected this request. Have you considered the damage this will cause to your pupils when they do not receive their lessons?'

'I will leave instructions and work. I am sure someone could sit with my classes for two days without causing permanent damage to any of my pupils,' I said.

'I find your request irresponsible,' he said, closing my dissertation with a slam. ' When I did my own doctorate in Sacra Theologia at the Gregorian University in Rome, my professors said that it was not necessary for a student to have extra time to prepare, because the defence was a mere formality; just a ceremony. However, I will grant you two free lessons on the day you go to the university. But, you must return in time for the last prayers of the day and resume your teaching on the next morning. Good luck, my son,' he said, stretching out his hand in my direction so that I could kiss his abbatial ring.

At that moment, I awoke. It was forty years since my meeting with that abbot and still the injustice of it haunts me. A host of different situations trigger the dream. Sometimes I can account for what has caused this repeating nightmare. At other times, such as last night, I have no idea why I should be dreaming about my doctorate again.

For many years Antonius wrestled with his conscience. Should he stay or should he leave and attempt to find a religious life nearer to his beliefs? As time passed, his discomfort lessened as he grew accustomed to the security and the pleasant aspects of abbey life. He became used to having the rhythm of the day decided by set hours of worship, meditation, private prayers, teaching, pastoral duties and meals. Many of his decisions were made for him. He liked and respected some of his confrères; their gentle, yet solitary ways. Special celebrations appealed to him; he loved the music and singing. He often found the atmosphere of the filled church moving. The abbey attracted fine organists and he established a rapport with some of these musicians. At times he switched off from the service and the abbot's sermon and daydreamed about other things; he sung hymns while his mind was elsewhere. After his grandmother died, he often imagined he saw her riding a bicycle between the ceiling rafters of the abbey church – an angel on rubber wheels. In her hand was a white bayonet with a label saying 'Made in Heaven'. Once he shocked himself by having a vision of her riding over the neck of a German soldier and calling out, 'Now I am twenty years younger, I can resist like a crazy man.'

By the time he was fifty, Antonius had overcome his internal debate. He examined and re-examined all aspects of his faith, and considered what he would do if he left the Order. He concluded that even if he relinquished his priestly life he would never become a layman, but remain a priest – perhaps a much damaged one. He had been formed, or was it deformed like a high class Chinese woman who has her feet bound at birth so that she cannot walk quickly or run away? The unbinding in adulthood would cause excruciating pain. As much as he disliked some of the Church bindings, he knew that he could never survive without them. He convinced himself that it was more courageous to stay than to go.

However, by the time he was sixty he developed another revolutionary idea, this time in relation to the ageing population of the abbey community. He noticed that when some of the confrères reached 65, they often went into a kind of physical and intellectual redundancy. They stopped their parish or abbey work and were destined to sit in their rooms wishing time away until the next meal and eventually their final journey to the abbey graveyard. Many of these men had a rich experience of spiritual and pastoral work; others like Antonius had studied for doctorates in their private time, which meant there was a wealth of unused knowledge in these old guys. Of course, some of them were becoming demented, but not all. It was time to communicate his ideas to the new abbot. After all, Antonius himself would soon be entering this phase of life and he did not want to spend his remaining years – as the Dutch say – 'sitting behind the geraniums'.

He read about a community of nuns where the culture was to keep the minds of the elderly active. No one stopped working at a certain age. The nuns who answered the telephone and worked in the reception area were in their 90s. They played board and word games. The convent found ways of extending the working life of all its community. God's work was lifelong and could be executed in many ways; tasks were modified so that the women did not lose their motivation. An eminent physician studied the community. This doctor found the nuns had much larger than average brains.

Antonius realised that this attitude towards the elderly was exceptional. Society in general had not worked out a good way of solving what to do with this growing section of the population.

In the 1960s, gluts of homes were built by the government for elderly people, who had nothing to contribute and could be looked after until death. The abbey was replicating society's solution. But, surely, better use could be made of the skills and knowledge if these old men continued to do God's work. Maybe they could be mentors, companions, perhaps they could write letters, record historical events, use their language skills, work in the archives, talk to visitors, and be subjects for medical and psychological studies. Antonius was buzzing with ideas when he spoke to the abbot who, from behind a desk piled high with books and papers, listened without expression to the suggestions. The reply was simple. The abbot told him that he was counting the months to the finish of his own six-year term of office. He wanted to be free of the abbatial burden of responsibility, which was so heavy that he developed a stooped posture as if he was carrying an increasingly heavy cross on the way to a personal Calvary. Although ten years younger than Antonius, the abbot thought that he was earning the right to a quiet life. He was not interested in thinking about his future duties, when he resumed his life as an ordinary priest. Without consulting the members of his community, he said he was sure that all those over 65 would feel the same.

Finally, Antonius gave up suggesting ways in which his community could change. He came to terms with the idea that his Order would eventually die out if it continued with its present regime. Incidentally, fifteen years later a new, young abbot introduced some changes based on the ideas of Antonius, who by that time had been moved to a Belgian abbey. Since finishing his teaching career, Antonius ensured that he kept himself fit. He regularly biked, walked, volunteered for pastoral work, helped adults with learning difficulties, visited the sick and dying, wrote articles for the Order, assisted and advised a group of local historians, regularly wrote in his journal and, with his brother's help, created his best-seller, 'Priests Dying'. He always claimed that he felt relieved that his confrères never elected him to serve as abbot. In a letter, Thomas summed up Antonius's position. Thomas wrote:

1990
'The trouble is, brother, you were always too intelligent for these guys. You outwitted them with your arguments. You disturbed them with your humility and you alarmed them with your temper. You felt frustrated by your various abbots because you made the mistake of expecting them to understand how to manage the complexities of their job; care for a variety of old buildings; arrange

finances; be aware of the changing spiritual needs of a community, and be a father to a group of precious priests, including one who is too bright. None had the advantage of having degrees in human resource management; they copied the authoritarian ways, which they have experienced in their predecessors. Your confrères would never want you as their abbot. They are terrified that you will change their safe ways of working and turn the abbey on its head. You were wasted teaching in that school, you should have been working at a university, challenging graduates to apply their knowledge of history to the serious world issues. What a lost opportunity! I hope it has been worth the sacrifice.'

Antonius had tucked Thomas's letter in a notebook. For years, writing had been his way of making sense of the world, exploring his feelings, rehearsing difficult communications and for explaining problems and mysteries to himself. In his book 'Priests Dying', he claimed that this regular habit helped him to remain sane, restrain his temper, keep his faith, retain an active mind and appreciate many aspects of his life.

Even after his book was published, he continued to write regularly in his small notebooks. It was as if the experience of converting his private journals into a public book, increased his capacity and desire to write. While at first he resented Thomas's editing, later he grew to appreciate and learn from his brother's skill. Antonius saw how his book had been transformed. Instead of his journal entries becoming briefer as he grew older, the reverse happened; he became more prolific. Even his slight dementia, which played games with his short-term memory, did not interfere with his ability to generate writing material. Antonius never asked himself why he was continuing to write after his book was published. Nor did he question for whom he was writing or what would happen to his work after his death. He wrote because he felt driven. Not to be responding to this instinct was alien to him. He wrote:

2007
   I am getting close to my 10,000th journal entry. Will I be able

to write something special for this occasion? I reread my first entry which I wrote when I was twelve. My grandmother wanted me to research the history of the Catholic and Protestant religions and tell a new story; one which would heal the past wounds. I never managed to fulfil her dream. What would she have thought of my book 'Priests Dying'? I wonder around in my thoughts. I start writing about one thing, forget why I started it, then drift off into another subject. That is the joy of keeping a journal. It is private and not meant to be read by anyone else. However, I know that my mind lets me down from time to time; I repeat myself both in my journal and in conversations. My grandmother did the same, the year before she died. I think I am becoming demented.

Since the publication of my book I received a lot of correspondence and requests to give talks. One arrived today from Piet van Rijn's Reading Club. They invited me to their tenth anniversary. Why do I get so nervous on these occasions? Will I ever get accustomed to doing this? The last time I spoke was to a Catholic women's book club in Amsterdam; I had chronic diarrhoea the day before. Amsterdam is a strange city – quite unlike the rest of The Netherlands. Yes Amsterdam. The so-called capital of tolerance; is there another option when people live so close to each other? They say 370 people per square kilometre. That is very crowded.

The Dutch are not particularly tolerant. Just listen to any conversation on a tram, in a train, in a shop, on a terrace, outside a church, and you will hear the anger, the anxiety and the criticism between different groups – Catholics commenting on Protestants, Christians being weary of Muslims, local people criticising migrant workers and the unemployed resenting the employed. Last year a filmmaker was assassinated because he was making a film about a Muslim girl. We also have the reputation of being liberal; possibly that view is based on a few thin ideas.

Either by accident or design, many tourists to Amsterdam visit the Red Light District; it is not difficult to find. A few steps out of Central Station and there you are. It is amazing how intriguing some visitors find this area. The prostitutes display themselves in the large bay windows of the houses along the canals. They sit astride chairs or stand in supposedly provocative stances, clad in revealing and erotic clothing – illuminated for all to see. Many Dutch people, including myself, are extremely embarrassed and dismayed when tourists describe, with enthusiasm and slight titillation, their visits to this area. Why do they bother? There are so many other more worthwhile things to see in the city, such as our famous paintings of the Golden Age and the collection of Vincent van Gogh's work. Even if you are not an art lover you can enjoy a trip on the canals to see the tall, narrow, gabled houses, the *Oude Kerk*, the bridges, the flower market, numerous beautiful buildings, and of course our bicycles – hundreds and hundreds of them. It is a long time since I rode a bike.

There are many sex shops in Amsterdam. Not many people would expect a priest to know about what they sell – but I do. The windows provide explicit displays of various sexual aids. I have heard several confessions in which some of these contraptions were described. Not that I have ever purchased anything like that for myself, or ever wanted to. Maybe some of my fellow confrères have been tempted – but not me. That is not to say that we do not experience sexual arousal. I am sure the majority of us do. Most priests and nuns are sexual people. We recognise it as a gift from God and see that as central to producing children. I would not make a good father, but I think I might have made a good companion for Wilhelmina. I chose to be celibate because I believe it is a way to be near to God without the distraction of family life. In some other faiths the priest may get married. I wonder how they manage.

In former years, sexual thoughts were described as a sin. The subject was taboo. But we are more enlightened now and have an understanding of how our bodies function, even though we chose a life of celibacy. Not that my generation talks openly about such things. It was quite different when I went to visit some of our missions abroad. There the priests were more open, talking about their sometimes inconvenient reactions and joking about the judicious use of ice cubes to disperse erections. I was quite shocked. I know that a life of celibacy does not guarantee a life without sexual arousal, nor does it mean that we will never feel attracted to members of the opposite or same sex. I think that it was the mention of this topic in my book which drew most criticism from some of my colleagues in the Church. Sometimes I think that I was too open in what I wrote, but Thomas insisted. He said that was what the general reader wanted to know. Was he right? These days I am more troubled by my uncontrollable digestive system which has a mind of its own (my gut brain) than by my dormant member.

I can still recall the disappointment I felt when my first abbot said that he was giving me the job of teaching literature and history in the abbey school. In those days, it was a seminary and we expected and hoped that many of the boys would choose to become priests after they completed their education with us. Since I had a degree and was preparing for my doctorate, it was thought appropriate that I work in education although I had no formal training as a teacher. I still had my grandmother's aspiration of rewriting Church history as my ambition.

As a young priest, it was my responsibility to talk to the boys about sexual matters relating to their adolescence and their future lives. I do not know why the abbot selected me for this task. I felt punished because surely he knew that I felt awkward about these talks. I watched the faces of the boys when I addressed them. Many looked confused. I knew from what some of them took to their confessions that they did not understand my sometimes oblique reference to sex. I was frequently worried that my words had a negative impact on those boys for the rest of their lives. As a priest and a teacher, I was expected to pass on the Catholic message about sex, procreation and the importance of the family, and this included certain codes of behaviour.

At school, the boys worked and played in groups of at least three, so that two never had a chance to become intimate. Several pairs of 'friends' were sent away from the seminary because they became too close. Their families were told that their sons could not manage the academic work and it was suggested that they sought other ways in which to serve God. I now realise that the message *numquam duo, semper tres* (never two of you, always three) became deep rooted in all of us and prevented many from having any close friends in school and later on in adult life. We lived in a religious community but were not emotionally connected with one another. The boys were told on their first night in the school to sleep with their hands above the sheets. This was very uncomfortable for those who were accustomed to sleeping with their hands tucked between their legs, under their arms or indeed cupping their genitals. It was yet another message about sexual matters.

In all, I spent over thirty years in teaching; I felt nervous before my lessons and my palms were sweaty when I was doing this work. In the early days, a number of our pupils went on to become priests but as the years went by, fewer and fewer heard this calling. Instead they chose different careers and some became parents themselves, sending both their sons and daughters to the new Abbey School (when girls became pupils it was no longer called a minor seminary). I never considered myself a good teacher. The work requires an extrovert. I am after all a quite reflective person, better working alone in a library or the archives than leading a group of students. I remain angry with the various abbots who told me that teaching is what God had selected me for. How did they know? I reluctantly followed their guidance as best as I could. It was a relief when the school closed and I became a redundant teacher.

2007

Since writing my book, I have received a lot of correspondence. Yesterday I was sent an invitation to talk about my book from Piet – what was his name? His Reading Club will celebrate some anniversary. I am repeating myself. I wrote about this yesterday. Wish that I did not get so nervous on these occasions. A doctor I saw last year said I was suffering from irritable bowel syndrome – which is aggravated by stress. Yesterday I had a chronic explosion in my digestive system and I do not think I was in a stressful situation.

It began, as usual, with a slight sensation in my lower back. I experienced problems in that region for many years and have seen an osteopath for treatment. However, this feeling felt different and I hoped it was a false alarm. The sensation turned into a familiar twinge, which registered behind my navel. Then there was a sharper sensation behind my anal sphincter muscle, a kind of bubbling like the bursting of tiny balloons inside my colon. I thought perhaps it was wind and it would pass. At that point, I offered a prayer that something more unmanageable would not develop. I felt the blood drain from my face and a layer of sweat spread over my nose, forehead, underneath my arms and on my back between my shoulder blades. I knew that if I looked in a mirror, a grey face would look back at me. My impulse was to find the nearest toilet. I feared I would not reach a suitable receptacle in a private place with time to drop my trousers. I felt a great pressure build up in my rectum and my ancient sphincter muscle would not withstand the developing hydraulic force. I felt sick and faint. Within the metres of my intestines, some demon cast a spell, which acted as a catalyst instigating a chemical reaction, converting the semi-solid contents of my intestine into an explosive mixture of liquid and gas, twenty times greater than its original volume.

I rushed to park myself on top of the receptacle, which would receive the explosion. Like the opening of floodgates, the muddy waters gushed from me, splashing against the sides of the pan with such force that some droplets bounced back and dampened my naked buttocks. This cascade was accompanied by embarrassing explosive sounds. My sphincter was stretched wide and scratched by the hard particles and the acid nature of the floodwaters. It closed for a moment like the iris of an eye responding to a bright light. The contraction stung. There couldn't be anything left in my internal tubes. I was wrong. Another gush of muddy water squirted forth. My digestive system was completely out of my control. My 'gut brain' was the director of operations, I was imprisoned on top, around, and beneath it, unable to bring my head brain in to control this situation. Prayers did not work.

In an instant, the odour of the muddy waters diffused through the air and I was sickened and exhausted by a gas of my own making. This time I experienced this in private. I dread the moment in the future when I soil my clothes and have the indignity of the presence of another who will choke on my fumes and pity my incontinence.

Thank God this is a private piece of writing because no one would be pleased to read about these details. Why are we squeamish about this particular bodily function when we tolerate so much literature and conversations about other activities, which bodies usually do in private?

2007

Since writing 'Priests Dying' I have become the recipient of bad memories belonging to people who feel unkindly touched by the Church. I received a letter from a reader saying how angry he was about his time in a minor seminary when his parents were told that he was not clever enough to be a priest and he was sent home. I was teaching at the seminary when this happened, though I was not involved in the decision to expel this boy and his friend. He said the story told to his parents was a fabrication created to cover up the principal's suspicion that he had become too friendly with another pupil. Concern about homosexuality amongst the clergy has been with the Church for centuries — the ever present fear that it will overwhelm those who take a vow of celibacy and corrupt the spirits of God's men.

The other day, my Belgian abbot told me in confidence that a visitor complained to him about sexual advances made to him by one of the priests. The complainant did not wish the matter to be taken any further, so the abbot respected this man's wishes. Apparently, this is not the first time that this has happened. It is a very sensitive issue and by not taking action, the abbot leaves himself open to charges of failing to do his duty. I am so pleased that I was never an abbot.

It was such a surprise to receive Piet van Rijn's letter. I remember him – not an outstanding pupil. He struggled with his reading and was famous for sometimes having his own version of the truth. I remember he lied to me once about his homework, or was that someone else? I think his father was a baker. It was a brief letter explaining that by coincidence some of his Reading Club had attended the abbey school and several of them gave me credit for initiating their interest in literature. I thought this to be an exaggerated compliment and I felt a tinge of embarrassment about their claim. The letter said the Reading Club would celebrate its tenth anniversary in ten months time and that they would like me to talk about my book, which they recently reviewed. I have an offer of accommodation, a car and a driver to collect me from Belgium and bring me back again.

I never wanted to be a member of a reading club; I cannot imagine that attending one would enhance my enjoyment or understanding of literature. My preference is to choose my own books and read them in my own time. Why do I agree to give these talks? I don't enjoy them. Yet my immediate reaction is to say yes. At 79 I still get very nervous. Now I have promised, I will not let these people down, especially as some of them are my ex-pupils. That would not be fair.

Since my brother Thomas, the clever editor, suggested a new format for these talks, they are not so daunting. However, my diarrhoea prior to speaking is getting more frequent. It is not the sort of thing that we talk about in my community. Nor do I like to bother the doctor. I must reply to Piet and send him suggestions for preparing his club members for my talk.

CHAPTER 4

The Journals

From the oak panelled communal telephone room in his Belgian abbey, Father Antonius spoke to his brother Thomas about Piet van Rijn's invitation. Thomas suggested that the Reading Club would be a good group to participate in the '2005 Writing Project', which they had developed in association with the Humanities Department of Erasmus University in Rotterdam. Although Father Antonius felt weary, he agreed with the suggestion and that afternoon he dispatched a letter to Piet.

Father Antonius van Aken
Sint Jan's Abdij
La Rochelle
Belgium
antonius-sintjansabdij@belnet.net
3/11/07

Dear Piet,

Thank you for the invitation to talk to your club on 3rd August next year. I appreciated receiving the names of the other members and their professions, together with some of the books which you have read during the last ten years. I compliment you on your wide choice. It is always interesting to have such details before talking to groups or reading their work.

With the help of Erasmus University, my brother and I developed the '2005 Writing Project', which arose out of my need to find the best way of responding to groups, like yours, who wanted me to talk about my book. Those who have taken part have said that it has helped them to understand the way I worked. In addition, it has provided an opportunity for a number of people to see their own work in print. To date we have produced fifteen different booklets, which have delighted the participant writers. Examples are to be found on the University website.

The idea is simple. We suggest that everyone writes regularly in his own journal for a few months before I come. From this work each person then selects one or two topics to develop as a contribution to a commemorative booklet. In order to complete the project in time for your celebrations, we would need to receive all contributions via e-mail or by post to the address above, by 10th May next year. My brother will edit and return the work for the authors' approval by 10th June. We allow one month for design and printing. The booklets containing a selection of members' writing will be ready in time for my talk and I will bring them with me on the evening of your celebration.

My brother, who negotiates the details regarding numbers of copies required and costs, will contact you at the beginning of July. The University provides a small subsidy and often a local company such as a bank, travel agent or bookshop, is willing to contribute towards some of the remaining costs. It is difficult to estimate the price of each booklet, but it is somewhere between €8 and €12, depending on the quality of the paper chosen, the number of pages and the number of copies required.

Please let me know if your members would like to participate. Suggestions for writing can be found on the University website.

The Erasmus University '2005 Writing Project' is a non-profit-making organisation and registered charity.

Best wishes

Father Antonius

On the University website were the 'Suggestions for Writing', which gave advice on making a start, tips for writing regularly, ideas for topics and items to avoid. Participants were encouraged to experiment with writing at different times of the day and with using different ways of recording their journals. The general message was to write regularly about anything. The promise was that the more they wrote the better their writing would become. After eight weeks or so, they were advised to stop writing and leave the journals unread for one or two weeks. After a pause, they should reread their work and select one or two pieces to develop for a final piece of writing which would be published in a commemorative booklet. There was a final caution which stated, *'Writing which refers to people or institutions in a way which we consider insulting, offensive or damaging, will not be published.'*

At the next meeting of the Reading Club, there was a short discussion about the suggested project. All eight members agreed to participate. Everyone was enthusiastic about producing an anniversary booklet. Within a week, the members, apart from Piet van Rijn, made a start on following the instructions from the website about keeping a journal, prior to developing a final piece for publication. Some found it relatively easy, because the first stage was private and there were no restrictions on content, spelling or grammar. They were invited to write freely – and they did. It did not matter to anyone else what was written. Others struggled to get started; some felt resentment at the task, others were devoid of ideas and one worried that an imaginary reader would sanction his writing. Some carried out the suggestion to write daily and experimented with different times, places and subjects. One or two went to the trouble of buying books about writing and keeping a journal. Many chose to explore private, personal and even secret aspects of their lives, believing that no one else had access to their writing without their permission. Some went to elaborate lengths to hide their notebooks and their computer files to ensure secrecy. Piet thought about writing and enthusiastically discussed the project with the taxi driver, but did not make a start on keeping his own journal.

The Journal of Titus Dekker

On most weekday mornings *Mevrouw* Dekker was to be found in her great kitchen preparing for the morning refreshment break. She could always hear when her doctor husband opened and then closed his surgery door at the front of the house. Then the large black and white marble hall tiles resounded with each tread of his hard shoes as he made his way towards his coffee. He often paused by the hall table to glance at, but not open, the post. Today he adjusted the arrangement of some wild daisies in an antique beer jug. As usual, he looked in the mirror then moved on. Ten more steps, before he turned a corner into a narrower, lower, but still chequered hall, where after nine more paces, he arrived at the kitchen.

Titus sat down, removed his shoes, wriggled his toes and placed his feet to cool on the well-worn stone kitchen floor tiles beneath the long, pine table. He frequently suffered from a foot fungus which made his lower legs hot, even when other parts of his body were cold. He wrapped his hands around a small cup of strong, black coffee while his wife stood leaning against an old, pine wall cupboard with a tea in a delicate bone china cup.

'Your feet are smelling again. Have you been treating them?'

'Yes... Why are you standing there? Come and sit next to me,' Titus said.

'I've bought you a gift,' she said, turning around and lifting a package from the shelf behind her.

'How nice, my dear. What is it?' Titus asked.

'A notebook especially made by your favourite book binders along the dyke. It's for your journal writing.'

He opened the package and gently took out the dark blue, leather bound book. He lifted it to his nose and breathed in the aroma of the hide. He carefully flicked through the pages; at least two hundred. 'It's exquisite, too nice for my scribble. I'll be frightened to use it.'

'Don't be silly. It will enhance your writing. When are you going to start?'

'I thought I'd write each day for half an hour after morning surgery.'

'You mean now?'

'Yes, if that's convenient for you,' he said.

'Do you want me to clear a space on the kitchen table?'

'No. I'll work in my room.' Titus held the book close to his chest.

'Do you think all that literature in your room will give you inspiration!'

'I hope something will.'

'I'm sure you will enjoy creating something unusual for the Anniversary Book. You are such an expert writer.'

'This is nothing like my usual work. I feel nervous about starting.'

In his very private room, on the first floor of his large house, Titus settled down at his desk. Apart from the occasional visit by his wife – but only at his invitation – no-one else entered this room; not his friends, not his children, not the cleaning woman, no-one. Beside him were the suggestions for writing he had downloaded from the University website and his new notebook; in his hand he held a pen. On the first page, he printed the date, making a note to himself that he should do this for all his entries. Around him were metres of shelves of dust-topped books and magazines which he shared with no-one.

Titus was proud that he was a founder member of the Reading Club and took pleasure in being part of this interesting group of men. He mostly enjoyed hearing different comments about the club's latest book and was known to modify his opinion after listening to those of others and even returning to a book in order to re-read and re-evaluate certain sections. When reading he made notes in a small book, which he took with him to the club meetings. It was still the original one, which he used on the first meeting ten years ago. From it, he could trace everything that had been read, and he was planning to list the titles in time for the anniversary. The celebration would be held at his house.

Titus had a strong sense of duty to the club. He had supported the anniversary project and now he wanted to create a significant contribution. This work should be different from his professional, scientific writing. For that, he preferred to do research in his room using his academic books, scientific journals or the Internet. However, if necessary, he would work in the library or study medical archives in the local hospital. Conclusions he could draw in odd places such as in the shower, walking to the shops, riding his bike or in discussion with a colleague or his wife. But this also occurred outside of his awareness; for example, he would wake up with an idea which had been formulating while he was asleep, or another one could develop while he was writing. The final stage was allowing the words which would best express his ideas to emerge onto the page. Once in that frame of mind, he had the sensation of being in a tunnel in which the rest of the world was shut out and only the writing process existed. He knew that this could only be achieved in his private room; this room. And he needed to have silence. He was not one of those people who wrote with a background of music. That interfered with his thinking. Even the ticking of his father's clock disturbed him; therefore it had remained unwound on a shelf in his study for the last fifteen years.

'But this journal writing will be different,' he told his wife. 'I'm not required to undertake any research. What's amazing is that I am beginning to have ideas at different times during the day, even during surgery. But when I sit down to record these items, they often disappear. I know I can't force them. I have to be in the right frame of mind.'

'This project means a lot to you,' she said.

'So does the whole club. It's one of the highlights of the month.'

Alone in his room, Titus waited for inspiration. Nothing came to him from the shelves crammed with unhelpful books and unlikely magazines. He knew that he must not put pressure on his writing frame of mind. However, nothing came to mind after he had written the date; apart from a small flower he had doodled in the corner of the page. The sounds of the house intruded – someone had just knocked on the front door and he could hear his wife walk along the hall, her shoes making a distinctive sound on the chequered marble floor. He re-read the suggestions for writing. He focussed on, 'A letter to or a conversation with a real or imaginary person'.

He looked around at the bookshelves in his office. Their contents were one of the reasons he did not welcome visitors into his private world. Then he rubbed his pen gently backwards and forwards along his bottom lip and scanned the interior of his mind for a starting point. The light perfume from the soap, which he had used to wash his hands, distracted him. It was important that he eliminated the smell of the surgery before he began writing. It did not matter what he wrote – yet it did. If he did not like it, he could cross it through or tear out the page and start again. But the notebook was beautiful and he did not want crossings-out on his first page, nor did he want to see the jagged remnants of a missing page every time he opened the book. He began:

Sweet Inspiration, where are you?

Titus paused. He was entering his writing tunnel. Then he continued:

Entry number 1

I just don't know how to start...

I have been writing for years; writing prescriptions, notes and letters to other doctors about patients.

I have compiled a number of articles for medical magazines and newspapers. I have had two books published and I am halfway through my next one.

'Too many sentences beginning with 'I',' he said aloud, 'but never mind.' He continued writing:

However, this daily writing task, which the Catholic priest has set the Reading Club, is challenging my writing skills in a way that nothing before has done. I do not know where to start.

I understand the suggested daily writing task. I think it is a very good idea for the reluctant and non-writers in our group. I can see how this might clear away distraction, which can block the creative process. I can see the purpose in writing directly to someone. I have read about a famous writer, whose name I cannot recall, who searches for new ideas by composing an imaginary conversation with his typewriter. 'Good morning, Typewriter. Do you have any good ideas?' Maybe I should start like that. 'Dear Father Antonius...', although he is not my father and in the days when I went to church, we did not address our leaders in that way.

When I agreed with this project I thought I would find it easy – but I'm not. Maybe I'll just skip this preliminary part, the daily journal. I really don't need to do this. I should be able to write something unusual for the anniversary book – perhaps something medical, or perhaps not. Surely, with all my writing experience, I will be able to create something special. I would like our club to produce a good booklet, although it is not compulsory to do any writing at all. On the other hand, the priest maintains that those people who have kept a journal for a while say that they have enjoyed it and their understanding of the way his book was written, had increased. I have heard that Joost and Huub are pleased with their journal writing, so at least two of the club members have started. I think that I should try it in the way that Antonius describes. It feels a bit artificial, rather like being back at school, although I did not go to a seminary like some of the other members in the group. I can appreciate that for a few people this task could be quite therapeutic.

Antonius almost suggests that we can write about anything which comes to mind. I might have difficulty recording some of the images which flash through my brain. They are too personal, too private and too intimate. Once committed to my computer screen, I am afraid that someone might read them. I have worked hard safeguarding my good reputation and it goes against my inclination to let down my defences and reveal parts of myself which may be viewed by others as less than respectable. I know my imaginary reader would be deeply embarrassed by some of my thoughts. When I consider some parts of my inner world, I too am shocked, but I do not believe that my thoughts are any more bizarre than those of the rest of the male population; including this Catholic priest. Maybe, I need to start at a safe respectable level, gain my confidence in this style of writing and then work my way slowly downwards or inwards to the core of my inner self. My heart is not in this project, but I will make a start tomorrow.

The following day, having seen fifteen patients in the morning surgery, Titus was having a coffee before beginning his journal.

'How did the writing go yesterday?' his wife asked.

'I didn't really get started.'

'Is my great doctor without inspiration?'

'I think I'll be better today.'

'Good luck.'

In his study, Titus re-read yesterday's piece and then wrote:

Entry Number 2

Dear Dr. Respectable,

It has been a pleasure, even a privilege for me to serve the community by being a doctor in this town for the last fifteen years. I enjoy many things about my work even if I have to give people bad news. They always thank me. I try to do my job as carefully as possible. I am beginning to look towards a time when I will retire and spend my days doing other things. I am tired of being respectable all the time. It is not as if I wish to break the law – to physically or emotionally hurt others. I would just like a rest from this constant expectation. I realise that a doctor has to be upstanding during all of his public life. However, sometimes I would like to be an ordinary man and not have to worry about my image. Even in the house, I am expected to maintain it. The surgery is in the front and my patients come through the hall where they can glimpse the kitchen, if the door has been left open. When we have people to do work in the house, they may see our private world and if it is not as expected, I know they will gossip. Some people probably find me rude, but I tend to ignore them and let my wife sort out our domestic needs. She even negotiated the framing of a print, which I bought when I went to see a special exhibition at the Tate Gallery in London.

I save my respectable face for the outside world. My family has become accustomed to this public interest in our lives. Now I am growing tired of it. There is one place in the house, which the family knows is my private room; this room, it is my own space. Especially my wife understands my need to have somewhere I can be alone. She never enters this room, unless I invite her and I always keep the door locked. It gets a bit dusty, but I don't mind. When she hears me sneezing several times, she suggests that the room needs cleaning. As much as I detest the sound of our vacuum machine, I do it myself – I never ask the cleaning woman to help me.

This room is devoted to that private part of my world which is not respectable. I feel very lucky to have a wife who understands this need. She has bought a number of the books for me, which I keep in here. She doesn't necessarily like my choice of literature, but she understands my need for an outlet from my public image. She is an eccentric woman herself and, like me, she has developed a façade for the outside world. I suppose that over the years I have become tired of always being a pillar of society, of conforming to its expectations of decency. The doctor is expected to have higher standards of behaviour compared with the man who cleans the station. However, we are both the victims of unconsciously held ideas, which dictate what we do privately.

Perhaps there is a part of me which is revolutionary, but I lack the courage to declare it publicly.

A few days later Titus and his wife were sitting in the great conservatory at the back of their house. 'How are you getting on with your writing?' she asked.

'It's more difficult than I thought.'

'Want to tell me what you are writing about? Or is it private?'

'The suggestion is that it should be private so that writers will be uninhibited.'

'But have you written anything interesting?' she said.

'I have written about respectability. Society's expectations.'

'Sounds awfully dull to me. Let yourself go, write about your inner thoughts. You're always writing serious stuff. Isn't the idea in this journal to loosen up before your final bit? Nothing to stop you writing anything – anything! For God's sake Titus, stop being so stuffy!'

Entry number 3

Dear Father Antonius – don't be shocked!

You won't believe it but one of my private interests is pornography and this includes erotica. You make some mention of these topics in your book. Remember the sex shops in Amsterdam? You will understand that I have always been careful to restrict this interest to my study. I enjoy it intellectually in the same way an anthropologist might be fascinated by the obscure queuing habits of the English. Pornography is about people, about what they are not expected to do. It can make me laugh, feel sad. Sometimes I am shocked, disgusted, horrified, excited, and aroused all at the same time. It can stimulate my mind and grab at my organs. To me pornography is more than naked bodies doing things to themselves and each other. By flaunting what is not polite and acceptable, it demonstrates the rules of conduct in our society. How clearly and simply it can show where the respectable edges of our culture end and where the unrespectable, disrespectable areas begin. Pornography frequently unsettles me – as the British would say, 'it gets under my skin and right up my nose'. It reminds me that people have desires and fantasies which respectability does not permit.

Antonius, is this the sort of thing you expected, when you encouraged us to write freely?

I know that pornography sets out to shock; to violate what society holds to be good taste and polite. Although erotica can be more subtle, even aesthetic, it too is about sex and power; quite different from the intellectual and emotional responses to so-called fine art. Pornography challenges our ideas about the way men and women should dress and what they should do both in public and in private. It makes a vulgar gesture to good manners and social conventions like an embarrassing child who turns his bottom towards the visiting priest and farts not once but twice. It is like the mischievous teenage scallywag who brings forth a gold vibrator, which she has found in her mother's cupboard. She waves it in front of the neighbour and asks her if she would like to have a 'buzz'.

Antonius! Can you understand that I believe many people enjoy pornography because it encapsulates their fantasies rather than their intentions? I appreciate that many objectors are fearful of pornography because they assume that those who enjoy it actually want to engage in pornographic acts themselves. I do not believe this is so for the majority. Perhaps you would tell me that pornography is often linked with violence. I can say with confidence that I have never been a violent man.

God, your God, gave most of us great sexual appetites. Some satisfy their hunger by viewing pornography. Mostly nobody else is harmed. There is a common fear that those who view pornography might abuse our children. I do not think that this is true of the majority of viewers. The atrocious fact is that children have always been abused. Priest, just look to your own Church! Isn't it better to accept that men and women have sexual fantasies and that some use pornography to enhance these basic instincts? Tell your Church to stop worrying about the girly magazine under a teenager's bed, or the erotic book in the spinster's cupboard and the celibate exploring the sex-sites on the internet. Instead, encourage your Christian community to address the real issues of the present and the future. If we are not careful, there will be too many people in the world and not enough food to feed them.

Antonius, this preamble is an introduction to my private collection of pornographic and erotic literature, which comprises intellectual treatises, together with some beautifully illustrated erotic books and pornographic magazines. Like many people, I keep my interest private. I await the framing of a print of Henri Fuseli's masterpiece, 'The Nightmare', which elegantly embraces many aspects of this subject.

Having finished his journal writing for the day, Titus came out of his private room, locked the door and met his wife on the landing.

'What's the progress with your writing?' she asked.

'It's getting better, but I don't want anyone to read what I have written.'

'No-one can get into your study without a key.'

'You won't let anyone in?'

'I never have in the past. Why should I do that now? Are you revealing some special secrets at last?' she said smiling.

'When will my print of Fuseli's 'Nightmare' be ready?'

'The taxi driver's wife said she would ask her husband if he could frame it. Now that they have lost their shop, framing pictures is a bit difficult. He will speak to a friend to see if he can use his equipment. Why do you like Fuseli so much? His work's sinister. I hate it,' she said.

'I thought I would write about Fuseli.'

'Why?' she said.

'I admire the man.'

'Try using your imagination a bit more.'

'I'll try, I don't find it easy.'

The next day after surgery, Titus began to write.

Entry number 4

Dear Henry Fuseli,

How kind of you to visit my study. Did you notice my coat of many colours hanging on the wall? I dare say, had it featured in one of your paintings, there would have been a delicate maiden tied up inside it or a mini monster leering out of the pocket or down a sleeve. Next to the coat, there is a space on the wall, waiting for a reproduction of your 'Nightmare'.

I heard that this picture represents a dream, which you had after eating undercooked pork late at night. I have treated a few patients with digestive complaints arising from eating partially cooked food. Many of them reported that not only did they experience pain but that their moods and rest were disturbed by vivid and sometimes frightening dreams.

I like your image of the pale medieval maiden clad in a diaphanous white gown, draped limp and still, across a bed. Is she dead, unconscious or asleep? You leave the viewer to decide. The rope around her wrist suggests that she might have been bound there. Half in the shadows, an ugly, brown, stunted creature with a huge head and small body, crouches on top of her. He has thick lips, a bulbous nose and eyes, which follow me no matter from which angle I look at him. I am not sure if that little monster has violated the young woman or is about to abuse her. Whatever, she looks powerless. When I first saw the crouching goblin, it was as if I could feel the weight of him sitting in that position on top of me. I was aroused by the idea of being draped over a bed with my hands tied.

Then, also in the shadows, you include that startled horse with eyes like eggs, ears upright in fear, and nostrils flared. She is the mare, the onlooker. Your English title is intriguing. Nightmare means a very intense type of dream. In Dutch, we have a similar word:

nachtmerrie. I read that, in your time, these dreams were thought to be caused by demons, called 'mares', who sat on the chests of the sleepers. Waking from a nightmare was usually accompanied by a feeling of terror, a difficulty in breathing and an inability to move – a paralysis. How clever! The mare refers to both the demon and the horse and the scene is at night; consequently, they are both nightmares. For a Swiss gentleman, you have certainly grasped the English love for what they call 'a play on words'.

I envy your varied life. I note that in 1761 you were a clergyman. At one time, I was also considering ordination. Now I do not believe in God. Like many of my fellow countrymen, I can speak several languages, but probably not competently enough to be able to become, like you, a translator and an illustrator of French, German and Italian books. I read that your job as a travelling companion ended when you were involved in a fight with your employer. You had a reputation for being high spirited; whereas I have a reputation for being a decent, but dull doctor. On the advice of that great English painter, Joshua Reynolds, you set out for Rome to become an artist. You stayed eight years. I too, had a chance to work abroad, but I lacked the courage to leave The Netherlands. As a charismatic man you became an influential leader to other artists; John Constable was your pupil. I have difficulty asserting my point of view in the Reading Club. Then finally, although a foreigner, you achieved entrance into the Royal Academy in London where you became the Professor of Painting. A professor – a title that I always wished I could have been awarded. Then your crowning glory was to be buried amongst the famous in St. Paul's Cathedral in London.

Is it true that 'The Nightmare' is an illustration of your failed romance or is it just some nonsense made up by an art historian? I think there are so many ways of seeing this picture. Does it matter if it is different from your intention? One of our local artists said a picture is begun by the artist and completed in the mind of the viewer. What do you think?

After my initial response to 'The Nightmare', I had several after-thoughts. What if, instead of an ugly goblin, you had portrayed a handsome young man with this young maiden? I wonder, would the viewer be so alarmed? After all, haven't we been conditioned to accept that sexual activities are the province of young, beautiful, slim heterosexuals? It is not the territory of the old, the ugly, the fat or the deformed. Only pornography is daring enough to show that sex is not restricted to an exclusive club, but derives from a universal appetite.

There in the shadows of the picture is the plump mare with bulging eyes; the shocked voyeur. It is not clear why the horse is looking so alarmed. I think she has been disturbed by what she has seen. You might find it a contradiction that although I like to see pornographic pictures of others, I would not like to be observed in my private moments. Perhaps it is a sense of decency, which dictates that we do not view each other engaging in intimate activities. Several hundred years ago, sex and personal bodily functions were not necessarily performed in private; the concept of disgust is a much more recent invention. The picture of 'The Nightmare' looks unnatural and this gives a feeling of unease. It suggests the experience of being seen by unseen eyes. Pornography gives us the mare's position.

In my fantasy I have created a different explanation. Perhaps the maiden is the powerful one who has forced the simple goblin into satisfying her sexual needs and now he sits on top of her, feeling confused and abused while she is resting. These would be difficult ideas to share with others. There is one person in the Reading Club who frequently claims that there is too much sex in our society; too much talk, too many pictures and far too much literature. Having read his book 'Priests Dying', I think it would be easier for me to talk to Father Antonius about this subject, than to one or two members of the club.

I had thought about describing 'The Nightmare' for my contribution to the Anniversary Book, but now I think I will choose something less controversial. Perhaps my father's coat of many colours would be suitable. It has a slightly biblical title.

In his study, Titus closed his journal for the day. His wife put her ear to the door. There was no sound.

'Are you still in there?' she said.

'Yes, I'm still here.'

'May I come in?'

'No. I'm coming out now.'

She heard him unlock the door from the inside. He opened it, closed it and locked it behind him. 'Still writing about Fuseli?' she asked.

'No, I have moved on to other things,' Titus lied.

'Good, now what is being explored?'

'That's private.'

'Writing about your dirty books, my dear?'

'You've never called them that before.'

'No, but I expect most people would describe them like that. What would the Reading Club say if they knew about your private collection?'

'Some would understand.'

'I doubt it.'

Titus had an emergency in his surgery next morning, which prevented him from writing at his usual time. Later, after his evening meal he continued with his journal letters:

Entry 5

Dear Coat of Many Colours,

Although I call you a coat of many colours, it would be more accurate to describe you as a patchwork jacket. My mother created you out of small pieces of material, which she cut from various items of my late father's old clothes. Your original belt was made from a black silk shirt and was really too delicate for the purpose. So I replaced it with a thick rope, which I bought some years ago for another purpose from the ship-chandlers at the entrance to the inner city. There in the shop window were neatly stocked tins of yacht paint and coils of ships' ropes. The interior smelt of varnish and rubber boots. I asked the shopkeeper to cut me two lengths of soft rope, a metre and a half long and to knot the ends to stop them from fraying.

Jacket, I like to wear you and to pass the rope knots at the end of your belt backwards and forward through my fingers, in the way old Greek men fiddle with their worry beads. Originally, I bought the ropes to please my wife when she declared an inclination to include some bondage in our lovemaking. She told me that she had often imagined herself bound, then seduced. When we tried to make love with her in a restrained position, she immediately complained that the ropes hurt her wrists and that actually being tied up had taken away her desire. Her pained expression soon dissolved into a grin. We were laughing so much that I had difficulty untying her. With her freed hands, she gave me a hug and suggested I throw away the ropes. She said that she would keep bondage for her imaginative mind.

My mother had taught me never to throw away good material, so I kept the ropes in my private room because I was sure that a good use would be found for them in the future. I am pleased I did. Sometimes, Jacket, when I'm wearing you, I tie the rope belt around me quite tightly and imagine that I am the maiden in Fuseli's painting.

During their evening meal, Titus said, 'It might interest you to know that the patchwork coat, which my mother made, was the subject of my writing today.'

'How nice.'

'I included the rope belt as well.'

'Did you write about why you had originally bought the rope?'

'Certainly.'

'Titus, don't tease me. You wouldn't put anything about me in the Anniversary Book.'

'I haven't decided yet.'

'You wouldn't dare.'

Titus's wife was out on the day when the taxi driver's wife arrived to clean the house which had ten rooms with high ceilings. She had never counted them, but the cleaner had told her husband that there must be over one hundred pictures hanging on the walls, some of which were beyond her reach and she needed to use steps to dust them. It was one of her least favourite jobs and she was not looking forward to this chore today. Along with her own cleaning equipment she had brought the framed picture of Fuseli's 'Nightmare'.

Entry 6

Dear Father Antonius,

I made a mistake. After all my years of experience in diagnosing and forming accurate impressions of people, I made a gross mistake. I allowed myself to be seduced into thinking that our cleaning woman was a devotee of Fuseli. I was completely wrong. Because she seemed to know somewhat about him, I assumed that she admired his work. I wanted to believe that I had found a soul mate; someone else to share my admiration of this man. Because of this desire, I failed to listen to my instinct about this woman. The embarrassment of what happened is fixed in my bones.

My wife had asked the cleaner if she could arrange for her husband to have my print of 'The Nightmare' framed. Unfortunately, she was out when the cleaning woman arrived with the picture wrapped in brown paper. This was the first time I had spoken to her, although I had seen her several times in the house assisting my wife. She is what I would call a handsome woman and when she first started to work for us, she became a regular feature in my sexual fantasies. This is not an uncommon experience for me. After a few weeks, she disappeared from my recurring thoughts and someone I had seen fleetingly at the airport took her place. I should explain that just because this woman featured in one of my fantasies that did not mean that I desired her in my private reality. Not at all. Like many people, I have sexual fantasies on a regular basis – many times a day. These experiences often involve both men and women that I know. Other times they incorporate strangers, even historical or mythical figures in sometimes bizarre and extraordinary activities. I know sexual fantasies are a universal phenomenon. When mine start to decline, I take that as a sign that I am unwell in some way.

I do not know why I asked this woman what she thought of the print. When her reply was knowledgeable, I regretted that initially I had misjudged her, just because she came to help with the cleaning. She was obviously better educated than I thought, she was familiar with the Gothic artists, and could tell me about the different interpretations of Fuseli's work and life. I felt angry at my own short-sightedness. I am so careful not to do this with my patients, but there in my private life, I had misjudged someone and ignored her too. I tried to compensate for my rudeness by asking her if she would come into my private room in order to hold the picture in its proposed spot. Had my wife been here, she would have probably protected me from myself. However, in her absence, we proceeded to my room where I unlocked the door and we entered. I saw the eyes of the cleaner scan the interior, and in a glance take in its contents and make a judgement about me. Probably, in a moment, I went from being the respectable doctor into being a despicable fellow with a pornographic library. I noticed that her posture changed and a slight flush appeared on her neck. I could sense that she felt nervous. For her sake, I wanted to get this task over as soon as possible. I did not want to add to her embarrassment.

She held the picture in front of her chest and continued nervously to tell me about my hero, Fuseli. She said that his work was eighteenth century pornography.

'He obviously hated women,' she said with disgust, then concluded, 'and he used opium!'

I asked her to hold the picture against the wall and I gave instructions for a slight adjustment. When it came to mark the spot, I began to be infected by this woman's anxiety and I fumbled about on my untidy desktop for a pencil. I glanced up and I could see that her arms were beginning to bend. At any moment the picture position would be lost. She asked me to hurry, otherwise she might drop it. I eventually found a pencil and moved quickly towards her. In reaching under her arm, I accidentally touched her bosom and felt the hard shell of her undergarment encasing her firm breast. A slight electric shock flew down to my groin area. She let out a small cry and her cheeks flushed. I grabbed the picture from her and apologised. I explained that I had rushed to mark the spot because I could see that her arms were aching. Her redness increased then, without saying anything, she left the room hurriedly.

On her way home from her weekly visit to her uncle, the doctor's wife saw her cleaner walking quickly away from the house in the opposite direction. As soon as she got inside the door, she spoke to her husband:

'What's the matter? I saw the cleaner walking very quickly up the road. She isn't supposed to finish working until 4.00.'

'There was a misunderstanding. She brought the Fuseli print. I asked her to help me. I was impatient to see it on the wall of my room.'

'You took her into your room with all those bloody books on show.'

'Yes. I didn't realise that she would get upset.'

'She is a good Protestant woman. I am sure she was upset to see your library. You idiot!'

'She told me she was interested in art. Surely she could manage a few nude bodies.'

'We've had this discussion before. Art, pornography. There's a difference.'

'There was also an accident.'

'What?'

'I asked her to hold the picture against the wall – I accidentally touched the side of her breast when I went to mark the spot.'

'You clumsy fool! You can be so single-minded. You don't think about the consequences. I've probably lost a good helper and a good friend.'

'Surely she's not your friend!' Titus said.

'The taxi driver's wife, as you insist on calling her – her name is Mieke – spends two afternoons with me every week. Apart from helping me with this bloody mausoleum, where we live, we often talk about different subjects. I enjoy her company. Yes, she is a sort of friend. I'll phone her later. I hope that she doesn't decide to leave. Sometimes I think you're just another bloody pervert!'

Later Titus agreed to send the taxi driver's wife some flowers and in the evening his wife phoned to see if they had been delivered.

'Mieke, I am very sorry about what happened with my husband.'

'I was very upset. I told Bob that I wouldn't be returning to your house.'

'I can quite understand. My husband made a mistake when he asked you to help him in his private study. We do not usually tell anyone that he is undertaking some research for Leiden University. He needs all those books for his work,' the doctor's wife lied.

'I thought he was a GP.'

'He is, but he writes medical books and reviews.'

'It's surprising what doctors have to do these days!'

'Not many people would understand why he has a collection of literature about the subject. I am so sorry if you were upset by what you saw.'

'I didn't know that there were people studying that kind of thing. Not for their work!'

'There have been quite a few studies already.'

'Did you know that your husband touched my breast?'

'Yes, he told me. That was an accident. He wanted to mark the wall quickly. He is very sorry and very embarrassed. He hopes the flowers he sent will express his concern.'

'They are beautiful.'

'Please Mieke, don't quit your job. I will miss you. I really enjoy you coming to the house. You're such a good friend to us.'

'OK, but I don't want to have to help your husband again.'

'Thank you, thank you.'

Several weeks later Titus decided to read to his wife what he had written in his journal. He omitted to include the sensation he had felt in his groin when he had accidentally touched the cleaner's breast; nor did he reveal the details of his sexual fantasies.

'What do you think?' he said.

'I like the idea of the letters to imaginary people. That's clever.'

'Thanks.' Titus liked it when his wife praised him.

'You've written a lot about Fuseli. That part sounds like a dreary art book. I like him even less now. There's not much humour.'

'I'm not really a humorous person.'

'True. What are you going to choose for the Anniversary Book? Please don't write about me being tied up.'

'Don't know yet.' He held his serious expression.

'You're joking.'

'Yes, I am.'

'Thank God.'

'Antonius encouraged us to be open in our writing.'

'You can't publicise some of that stuff from your journal. You'd be taken off the register of doctors.'

'Now, who's joking? I might talk to Joost about what he has written.' Titus put his hand in his pocket to retrieve the key to his study. 'I want to show you where I keep my journal. Promise that in the event of my death you will destroy it and all of my notebooks and my pornographic magazines.'

'You're being very dramatic. Stop worrying about someone else reading your writing. I am sure there are more intimate secrets and shocking disclosures in some women's magazines,' she said.

'I insist.'

'OK. I think you're making this bigger than it is.'

'Let's change the subject?'

'What do you think the others have written?' she said.

Titus thought for a moment and then said, 'Joost will create something about art; Bert and Huub will focus on their shops; Paul obviously will produce something about education; Hans will make a joke or a comedy and Milo will write about religion.

I don't expect Piet will do anything other than make up an excuse why he hasn't completed the task. He doesn't have much commitment to the club.'

'I thought you told me that when the club read 'Priests Dying', Piet had printed his comments and the others were impressed by his commentary.'

'That's right; maybe I'm wrong about him.'

'You're wrong about everyone,' she continued. 'Look at what you've written so far. Who'd guess that our upstanding doctor has such an erotic secret? Don't you think that the others are capable of writing about some surprising subjects?'

'It'll be very interesting to see what goes in the Anniversary Book,' Titus said, smiling at his wife's comments.

'It would be far more interesting to read what is written in the journals but stays out of that anniversary booklet,' she replied.

Every day Titus wrote his journal about a wide range of subjects: his patients, the death of a neighbour, his dreams and an imaginary visit to Fuseli in his studio. He recorded his visit to the Rijks Museum gallery at Schiphol Airport where he had seen a painting by Jan Adriaensz van Staveren. It showed a seventeenth century doctor holding a sample of a patient's urine to the light. Titus knew that this was how doctors of that time analysed symptoms. They were called *'piskijkers'*, which today would be considered a vulgar term. He wondered if any of his dissatisfied patients referred to him in that way.

Furthermore, he recorded his impressions of different rooms in his house and the plants in his garden. He reflected on his collection of paintings by old Dutch Masters. Some pictures had been in his family for generations. They dated back to the Golden Age in the Netherlands, when there was great prosperity and many of the houses had paintings, which were either commissioned or bought directly from the artists' studios. Many of the innocent looking Dutch interiors in the paintings were laced with symbolic items – skulls, burnt candles, hourglasses, and little worms on top of aged books – all representing the passing of time. Sometimes an artist would express erotic ideas with a lute or certain fruits. A dog was a token of fidelity.

Titus grew accustomed to the daily writing. There seemed to be so much to write about; there was material everywhere. Sometimes he would wake up in the middle of the night with an idea and would lie in his bed wondering whether to get up, go down to his room, take out his journal and start writing. Even when talking to a patient, a writing idea might come to mind. He became so enthralled with the writing project that he addressed his Rotary Club in one of the five minute slots given to members who have something of interest to impart. His description was so convincing that a number of members placed orders for the Anniversary Book. He also wrote an article in the Rotary Magazine and listed the suggestions for writing on his club's website.

After a few weeks, his wife stopped asking about the progress of his writing. She did not tell him that she was getting fed up with the project. Titus was becoming a 'journal bore'. He was undeterred by his wife's lack of interest; he was more concerned about what he would choose from his ample journal, to be developed as a final piece for the Anniversary Book. If he wanted to be modest and respectable then he should pick safe subjects. If he followed Antonius's suggestion, he would be bold and honest. Was this an occasion where he could reveal a little of his private self or not?

The Journal of Huub Schevers

Huub Schevers, the retired owner of a cleaning firm and current proprietor of an antiques shop, was the only single man in the Reading Club. The members did not know much about his background and they were unaware that for a number of years he had been writing for his own pleasure. Some of his short stories had even been published in various magazines. He lived alone in an old narrow house, which was between the museum with its onion tower and the medieval Cathedral. The ground floor was converted into a shop where Huub displayed his stock of antiques. It was beautifully arranged, smelt of furniture polish and was subtly lit by four table lights with green shades. Huub was comfortable with his antiques, he felt at home with the ensemble of their sounds; the mouse squeak of the small French china cabinet as its doors were opened, the dainty bell chimes of the silver teapot when the lid was lifted, and the tinkle of a triangle as fine bone china cups were replaced on their delicate saucers.

Cleaning these treasures was a very important job. Huub experienced it as an opportunity to care for and enjoy his possessions. Although he liked to do this himself, he was pleased to have the assistance of a Turkish cleaning woman.

'I love your things, Mr Huub. I like to clean them for you. You see I am very careful.'

'Which is your favourite, Leyla?'

'I like so much the brooch with the wings.'

'The dragonfly. My favourite too. My grandmother left it to me in her Will.'

'Will, what is Will?'

'That is a paper on which people write to say who should have their things when they die. Usually people pass on their treasures to their children.'

'You have children?

'No.'

'Mr Huub, can I ask you something?'

'Certainly.'

'Why you never did marry?'

'I never found the right person.'

'Didn't your mother look for a nice wife for you?'

'No, unfortunately she didn't.'

'I think you make a lovely husband and a good father.'

'Thank you.'

'I have told my husband. Kemal, I said, Mr Huub he should marry. He would make lovely man for a wife. I have a cousin...'

'Thank you. I think it's too late now. I did love a woman a long time ago. I don't think I could share my house or my life with anyone now. I don't like noisy children.'

Huub was very happy with Leyla's help. He had the impression that his previous cleaner, the taxi driver's wife, did not respect his belongings. She once installed a lavatory cleaning block in his outside toilet without consulting him. The product made his garden stink and its odour penetrated the shop's atmosphere, shrouding his possessions in an ugly smell, which masked the subtle perfume of beeswax polish, but failed to take away the faint impression of boiled sprouts.

At the back of his shop was a small, tidy, but not so elegant kitchen which housed an old sink, a cooker, some chipped enamel utensils and a few cupboards, circa 1940. Outside the back door was a toilet, with a stained lavatory pan, a high cistern, a pull chain, a door with a latch, but no bolt. Beyond was a tiny walled garden with a raised pond, a wooden seat and some potted plants.

Inside the house, up some steep narrow wooden stairs, was the living-room where Huub did his accounting, his writing and ate his evening meal. A bath was installed on the landing and a cupboard converted into a toilet. In the roof was Huub's unheated bedroom containing a single bed and some old furniture. Beside his weary leather armchair in the living-room, a neat pile of local papers waited to be read; inside a small nineteenth century display table with a glass top, was his collection of dragonfly *objets d'art*. The centrepiece was a brooch, Leyla's favourite, an elegant Art Nouveau corsage, of a woman emerging out of the insect's mouth. She was green and bare breasted. In place of her arms, she had a pair of beautiful jewelled peacock patterned wings. His grandmother had willed it to him. He had no idea of its worth, nor did he care. Daily, using a clean white handkerchief he dusted the glass top of the table and let his gaze linger on this, his prized possession. When he found his former cleaner, the taxi driver's wife, scrutinising his collection, he had been cross.

'Please put that brooch back in the cabinet,' he had said to her.

She looked sideways at him, shrugged her shoulders and slowly replaced the treasure. 'Please yourself,' she had said, 'I did not realise that you liked women's jewellery.'

'I like beautiful things, whether they were originally designed for men or women.'

'Have you ever worn it?' the woman asked.

'Of course not, it was left to me by my grandmother.'

'An unusual thing for a woman to leave to a man. I can't imagine my husband owning a thing like that.'

Huub felt upset by the conversation. He perceived her comments as a kind of judgement on both his collection and himself. This act confirmed his intuition that she was a nosey woman and he later found an excuse to terminate her employment.

Huub was acutely aware of the noises in his environment. It was as if his brain was criss-crossed with taut wires, which reverberated with every sound around him. His ears seemed to be tuned to receive full volume and his mind did not filter out those barely audible vibrations which most people do not notice, such as the striking of the Cathedral clock, the idling of an engine, the click of the latch, the hum of a washing machine from the house next door. In some ways, he was thankful not to live with the noise of a family. He hated the sound of crying babies. When his neighbours made a lot of noise, he slipped a note with complaints through their door.

However, music was different. It could stir in him a range of unique sensations and moods. Melodies would enter his very core and produce feelings which he could not describe. There were no words. A selection of classical music was a central part of his life; like his antiques, his dragonfly collection, his tiny pond and his numerous cups of strong black coffee. In contrast, he loathed other noises such as shouting, banging, pop music, someone singing an old drinking song out of tune, a shrill voice, the intercity train rushing through a station. These caused him auditory pain and he would cringe, wince and cover his ears against those intrusions in a way that observers would think he was exaggerating; simply because they did not share his experience of sounds.

Huub was not daunted by the writing task; although he moaned about it in his usual fashion, in the same way as he would object when the club chose a thick book. It was his habit and the club members were accustomed to hear his complaints. Most were unconcerned about his negativity because his insightful comments about reading often introduced new perspectives into their discussions. Yes, he could be a bit pompous, but mostly that feature appealed to and amused the others, who were impressed by his capacity to read books in several foreign languages, which he had learnt in later life.

Having read the writing instructions, he selected a restful piece of music to play in the background; he sat down on his garden seat with his notebook on his lap and began to write. This was how he created his other stories – notebook first, then he continued on the computer later. He found out that he could write in many different situations. The garden today was ideal. He started immediately.

Writing

I have been writing for a long time. A few of my stories have been published and I have read a lot about writing. I have kept a journal and notebook for many years. When I write I usually begin with a small impression I have of a person – it is not necessary that I know that person well. Real people are my beginnings. If I know them very well it could be a hindrance. That's not to say that I have not used family and friends as starting points, but once I begin writing the real person disappears and another one from my imagination takes his place. Initially I like to use the real person's name as an anchor to the character and later, when I have created a different person, I choose a new name. A sophisticated idea, I don't think some of the Reading Club will understand.

'Not a wonderful beginning,' he mumbled to himself, 'but I could develop it later.'

Huub had spare time enough to devote to writing because he only opened his shop on Thursdays and Saturdays and even then he did not always see many customers. He had often started his stories on these days. For a moment, he was distracted by a damselfly, which was drying itself on a leaf in his pond. He knew these creatures well. Something from his childhood came to mind. He wrote:

The damselflies 1

One of my earliest memories is of the pond in my

grandparents' village. During the late summer it attracted many dragonflies. They flew in ones and twos above the pond, hovering and turning like acrobatic helicopters. Some of the older boys would catch them and attach a string to the end of their bodies so that they could not escape. I always thought that very cruel. When I moved to my present house, there wasn't sufficient space to build a big enough pond for dragonflies; instead I made a small one, which was just large enough to attract the smaller relatives, the damselflies. Each year I watch them emerge from the pond and turn into beautiful flying insects.

Today, I looked up from my book and into my raised pond. A very young damselfly was drying itself in the afternoon sunshine; a clay brown, translucent creature with crumpled wings and a kinked abdomen, no longer than a pin, no thicker than a matchstick and half the size of its mature winged relatives hovering around the pond with their bright colours and confidence. The newly emerged insect looked like a piece of decaying leaf. Using its delicate legs it clung to the aerial flower head of a half submerged water plant. Sometime earlier in the day it had squeezed itself through a split along the back of its nymph case where it had been entombed in a protective fluid for two weeks. It emerged into the air looking like a tiny, wet, silk dress, which must be drip-dried. The transparent silver-tinted paper tomb where it had been metamorphosing was attached to a reed. There were several of these static cases on the water plants. It was difficult to tell which were empty and which ones still had new adult damselflies inside.

The newcomer was vulnerable, its wings and body not yet ready for flight. Unkindly I prodded it with a stick to see how it would react. In response it moved slowly to the other side of the flower head and clambered on top of a lily petal. At a further poke, it released its light grip and plopped into the water. Unintentionally I had pushed it in. It thrashed about for a few seconds before being engulfed in the mouth of one of my usually shy fishes.

A few days letter, Huub continued with his writing.

Damselflies 2

After emerging from their nymph cases these insects begin to eat, then they shed their skins a few times, they mate, the females lay their eggs – and then they die. That's it! THAT'S IT!

Isn't this a shorter version of the human life cycle? Most people have children, they live for a while longer and then they die. Except for me, I haven't had children. This was never a very strong desire; maybe once it was. Had the right opportunity arisen, I would not have refused. Could I have tolerated the noise? I will never know; not now. Sometimes I get upset by the assumptions people make about my partner-less and childless life. I am often informed about other people's families, as if being without one of my own, I am somehow less than human. Why should I have to justify my existence as a single person? There is more to life than having kids. Sometimes I have lied and said that I had a wife and child who were killed in a road accident. That silences people. If they start asking for more details, I say that I would rather not talk about that aspect of my past. Yet I once loved a beautiful woman, but I sent her away.

Later on that evening, Huub looked at some old photographs he had made of the damselflies in his pond. He also read a few pages from his book about insects before continuing his journal.

Damselflies 3

Damselflies have very complicated lives. I have watched how the males get to the pond before the females and defend their territory against rivals. The females arrive later when they have some eggs ready to be fertilized. I noticed two damselflies coupling, locked together in a heart shaped wheel on a branch overhanging the pond. At first, this appears to be a male dominated rough mating in which the male, using claspers at the end of his long abdomen, grabs the female by the scruff of her neck. Then he offers up a segment of his abdomen, where his sperm are stored, to her genital area. Many males do not let go of the female's neck until the fertilised eggs have been deposited on a plant below the surface of the water. However, I have found out that the damselfly mating is not so one-sided as it appears. If a male of a different species, or one that she does not fancy, grabs the female, she refuses to co-operate; the male gets the message that he is unwelcome and releases her.

Life is tough in the insect world. In some species, unless the males are involved in the protection or rearing of the young, there is a chance that the females could eat them, during or after mating. For example, the female praying mantis will sometimes eat her mate. When the male damselfly takes the female by the scruff of her neck, this prevents her from eating him. After she has received the sperm, the female damselfly disengages her abdomen and the heart-shaped mating wheel is broken. In some species that come to my pond the male continues to hold onto the female. The pair remains in this position – locked like static acrobats. The male keeps his abdomen erect, so that his body is several centimetres above the female, whether she is still on a leaf or hovering in flight. He is in a trance and will not let go, even when threatened with a finger or stick. The female below him settles on the edge of a lily leaf and by bending her abdomen beneath the water, deposits the tiny eggs under the surface of the leaf.

There amongst the pictures of the damselflies was one of a young woman. Huub propped it up on a shelf and next day he wrote in his journal.

Damselflies 4

Twenty years ago, I knew a girl who was delicate like the damselfly; words or a gentle embrace easily crushed her tiny slim body. When I was with her, I often felt like a clumsy bullfrog. She was loving and gentle. I was half seduced by this damselfly as she hovered around me with her black lace wings and her colourful body. But my very guarded self questioned her closeness. Her beautiful kindness penetrated my secure outer shell and I felt overwhelmed and out of control. Her nearness created a conflict within me. I wanted her company, but at the same time, I was confused and longed to find my familiar secure self, which had been imprisoned in a castle wall of my own making. The damselfly had entered my keep and my very foundations had been rocked.

I know that I was foolish but, at the time, my feelings seemed so real. It was as if, close up, she became like an armoured tank with jaws like a mechanical crusher. I became frightened. I asked her to fly away, just for a while, so that I could get her in a proper focus. I felt exposed. My request crushed her delicate wings. During her absence, I pined for her company. I knew I liked her, but she came too close to my inner core and she wanted something, which I could not find within me. I did not want to tell her that in my mind I was both magnifying and reducing her. It is said that the male damselfly holds the female by her neck to prevent being devoured by her. But even in this position, the male is exposed to the free will of her abdomen, which could strike him where he is most vulnerable.

I knew then that a damselfly lives only for a few months, yet I still let her go. I do not know what happened to her. Maybe in my dismissal I accidentally crushed her, perhaps she found another mate or, like all damselflies, at the end of the summer she shrivelled up and died.

When Huub had finished his writing he looked again at the picture of the young woman. Then he tore it up and threw away the pieces.

The following day Titus came into Huub's shop to buy a special cup and saucer for his wife. Accidentally he had chipped the china one that she always used. He knew she hated drinking tea out of a glass mug. When the replacement was chosen and wrapped, Titus asked,

'How's the writing going, Huub?'

'Not bad. I'd rather be doing other things. I've got a shop to run.'

'What sort of things have you written about?'

'The joys of being single. What about you?' Huub asked.

'I've described one of my favourite pictures.'

'Which one?'

'One of the old Dutch masters which I have in my house,' said Titus untruthfully.

'Art. That's not my favourite subject. I prefer practical things, beautiful practical things, old things like the cup and saucer you have just bought. What could be more exquisite than to sip tea from such a cup?'

'Any idea of what you are going to write for the Anniversary Book?' Titus asked.

'Yes,' said Huub, 'I'm going to write a love story.'

'Had much experience of love?'

'Plenty. That's why I am a single man.'

Huub became accustomed to write in his journal every day.

The Cleaning Business

As a child, I was always very tidy. I took after my mother whose main mission in life was to keep her house and family looking neat. My father was not by nature like this, but years of living with my mother taught him that it was less bother to go along with her ideas than confront them. I always kept my room tidy. My brothers and sister were unlike me. After her stroke my mother was unable to continue being so orderly. I looked after the house, no-one helped me.

When I left school, it was without any success. I blamed the teachers. My mother was especially upset. She always had the notion that my extreme desire to create order in my room was a sign of my intelligence. She was wrong.

I was given a job with my uncle's company, which cleaned the local factories and offices. It was tough work, a much bigger project than looking after my own room. Many places had to be cleaned before the workers arrived and after they left. During the day, the firm undertook cleaning of stations and local authority buildings. My hands quickly became permanently red and puffy. There were splits in my skin, which refused to heal. I regularly got splinters from the old brooms and I soon acquired a recurring backache. I learnt early on in my career that people generally ignore cleaners. It was as if we were not there, invisible.

Promotion

After a year of this work, I realised that my uncle's business could be improved. Initially I was very nervous about speaking to him, but my mother encouraged me to share my ideas with her brother. He listened to me and some of my suggestions were accepted. In the following year, he gave me charge of two female cleaners who worked at the ship's engine factory, near the river. Again, I felt nervous, since both women were of my mother's age and I wondered how they would accept me telling them what to do.

By the time I was twenty-five, my uncle had given me a lot more responsibility in running the company and we had taken on more staff and negotiated new contracts. It was tough. When I was thirty, I was made a partner. It was the year that my mother died. By then the company had moved into new offices and I had my own room with a telephone. I still undertook some cleaning work if someone was away, and each year I made sure that I worked alongside every one of the cleaners. Although I was the younger director, I earned the respect of our employees. I had begun my working life at the bottom of the ladder and not skipped a rung on my promotion to the top.

After my mother passed away, my uncle told me that his intention was to leave me the company when he died. He never married and had no children. In preparation for the time when I would own the company, he became a non-working partner and withdrew himself from the office. Initially he wanted to be consulted on all business matters. Later, when he saw that I could be trusted, he left it to my discretion to update him on our progress and seek his advice if necessary. It was a huge responsibility. He continued to draw a salary. In the small house he bought near the museum, he intended to open an antiques shop.

This arrangement was successful. Having taken advice from a good business solicitor and a reputable accountant, I made a few changes with my uncle's approval. I wanted to be able to give some security to workers who had been with the company for some while. I kept up to date with the health and safety regulations and I inspected new premises to ensure that there were no unnecessary risks for the cleaners. I was careful in my choice of cleaning products and equipment, long before there was a general awareness of such potential hazards.

My Own Business

My uncle died two years after my mother. Not only did I inherit the cleaning firm, but also his little house. At thirty-seven, I was a fortunate man. The company continued to flourish and I became a respected member of the community, being elected as a member of the local council when I was forty. This meant more work. The only thing I had not yet acquired was a wife and family. Publicly I stated that I had been too busy. Privately I knew I was never sufficiently attracted to either a woman or a man to want to share my life. The thought terrified me. There was somebody once, but she came too close to me. Both my brothers and sister tried hard to find me a partner, but I resented their interference. Their intrusion curbed what little sexual appetite I had. I know many people say that I am gay. I am not gay, I think I'm heterosexual. Maybe I am neither. But it doesn't matter. I prefer to be alone, but certainly not like Father Antonius – living in a religious community. I would hate that!

The Antiques Shop

I was pleased to sell the cleaning company when I was fifty-five. I was tired. I followed my uncle's idea of having an antiques shop at the front of the house. Of course, it is neat and tidy, but I am not so bothered about the appearance of the rest of my house. I never invite anyone beyond the shop boundaries. When I entertain the Reading Club, which I find such an effort, I clear the largest table of antiques and we sit around it in the shop. It is just about big enough for eight people. I could not manage another person. Once, my Turkish cleaner made some delicacies for a meeting. I thought the food was delicious, but I noticed that several people did not try what she had prepared. They're such a conservative bunch! Now I only provide a few nuts and some ordinary wine when I am the host.

I go to antiques fairs where I meet other dealers and I open my shop on Thursdays and Saturdays. I do not sell much. That is not important. I have always liked to handle old things – to clean and care for them. I read a lot. Ten years ago when Titus came into my shop to buy a gift for his wife's birthday, we had a conversation about starting the Reading Club, which we did together with Joost. I enjoy our monthly meetings, although some of the newer members are quite annoying.

My Turkish Cleaner

I employ a Turkish woman to keep the house clean and tidy. I pay her well because she deserves a good wage. Halfway through the morning, we both stop what we are doing and drink a coffee together. We talk about various subjects. I have told her that I was once a cleaner and I inherited my uncle's company. She confided in me that she was once a primary school teacher in her country, before she came to The Netherlands with her husband, ten years ago. She works for other people in the neighbourhood, but she is discreet about what she shares with me. I appreciate that and feel confident that she is careful not to talk about me.

Like other members of the Reading Club, I once employed the taxi driver's wife to do my cleaning. Her work was satisfactory, but I found her rather nosey, especially about my past and my collection of dragonfly memorabilia. This woman gossips about other people; I do not like that. I prefer my Turkish helper, she is very careful with the antiques. I can see by the way she handles them that she likes them too. She was enthralled the first time she saw the dragonfly brooch. I have arranged to leave it to her in my Will.

Her husband works for my old company. I spoke to him when he was cleaning the station – it has always been an awful place to look after. I did that work myself once. I still see every environment as a potential place to clean. In the station there was rubbish everywhere; pages of free papers and empty beer cans in the waiting-room, many indelible spots of chewing gum on the floor, a stench of urine in the lift, an excess of dirty, inaccessible windows and a herd of careless, unappreciative passengers who are unaware that a cleaner is trying to keep the station clean, safe and tidy. I sat in the glass waiting-room looking out at the river in the distance. Our town drunk, Gerrit, was there with his shopping trolley. I think anyone who works there could write a book, or at least a short story about those who come to and from the station.

The Journal of Joost Kuijpers

Joost Kuipers, co-founder of the Reading Club, and a professional artist, lived in a large, mellow, yellow brick house with a walled garden and an unobstructed view of the Cathedral. With the aid of a government grant, this eighteenth century property was professionally renovated. An art gallery, with large windows onto the street, occupied most of the front downstairs area; while at the side, an old kitchen had been transformed into a studio where languished a number of unused canvasses, an assortment of finished paintings, several easels, a large pot of brushes and a library of art books. In an old still life arrangement, a collection of shrivelled and decaying vegetables was slowly dying, apart from a crown of garlic which, without water, was sprouting a head dress of light green leaves from its centre parting. Everything appeared to have been arranged in an artistic rather than a functional manner and naturally the studio smelt of old oil paint.

Joost's wife, who managed the gallery, was slim, angular and elegant; she moved like a straight-backed ballet dancer. Joost was equally slim and angular, but he walked with his head bowed and his spine slightly bent. Far from looking elegant, he had the appearance of a worn-out drummer from a 1960s rock band. Most of his pale face was hidden by a walrus moustache, bushy eyebrows and a long fringe of jet black hair. His eyes bulged and his Adam's apple protruded. He had a sallow complexion and a long, beak-like nose. The taxi driver's wife nicknamed him the crow. About the town, he usually wore a once-white t-shirt, which had a stretched neck and fluted sleeves, plus a pair of paint-splattered loose-fitting jeans. Some people said that Joost with his scruffy appearance and his wife in her smart attire, made an unlikely couple. Nevertheless, they were often to be seen walking hand in hand in the city.

Joost took readily to the idea of keeping a journal. Using a sketchbook and a black ink artist's pen, he wrote and drew in his spare moments – on train journeys, in his garden and in his studio. Each page was a pleasing composition of words and pictures. Even the errors were artistically corrected. Only later, when he was preparing his piece for the Anniversary Book, did he set aside his sketchbook and use his computer. Having made several sketches of his first school, he wrote about some of his earliest memories. It was later that he gave his writings the title of 'Pictures from a Life'.

My First Day at School

I was born in a remote part of Kenya where my father was working. When I was five, my parents took me 200km in a jeep to a boarding school. I was told that I needed an education, but I could not imagine why that was necessary. Surely, my mother could teach me everything I needed to know. Already I was reading and able to count to twenty. My father taught me to ride a pony. The school claimed to be international, but only white boys were accepted, mostly British. I was the only Dutch child in my year, together with two French and three Afrikaners; we were sometimes referred to as 'the foreigners'. This pseudo academy of excellence was in the White Highlands and run by a strict Scottish Protestant couple – Mr and Mrs MacBayne.

I can recall my first day vividly; the whitewashed square school buildings, the surrounding countryside, the other pupils arriving with their parents, our principal, his wife, and standing behind them a line of black, dusty faced workers with wide eyes and bright teeth. There were six small classrooms in one building and in the other were four dormitories, which were named 'cars',' trains', 'ships' and 'planes'. Together with the fifteen other new boys, I had my metal-framed bed with its strange smelling mattress, in 'cars'. At first, I felt very confused because I could not understand what the adults or the children were saying. My mother told me that I was going to an English school; I knew a few words of that language, but I did not realise that I would not understand what anyone was saying. Although there were two older boys from The Netherlands in other classes, we were not allowed to use our mother tongue. Fortunately, the boy in the next bed to mine offered me a sweet. His name was Tommy Little. We stayed friends throughout our time in school. He was an English boy who looked after me when I did not understand what was happening.

The Pains

Mr and Mrs MacBayne, or the 'Pains' as the boys secretly called them, had their bedroom in the middle of the four dormitories. If there was a disturbance during the night, one of them would appear. To them noise signalled misconduct and misconduct required immediate correction. It was as if they spent much of the night waiting for a punishable crime to be committed. Once caught, guilty or not, the alleged perpetrator would be grabbed by the throat and shaken. Not even the toughest pupil could endure this in silence. The screaming, choking and crying extracted by this brutal punishment was always loud enough to wake the occupants of all four dormitories. This dangerous method of restraint frequently left a temporary mark on the necks of the victims and an indelible impression in the minds of us boys.

I remember Tommy had a favourite toy bear with a secret pocket in which he kept a long cream coloured silk underslip belonging to his mother. Every night when he went to bed, he would cuddle his bear, put his hand into its secret pocket and feel the underslip. I think he found the smooth material very soothing and it reminded him of his home. It was his comforter and when he thought no-one was watching he would take out a corner of the silk and gently rub it around his mouth and nose. In this way he would drift into sleep. Every holiday he would take the bear and the garment home to be washed and he would bring them back to school clean.

Once, one of the older boys stole the underslip and put it on over his pyjamas. The thief paraded through our dormitory, pretending to be a woman, and the older boys started to whistle. Tommy raged, he punched the boy and shouted at him to take off the garment. The noise soon came to the attention of the 'Pains' who rushed into our dormitory to see what was happening. Mr MacBayne seemed most upset by the boy wearing the underslip. He told him to take it off and then he grabbed the offender by the neck and shook him.

'Good Protestant boys do not wear women's clothing,' he yelled in the culprit's ear.

Mrs MacBayne picked up the underslip. Her husband scanned the room to ensure everyone was back in bed and his eyes alighted on me.

'Wipe that smile off your face, Laddie,' he said.

I did not understand this English expression. I knew wipe; that's what I did when I washed my face or used toilet paper on my bottom. I knew smile; that's when my face creased up when there was something funny. What did he mean? There wasn't anything funny about what had just happened. I wasn't smiling, I was frightened. What did he expect me to do? I was too scared to ask. Using both hands I rubbed my face, hoping that was what he wanted, and then I feigned a smile.

'Don't you ridicule me, boy,' he shouted.

I didn't need to understand this new word ridicule, I could sense his anger. I began talking in Dutch. I was so terrified.

'Leave him alone,' his wife said. 'He's not being rude; he doesn't understand what you mean. I think the boys have had enough lessons for tonight.'

There was a long silence while we all held our breath, wondering what would be our headteacher's next move. Thankfully it was to return with his wife to their room, leaving the dormitory filled with the electric silence of fifteen terrified boys.

The next day I realised that Tommy would be distressed without his comforter, but I also knew that Mrs MacBayne would not give it back to him. The only chance for retrieving the treasured garment was if it had been thrown away in the large bins behind the school. We were not allowed in that area, but the women who cleaned the school went there daily. I asked Gladys, our kind dormitory cleaner, to look out for the underslip in case it had been put there together with the rubbish to be burned. I said that if she found it I would give her one of my favourite little cars. The following day she had retrieved the garment. I offered her my toy, but she said that I should keep it for myself. Tommy got back the underslip and returned it to the secret pocket inside his bear. He said I would always be his best friend and he added that his mother would have been terribly upset had he lost her silk underslip.

Nude Bathing

There was a pool next to the schoolhouse and every day we had to swim in the nude. Sometimes when the water turned green, Mr MacBayne would call for one of the black workers to test it and add some chemicals. I do not think anyone really understood how to keep a pool clean and safe. Once or twice, a number of the boys had sickness and diarrhoea and then the local doctor insisted that the pool should be closed for a few days until one of the white guys from the local town came to fix it. We swam in the nude, which was very difficult for some of the boys who came from families where they had never seen anyone without their clothes. The Pains took it in turns to supervise the swimming. I did not like the way Mrs MacBayne looked at me without my clothes; only my mum had seen me in the nude.

Mr MacBayne taught us Mathematics. He was a strange looking fellow. His bottom lip was thick and curled out from his mouth as if wrapping itself around an invisible pencil. The moist, pink area protruding outwards gave the impression of a permanent pout. The remains of his last cup of coffee always left a thin black tidemark stretching from one corner of his mouth to the other. It was as if there was something inside his head pushing parts of his face outwards, because his cheeks were puffy and his eyes bulged. He looked like a hippopotamus in a dark suit. When Mr MacBayne was annoyed, he let out a sigh, which vibrated his bottom lip against the top. Occasionally during these expressions of exasperation, tiny droplets of saliva would spray out and land on nearby objects and people.

Mrs MacBayne was not quite as ugly as her husband. Her lips were thin and she had a high-pitched voice, which rang through the school when she was angry. She wore her hair pulled tightly back in a bun. The most striking thing about her ashen face was a large mole on the side of her chin, which sprouted three black hairs. Sometimes the hairs would disappear and the boys would start a whisper that the forest had been cut down. Then after about four weeks, the hairs had grown again. Sometimes, while we were working, Mrs MacBayne, would be daydreaming and she would start to fiddle with her three hairs. When they were at a length that they needed cutting, she would get hold of them between her thumb and forefinger and try to pluck them out. This was never successful but she would spend a lot of time tugging, unaware that most of the class were watching her.

An Artist at Six

The couple were religious fanatics, believing that chastisement was a way of bringing us boys closer to God. We worked hard every day at our lessons, including all day Saturday, and on Sunday we studied the Scriptures. Parental visiting was restricted to once a term. The 'Pains' claimed that anything more frequent would disturb our studies.

I had a skill which Mrs MacBayne admired. At an early age I was very good at drawing. When we were asked to draw a picture of one of the stories from the Bible, mine was usually held up in front of the class, as the best. I think this ability prevented me from being in any serious trouble with the 'Pains' and unlike my fellow country boys in the Netherlands, who were told to be modest about their achievements, I grew accustomed to having regular praise for my pictures. In that way I came to value my drawing skill and I decided by the age of six that when I grew up,

I was going to be an artist and make pictures like the ones in our school Bibles.

The food at the school was awful, but we were hungry, so we ate it. All the boys were slim because we lived on minimum rations. Eventually I got used to drinking sour milk, but at first it made me sick. Bullying was rife in the tradition of the English public schools. I see now it was only to be expected since the 'Pains' bullied us. I tried to tell my parents about my dislike of school, but each time I did, my mother became upset and tearful and left the room. My father asked me not to distress her with exaggerated stories. He said he was very proud of me, because I was following in his family tradition of going to a boarding school. Frequently he told me that boys without a good education turned out to be bad men.

A Horrible School

I got used to living in the school environment, accustomed to avoiding trouble by keeping quiet and I learnt not to show my feelings. I was never bullied, thanks to my friend Tommy who made sure that I was always included in the main gang with him, but I witnessed some of my classmates being tormented by the older boys and I felt helpless to do anything in case the bullies set about me.

I spent four years at that school, only coming home during Christmas, Easter and for the long summer holiday. I have mostly awful memories of those days; of missing my parents. I felt rejected when they sent me away to school. Of course, I could not articulate that then. We returned home to the Netherlands when I was nine and I went to an ordinary Dutch school. But those early years had a great impact on me. I still conceal my feelings. I am able to keep a straight face. Today my moustache – which I first grew in the 1970s – hides much of my face. I know that some people say that I am a miserable man.

Hard Times

I have become an artist, a few might say that I am quite successful and respected. I have a fine studio attached to an elegant house. I have a good-looking wife. We do not have any children; neither of us really wanted them in our lives. I lecture in Art at Utrecht University and have my own style of painting the local landscapes. Each year my wife and I open up some rooms in our house to public view, as part of the local 'Art Route' and we invite visitors to see examples of my work in the studio and the gallery. When I am not painting, I like to cook. Each day I take my small shopping bag to the supermarket, to collect things for the evening meal. I also like to read; that is why I am a member of the Reading Club along with those other middle-aged men.

After the evening shift, the taxi driver was back in his flat talking to his wife. 'I saw Joost Kuijpers in Amsterdam today. He was going into one of those old houses with lots of studios, just off the *Zalm Straat.*'

'What were you doing in that area?'

'One of my clients has a house there. We were having coffee before we drove back. I saw Joost with a portfolio. My client says he has seen him a few times. Apparently, he paints portraits of the locals.'

'I thought that was an area for prostitution.'

'It is. That's how he makes his money now.'

'Aren't his landscapes selling any more?'

'Apparently not.'

'Painting prostitutes! I wonder what his posh wife says about that?'

'If she knows.'

Joost continued with his journal.

Unsold Pictures

During the last ten years, my style of painting has lost its popularity. This has resulted in my work getting stacked up in my studio and not being sold. Each year for the 'Art Route', I dust my pictures and rearrange them, hoping that they will look as if they have been freshly painted. That is the impression I try to give, but the reality is that no-one wants to buy my work any more. I used to be a full time lecturer at Utrecht University. This gave me a steady income which I supplemented by selling my landscapes. However both of these sources almost dried up. The lecturing was reduced to a few sessions a week – hardly enough to pay for our food. I began to feel desperate about the upkeep of our house. It was at this time that one of my ex-students asked me if I would be interested in painting a portrait of his friend.

There is a huge difference between painting landscapes and portraits. I was on the point of dismissing this idea, when I remembered that I had enjoyed doing this work during my college days and I had even sold a few pictures. I said yes and agreed to meet the friend to discuss what he wanted.

I liked this young man immediately when I saw him. His skin had a soft glow and he reminded me of my old school friend Tommy Little. We instantly got along, unusual for me, since I am very cautious about new people. I told him he had beautiful hands and classic cheekbones. Maybe it was because of my compliments that he felt he could trust me. Within half an hour, he told me that he was a transvestite. I was shocked. I had never knowingly spoken to one before. When I heard the word transvestite, I called to mind images from the pornographic magazines on the top shelf of our local tobacco shop. Once I flicked through a 'Rustler' magazine before its copies were covered with plastic sleeves to prevent peeping without paying. I was horrified at the grossness of the cartoons and the photographs. I could accept homosexuality, providing that no man made sexual advances to me; but I didn't understand why a man would want to dress up in women's clothes.

Eduard told me why he enjoys being a transvestite. His attention to the detail for his female clothes and make-up is fascinating; like the awareness an artist has towards the subject of his painting. I am intrigued by his desire to be smooth – his skin, his hair, his chin, his chest, his legs – in a way that women supposedly want to be. The wish to be very feminine in mannerism, in voice, in perfume, is a real compulsion for him. He wants to be slim. He was pleased that he had reduced his waistline by several centimetres. He has a strong urge to dress up and live out his fantasy and to be transformed into being something quite different from the stereotypical male. He does not want to be a woman; being a transvestite is his way of enjoying some feminine longings. He wants to keep his penis, even if in a pose he pushes it between his legs.

Like Cooking

For centuries, portrait painters have flattered their subjects. By changing lines, softening shadows and enhancing colours they have delighted their patrons. Was it possible for me to paint a fine picture of this person? Could I convey his desire to be feminine, when I was uncomfortable with that idea myself? How would I feel seeing him dressed in women's clothes? I could not predict my response.

I asked him, 'How would you like me to paint you? Do you have a favourite outfit or pose?'

'I've several. I'd like to show you all of my special outfits so that we can choose the best for the portrait.'

At this point I felt uncomfortable and I told him, 'I'm happy to do that but I want you to know that I'm heterosexual.'

'You don't have to tell me that. It's obvious. I'm heterosexual too. Transvestites aren't necessarily gay guys. Some of them are straight.'

This confused me so I said, 'I'm sorry, I've never met a transvestite before and I don't understand your...what you do... your sexuality.'

'That's OK. Not many people understand us, that's why most of us keep our preferences secret. I'll try to explain. Do you have any hobbies?'

'Yes, I like reading and cooking.'

'Let's take cooking,' he said. 'The appetite for food and sex are similar in many ways. Would you agree? Imagine how you'd feel when living in a society where men were forbidden to go into food shops and select and buy food. Just think about what you would be missing. No touching, seeing, sampling or smelling the raw ingredients. I know an artist who says that he becomes almost orgasmic when he sees a nice display of vegetables. And in that fictitious society, not only is shopping forbidden but cooking too, so you're not allowed to mix the ingredients and to experiment with new recipes. Men only eat the end product; all that sensory excitement, buying and preparing is for women only. In a similar way, transvestites like some feminine things which society dictates aren't for men. Many of us seek to enjoy ourselves in private where we can taste experiences which are forbidden to us.'

'That's an interesting analogy,' I said, still aware of my strong feeling of ambiguity. I returned to the commission. 'I'll take some photographs then you can choose which outfit you would like to wear for your portrait.'

He suggested that when he is wearing his feminine outfits, I should call him Edwina.

Strong Feelings

I remember what I experienced when I first saw Eduard dressed as a woman – ambiguity, revulsion, pity, maybe a little fear, a disharmony that had nothing to do with my belief that people should have freedom in these matters. It was an instinctive reaction. This human was neither male nor female and was violating one of the first distinctions I make about a person. My reaction reminded me of the feelings I had about certain severe disabilities.

My sister works in a day centre for adults with special needs. She cares for and loves her charges. She is so natural in her approach. I always envied her attitude and wished I could be the same, but it upsets me to see people with profound handicaps; I am terrified. I tried to hide my reactions, but my sister always saw my fear and became angry. She said that I should undertake some voluntary work in her setting, in order to get rid of my prejudices. She never understood that I wanted to be different, but my emotional response crippled me. I experienced a similar reaction when I saw Eduard dressed as a woman. It wasn't my wish to have a strong reaction. I endeavoured to act calmly and professionally.

Six Outfits

A few weeks after our first meeting, I rented a small studio in a back street in Amsterdam. Eduard arrived with a case containing his female clothes. I set up my camera and we began our session. He had six outfits for six different characters. The first one was what he called his 'slinky look' which comprised a long, tight, black silk dress with a slit up the side; the top of the garment was filled out with a pair of false breasts which he yanked about until they exactly fitted into the bodice. He kept touching his hair and feeling the smoothness of his red nail varnish. He had so many mannerisms which I recognised from my female friends. Yes, I felt shocked – I had been brought up to believe that men should not wear women's clothing – but I was overwhelmed by this amazing creature, who was still Eduard. By the end of the morning, I had seen all of his outfits: the nurse, the young nun, the waitress, the leather look and the New York City girl. By far the most attractive was the last character. For this he wore a plain black sheath dress with red accessories; shoes, belt, beads and small shoulder bag. I took many pictures. We agreed to meet again and choose which outfit he would wear for the portrait.

The Contract

We met two weeks later in a quiet café near Amsterdam Central Station. Eduard was wearing light brown trousers and a red check open-necked shirt with a white tee-shirt beneath. He was delighted with all of the photographs and explained how difficult it was for transvestites to acquire images of themselves. He told me that it was risky for them to take self-portraits in their own homes. Many went to hotel rooms, but it was not easy. He told me that a number of transvestites like to see their pictures in the advertisement sections of transvestite magazines. Apparently it is all part of the excitement. He had once done this himself and had been dissatisfied with the quality of his pictures. Now, in addition to painting his portrait, Eduard wanted to buy all of my working photographs.

The Feminine Portrait

He had chosen to wear the long, black, silk dress for his portrait. He said it was the most feminine and elegant of all his outfits. The bodice was tight and the skirt fell into soft folds from his hips to the floor. It was a beautiful garment which fitted him well. His false breasts filled the top of the dress, but there was no suggestion of a cleavage. The dress had long sleeves, which emphasised his angular shoulders, which he hunched as he pretended to flirt with me. He had long arms, large hands, square nails painted with bright red varnish. Down one side of his dress was a split, which allowed a glimpse of a hairless thigh. I thought his high, black, shiny boots emphasised his large feet. Suede would have been more flattering. His hair, a realistic wig, was a mass of blonde, shiny curls.

His make-up was heavy: bright red lipstick, thick dark lashes and a blusher which emphasised his high cheekbones. Even though I asked him to remain still, every now and then he insisted on pushing his lips out as if getting ready to give some imaginary suitor a kiss. He filled the studio with his expensive perfume, which lingered long after he had gone. In our conversation prior to the painting he said that he always wanted to look very feminine but because of his height and shape that had been impossible. He asked whether I could make a beautiful portrait, even though he realised that he could never be a beautiful woman. Working from several photographs I modified and softened some of his features and I gave him a hint of a smile.

I worked long on the portrait. Eduard agreed to my suggestion that I give it a seventeenth century flavour. Following the ideas of painters of that time, I included some everyday symbolic objects around the edges of the picture; a burnt-out candle, a book and an hourglass symbolising the transience of life, and a lute with its erotic connotations. I included a small boy in the background. As was the custom of the time, he was dressed as a girl.

I liked Eduard from our first meeting and I was determined to make him look feminine, since that was important to him; yet he should still be recognisable as Eduard. I wanted his portrait to be an aesthetic piece and that is what I believed I produced. He was delighted with his picture; particularly the inclusion of the small boy wearing a girl's dress.

I did wonder where he was going to hang the picture, but I chose not to ask him.

The Business

Eduard paid a fair price for my work and then suggested that we went into business together. According to him there was a good market for photographing and making portraits of transvestites. He would find the customers and arrange the studio if I came regularly to Amsterdam to do this work. We could offer our clients complete security of identity and make some money for ourselves. Eduard took responsibility for renting a little studio behind the Central Station. It was a miserable looking place, with poor lighting, and it smelt of stale paint and old cigars.

However, the ambiance of the studio was transformed when Eduard had it decorated; it looked bright and airy and was fragrant, as if someone had just got out of a perfumed bath. He bought a few items of furniture and made sure that there was a large, well-lit mirror for our clients to apply their make-up and adjust their dress and ensure that their breasts were evenly placed. He also provided a little screen, make-up remover and tissues for them to use at the end of the portrait sessions.

For the last ten years, I have painted numerous transvestites in various states of dress and undress. Although some people may consider some of my work as verging on pornography, my aim is to create aesthetic pieces. In some of the portraits I allude to the story, the drama and the secrets of that person's life. But not every picture has to tell a story. Sometimes I paint a picture without the intention of conveying anything else but a feminine impression.

I have concealed this work from my friends in the same way the transvestites follow their dress preferences in private.

Salvador

Over the years Eduard and I have become good friends. I spoke to him once about my fear of people with physical handicaps. He said he thought that my sister was right and that I should volunteer to do some work for her. For two years now, I have been running art classes for both the clients and the staff of the Centre for Adults with Special Needs.

Salvador has a handsome head of dark hair and thick, black eyelashes. One of his deep brown eyes is slightly larger than the other. The smaller one does not see. The right side of his body is still, and one hand, which is permanently curled, rests on his lap.

He spends most of his time in a wheelchair, which he operates in a jerky fashion with his good hand. He has long, elegant fingers, which often open, close, stretch and wave about, seemingly out of his control. His mobile side can manage large movements, which are often exaggerated and twisted. When he smiles, which he does frequently, his head and upper body move through a wide unnecessary arc. His pleasure is conveyed through noises which, to those who do not know him, sound like grunts and groans – not recognisable words. When I first met him I was disarmed by his appearance, and embarrassed that I could not understand him. Fortunately my clumsiness at our first meeting did not prevent Salvador from addressing me.

He came towards me in his wheelchair. I knew he was talking to me, but I could not understand his sounds. A very small woman beside him said,

'Salvador says hello.'

I held out my hand in greeting. It took a few moments before his swaying hand caught hold of mine. Then he said something else.

'I don't understand,' I said apologetically.

'He says you're hand is wet and shaking,' said his interpreter.

I rubbed my hands together and felt their sweat and their tremble.

'I feel nervous,' I said.

Salvador's body lurched from left to right so vigorously that I feared he might fall out of his wheelchair. Then he thumped the arm of his chair with his good hand and grinned to reveal a pristine set of teeth. He made some more sounds. I realised that he was laughing at me. I looked to the woman to translate.

'He said there's no need for you to shake; he's the chief mover and shaker around here.'

I smiled.

'He says he's come here to paint. What are you waiting for?'

I looked at his hand, which was moving about wildly and wondered if he would have sufficient control to hold a brush or pencil and then make contact with the paper or canvas.

'Does he like painting?' I said, addressing the woman.

'Ask him,' she said.

'Do you like painting?' I said, looking at him.

More excited groans, then, he gave a thumbs-up sign, which wavered in the air. He thumped his chest and bellowed something indistinguishable at me. I looked to his small companion for help. I felt hopeless.

'He says he's an artist. He used to be Van Gogh.'

'How do you know what he's saying?' I asked the woman.

'That's what he said – isn't it Salvador?'

Salvador bellowed, swayed and hoisted his thumb in the air.

She continued, 'He said, before he was born as Salvador, he was the artist Van Gogh.'

'In a former life?' I asked Salvador directly, not knowing if that was what he believed or if he was making a joke.

He thumped the arm of his wheel chair and groaned with delight. The top part of his body circled and twisted and his thumb went in the air once again. He was joking! Apparently satisfied that I would now start the lesson he reversed his wheelchair and returned to his place in the class. I began by introducing myself and inviting everyone to begin drawing or painting.

Salvador has regularly attended the art classes. Often he goes over the edge of his painting and once or twice he has punctured a canvas, but he has produced some interesting pictures, including a portrait of me, which is hanging in my studio.

After one of the meetings of the Reading Club, Joost and Titus were walking home.

'How's the writing?' Titus asked.

'I've enjoyed it. I started out thinking that I would do some portraits in words of several people that I admire. Instead I explored my childhood memories.'

'Pleased with what you wrote?'

'I felt a bit unhappy when I realised how I had been influenced by those early days. I had a very harsh school life from the age of five. We lived in Africa. It was better when we came back to The Netherlands. I was nine. Then I went to an ordinary school.'

'Sorry to hear that. How's your painting?'

'I've had a tough time selling my pictures recently. I've been doing some private work in Amsterdam. I've written about that in my journal.'

'Interesting, will you include that in the Anniversary book?'

'My partner prefers that I don't publicize it.'

'That's unusual.'

'Yes, he is.'

Perhaps Titus did not understand, or maybe he could not be bothered to find out more. He asked, 'Any idea about what you will write for the book?'

'Yes. I know a young man – Salvador – at the Adult Day Centre. He's got a great sense of humour – loves painting. He's painted my portrait. I want to write about him.'

'I know him,' said Titus, 'he's one of my patients. Can't understand anything he says. One of his carers has to translate. He's very badly disabled. I am surprised he has sufficient control to paint.'

'He's good in a naïve way.'

'His family lives in the area. Do you think they would be happy to read about their son in our booklet?'

'Is our book going to be distributed widely?'

'Quite a few people outside of the Reading Club have ordered copies. Could be that Salvador's parents get to read what you have written.'

'I hadn't considered that. I thought the idea was to write freely.'

'Yes, but we were asked not to include anything which might upset someone else.'

'Perhaps I should choose another subject.'

'I think you should.'

'What have you in mind?' Joost asked.

'It's difficult. I've written about lots of things, which I wouldn't want people to know about. They might misunderstand. I write professionally so I feel I want to be modest in what I choose.'

'Don't be too modest'.

The Journal of Paul Bazelman

As a young man, Paul had a sumptuous head of brown hair, which by forty had receded, thinned and turned grey. At forty-five, he was prescribed his first pair of spectacles, which he wore a few centimetres from the bridge of his nose, giving him the option of looking through the glass or over the rims. At fifty-five his neck had thickened, he had given up trying to spread his thinning hair evenly over his scalp and had taken to shaving his head every Saturday. By Friday, his scalp looked like a shadowy egg.

Even when they were young, Paul and Venus Bazelman made an unusual couple. He was slim, pale and quiet. Although she was now well-built, even voluptuous, Venus had been slim in her youth, but she had always been noisy and playful and had not stayed in teaching for long. They had one child, a daughter who, having inherited her mother's sense of adventure, was working her way around the world with a mature woman friend.

Over the years, Paul had grown serious and engrossed in his career. He had worked at the Ministry of Education for the last fifteen years. Before that he was a teacher in a grammar school. He and his wife no longer enjoyed an intimate life. Either through the pressure of work, a consequence of his age or for some unknown reason, Paul had experienced a long period of impotency. At first Venus did not care, as long as during their love making, she achieved an orgasm for herself. She teased him, told him that she had read about his condition and terrified him by saying that his erectile tissue was ageing, with a kind of fibrosis.

'You've lost your elastic,' she said to him with a laugh.

This comment had extinguished any vestige of his sexual confidence. He felt humiliated and cursed like his medieval ancestors who believed that impotency was a spell from a witch who was acting in proxy for the devil. Venus gave up initiating their intimacy and Paul, unaccustomed to talking about their sex life, could not find the words to express his difficulty to his wife. He was too shy to speak to Titus, his GP, and he did not consider doing his own research into his problem. He took his wife's view about his faulty plumbing and accepted his situation as fate. He was pleased when she stopped referring to it or expecting him to engage in sexual activities.

Paul took his membership of the Reading Club seriously and believed that his critical analyses of the club's books were often more insightful than the ones he read in newspapers or literary magazines. Although he was able to offer reasons why it was not a good idea to undertake the writing project, he went along with the majority decision and planned to dedicate several afternoons to preparing his entries for the Anniversary Book. Initially he decided that it was unnecessary to keep a journal; instead he would concentrate on his final submissions. The idea of recalling his schooldays appealed to him. He was one of the Reading Club who nominated Father Antonius as being the main inspiration for his love of literature. He enjoyed 'Priests Dying', recognising himself in the stories of the junior seminarian. Paul made a start by recalling something from his schooldays. He wrote:

Homework

I hadn't done the homework which Father Antonius was asking

for in front of the class. I lied – said I'd done it. Said I had left it in the study hall.

'Then go and fetch it,' the priest demanded.

Outside of the classroom I scribbled a few lines on a piece of paper. I gave it to the priest. He looked straight at me. I was frightened.

'If this is your homework, you should show it to the Principal, see what he thinks.'

The Principal said some sharp words and when I tried to defend myself he hit me around my head. It hurt. It still hurts. My anger shot out.

'I don't like it here. It's like a prison,' I shouted.

'This is not a prison. You're free to leave whenever you want. But if you are staying you are suspended from your lessons for a day. And no smoking for a week. In your free time you can read and copy out an article on prison life.'

I cried. I was angry and humiliated.

I met a fellow student, a junior seminarian. Not so young, twenty. He had already been in the school for nine years. Not bright enough to move on to the major seminary. He didn't attend many of the lessons – instead he assisted the music professor. Bart had a deep voice and huge hands. He asked me what had been going on. He was kind. We went to the music room. He sat in the professor's chair; I sat on a music stool. He opened a cupboard and took out a large box of cigars. Everyone smoked openly in our school – both priests and pupils.

'I think it would be a good idea for us to have a smoke. You tell me your story,' he said.

I told him I had never smoked a cigar, only cigarettes.

'This is different,' he said, 'your situation requires something stronger.'

So there we sat, he puffing at his cigar like the Principal and me coughing. I was trying to copy Bart.

After I told my tale, he said I should be his assistant – the music master's assistant assistant. I liked that job. It had some advantages – including the occasional cigar. The post also came with some chores, Bart's chores, which I undertook. I did not mind because I liked Bart. The music area, when not in use, was one of the quietest places in the school.

When I was back home for the holidays I visited the nearby Cross Friars Priory. There, I became acquainted with a senior seminarian, who was about twenty-four and not yet ordained. He played the organ. He was very kind to me. I told him about the homework and my view that my school was like a prison.

'Come to our priory. We also have a minor seminary,' he said.

I was very keen on this idea. When I told my mother she appeared not to listen. Without my knowledge, she telephoned the prior of the Cross Friars and told him what had happened. He made the young organist say sorry to my mother by letter and also give her a box of chocolates. Then the prior transferred him to another monastery. I thought this was my fault. My mother was a powerful woman in those days – much like Venus is now.

I returned to my seminary to continue my studies. I remained angry with Father Antonius and furious with the Principal for many years. It was only when I became a teacher that I understood how frustrating educational work can be.

Paul reread what he had written. He made no allowances for the fact that this was his first attempt at writing in an unfamiliar way, and judged his effort as being a poor attempt. It was one thing criticising other people's work and a completely different thing to write oneself. He concluded that it would be inappropriate to embarrass Father Antonius with this story. He deleted what he had written and began again:

Day Order

At 6.30 every day, the dormitory brother, our night guard, would wake us. By 6.50, we were marched around the inner yard between the school and the chapel. We walked in silence, in all weather conditions – hot sunshine, heavy rain, snow and below zero temperatures. After this exercise we went to the Study Hall, where the Spiritual Father gave us a talk on the saint of the day; most of the time he paid careful attention to chastity. In the same way that Father Antonius described his early lack of understanding on the subject, it took me two or three years before I understood what the word meant, although I realised from the beginning that it was significant because the Father frequently became angry and excited in his deliverance. White slime would build up in the corners of his mouth and at the height of his performance tiny droplets would be propelled into the air. He was an ugly man, whose main job was to ensure our spiritual education. He frightened me. I decided then, that if ever I was going to be a priest, I would not be like him.

At least once a year, all the boys had private interviews with the Spiritual Father, to check their progress. At my first talk, I was twelve when he asked me about chastity; how I estimated the level of my calling and if I had any special friendships with other juniors. I did not realise then, but he was finding out if I had any homosexual inclinations. In the second year he asked me if I knew how the human body was made; did I know about specific parts around the 'under belly'. I told him I was not informed.

'Your mother should have told you.'

Using very vague terms the Spiritual Father instructed me about procreation and the job of 'the special instrument'. I sat for a long time. What he said terrified me. Is that how I had been conceived? I was pleased that I was going to be a priest and would not have to do that sort of thing. When I returned home, my mother was very angry because the Father had contacted her saying that she had failed in my education.

She said, 'I told you about that,' but I did not remember. Perhaps I wasn't listening or had not understood her explanation. It was never mentioned again.

Every year, all of us went on retreat to a different monastery. I remember that the Jesuits and the Franciscans talked more freely about chastity. However, I did not learn the word penis until I was eighteen; prior to that my special instrument was nameless or 'it' – 'it' because it was associated with sin.

The vague talks were of no help when it came to my night-time emissions. I was fearful to tell anyone because I sensed it was a sin or that something was wrong with me. We wore our underwear day and night for a week. Having a thorough wash or showering was not emphasised. We became accustomed to the odours of each other, the holy fathers and brothers. I did not learn about deodorants until my late twenties.

At 7.15, we went to the chapel. Mass was conducted at the altar end where we sat in class and alphabetical order. At the other end were two confessionals in which a priest had a middle compartment and on either side of him were two boxes for those confessing. Every day, two confessional fathers would come from the abbey to the school chapel to hear the confessants who were gathered in the back pews waiting to lighten their souls. Each priest could manage two boys at a time. When the first confessant had finished whispering his sins, he would have to sit in silent contemplation, while the priest heard the boy on the other side. When the priest had finished with sinner number two, the first boy would receive his response and the confession, for him, would be concluded. Enlightened boy number one would leave the box and go to his place in the front of the chapel to join the Mass. The priest would then address the other confessant. At the other end of the chapel, those who were participating in Mass would also be observing those going in and out of the boxes. Not only could they see who the frequent sinners were, but also they could tell who had committed the greatest sins by the length of time it took to make the confession. I am sure that sometimes the priests became confused with this double system and issued the wrong penances.

By the time I was nineteen, I was at university having decided that I did not want to become a priest. I got to know a girl, not Venus, a fellow student. We only talked and I did not know what to do with her. I became very worried when my mother came to hear about this relationship. She said that my studies came first and there would be time afterwards for other things. I wrote to my former confessional father and asked for some advice about how I could manage the restrictions of my mother and my own interests – if not longing. He replied that I should listen to my mother and resist the temptation of young women.

I feel angry at the way the youngsters behave today. They meet someone and in no time they are jumping into bed with each other. My daughter is nineteen and instead of finishing university she has gone off with a woman friend who is ten years her senior, travelling around the world. I suspect their relationship is more than she is telling me.

Even married people do not keep loyal to their spouses. A man at the Ministry talks openly about his mistress.

I am saddened by the doom of my early years; the mental and spiritual struggle. I feel angry that I was naïve and inexperienced. It was no preparation for life. When I compare my early years with the way young people behave today, I feel wretched. They are dark pages in my history.

This recollection caused Paul to become tearful. He took a handkerchief from his pocket, wiped his eyes and blew his nose. Nearly fifty years on, some aspects of his seminary days still pierced his hardened exterior and reached the softer man within. He was sorry that he had explored this subject so thoroughly. When he started to recall his days at the seminary, he had no idea that he would feel so upset.

Yet again Paul ignored the advice on writing, which was to wait until all journal entries were finished before choosing which themes to develop. As he pushed his handkerchief back into his pocket, he had already decided that he would not be using what he had just written as a basis for a submission to the Anniversary Book. It was too painful to relive those days again – he deleted the story.

He needed some air. Downstairs, he went into the garden and strolled behind the summerhouse where he could not be seen from the kitchen where Venus was putting black varnish on her toe nails. As he smoked an illicit cigarette he looked into the neighbour's garden. Why had he become so upset? He leant down to pick up a ball, which belonged to the children next door. For a moment he held it, and then he threw it over the fence. He extinguished his cigarette and flicked the butt into Mrs Lentjes's garden; his other neighbour. She was now unable to walk to the part where Paul threw his cigarette ends. He had created a small heap.

Back in the house, Paul leant on the pine table and glanced at the post which was balancing on top of some bills, a literary magazine, last week's free paper, and a shoe box. The table was cluttered, but he was not in the mood for tidying. This was Venus's job. He needed a drink. Upstairs in his room he poured himself a strong black coffee, lit another cigarette and went over to the window to ensure that the smoke went outside. Ever since he had started smoking at the seminary at the age of twelve, he held his cigarette between his thumb and his pointing finger, using the other three digits as a shield. As a boy, he became adept at concealing a lit fag in his trousers, by pushing the sides of his pocket open with his middle and little finger. Sometimes it got a little hot in there and once his hand was burnt when a boy bumped into him. Paul looked down at his cigarette and remembered how smoking featured in his early life. Perhaps he could write about that.

He recalled that smoking was not discouraged in the school. The boys were allowed to smoke at set times during the day; after Mass, after breakfast and after study. At other times it was banned; but for some it was at those times that the desire to have a smoke was at its strongest. At mid-morning, the boys were taken along the abbey and through the village. Smoking was not permitted. They walked in a line of twos and threes. The ones in the middle would often chance to have a drag because they were more concealed than the ones following the leading priest or those preceding the escort at the rear of the group. If caught, the offenders were sent to the vice-principal who issued a punishment such as 'no smoking for one hour during a time when it was allowed'. If the prohibition was ignored, then an additional five-day ban could be issued.

The vice-principal ran the little shop where smoking accoutrements could be bought. Paul recalled the cigarette brands of those days: 'Chief Whip', 'Golden Fiction', 'Miss Blanche', and 'North State'. They were sold in packets of ten or twenty. Sometimes his parents gave him money to buy cigarettes and he always got a packet from them at the beginning of December as a present for the festival of Santa Claus.

Nearly all the boys smoked; those who did not became passive smokers. Every priest and every brother smoked pipes, cigars or cigarettes, both in the lessons and in the study hall. Paul remembered that Father Antonius once smoked a pipe. He used to tap the end of it on his forehead when he was thinking and grit his teeth on it when he was angry. Paul recalled the unpleasant Latin and Greek teacher with the rough manners, who had a cigar in his mouth throughout the lessons. Paul was sure that this man did not like him, because he was never selected to read out his work.

Paul remembered another cigar smoker who came from the eastern part of the country. He had a dialect, which amused the boys; but they had to be careful not to smile in front of him. There were many times when he accused them of mocking him. He also smoked in lessons and when he inhaled he hiccupped, and then with his piggy eyes scanned the room to see if anyone was laughing at him.

Up until the 1970s, when he was a young history teacher, Paul smoked in class. In many ways he regretted his habit, which was now an anti-social activity. How times had changed. In some adverts from the 1920s, cigarettes were promoted as being healthy. Although he had sufficient material to write about smoking, he decided that he did not want to draw attention to a habit which he tried to keep private. Even the slight anger he felt towards the anti-smoking lobby did not provide him with sufficient impetus to write about this theme; he decided against it.

Although Paul had given a lot of thought to his submission for the Anniversary Book and had written a few unsatisfactory pieces, which he had deleted, he had nothing to show for the time he had expended. Eventually he decided to follow the advice, which was to write a journal from which some material could be used at a later date. He opened a new file on his computer, named it 'Journal' and began writing:

My initial reaction to the task is a feeling of resentment. Surely, the Reading Club is for enthusiastic readers not for would-be writers. I am a historian; I deal in facts, not thoughts and feelings. At the seminary school, I hated any kind of essay writing. I imagined I had left all of that behind me. Am I really expected to undertake work set by my old teacher? I could say that I do not want to do it or that I couldn't think of anything or that I had no time. At school, I used to make excuses as to why I had not completed the set assignments, but the fathers always had counter arguments. To avoid the embarrassment of being singled out, I did my work like everyone else. I certainly did not want to be sent home, on the pretext that I was not intelligent enough to be a priest. Two boys from my class were dismissed – officially it was said that they could not manage the work; rumour had it that they had become too friendly. It is hard to imagine that I wanted to be a priest when I was twelve. I wonder what my life would be like now, had I been ordained. I cannot imagine leading a celibate life devoted to prayer and poverty. But in practice I am like a celibate now. I do not even believe in God any more; or do I? So what shall I write? Where to begin?

At this point Paul looked up to see Venus standing in one of her many provocative poses at the entrance to his study; one hand on her hip and the other stretched up and holding onto the door frame.

'How long have you been there?'

'Long enough,' she said. 'Not going so well?' she asked, dropping her grip on the frame and adjusting her jacket.

'No.'

'Let me guess what you've been writing about.'

'Have you been looking in my computer?'

'You know that I don't know or care about how that machine works.'

'I've seen you at this computer.'

'Only to look at photos.'

'What's your guess?'

'The seminary.'

'Why do you say that?'

'You often talk about it, especially to other men who have

had the same ordeal. When you get together with some of those old seminary boys, you talk of nothing else.'

'What do you mean, ordeal? They gave me a good education.'

'Maybe, but they treated you like shit, ruined your boyhood. As a result you are rubbish socially. The Catholic attitude towards sex has stayed with you all of your life. You're even frightened to talk about it, as if it were a sin.'

'That's a cruel exaggeration.'

'Yet you still send them money each month.'

'I feel attached to the Church.'

'Why?'

'I don't know.

'You're so critical of other things, yet you accept what they did. Why are you loyal to an institution which so damaged your life?'

'Non-Catholics don't understand. That's what I told Hans at the Reading Club after we had read 'Priests Dying'.'

'What did he say?' A slight flush crept up Venus's neck at the mention of Hans's name. Paul saw it but did not react. When his wife was in this mood she could be scathing. He decided not to provoke her by drawing attention to a sign that might suggest that she was embarrassed. 'I argued with him,' Paul said, 'he was quite rude to me.'

'Touched a nerve, did he?' She placed her hand on her neck to cover the hot rash.

'He lost his temper. I didn't understand what he was going on about. Titus intervened and he quietened down.'

'Seems he doesn't like you.'

'I don't know why. I'm always very civil to him.'

'Smoking will be your other subject. You're always banging on about it.'

'I have been thinking about it. Everyone smoked when I was at school.'

'You've told me that a hundred times.'

'You sure you haven't been looking at my computer?'

'I don't need to. I know you so well.'

'I wish I could say the same about you. I still find you a mystery.'

'Good,' Venus said as she turned around and left Paul to continue with his journal. He pondered a while, and then he wrote:

In the instructions there are many suggestions. One is to complete at least one or two pages each day about anything which comes to mind. I can't see the point of that. There has to be a proper subject. Another suggestion is to write about some memories from my schooldays. I have done that a few times and nothing was agreeable to me. I know that Father Antonius wrote regularly since he was in the seminary. Another suggestion is to write about a significant incident like a family occasion or a simple observation of a person or a thing. I have to say that none of those things inspire me. I really am quite blank about what to write. Apparently, Titus has been writing a journal every day and has thoroughly enjoyed it. I expect at school he was a *Brave Hendrik*; a real goody-goody, always doing what was asked of him. I have heard that Joost and Milo have written about their days at school. I thought this writing was supposed to be private. Why are people talking about what they have done? I could write about the view from my study. The garden looks beautiful now. I am very proud of it. But some people might think that I am boasting.

Although Paul was not pleased with what he had written, he decided to follow the advice and kept what was on the screen. Perhaps he could develop some aspect of it later. What else could he write about? His first day at school came to mind. But not now. He had already spent much of the day writing pieces which he had deleted. Perhaps later in the week. Next Wednesday he had some free time and Venus had said she would be out for the day. There might be another opportunity sooner. Paul decided he could concentrate better when his wife was not around.

A few days later Paul was in his study scrutinising some ministerial reports. These days he often worked from home. Venus appeared in the doorway wearing a jacket.

'I'm going out for the day,' she said.

'Anywhere interesting?'

'I've a few people to see and then I'm having lunch with my sister.'

'Could you collect a book from *'Boeken Boeken'*? Just give my name. They'll know the book.'

Venus nodded.

'When will you return?' Paul asked.

'About five.'

'I might go out myself later on.'

He remained seated at his computer and stretched out his hand in the direction of Venus. She did not move towards him as he had hoped.

'Goodbye,' she said from the doorway, pulling her jacket down on both sides. She did that with many of her clothes. According to Paul, Venus always bought her clothes a size too small, which meant jackets rode up her body and jumpers often revealed areas of flesh which were meant to be covered.

'Can't you be bothered to give me a kiss?' he said quietly. 'You don't even want to touch me.'

She yanked her jacket down again, walked quickly towards him, and placed a cupped hand over his genitals.

'Not like that!' he said, pushing her hand away. 'Don't be unpleasant. I'm not unpleasant to you.'

'OK, I won't do that again.' She kissed the top of his head.

'How's the writing going?' she said.

'Still difficult. I thought about my first day at school.'

'That's history. Almost half a century ago.'

'Not that long.'

'Write about something in the present. Something shocking! History's boring. Give those old buggers a fright.'

'I assume you're referring to the Reading Club.'

'Certainly.' She patted his head and left the room. 'I'll be back at five.'

Later that day something happened to Paul which could only be described as a life-changing event. It left him with a confusion of feelings. He wanted to write about the complete episode. Not that the event, the build up to it, or its aftermath, would make suitable material for the Anniversary Book. He could never tell anyone what he had experienced. No, it was more that he wanted to recall what happened when he decided to go into his attic to look for a photograph of his first day at school. It had been extraordinary. He thought that if he wrote about it he could take some distance from the event and stop the flashbacks, which were making him sweat and causing his heart to race. He especially wanted to write about the silk underslip – potentially the most disastrous part. However, he decided that he would record everything from the time Venus went out to the time she came back. This had nothing to do with the Anniversary Book. This was for his benefit; not for anyone else to read. It was no good trying to write with Venus about. He would have to wait until next Wednesday, when she was again out for the day, before he could start. In the meantime, in his mind, he went over and over what had happened to him.

On that Wednesday, Venus left the house at 8.00 and Paul immediately started writing about the day which changed his life. Two hours later, he was interrupted by the taxi driver's wife who arrived to clean the house.

'My wife's out. She's left you a note.'

The cleaner put down her basket containing a selection of clean rags and her own rubber gloves. She read her instructions. 'She wants the usual,' she said. 'Is she going to be gone long?'

'All day.'

'I'll get started.'

'No need to do my study. I'll be in there working.'

'Please yourself.'

Paul had been at his computer for a few hours, completely absorbed in writing about his significant event. The study window was open to extract the smell of his cigarettes and cigars – Venus forbade smoking in the house. The cleaner began working her way through the three bedrooms. Although he was aware of her noises, they had not prevented him from writing freely. The background sound of the water being turned on and off a few times and the lavatory cistern being flushed, did not interfere with his words flying onto the screen. Paul had closed his study door as a sign that he did not want to be disturbed. He had written several pages and, after completing the final paragraph, he was partly through rereading the whole piece. What an outpouring it had been!

It was during the vacuum cleaning of the hall outside his study that the doorbell rang. Paul decided not to answer it. The machine was switched off, so he assumed the taxi driver's wife had gone downstairs to answer the door. He continued rereading his last sentences. The machine was switched on and after a while the doorbell rang again. Still he did not want to move – what he was doing was far more important than answering the door. His idea had been to exorcise his demon feelings and to turn his experience into something positive. The process was working and he did not want to stop now. He had just reached a special part of his story when, through the open window of his study, he heard his neighbour calling to him.

'Paul, I know you're in there, I've lost my key and I need to come into your house before I have an accident.'

Paul gave an exaggerated sigh and with a great measure of resentment, he got up from his computer and looked out of his study window to see Mrs Lentjes leaning on her walking-frame and making a gesture, which he knew meant that she wanted to use the lavatory. He sped downstairs and opened the front door. The old lady lifted her walking-frame over the doorstep and trundled it quickly towards the downstairs toilet. When she came out, she told Paul that Venus kept a spare set of her keys on the rack. He looked but it was not there.

'Try her long coat hanging up in the hall.'

Following Mrs Lentjes's advice, Paul looked in several places, but the spare keys were not to be found.

'Then I think you'll have to use your long ladders and climb up to my bedroom window and get in the house that way,' she said, looking as if she was very satisfied by her own suggestion.

Paul hated doing this. He was not an athletic man; he became dizzy at heights and felt very unsafe stretching across the gap between the ladders and a window. However, it seemed there was no alternative – except to have the old woman waiting in his kitchen until Venus returned home.

'Would you like a coffee?' he asked his neighbour. The old lady nodded.

'Could you make Mrs Lentjes a coffee,' he called out to the taxi driver's wife, 'she's locked herself out and I have to use a ladder to get into her house.'

'What, right now?'

'Yes please.'

Managing the long ladders was not an easy task for one person; but there was no-one else around to help. Carefully, Paul rested the ladders against Mrs Lentjes's wall and slid the extension up until it reached just below the open window. Having made sure that the base of the ladders was secure, he made his way up the rungs. At the top, he squeezed his arm through the open window in order to release the catch. He then descended the ladder a few rungs in order to open the window fully. Next was the tricky manoeuvre, which was to climb to the top of the ladder and swing one leg over the last rung and onto the inner sill. Holding onto the window frame, he bent down, at the same time pulling the other leg through the window. There was a moment in which he felt he was going to fall. He could hear his heart beating. When he touched the bedroom carpet beneath his feet, he knew that he was safe; safe but sweating and shaking. He sat down on the bed. Mrs Lentjes needed to have some spare, spare keys. He would not do this again – ever! He glanced at the bedroom with its heavy furniture and its floral bedspread and its old-lady smell. The half-empty medicine bottles on the dressing table and the large packet of incontinence pads in the corner reminded him of his mother. Below in the kitchen he found a set of keys on the table. In turn, he tried each key in the front door lock until one of them fitted. He put the keys in his pocket, took down the ladders and lifted them back to his shed.

When he returned to his house, more than twenty minutes later, the taxi driver's wife was standing by the kettle, waiting for the water to boil. It seemed that she had not immediately made a coffee for Mrs Lentjes. Paul was invited to have a drink with the two women, but he refused. He wanted to get back to reading his writing. When he reached his study, he found the door was open; he thought he had left it closed. The pile of the carpet was raised. The taxi driver's wife had been in his room with the vacuum cleaner and her nosiness. His computer had gone into hibernation and when he gave it a tap, his writing reappeared. Thankfully, it had not been lost. But was this where he had left off or had the taxi driver's wife been reading his writing? He could hardly ask if she had been looking on his computer. He scrolled back to the beginning, re-read his story and hoped that the cleaner had not seen it. He had written:

My first day at the junior seminary

I cried, I did not want to leave home. My box of treasures, my stamp album, my collection of foreign coins and my grandfather's old cashbooks from his cheese shop – I had to leave them behind.

Looking for the old photograph

I remembered that somewhere in the attic there was a photo of me from that first day, wearing my big suit. Although my mother had turned up the hems on the sleeves and the trousers, she had not been able to lessen the width of the shoulders, which drooped onto my upper arms. Nor had she been able to take away the excessive amount of material in the front and back of the jacket. The trousers were prevented from falling down by the use of one of my father's belts in which my mother had pierced new holes with a kitchen knife. She had chopped off the surplus end and Papa was furious with her. He said it was his best belt.

Either the photograph was in an old album, or in the box

containing a few of my mother's possessions, which my sisters had left for me after she died. I am sure that they claimed the best things for themselves.

I remembered that one of the other parents had taken the picture as we stood in front of the Abbey Church. There was a horse and cart in the background and maybe one of the priests was there as well. If I found the picture, some memories would be stirred. I recalled that my mother wore her Sunday hat, which was squashed on the bus journey because someone sat on it. I could not remember whether my father came with us. In the dormitory, my mother asked if I could sleep near a window; my breathing could be troublesome. One of the brothers said that the cells and the boys' numbers had already been allocated. Arrangements could not be changed. I remember how my mother had raised her eyebrows; she was unaccustomed to having her requests denied. The brother said that there was always plenty of fresh air in the dormitory and he was sure that I would have no breathing problems in the allotted cell.

There certainly was a lot of fresh air; it was extremely cold at night. We were told to sleep with our hands above the sheets. I remember that my hands felt like the marble counter in my grandfather's cheese shop. My identification number was 35. I kept it throughout my school days. Our dormitory brother told me it had been the number of the present abbot when he was at school. I felt very proud.

My mother's box

We do not go into our attic very often, but I was able to locate the box. On opening it, my first impression was not of my mother, but the smell of my grandparents' house. I wondered if the box had been theirs originally. It had a sharp odour, which touched the back of the nose – an infusion of damp dust, concentrated dirt and stale cheese. Inside was one piece of jewellery – a small gold cross. I never saw my mother wearing it, although she owned several crucifixes. I decided that my sisters had probably taken the best ones. There was a very old picture of a wedding group, one of a young man in priest's clothes and a small suede pouch containing some buttons. I wondered why my sisters left me these things. I told them that they should take what they wanted from my mother's possessions because they had been much more involved in her care. At the time, I did not want anything. There was also a small leather purse with worn corners. Inside was a stiff black silk hankie containing a tiny tooth and a quiff of hair; perhaps belonging to a child; perhaps from one that died. When I looked at the contents of the box, I felt sad; not at the loss of my mother, but at what remained of her in these few things. I wondered then if I should write about this, instead of my first day at school.

The Photograph Album

Underneath the box I found an old photograph album. As I picked it up, I felt a film of sticky dirt on its cover. I flicked through the black pages. There was a smell of death. Many of the old photographs had been taken out. One snap was of my sisters and me at a birthday party. Someone had cut out my face so that my headless body remained. I felt upset. Did one of my sisters do that? Someone hated me at the time. I wondered if she still does. The culprit was in a vicious mood because the angles of the cut are jagged and hurried, as if done in a temper. The cutting instrument had damaged the page underneath. Another picture had been cut in half, removing the end person from the group. I could not tell if I was the missing person. Fortunately my sisters left some pictures of me with my parents. I found one of my first day at school; not quite as I remembered. It showed an old car in the background, not a horse and cart; it was in front of the abbey building, not the school, and the priest in the picture was a very young looking Father Antonius. I removed two of the photographs from the album, and then went downstairs towards my study. I would write about my first day at school.

The Walk-in Wardrobe

At the opposite end of the corridor to my study is my wife's special room. It is a replica of a walk-in wardrobe that she saw in a hotel where we stayed in Florence.

140

'This is what I want in my next house,' she declared.

On both sides of that small room were shiny metals rails and matching coat-hangers, which jangled when clothes were hung upon them. Beneath the rails were drawers and shelves at sitting level. The lighting was directed up to the ceiling by lamps concealed behind dropped coving. On all four walls there were mirrors of tinted glass. The whole area smelt of suits, impregnated with stale cologne, body odour, and hotel cleaning products.

'There's a place for everything,' Venus said, as if visualizing her own walk-in wardrobe. A place for everything appealed to her tidy-mindedness. On the inside of the door of one of the long cupboards was an ironing board. As the door opened, the ironing board became erected. She said that this was a must in our next house. When we eventually moved, I was keen to have a spacious sunny room for my study. I do not think Venus really understood why this was necessary for me. She said little about my request, but reminded me that she wanted to have a walk-in wardrobe. I have often thought that she insisted on this obscure room for herself as a protest at me taking the best room for myself.

Our walk-in wardrobe was built by splitting one of the bedrooms in two. I have always considered it was an unfortunate waste of space because not even a very tiny bed could be fitted into the remaining part of the room, which became a store where things which do not have a home are put, on the assumption that a permanent place will be found for them sometime in the future. However, once there, that is usually where they stay and neither of us bother to organize the room, nor its contents.

Venus keeps her wardrobe very tidy – much tidier than she keeps the house – with neat rows of dresses, blouses, jackets, coats, skirts and trousers all in their own groups and each group arranged in colour order. Venus's choice of colours is outrageous – vivid reds, pinks, oranges, yellows, bright greens and purples. I have told her that I like to see her in more subtle colours. She did experiment with some of my ideas, but after a while she went back to her own choice. Her shoes too are in neat rows and have shoetrees in them so that they keep their shape; even her trainers, which she wears for summer walking, are in the line-up.

I detest these. I have told her frequently, but nevertheless she insists on wearing them. I am sure that she does that to annoy me.

The Black Silk Underslip

On my way to my study, I noticed that the door of the walk-in wardrobe was open and that the strap of a black silk underslip was hanging out from a half-opened drawer. It was spoiling the tidiness of the wardrobe. Since none of my things are kept in there, I have no reason to enter her domain. However, I felt drawn inside in order to tuck away the offending strap.

I put the photos of my first day at school on top of a small cupboard to free both my hands. As I opened the drawer further, I got a waft of Venus's smell – her perfume, her body, her in an aroused state. I picked up the underslip and held it against my face. I have always enjoyed the cool dampness of silk. Through the fibres, I inhaled the trapped air, unlocking the variety of hidden smells. A subtle aphrodisiac went up my nostrils and travelled deep into my lungs. *Hemels!* In the peace and security of the house, I was in heaven as I rubbed the under slip around my face: at the same time, I was reworking one of my favourite sexual fantasies, which I had not had for a long time.

This combination led me into a pleasantly ecstatic state. I used the garment like a flannel, wiping it around my neck. I became intoxicated by my own arousal. I wanted to feel it all over my body so I removed my shirt and my t-shirt and passed the silk under my arms and then gently backwards and forwards over my nipples; this is an erogenous zone for me. When I first discovered this area, I was concerned about my masculinity. Therefore, I was relieved when I read in a psychology magazine that many men enjoy this region of their bodies.

I was aware of a growing pressure beneath my belt as if a certain part of my body – my special instrument – was demanding to be rubbed with the underslip. I breathed in, in order to undo my belt and then the zip on my trousers. I pushed the garment into my pants and felt it sticking against the moisture of my groin. I removed all of my clothes and looked at myself in the mirror.

Reflected back at me was this middle-aged man massaging his body with a piece of female underwear. Was that really me? I was excited by my own reflection. I was doing something which had been forbidden in my boyhood. Good boys don't play with themselves!

In this aroused state I imagined that one of my familiar fantasy nymphs was telling me to try on the black underwear. Why not? With a great struggle I pulled the underslip over my head and shoulders and pulled its skirt down over my knees.

What gave me great pleasure was to see my growing erection pushing against the black underwear and to feel myself restricted by the silk. The top of the underslip was sagging. It was used to being filled by Venus's breasts. I went to the underwear drawer, pulled out some more silk items, and stuffed them into the top of the underslip – each time deliberately touching my nipples. Now I too had breasts – fine false ones – and something protruding against the lower part of the garment. For the first time I understood why some men like to dress in women's clothes.

I looked down at the make-up shelf. I had watched Venus using lipstick and often wondered what it would feel like to smear something creamy across my lips; perhaps an erotic thing to do. I was contemplating whether to try it, when downstairs, in the reality of my everyday life, a door banged and my arousal was painfully punctured by the fear that someone else was in the house.

Hiding

'I'm home, I've got your book and we have a surprise visitor.'

It was Venus. She had said that she would be out all day. She never comes home before the time she says she will.

'Where are you?' she called.

I panicked, grabbed the hem of the underslip and attempted to pull it over my chest. In that moment I had started to sweat and the material clung to my body. With both arms across my chest and the garment over my face, I was stuck. It would go neither up nor down. The extra padding had acted to tighten it. I tried tearing the material by widening my shoulders and pushing out my arms, but the silk was too strong

143

I could hear Venus's footsteps on the stairs. When she is on a mission, she travels up two steps at a time. I could hear her go along the landing, calling out,

'I've got your Reading Club book.'

She came nearer and nearer. I made a decision that it was better to pull the underslip down instead of up. At least I could see. I could hear her footsteps go into the bedroom.

She repeated, 'Where are you?' This time there was less enthusiasm and a little annoyance in her voice.

I hoped that she would not look into her walk-in wardrobe. Unfortunately, the door was a little ajar and I was afraid to close it in case she saw it moving. Also, I did not want to chance hiding behind the clothes because that would set off the jangling metal coat-hangers. I crept into the corner, praying that she would not see me. I then became aware of some other footsteps, quieter and slower than Venus's. The visitor was upstairs too.

'He must be in the garden. Let's go and have a coffee,' I heard her say.

'Fine,' said a man's voice.

The visitor passed the wardrobe without looking inside. I do not think he saw me, either through the open door or through the gap between the door and the frame. I could not see who it was.

When I heard them talking in the kitchen below, I crept along the landing and into the bathroom where I locked the door behind me. Looking into the mirror I saw I was sweating and red in the face. I found a pair of scissors and cut up the side of Venus's slip because I could not get out of it any other way. I screwed it up and stuffed it into a cupboard behind some bath towels, making a mental note that I would destroy it when Venus was not around. I got into the shower and turned it on. The coldness of the water took away my feeling of nausea. What would have happened had Venus or her visitor seen me wearing the black silk underslip?

Paul looked up from his reading. Had the cleaner read what he had written? He could hardly ask her. What if she tells his wife, or her husband or anyone else? If she has seen it, what could he do to stop her telling other people?

The taxi driver's wife was putting on her coat. She had picked up the envelope containing her pay and was about to put it in her bag.

'We really appreciate the work you do for us in our house,' Paul said.

'Do you? It's good of you to say that. Many of my clients never even say thank you after I have cleaned their houses.'

'It must be tough work. We have so many rooms.'

'Yes,' she said with a faint smile.

'What I really appreciate is your discretion. You don't tell other people about how we live. I don't like it when people do that.'

'I agree. I told my husband that when he is a member of the Reading Club, I don't want all of you coming to our home and seeing how we live.'

'I completely understand that. There are some things which I like to keep private. We're all different.' He had both his hands deep in his pockets.

'We certainly are,' she said.

'I would like to show my appreciation for your hard work and loyalty. Would you accept this and buy something special for yourself.'

'Fifty euros! Thank you.'

'I can rely on your discretion?'

'Certainly.'

Paul returned to his writing, hopeful that even if the cleaner had seen his story she would not tell anyone. Now that his experience was written down it seemed different; as if someone else had told it. Strangely it no longer felt so dreadful. Not only was there an overwhelming feeling of relief at not being discovered wearing Venus's underwear, but there was a new perspective, a realisation that he had achieved an erection in that walk-in wardrobe. Surely that was a sign that his impotence was temporary; that it was psychological rather than physical. Nothing to do with his 'plumbing', as Venus had suggested. This was something to celebrate. He decided he should take his wife away for a short holiday to see if they could enjoy some intimacy again. Paris seemed the ideal destination.

He went over to the window to smoke a cigarette and to reflect on the fact that he still did not have any suitable material for the Anniversary Book. A couple of hours remained before Venus returned. It occurred to him what to write. He stubbed the end of his half finished cigarette against the outside wall of the house, then flicked the remainder in the direction of the street. It fell short of its intended destination and Paul smiled as it landed in Mrs Lentjes's garden, in between the petals of one of her prize roses. He thought for a few moments about his mother's box, and then he wrote:

The Contents of my Mother's Box

Why am I keeping these few things? Do I need a reminder that I did not look after my mother towards the end of her life, that I left this task to my sisters who have been bitter towards me ever since? Did they expect me to have my mother living in my home? Did they think that I could visit her as much as they did, even though I lived a long way from her? Why do we feel the need to keep the stuff of the dead? I do not need a reminder. I have good memories. After I have written about the box, I will throw away these last trinkets. They have no function, no intrinsic value, they are meaningless. I do not want to keep them; I have been hiding behind the junk of years, pretending that I require certain things in order to function. Layers of dust and grease have been clogging my arteries, the hydraulic pressure in my vital member has been lost and internal layers of mental debris have caused cirrhosis of my mind. What will be left when I am gone? Will my daughter cherish a small box of useless items, which smells of old dust and sour grease? This room, this house has many objects, which I keep for no practical purpose. I will stop writing and start to clear out some of this rubbish in my life.

Paul saved his piece of writing and closed his computer; he then filled four large plastic sacks with old books, clothes and shoes.

He went into the attic and brought down a fold-up bed, a box of toys, a child's bicycle seat, a dog basket and bowl, two old tennis rackets with broken strings, and an old typewriter, followed by several framed posters, a box of china, a pair of his father's rusty ice skates, and a bag of carnival costumes. He loaded all this into his car and delivered them to the charity shop, the *Kringloopwinkel* where Piet van Rijn was the manager. A part-time assistant was there; her job was to assess the worth of items which were antique or collectable, and to sell these on to shops. When this woman saw Paul's various sacks she stopped what she was doing and took them from him. Piet welcomed him and started to talk about the latest Reading Club book while the assistant, within Paul's view, began to rummage through his possessions. Although everything had remained dormant and unloved for years in his attic, Paul suddenly experienced a feeling of attachment for what he had just given away. He felt uncomfortable as the woman started to examine each item; she was like a vulture prematurely pecking at his body before his death. The assistant showed no regard for the fact that these objects might still hold some sentimental value. She remarked that he had had a good clear out and asked if he and Venus were moving. What an intrusive question! He saw her put to one side certain trinkets as if they had some worth and she would be taking them to sell for her own profit. He felt cheated and thought that he should get the money for them and not her. He disliked her coldness, the rough way she was handling his things. Didn't she realise how brave he had been to tear these items out of his life? He would have preferred that she had taken the bags from him; removed them from his sight before she began her work. Her manner gave him the impression that she was doing him a favour in receiving his things, rather than the other way around. She had not even thanked him for his donation.

Probably Piet saw Paul's disquiet and said, 'One man's junk is another man's treasure. Clearing out is a sign of progress. Think of it as a boil bursting. It hurts a bit and lots of awful stuff is dispersed, but then new flesh grows.'

Paul looked at Piet and decided that he was talking nonsense, but kept that thought to himself.

When Venus arrived home, Paul disclosed that he had been clearing out some things and suggested that she did the same. Moreover he invited her to go to Paris with him, as he had decided that they both needed some new clothes.

Later, when he looked for the black silk slip, which he had hidden in the back of the bathroom cupboard, it had gone. The school photographs had also disappeared from where Paul had left them in the walk-in wardrobe.

A week later, the taxi driver and his wife were at home.

'Venus Bazelman gave me a beautiful black underslip which had been cut down one side. She told me a friend had bought it for her from Paris. She didn't say who, but I think it was Hans van den Elsen.'

'How do you know it's Van den Elsen?'

'I've heard her on the phone and I've seen them in the book shop. She must think that I am blind. She asked me if I could use the underslip as a rag for cleaning.'

'Can you?'

'Of course not.'

'How did it get damaged?'

'She made a joke saying that her husband must have torn it when he was wearing it.'

'What a ridiculous thing to say.'

'Yes it would be, if it weren't true.'

'What do you mean?'

'I was in Bazelman's study dusting his desk. On his computer he had described how he tried on his wife's underwear to give himself a thrill. It got stuck on him and he cut himself out. Before I left he gave me fifty euros because he thinks I am discreet.'

'That's weird. What sort of a man would do that?'

'I did warn you about these guys. And you still want to join the Reading Club?'

The Journal of Hans van den Elsen

Like many Dutch men, Hans van den Elsen was tall, slim and long limbed. He moved gracefully and had the charm of a Frenchman. Since he was a child he had bitten his nails, and although he had long fingers, they had soft, round ends, which together with his stunted nails prevented him from looking completely elegant. On his visiting card, he announced himself as a 'Business Consultant'. What it did not reveal was that he had studied at Harvard Business School in the USA. His Dutch colleagues would consider this piece of information ostentatious. Primarily he worked with organisations who wanted to streamline their administration departments. For this work he received a fat fee, plus commission from the computer companies whose products he recommended. Mostly the results of his interventions were new systems, redundant software, a change of furniture and new routines, retraining, relocation and the rearrangement of the hearts and minds of the owners, if not always their employees.

In his business persona, he was very like Cia, his wife – tough, intelligent and efficient. However, when it came to their personal and private lives they were different and had grown apart. Cia had cultivated a wide circle of gossipy friends; she had an over-interest in her own appearance and their daughter's social life. At first Hans went along with these domestic developments, enjoying the security of a routine, the intimacy, the family, owning a house, developing a career – he had even stopped smoking. Now he found his home life shallow and monotonous. He was no longer interested in his home, which contained many pieces of once-prized, but now uncherished Swedish furniture.

He enjoyed the Reading Club. It was a change to be amongst what he jokingly described as pseudo-academics, instead of top business folks. He enjoyed engrossing himself in the chosen books and hearing what others thought. When he was reading he didn't bite his nails. It was through certain books that he had been reminded of deeper feelings, which he had not experienced for years in his own marriage. He had grown out of love with his wife and was entangled in another relationship.

Hans followed the suggestion of experimenting with different ways of recording his journal. Some of his jottings went into a note pad, which he kept between the stationery in the bottom drawer of his desk. He used some pages in the middle of a spiral-bound note pad, which were meant for his daily list of 'things to do' – this was always kept in his brief case. Once he had written some observations on the back of a menu, folded it in four and left it somewhere, but he had forgotten the place. A small black moleskin book, which was similar to his address book, contained some of his most revealing thoughts and he stored several entries on his computer and saved them under 'Accounts 10'. Listed in 'My Documents', was a file named 'Journal'. Much of the other work was on his company's laptop, which required a password to open.

Hans had always been intrigued by the dynamics of the Reading Club and he spent several hours describing its activities, which he had observed since he joined the club five years ago. He wrote:

The Reading Club
One night the club met in the old kitchen at the back of Bert de Lange's wine shop. It was my first visit to this part of his

premises and I was surprised to see the largest and oldest table I have ever encountered outside a castle or a museum. Apparently, this is where Bert hosts his wine tasting evenings. I have never been invited to one of these gatherings, although some of the club are regulars. Probably my name is absent from the guest list because I usually purchase my drinks from Albert Heijn, our main supermarket or I bring a supply back from France or Italy when I have been working in these countries. Bert's prices are high. Sometimes Cia buys a bottle at his place, when she is going to visit a friend. The purchase is always wrapped in tissue paper, and then placed inside a narrow brown paper bag bearing the shop's name.

Once a month, three of the club members play billiards together. I have not been invited to join that group either. It's probably because they don't understand my sense of humour.

I arrive at the Reading Club meetings at 7.00 precisely. I'm always punctual, whatever I'm doing. Good old Huub Schevers is usually the first to arrive. Sometimes he is twenty minutes early. That must be a pain in the arse for some hosts. Huub can be such a fussy old fart. He usually parks himself opposite the host. Paul Bazelman is also an early bird. He's a prissy tart. He often sits next to Huub. Titus and Joost, who are obviously good mates, usually arrive together, looking as if they have already discussed the book of the evening. That pisses me off. They shouldn't do that. I advise companies to avoid this – transparency is much better than perceived conspiracy. The two friends usually sit next to one another and opposite Huub. They're the hub of the club!

Although I know Paul Bazelman, I never like to sit next to or opposite him, but always at an angle, where I can see him in my peripheral vision. Since I am screwing his wife, I don't feel inclined to face him. One could easily get into a row with him. He can be so cantankerous. Milo Jansen and Piet van Rijn are usually the last to appear. So the early birds can pick their seats and the late ones have no option but to occupy the remaining chairs. It is interesting to observe how often the arrangement of members around the table is the same.

In my consultancy work with troubled organisations, I frequently suggest that people change seats during a difficult meeting. Sitting in the chair of another person can change a point of view – it has a posh name – 'Gestalt for Businesses'. I usually say, 'Bums up and move around guys!' Of course, I would never use this language or make this suggestion to the members of the Reading Club because I am keen not to confuse my business role with my private life. I'm there for relaxation and to enjoy myself.

Several people bring with them their own copy of the book of the month. Others have borrowed theirs from the library. Occasionally Paul finds one in a second-hand-bookshop and will croak about his bargain. Books are taken out of pockets; others are in plastic carriers or in their original paper bags from *Boeken Boeken*, our local bookshop. Milo always brings his copy in his battered brief case. Some books look as if their owners have not opened them. Perhaps they have been read with a lot of care. A few have damaged covers showing that they have been well travelled: jammed into pockets, rammed into bags and read in snatched moments in busy lives. No doubt, some books have been read directly after they were collected from the bookshop or the library, while others may have been finished a few minutes before the start of the club meeting. Piet's books often look in pristine condition. Usually his hard backed volumes give a little squeak when they are pressed open and some of the pages stick together slightly, suggesting, to the more cynical members, like me, that he's not read them. We all know that Piet lies about his reading.

You should see Huub's books! He's a messy animal. He highlights words with a pink marker, writes notes in the margins and bends over the corners of the pages. Every time Milo sees one of Huub's abused books he raises his eyebrows as if he is witnessing the disfigurement of a religious artefact. Some bring notebooks in which they have written comments. When we discussed 'Priests Dying', Piet read from several pages of typed notes. We were all impressed, even though it was long winded. However, I wonder if anyone noticed that Piet made reference to the elders from the Protestant Church. As far as I know he is a lapsed Catholic and probably now an atheist. I am suspicious that he had a ghost writer working for him.

Either the host or his wife undertakes the ritual of greeting the club members. If their entrance hall is large enough, the couple may come to the door together to welcome us. Titus, who can show off like a peacock, together with his pleasant wife, likes to do this. Some wives are quite formal in their greeting, preferring to extend a hand to the visitors. Others are more relaxed and give three kisses on alternate cheeks to those they know well and a handshake to others. In that way each woman can demonstrate her own 'pecking' order. Some wives do not appear at all when club members arrive. They either stay in another room or use the opportunity to spend an evening out with their own friends. Others tend to linger while serving the drinks and the food, as if they want to be part of the evening.

The host or his wife lays out some refreshments, either in the centre of the table or on a side cupboard. The amounts vary. Titus is the most generous in offering coffee, tea, wine, biscuits, nuts, *bitterballen* (meat balls), finger-sized pieces of '*oude kaas*' (mature Dutch cheese) and garlicky olives. Huub, although he eats like a pig in other people's houses, is frugal when entertaining, rationing the drinks to two glasses of thin, sour, red wine. Once his Turkish cleaner made some snacks, which were very spicy and only half were eaten. I think he was offended and since then he only offers us stale peanuts.

At the only time I hosted the club meeting at our house, Cia, my extrovert and untypical Dutch wife, took it as a great social occasion in which she was going to excel in her role as the hostess. Even two members she had only seen once were greeted with three kisses. She asked about the members' wives and families and continued her conversations when everybody was sitting at the table ready to start the meeting; she fussed around like a mother hen. After an hour, when we were in the middle of a very interesting perspective on the book being given by Milo, she came in with a second round of coffee and slices of *vlaai*, the cake which is rich and difficult to eat without getting cream on your fingers, your shirt and your book. I could see Milo was upset because for once he had the full undivided attention of the group. At the end of the meeting when we had reached the point where we award a score to the book, Cia chirped in yet again to ask if anyone would like another drink. As members left she tried to engage them in conversation.

When Paul was leaving she said to him, 'The next time you see me on the terrace having a coffee, don't walk by, come and join me.' He hopped away quickly.

When I spoke to her after about her intrusion, she laughed, saying that she was sure that the guys had loved her attention.

'I had them all eating out of my hand,' she said, as if she was referring to a group of farm animals.

I have never volunteered to have a meeting at our house again. Instead, I present whoever is hosting the meeting with two bottles of wine and a bunch of roses, which I collect from the commercial greenhouses at the back of my garden. Sometimes I take some small edible treats, which I buy on my travels. Two other members do not invite the Reading Club to their homes. Both say that they do not have sufficient room or a table big enough to seat us all. Milo is one who makes this excuse. I have been to his house. He has a huge room with a large table at one end, where ten people could sit around easily. His wife, I have heard, does not like the idea of an all male club. She has the reputation of being a staunch feminist. Neither does she approve of the Women's Reading Club which some of the other wives attend. You should hear what Venus Bazelman says about her.

I like the idea of an all male club. Just occasionally, I prefer to be amongst the fellows. Women change the atmosphere. They should not make an appearance on the club evenings and that has nothing to do with me not liking and not admiring some women very much (I have heard people call me a ladies' man, although my wife says I am a sewer rat).

Women change the flavour of a group. I am not sure that I would want to discuss sexual matters and sensual feelings if there were women in our club. The quality of the debate, which we had about Ian McEwan's 'On Chesil Beach', would not have been achieved in a mixed group. I was surprised by Bert's opening comment. Usually he doesn't say much and when he does, he tends to follow what others have said before him. A bit of an old sheep. He said he found the book too explicit and that he was not interested in reading about the details of an unconsummated wedding night. He went on to say that he preferred intimacies described in a more subtle way. I experienced the book quite differently. I found that I identified with the fears of the young bride as well as the desires of the young man. I enjoyed the details and thought the book was beautifully written. I wish I had been the one to recommend this sensitive and tragic tale and, for once, I did not joke about the story.

Titus occupied much time in explaining his point of view, which annoyed me. His intellectual commentary could have easily deadened my impression of the book. Huub, who reminds me of a pig sometimes — intelligent but not very beautiful — said he found it pathetic. How could he use such an inappropriate word? He joked that the simple insects in his pond make copulation seem so much more natural than the clumsy activities of the couple in the book. I wondered, had Huub ever coupled with anyone? I wanted to say that I had identified with the loneliness of the hero and with the young bride's fear of intimacy, but that would have revealed too much about me. Milo issued his usual complaint about there being too much sex in modern literature, on the TV and in the magazines on the top shelf of the paper shop. We have heard it all before, like an early morning cockerel repeating his message to the world. Then in a more gentle tone, he said:

'These things are private.'

Milo is an unusual fellow; although he annoys me with his anti-sex literature campaign, there is something likeable about the man.

Joost made a telling remark. Now he's a bright fellow. Doesn't say much but, when he does, he's clever; like the crows who scrape up squashed animals along our road without getting killed themselves. They don't look very special creatures but apparently they are the most intelligent of birds. Joost said that in the past he had read so much about sex — vibrant, lustful, tender, successful, satisfying sex – that he felt pleased to read a delicate description about what can happen between two people when their coupling goes wrong. I had not thought about that point of view. After the meeting, I went home and reread the book in one sitting.

Once, Piet van Rijn invited us to have our meeting at the *Kringloopwinkel*, that charity shop he manages. None of us had been there before; I could never become accustomed to buying second-hand things. I don't even like borrowing books from the library. I would rather purchase my own copy. That evening we were reviewing 'Animal Farm.' It had been my suggestion.

Piet's shop is a huge place – a redundant flower warehouse, now superseded by a much larger, modern, purpose-built, automated flower processing plant. Here roses, which have been cut by machines in the adjacent greenhouse, are sorted and trimmed and then packed into long cardboard boxes and loaded onto trailers. The rose grower decided that the old warehouse was too good and too expensive to demolish. Now he lets it out to Piet's charity for a fair price.

At a glance, I saw that Piet is an inefficient manager. On his desk was an untidiness of notes and memos, an ashtray full of cigarette ends, a half-filled coffee cup, a sketchbook, a pot of artists' pencils and an in-tray heaped with unanswered correspondence. This was quite the opposite to the desks in today's paperless offices. Computers may be here to stay, but Piet did not have one. However, I observed that his part-time assistant had a PC and that her desk was tidy. It was obvious that she is the one who really runs the business. With some pride, Piet told us that people donate their unwanted possessions to his shop. Some items are sold locally and some are transported to third world countries to help people there improve their lives. I knew that this did not make business sense because mostly sending other people's junk abroad is not a viable option. The cost of transportation is greater than the value of the goods, even when the airlines give special rates for charitable work. I am sure that what is not sold in the shop is collected by recycling companies who separate the various materials and sell them on to manufacturers for remaking into 'new' garments and products. Surely, Piet must know how the business works. Was he trying to impress us?

After the club meeting, which turned out to be very enjoyable, the members looked around the shop and some bought a few second-hand items – but not me.

While the early arrivals at the club meetings await the late comers, some inconsequential news is exchanged about the weather, the traffic, the height of the river, holiday travel – all safe subjects, but it can become quite noisy. There is never any gossip during this part of the meeting, because this is not a friends' club and we do not necessarily know the circles in which the others move. That is not to say that we never gossip, most people do, but we are circumspect about when we do and with whom. If we happen to meet one of our fellow members outside the meeting, we may greet each other like friends and exchange comments about another member, but only if we are sure it is safe to do so. The other thing we do, when we see a member in a public place, is to exchange some remarks about the book we are reading. I guess that this is to let others within earshot know that we are members of an exclusive club. Outside of the meetings, Milo and Piet are often the subjects of our small talk; usually in an unflattering way. They are the scapegoats of our club; the *zondebokken* (the goats that carry away the sins into the desert). Such people are usually positioned on the edge of a group and in that way show its parameters. This arrangement may bring a sense of confidence to those at the heart of the matter, but can be unpleasant for men like Milo and Piet who are treated differently from the rest.

Usually Titus decides the right moment to stop the chatting and begin the meeting. He takes an audible breath, grows a few centimetres and taps on the side of a glass with his pen, which he keeps in his hand throughout the meeting, looking as if he is about to write a prescription or make a note on a patient's file. I often give feedback to senior managers about holding their pens when talking to subordinates. It can give the impression of being in the role of judge. Of course, our doctors no longer write with pens on paper. Via a computer link-up, they pass on directions for medication to pharmacists and they record notes directly on individual computer files. Titus tentatively suggests we begin. We all look to our self-appointed leader to fulfil this duty.

Everyone has something in front of him; a copy of the book, a notebook, a piece of paper – something to show the others that he has participated in the group task. The book will have been selected at the previous meeting and Titus will have influenced the choice. If challenged, he would probably say that he tries to facilitate a democratic process. He is not so skilled. Doctors engage with their patients superficially for a few minutes. They cannot afford to listen properly or for too long. They have to be judgers; they are foreigners in the minefield of the democratic group process.

The one who recommended the month's read begins by providing a summary of the book, followed by reasons for his choice. Here is another interesting process in terms of whose suggestion is accepted. During the selection, Titus, Joost and Huub look backwards and forwards between each other and monopolise the discussion. If one of them proposes a book or an author, the other two persuade the group to approve. If others have a suggestion, the trio will make a decision, based not so much on the book itself, but more on the person recommending it. Then they steer the group towards this member, while talking over and not giving eye contact to others. Like in many business meetings, this often appears to happen outside of everyone's awareness. Occasionally, there is a demonstration of token fairness, in which an outsider is given a chance to have his book read. In group analysis, such a ruling triumvirate is known as exclusive shared leadership; it can be powerful, but it is often destructive to the group function. I encourage companies to aim for an inclusive leadership, which gives everyone a chance to experience different roles.

It is interesting to see which types of books are proposed. A confident reader will recommend one he has genuinely enjoyed; be it relaxing, absorbing, fun, intimate, challenging, enlightening, or providing a true escape from ordinary life. Others want to demonstrate their intellect by suggesting obscure and difficult books with an academic flavour, or novels which have an overbearing psychological or philosophical basis. Some like to display their maturity in proposing books which are explicitly sexual. I wonder whether that is done just to challenge Milo. It would be interesting to understand the motives behind the choices – for some these will be hidden even from themselves, somewhere deep in their unconscious minds.

Listening to others when they comment on the book of one's choice can be tough, if not excruciating, especially for those who feel passionate about their recommendation; as if they had written it themselves or adopted its spirit as their own. Although everyone listens in silence to the comments, different opinions are communicated through facial expression and body movements. A disapproving glance, a raised eyebrow, an unconscious nodding, a posture of attention, an inattentive gesture; it is easy to discourage or encourage a speaker. I am frequently surprised by how nervous some fellows become when it is their turn to give an opinion. In my business, I often encounter performance anxiety. It can result in the speaker having sweaty palms, an audible heartbeat, knocking knees and a dry throat. Even Titus, our peacock, gets nervous when he has to introduce a book of his choice.

Sometimes members have disapproving expressions on their faces in anticipation of what is going to be said. Here comes Huub with his usual complaints! The book was too thick, the library only had an old edition; or worst of all, it was too academic. Even in regard to slim 'On Chesil Beach', Huub was able to moan that he had to buy a hard-backed copy, which had cost him €17; far too expensive for such a small volume. Paul is also often greeted with looks anticipating his critical analysis of the book's content and style.

We expect Milo to complain about explicit sex. His usual song. Venus Bazelman has some theories about Milo. In her view he is either asexual or terrified by his over-active erotic imagination. She says that he probably looks at porn on the internet. I think these suggestions are unkind and unjustified. A solicitor friend told me that he has handled several cases in which compulsive internet viewing of pornography played a significant role in divorces. I do not know if Milo is aware of the multi-million dollar market that now exists and of the millions of pages of porn which can be found on the internet. I have come across pornographic material downloaded on computers belonging to companies where I have worked. In my view, Milo's overt religiosity does not go down very well with the members, especially those who have chosen to be atheists; mostly we stop paying attention when he gets into his imaginary pulpit.

I can see from his expression, his questions and his comments that Titus listens carefully to the opinions of others. Occasionally he makes notes. Sometimes he looks up as if he is developing a new perspective on a book, based on another man's ideas. In this way, he is achieving the main function of the Reading Club, which is to hear and take account of the views of the other members. However, there are always other agendas when a collection of individuals agrees to function as a group. Sometimes the whole business gets a bit too serious for my liking and I make a joke; often I am deliberately silly, other times I am a bit crude. I don't do this at work, although I encourage companies to create opportunities for fun. People work better if, from time to time, they can laugh at something amusing.

After everyone has had an opportunity to give his opinion, there is a free discussion about the book. Often people who were nervous in the first part of the meeting become articulate in this session. Titus loses or relinquishes his control over this part and Joost assumes the role of facilitator; for example, when he senses someone is prevented from talking he provides them with an entrance by saying:

'Piet, I think you want to say something', or, 'Paul would like to speak.'

I never intervene. I do that at work, but I want to be here in a different capacity.

Huub is our timekeeper; he will say to Titus:

'Shouldn't we be thinking about the book for next month?'

Time keeping is vital. Most meetings go on for too long. I tell companies to decide on the time they want to spend on their agenda, and then halve it.

There is a security and a danger in having fixed roles in a meeting. We have Titus the leader; he, Joost and Huub influence the choice of books; I am the joker; Milo is the moraliser; Paul is the critic; Bert provides us with good wine; Piet is our loveable liar; he and Milo are the club's scapegoats. I have observed many hierarchical groups in which either the leader is too frightened to relinquish his power or where the others do not want the responsibility. Mostly these arrangements do not facilitate growth and learning. Only when all members take turns in the different roles will the group evolve, and become a healthy organisation.

At the conclusion of the discussion about 'Animal Farm', Titus made an attempt at a joke (an unusual event!). He said that 'All members of the Reading Club are equal.'

To everyone's surprise Bert replied, 'True, but some members are more equal than others!'

As long as individual needs remain greater than the group function, the group will fail to learn. I am surprised that this club has survived for so long – almost ten years.

'Animal Farm' was well received. It is a clever metaphor. After all, we're all animals.

A few days later, Cia was in the mood to gossip. Having heard from the taxi driver's wife about the events in the doctor's private study, she was eager to pass the story on to Hans.

'The taxi driver's wife told me that your respectable Titus touched her breast in his den of pornography.'

'What are you talking about?' Hans replied without looking up from his newspaper.

'Did you know that your doctor member has a large collection of pornographic books, magazines and pictures? He has more porn publications than the newsagent on the corner of the Water Straat.'

'What's wrong with that?' Hans said, before rustling the maximum amount of noise which he could generate from turning the page of his newspaper.

Cia ignored the hint. She liked to bait her husband with stories against the Reading Club members and so she continued:

'Do you look at porno pictures?'

'No, not since I was fifteen.' Hans paused and then added, 'I'd like to read my paper.'

Cia ignored his statement, 'I would have thought that you out of the entire club would be the one to have a secret like that. Although I can imagine Huub has gay literature.'

'How do you know that?' Hans was irritated that Cia had ignored his request for an opportunity to read his paper.

'The taxi driver's wife told me that he is a homosexual.'

'So what if he's gay?'

'Don't pretend to be so liberal. What would you say if Huub put his hand on your thigh? I know you'd hate that.'

'If he is gay, and I am not interested whether he is or isn't, I am sure that he does not go around touching men's thighs. You are so narrow-minded. What do you know about homosexuality?'

'One of my good friends is a lesbian.'

'Who's that?' he said, surprised.

'She likes to keep that information private.'

'Then why did she tell you?'

'She trusts me not to tell anyone,' Cia said smugly.

'She's taking a risk. Doesn't she know you like to gossip about others?' Hans said, wondering which one of Cia's friends was gay.

'You're not above passing on details about others,' Cia snapped. Then she added, 'But I'll tell you something else, Milo is an overtly sexual man.'

'I wasn't asking you to give me your opinion and he can't be because he is always complaining about too much sex in the books we read. I'm not interested in gossip.'

She ignored the response. 'The other man who is a bit deviant is Joost.'

'This is nonsense. How can you believe all of this tittle-tattle?'

'I don't believe, I know.'

162

'Who said that?'

'Jung.'

'Since when do you know about Jung?'

'My gay friend told me.'

Hans glanced sideways at his wife. He decided that he had endured her company for long enough. It was 11.00 p.m. He put down his newspaper and got up from his seat.

Then Cia said, 'Did you hear what I said about Titus touching the taxi driver's wife's breasts?'

'Yes, I heard you, and as I said, I'm not interested in gossip. I'm going to do some writing now. Sleep well.'

Eighteen months ago, Hans had withdrawn himself from the marital bedroom on the pretext that, since he woke regularly during the night and liked to read, have a drink or listen to the radio, he did not want to disturb Cia who was a light sleeper. That was half true; the unspoken reason was that he no longer wanted to lie down near to his wife. Yes, she was still good looking, smart, meticulously clean, showering once and sometimes twice a day, bathing several times in the week, visiting Wim the hairdresser and beautician; but none of these things made her desirable in the way she once was. He knew other men found her attractive; he had watched admirers at parties and on the Town Square terrace flirt with her. In his fantasy, the worst thing about Cia was her smell: layers of stale perfume, make-up, sour skin, breath and body odour; aromas which were not washed away by her frequent bathing. It filtered up his nose and diffused onto his tongue so that he often felt sick to be near his own wife.

She was at her worst at night when she snored, farted, grunted, talked and laughed in her sleep. It was as if a nocturnal hag-like spirit inhabited her body as she slept. Yes, he could recall the good times, the fun, the intimacies, the house building, their daughter, and their successful separate careers. But remembering was like viewing a poorly edited old black and white movie. The difference being that this film memory was silent and Cia was not. Missing were good feelings, pleasant smells, refreshing colours and the music of a vibrant relationship. He wondered if they ever existed.

Now he loathed the feel of Cia's skin, which had grown tough in parts through excessive exposure to the sun; in other areas her flesh was soft, puckered, and flabby. He especially hated the area around her navel, once the eye on the world, now invisible down a shaft of white blubber. It was the colour of goose lard. Just before he closed the door of his study, he heard Cia begin a conversation on the telephone. Was she phoning her lesbian friend to report that she had not disclosed her name?

Hans ignored the instructions for writing which suggested leaving the journal for several weeks, before rereading and deciding which theme to develop. On the day of its creation, he reread the piece about the dynamics of the club, several times, before assessing that it was too long, too serious and that some of the members might not like to see themselves described in the way he had written.

Some wives spoke critically about the Reading Club, either because women were excluded from joining or that their husbands talked too much or not enough about what went on. Several ridiculed the journals by saying that the men had been set a schoolboy task. Others were curious and uncertain; they wondered if their husbands had written about them, their private lives or indeed about information to which they were not privy. Would their secrets be published in the Anniversary Book? Emotional vulnerability soon translated itself into mistrust and several wives toyed with the idea of searching and reading these private documents. None were more determined than Cia, who planned her hunt like a military campaign. She knew exactly what she would find; it was only a matter of locating the evidence. Laden with curiosity and the suspicions of an unhappy wife, she went in search of Hans's journal. She assumed it would be located in one place; either on the computer or in a special book. She went through his shelves, opening books where it might be concealed, and then carefully replacing them in their former positions. The result was that she found nothing. She failed to look thoroughly through her husband's stationery drawer; she overlooked his moleskin book because she thought it contained addresses; she found a ringed notebook, but only opened the front pages containing lists of jobs. However she did make two discoveries. The first one was entitled 'The Reading Club'. She scanned the first page, missed the references to Venus, considered the piece boring and decided that this was not what she was looking for. Her second discovery, hidden in the 'Journal' folder on his computer was exactly what she had anticipated. Hans had written the following:

She looked my way several times. I became aware of a sensation in my abdomen, as if there was a wooden spoon gently rotating my intestines. It was not a new feeling, but it was one that I had not experienced for some time – some years, many years – a stirring, which grew stronger as our gaze lasted beyond a respectable glance. As it strengthened, it was as if my insides were being pulled out by a pleasurable pain of longing or a gentle lust. This was my dormant libido resurrecting itself after years of domestic imprisonment. It was reminding me of a feeling that I had not realised that I was missing. My exiled lust and desire, which had been put on ice, filed away for good, shrivelled up by the priorities of work, making a home and growing a family - was awakening itself. Within a few minutes, I felt a new kind of aliveness; I was desiring and desirable. My God, she is coming over to talk to me. My whole body was crying out for this woman. I felt sick, I want to die, I want to live.

A few spaces had been left, then this quotation:

'In our erotic life...it is not possible to work at a relationship, any more than it is to will an erection or arrange a dream. In fact when you are working at it you know it has gone wrong, that something is missing.' (Adam Philips, Psychoanalyst)

Although brief, the evidence fed into Cia's bank of suspicions where she was accumulating an account, which she intended using to pay back some of the hurt which Hans had caused her. She was only waiting for the right moment.

However, Cia did not discover what Hans had saved in 'Accounts 10'. He had written:

Titian painted Venus a number of times. My favourite is Venus of Urbino. It is said that a prostitute was his model. She was thick around the waist and had small, not yet fully-matured breasts with erect nipples. Her skin was creamy, soft like an infant's bottom – silky, warm, spongy, squashy, welcoming, inviting – she had the makings of a big desirable woman of her time.

I have my secret Venus, we are lovers, we are married, but not to each other. In one of my fantasies she becomes Titian's Urbino woman draped on a bed, propped up on some pillows, so that the front of her body is exposed. In one hand she is holding a bunch of flowers, while the other hand with curled finger lies softly across her pubic area, as if she were in the act of caressing herself. She is gazing at me, unashamed and sensual. She is completely naked. I imagine myself nuzzling between her fleshy folds and finding both comfort and arousal there.

I know that some commentators, in their analysis of this picture, have remarked on the domestic scene in the background, where another young woman is looking into a large marriage chest and in the foreground is a sleeping dog, which is said to symbolise fidelity. Others have commented on the pubic area, which was judged to be the focal point. Still more have remarked about the composition, the light and the colours. I think that is artistic waffle avoiding the fact that this is an erotic picture.

My Venus, my lover, is not slim and she defends her chosen shape with the ferocity of a feminist. Like her counterpart in Titian's picture, she gives the appearance of a woman who is comfortable and confident about herself and stares back at the viewer encouraging him, daring him to enjoy her nudity. When I shared the details of my fantasy with my Venus, my lover, she mocked me; she declared that she was nothing like Titian's portrait. She said:

'This is an instructional picture for a new young wife. I am middle aged and I have been married for twenty years. She comes from a rich family who have fattened her up for marriage because to be skinny was a sign of a poor heritage and the thin ones often did not ovulate; consequently they were not the most fertile. I am well-shaped because I love food and drink and I choose not to be careful with what I eat. She is probably not as fit as me because she has been kept at home since her betrothal. I am out of the house as much as possible walking, cycling, dancing, going to the gym, making love in secret places. I read that this painting was meant to be a gift for a new wife and not a 16th century pornographic portrait as a number of ill-informed art historians claim.'

She continued, 'The message which the artist is giving, on behalf of the commissioner, is to inform the new bride of the delights of domesticity, as pictured in the background scene and fidelity as symbolised by the sleeping dog. Further instruction is that she should be sensual and available to please her husband. Finally she is encouraged to arouse herself so that she and her husband could climax together. The belief of the day was that conception was only possible if husband and wife achieved simultaneous 'emissions'. Finally she added, 'The most bizarre aspect of those times is that both medical and religious leaders were insisting on this practice. Isn't it a pity that the Church has not retained this liberal attitude towards masturbation?'

In his ringed notebook he had written:

On the way to the station, I asked the taxi driver if he knew the work of Titian from his days in the picture framing shop. He said he was familiar with some of his work but he did not know Venus of Urbino. He remarked that it was unusual to hear a Dutch woman with the name of Venus and he asked me if I knew Paul Bazelman's wife. I said that she was known to both my wife and me.

He really is an enormous fellow, tall with a large belly, which just fits between him and the steering wheel. To get into the car he has to breathe in and squeeze his stomach around the end of the wheel. The seat needs to be a long way from the steering wheel. When he is in the driving seat his arms are stretched out straight to reach it. He looks permanently uncomfortable with that great weight in front of him. He has large glasses, which were fashionable in the 1990s, and he is very chatty. He hinted to me once that he would like to join the Reading Club, but I ignored him.

On his company laptop, Hans created a new file and typed:

My Venus doesn't seem to worry that we might be seen together. I can't get this woman out of my mind. Her image is there when I wake and in most of my thoughts during the day. I am consumed by lust and desire. I want to be with her all the time. I don't know how I manage to work and function as a family man. Fate played a heavy blow when I was tricked into believing that my feelings for Cia were love. They never have been. We were only ever good companions and that was before I knew what it was really like to ache for someone. I am helpless. I don't want to eat, but somehow I have a lot of energy for loving and for contriving ways for us to meet in private. Even a fleeting glimpse of her gives me pleasure. The Greeks called this a sort of madness. Yes, that's what I have. Sometimes I think I am losing my mind.

When she first spoke to me eighteen months ago, I became captivated and I have remained that way ever since. From that time onwards she has haunted me like some mythical siren, an elusive Venus, tempting me to set aside what I believe about how I should behave as a family man. I have stopped trying to justify my actions to myself. I am obsessed. I have never loved anyone like this before.

Under 'Accounts 10', he further wrote:

Yesterday, as planned, we met at the bookshop. We often go there because it is where people can linger and read books and it is quite natural to glance at the other customers. I was there by 10.00, I bought my copy of the next Reading Club book, and I was pretending to study the history section. Venus arrived at

10.30 and collected a copy of the same book for her husband. Then she went to the opposite side of the shop and began looking at the self-help section. When I was sure that no-one was looking at us, I glanced up and held her gaze for just a second. It was enough to send a lustful ache into my groin. She opened her mouth slightly and then ran her tongue along her bottom lip. She knows that I find this very erotic. After a few more furtive glances, we engaged in a conversation which was not quite loud enough for the woman behind the counter to hear.

'Are you wearing the black silk underwear which I brought you from Paris?'

'Everything, the black bra is cupping my breasts.'

'How's the husband?'

'Paul is at home struggling to write his contribution for the Reading Club booklet. I'm sure he could do with some inspiration from you. Would you like to join us for a coffee?'

'I'm not sure.'

She ignored the reply. 'Have you been writing?' she asked.

'Every day,' he lied.

'About what?'

'About our passionate love affair,' he joked.

'That should make good reading for all of those so-called respectable gentlemen.'

'You know I wouldn't do that.'

'I would,' she said, 'but I would hide the identity of the lovers. Get them all guessing. Will you come for a coffee?'

'Isn't that a bit indiscreet?' Hans said.

'You've a lot to learn about how to conduct a secret liaison. People who are having an affair would not issue such an invitation. Only those not having an affair would think it quite normal to go to a friend's house for coffee.'

'Really!'

'Yes, so no-one will suspect if you come home with me.'

'Are you sure? I don't want to be a distraction for a fellow writer.'

'All this writing you guys are doing is a complete waste of

time. Each is sicking up his inner secrets. What's the purpose? It's as if you're all good little Catholic boys pouring your hearts out in confession. What difference will it make to anyone? Perhaps this Anniversary Booklet which you are writing should be called 'Confessions of a Reading Club'.

'How do you know what's been written?' Hans said.

'I have my sources.'

'Who?'

'Cleaners, taxi drivers and other wives. I've read some of Paul's writing. A lot of nonsense about his schooldays.'

'Has he shown you?' Hans asked.

'No, I read it on his computer. It was in the delete box.'

'I hope my wife hasn't found my writing,' Hans said, finding a tiny piece of nail on his ring finger, which he could bite.

'She probably has.'

Hans pressed the little finger of the other hand against his teeth in an attempt to find something there to nibble.

'She'll find out about you, about us,' Hans said.

'She knows already. Stop making a fuss.'

Hans looked at Venus and shook his head. 'I never know when you are joking.'

Venus shrugged her shoulders and ran her tongue over her bottom lip.

'Stop doing that!'

'I thought it turned you on,' Venus grinned. 'There's a slight chance that Paul will be out this morning. You could come home with me and see for yourself exactly what I'm wearing underneath my clothes.'

Hans hesitated, and then said, 'I'll just come for coffee.'

'Good. I have to go to the pharmacy first. I'll meet you at the river end of our street.'

Hans stood next to Venus as she opened the front door of her house and called out to her husband. There was no reply.

'His hearing is getting bad,' she said with a smile, 'let's go upstairs and look in his study.'

'I'll wait here,' Hans replied.

'Certainly not, follow me!'

She ran up the stairs two at a time, calling out as she went. Hans followed slowly.

'We have a visitor.'

There was no reply.

'Maybe he's popped out,' she said in a matter-of-fact way. Then she whispered, 'He could be in the bathroom. These days he suffers terribly from constipation.' She grinned.

Later that day, while his wife was out, Hans typed the following account into one of his computer files:

I felt very uncomfortable being upstairs in their house. This is where another man and his wife, my woman, were intimate. I tried hard not to think about his hands on her body.

I had asked Venus where she would hide the black silk underwear which I had bought for her. It was then that she told me about her walk-in wardrobe where she keeps all of her private and precious things. I knew it was in the middle of the landing. She had talked enthusiastically about it, so I was hoping to get a glimpse inside. By the time I got to the walk-in wardrobe she had disappeared. The door was a little ajar. I glanced in to see two neat rows of clothes in the half light.

Then I saw Bazelman. He was crouching in the corner with his backside reflected in the mirror. An ugly toad wearing a woman's black underslip. Was it the one I had brought Venus? Yes I think it was. I wanted to laugh. He could not see me. I pretended not to see him. I did not want him to know that I had spotted him. I might be screwing his wife. That is enough damage for any man to tolerate. No need to expose his secret transvestite tendencies.

I decided that Venus had lied to me when she said she was wearing all of the Paris underwear. How could she, because the toad had on the most expensive part, that black underslip?

My instinct was not to tell her what I had seen. Perhaps she knows, maybe she helps him with his obsession. Probably they shop together to buy clothes to satisfy his fetish. I thought that he was a respectable man. He is weird. Do I trust her any more?

Several days later, Cia and Hans were sitting opposite each other in their living room. She was reading and he was looking at the notebook in which he had recorded some of his observations from a bicycle ride he had taken along the dyke road into town. He planned to submit this piece for the Anniversary Book. Although he was concentrating on searching for some words to describe his journey, every now and then he became distracted by thoughts of his visit to Venus's house. The image of Paul kept repeating itself; the toad in black underwear. Perhaps he could write a toad story? What a household!

As if reading his thoughts, Cia said, 'You didn't tell me that you visited the Bazelman's house on Monday.'

'How do you know about that?'

'The taxi driver's wife told me when she came to clean the house today. Venus gave her some old clothes and asked if she wanted to use them as dusters. That woman is so wasteful. Apparently there were some perfectly good items of clothing, including a collection of French black silk underwear. I thought that most people knew that only cotton material is of any use for cleaning purposes.'

The following day Hans phoned Venus to tell her about the conversation about the underwear, which she allegedly gave to the taxi driver's wife.

'Do you think that I'd give away what you bought for me?' she said, with a laugh in her voice.

However the seed of doubt had been sown in his mind. Hans was not convinced by her reply. Uncertainty was beginning to nibble away at his trust; but his lust had not abated.

'Can we meet at the weekend? I don't find phone calls very satisfactory. Cia is going to visit her mother on Sunday; I'm not going with her.'

'Sorry, Paul's arranged a trip to Paris. He wants to buy me

some new clothes. I'll contact you next week. Bye.'

Venus put down the phone before Hans could reply.

For a moment he was numbed. She could have said no to Paul, or that she did not want to go. Hans was angry and jealous. He had not believed Venus's explanation about the underslip. This was the second time that she had lied to him about the gift. In total the underwear had cost him €250 and a lot of anxiety when he smuggled this into his house, then out again. As his dissatisfaction grew, so did his ideas about Venus and her sexual relationship with her husband.

A few days later Cia and Hans had a conversation which he described word for word in his journal. He typed it out on his computer and stored under 'Philips Closure Account':

Shit! I am in a mess. It is bad enough aching for a woman I distrust; now Cia is on the wrong side of my defensive wall. Last night the following chapter in this saga was played out.

I thought Cia was engrossed in her reading, but she looked up from her book and said,

'What are you going to write about for the Reading Club Anniversary Book?' Her question was asked in a light tone, which was laced with a suggestion of an ulterior motive.

'How did you know about that?' I said.

'Titus's wife told me.'

'Isn't anything private?' I replied immediately, despising the way women gossiped to each other. 'I expect the whole town knows what goes on in the Reading Club. Why does Titus tell his wife everything?'

Cia's way of conversing is to ignore those comments she does not like and repeat her original question. It is a clever and aggravating technique and I had never learnt how to deviate her from this way of talking.

'You haven't answered my question,' she repeated,' what are you going to write about?'

'It is not compulsory to write anything, it's only a suggestion from the author who's coming to talk to us, so that we can experience keeping a journal. He kept one for fifty years and then turned it into a book.'

I sensed Cia looking up from her book and watching my face. I was not sure what would be her next line, but I had a bad feeling that I was not going to like it.

'Why don't you write about the love of your life?' she said, her voice like hot chocolate containing slivers of razorblades.

I did not answer directly. This was one of her traps. I wanted time to think about how I could change the subject. I continued to stare down at my book in the hope that she would think that I was still reading, but I could feel those penetrating eyes like laser beams dissolving my defences. I did not have to look up to see her expression because I knew exactly what face went with each of her tones of voice.

'Are you suggesting that I write about you?' I said without looking up.

She laughed. 'You were a bit too slow with your answer. I wasn't referring to myself, but to the real love of your life.'

I realised that this was getting serious. I didn't think that she was directing me to give her a compliment; this was something much more devious than that.

I do not know why I said, 'Who're you referring to?' As soon as the words came out of my mouth, I knew that they were a mistake.

'Forgotten her name?' came the quick reply.

She knows something, I thought, but how could she? I am so discreet.

'Would you like me to remind you?' she said. Now the knife was in my back and she was just about to give it a painful twist.

'Whatever are you talking about?' I pretended to be cross, but she knew the difference between my real and fake anger. I guessed that she would not believe my protest.

'That's not a very convincing response.' Then came the voice, which implies that she knows everything. 'If it wasn't true you'd be laughing at my suggestion, not going on the defensive.'

She's too clever, I thought.

Cia continued, 'Whatever you say, I know that you're in love with Venus.'

174

I feigned surprise.

'Your face betrays you whenever we meet her. Your nostrils flare and your voice changes. Your eyes linger longer on her than on other women. Your stare goes from her face down to her breasts and back to her face again. You're in such a trance that you're not aware of what you're doing—you're like some old gorilla in the middle of the mating season.'

'You're crazy. I don't look at other women,' I lied. Of course I do.

'Yes you do. You've always looked at other women. Most men do. You don't realise you are doing it. It's a natural instinct. Some men are better at hiding it than others. Once you used to look at me like that – not any more.'

In my mind, I replied. Yes, that was in the days when you were worth looking at.

'Where do you get these ideas from?' I continued to imply my innocence. I was hoping that this was not going to go in the direction I feared. My life, our lives, were at stake here. I could ruin everything by saying the wrong thing – if all was not already ruined.

'I'm not the only one who has noticed. Sonja Mulder said she has seen you look at Venus in a special way. Women notice things like that.'

'So Sonja has opened her big mouth again. That woman's a witch. Now all of the Reading Club and probably the whole town will have heard. Why didn't you notice this so-called attraction yourself?' I was not sure that this was the right question; she was bound to have a smart answer.

Her voice took on another quality. 'Something has been wrong with our marriage for a long time, I didn't know what it was.' She continued, 'I wasn't looking closely at the signs. I spoke to Sonja who's very sensitive to these things and she lent me some books about reading faces. I know you are obsessed. When I realized the situation, other things began to make sense; for example, your lack of interest in me sexually, I thought it had to do with your age. No, it was because you were lusting after someone else.'

'You're crazy and that Sonja's an evil woman.'

175

'Don't waste your breath telling me otherwise.' She paused and the tone of her voice changed again.

'Let me ask you a question. Do you love me?'

I paused. It was a long pause. Then I sighed. In that moment I gave up the struggle of pretence and gave in to my intuition, which was to tell the truth, just in the way that my parents had drilled into me when I was a child. So, disregarding the consequences of being honest in this situation, I let down that defensive wall that I had built up over the years against Cia's questioning and said quietly and gently, 'No, I don't think I do anymore.' Then I left the room.

At breakfast the following day, Cia did not mention the previous night's conversation. It was as if nothing untoward had happened. She was dressed for work and said that she would be late that night because she was meeting some friends for a meal. Did Hans dream what had happened yesterday? What was going to be her next move? He knew her too well to assume that last night was the end of the affair. She would be thinking carefully about her following step. Two days later Hans found this letter on his study desk. Cia had gone out to give him a chance to read it:

Dear Hans,

I have realized for some time that our relationship has been a difficult one. We argue a lot and do not seem to have the pleasure in each other's company which we had when we were first married. I know that I have blamed you for that but I also realize that I have to take some of the responsibility for how our lives have changed. I understand that the passion of youth dies and other priorities take its place, some of which have united us as a couple, while some have pushed us apart. We have both devoted a lot of time and energy into building our home, caring for our family and developing our own successful careers. The result is that we have neglected our relationship. I accept that I have done that as much as you have.

I know that I have not always been a good wife to you. I

prefer to do different things and I have a wide circle of friends, some of whom you do not like. They give me what you have never been able to provide.

Now there is another dimension to our marriage, which threatens to destroy it and us. I feel very angry with you – not because you have found another woman attractive – I have had my head turned several times by different men. But you have followed your desire and have allowed yourself to become obsessed by your own passion. I have never let that happen to me, I thought too much of you to allow that. I am very frightened that you will do something impulsive, which will destroy everything we have.

By chance, on the computer, I found a piece of your journal about relationships. So I am aware that you are sceptical about working at ours, but I am sure that it is worth a try. Trust me. Consider the alternatives. Are you thinking beyond today? When I say a try, I do not mean spending hours discussing what went wrong so that we can blame each other all over again. Instead I suggest that we have a weekend together, away from here, where we can stroll in different streets, see a few sights and enjoy some delicious meals. I know that you are very fond of Paris. There is a small hotel near *Sacré Coeur*, which has a large double room free this weekend. I have made a provisional booking. Please say you will come with me. No rows, no blaming, no inquisition – just being together.

Love Cia

Hans was troubled and suspicious of Cia's response. He found it sickly, like eating a cream cake after drinking a sharp wine. Having received her letter, he lost his motivation for keeping a journal. In vain, he probed with his teeth along the margins of his nails to see if there was some morsel on which he could chew.

Two days later, he met Huub.

'What's our famous business consultant found to write about?'

'I've lost my enthusiasm for the project.'

'Surely not, you usually have so much to joke about at the club meetings. You must have written something.'

Hans paused for a moment. 'The dynamics of the Reading Club, a cycle ride, a picture by Titian.'

'Not another art lover,' Huub said as a bored expression flashed across his face. 'Our booklet will be full of descriptions of old pictures. Is Art becoming the new religion of the middle classes?'

'God, I hope not. I don't know if I will submit anything,' Hans said.

'You must, for the sake of the club.'

'I haven't decided on my final piece yet. I may not write about an art work if others are doing that.' Hans chewed on a piece of skin at the side of his right thumbnail.

'And what has our shop owner written about?' Hans asked.

Huub grinned, 'The damselflies in my pond.'

'Is that an interesting subject?' Hans looked doubtful and nibbled on the side of his other thumb.

'It's a metaphor. I want to make the point that there is more to life than having kids.'

'A metaphor. That's a good idea. I have written about the dynamics of the club. When I re-read it I found it was like a business essay; long-winded and boring. Maybe I could use animals in a story. That would be much more fun. Thanks for the idea, Huub.'

'I seem to have inspired you.'

'Yes. Look out for some animal stories.'

After his conversation with Huub, Hans went back to his writing. He found it remarkable that even though he felt like shit, he was confused, embarrassed, jealous, and resentful – you name a negative emotion and he had it – he was able to produce several pieces of writing. This gave him rest and distraction from his pain and incidentally he found some pleasure in the creation of four pieces of writing: 'The Cycle Ride', 'Love Smoking', 'Dutch Barn Animal Reading Club' and 'The Common Toad'. Just before the suggested weekend in Paris, Hans was very relieved that he developed bronchitis and this gave him a reason not to accept Cia's invitation.

As he grew more agitated by the events of his life, he started to chew parts of his flesh so that he exposed two small circles of pink under-skin on his right hand thumb, just below the nail. The wounds became so raw, painful and embarrassingly conspicuous, that he covered them with sticking plasters and took great care not to allow any of his expensive cologne to come into contact with these mutilated areas.

The Journal of Bert de Lange

The door of the *Wijnwinkel* was dark green and very shiny. Above its large, brass letterbox, a sign writer had inscribed the name of the owner, *Bertrand C. de Lange*, in gold italics. The top half of the door had six panels of bevelled glass, each providing a different glimpse into the shop. Every day Bert unlocked his premises, polished the front door, swept the pavement and watered his two bay trees outside. On Wednesday evenings Bert's cousin, the taxi driver's wife, cleaned the shop's interior.

When the shop door was opened, it nudged a brass bell, which was suspended on a spring. The contraption nodded up and down a few times and tinkled lightly like an altar bell; not too loud to be annoying, but loud enough for Bert to hear when someone had entered the shop. This time it was the doctor's wife.

'Good morning *Mevrouw* Dekker. How can I help you?'

'I'd like a sherry glass.'

'Just one?'

'One of those nice glasses which I bought from you last year was broken by our cleaning woman.'

'Ah! You mean my cousin, *Mevrouw* van Dillen.'

'It was an accident. She is always very careful.'

'She cleans here too and I am very selective in what I ask her to dust. For example I do not allow her to handle a bottle of *Petrus* worth €850 and other rarities like the 1900 Port; that would fetch €2000 at auction.'

'Expensive bottles.'

'That's the business.'

'I trust your cousin with everything.'

'Not your secrets, I hope.'

'You don't have a very high opinion of her.'

'My cousin likes to gossip. In the past, I have been the subject of some of her stories. She caused some trouble when my parents were alive.'

'I thought she was a discreet woman.'

'Not in my experience.'

'She is very thorough with her cleaning. We have a huge old house. She helps me a lot'

'So you would like another sherry glass? Just one?'

'Just one.'

The bell and the other internal brass fittings had their weekly clean, along with the displayed bottles of wine, champagne, liqueurs and spirits with their colourful labels. The shop boasted a grand selection of different Scottish whiskies with strange sounding names. Its walls were lined with oak shelves which, together with the counter, were wiped regularly with a damp cloth. To the right of the entrance door was a table display of expensive, yet unpretentious glasses. These also had a weekly polish. For the customers, the overall effect inside the shop was of being like privileged viewers to a private collection of treasures. Consequently, people often spoke in hushed tones, as if they were in a museum or in a church housing a holy relic.

Behind the shop were several rooms; one of these had once been the family kitchen. The house had a number of cellars whose temperatures were just right for storing vintage wines, ports and champagnes. These expensive bottles were allowed to gather dust as their value increased. The rooms upstairs, once the family bedrooms, were now used for storage. In some ways it was a waste of an elegant family house whose upper back windows looked out onto the harbour and beyond to the great river.

When Bert was six, his family moved out of the wine shop house, and into rented accommodation. Neither of his parents wanted to live in the place where their twin daughters had died within a few weeks of each other. The first tragedy happened when one of the girls became ill. Bert's mother wanted to take her to the doctor, but her husband made light of the child's symptoms and assured his wife that the little girl would be better the next day. She was not. When the GP saw the child he sent her to the hospital, but by then it was too late; she died two days later of meningitis. Bert's other little sister was killed a fortnight later when she ran out of the gate in the back wall of the garden straight under a van which was delivering fruit. Someone had left the gate open. Bert's father thought that he had closed it and Bert's mother knew she had not used the back entrance for several days.

In the case of the first little sister the GP had said that delaying the child's visit to hospital had made no difference to her life chances; when the second had her fatal accident, the police constable stated that it had been an unforeseen situation. But their words had made no difference to Bert's mother, who blamed her husband for the death of their daughters. Bert's father never relinquished his guilt, except when he was drunk into oblivion. At a very early age Bert learnt from him how to feel guilty.

The most awkward part of moving out was caused by the great table which had been in his mother's family for years. It required the assistance of a carpenter to dismantle and reassemble the old wooden colossus. No-one in his mother's family knew its origin. People assumed it had come from a large country estate house, because nothing smaller would have had sufficient space to take it comfortably. Nevertheless, Bert's mother was adamant that she would neither part with the table nor have it made smaller.

After her husband's death, Bert's mother decided she wanted to live in a small flat near to her eldest daughter in Dordrecht. As many items of furniture would not fit into her new home, she donated various pieces to the *Kringloopwinkel*. Piet van Rijn was very kind and removed everything with care, suggesting that some families in the Third World would be forever grateful for the proceeds from her donation. Little did Bert's mother know that her furniture did not sell; Piet could not even give it away. Since it was far too bulky to transport to those needy families, Piet had it all broken up and burned at the back of the shop. Everything went up in smoke, except the great table, which Bert's mother had kept back because her daughter-in-law agreed to have it in her home. Again a carpenter was called to dismantle and reassemble the heirloom in Bert's house. It was going to be a surprise. It certainly was, because once re-built the table was much larger than the two women had envisaged. Seeing her mother-in-law's worried expression, Bert's wife reassured her that the family would soon get used to the table and enjoy adding to its history.

At first neither Bert nor his three children liked the table occupying so much space in their main living-room. However, as predicted, they became accustomed to it and used it, not only at meal times, but also for all sorts of other activities, which their previous small table would not accommodate.

When he was twenty-one, Bert left university with a degree in Art and Design. His ambition was to create smart interiors for offices and hotels. At that time the *Wijnwinkel* was running at a loss because his father was drinking heavily; by the afternoon, he would leave the shop, go home and fall asleep with his head on the great table. Bert's mother refused to enter the shop and help with the business after her daughters had died. To prevent bankruptcy Bert agreed to run the shop for a year or until they found a manager.

Under his lead, the business began to make a profit, but it was never sufficient to employ a manager. Bert stayed, exercising his flair for interior design in creating efficient storerooms, refurbishing the shop's interior and rearranging the displays. People then, as now, went to the shop to buy bottles for special occasions, rather than for everyday use. For that, they used the local supermarkets. The sales from the shop never made a large profit. Bert's wine tasting evenings for connoisseur customers were more lucrative. Titus, Huub and Joost from the Reading Club received regular invites. However, Hans was never asked because he had a strange sense of humour; nor was Paul on the guest list because he moaned too much; nor Milo, because Bert thought he was rather a strange fellow; neither was Piet, likeable though he was; he would probably get drunk on the free wine. These tasting evenings resulted in most of the customers ordering a few bottles and some bought several cases of wine, which they had sampled. Later Bert began importing fine wines for a range of established customers and storing them until they could be auctioned at a good price.

When his mother died, Bert and his wife decided to move the old table out of their average sized house and back into the shop. They planned to buy some modern furniture for their home and finally create a living space which had harmony as well as comfort; a place in which they could relax.

Yet again, the old table was dismantled and reassembled in the old kitchen of the former family house behind the wine shop. It was on the table, in the peace and quiet of the shop, that Bert wrote his journal entries; sometimes a sentence, the next day a paragraph – so on until he had completed his story. He wrote:

The Drunk at the Table

I am sitting in my father's place at my mother's old oak table. When I close my eyes, I can recreate his alcoholic smell in my memory and visualise him becoming impatient. He wants a drink.

My father always had a negative attitude towards me. I only

wanted to receive his pride. I have lost that opportunity now that he is dead. Most people say that he drank himself to death. At the time, I did not know how to handle his excessive drinking, my mother's helplessness and my own angry feelings.

It is a long time since I suggested a book for the Reading Club. My last attempt proved to be very unpopular – not one person had anything positive to say about it. I read this book years ago, just after my father died. Had I known about this before, it might have helped our family to cope with what I now prefer to call his disease – his disease of addiction. When my father was alive, I blamed him for being selfish, unkind and out of control. I felt bitter, angry and resentful towards him.

After I read this book, I felt relieved, different, enlightened. Instead of thinking my father had been a selfish drunkard, I could now say that he died of a disease – Korsakoff's disease – which sounded more respectable than saying that he drank himself to death. Perhaps some people still say that about him.

I wanted to share my feelings and discoveries with the club members. However, I was naïve to think this book would have the same impact on them as it had on me. They were very critical; even Joost, who always finds some redeeming features in our books, did not say one good word about my choice. Piet, who rarely finishes a book, had made up a story about why he did not like it. When my choice of book was attacked, it felt like an insult; an insult to my intelligence. I wanted them to think differently about my father's demise. I resented their comments; I felt humiliated as if I had been the author, not the book's proposer. They were very unkind about my choice. I was criticized for recommending an English author because, as one person said, there were cultural differences which did not apply here in the Netherlands. Paul said that the book was not a novel, but a self-help book for addicts, implying that no-one in the group could possibly be affected by addictions of any kind. It was true that the book explained a process of recovery, but of greater significance to me were the numerous autobiographical sections, which in my opinion were well written – brilliantly written. It was in reading about the author's own experiences that I found a sympathetic comparison to my father's condition.

As usual, Paul was damning in his judgement. He did not accept the writer's suggestion that some people suffer from an addictive disease from which there is no cure.

'Of course there's a cure,' he said, 'they have to stop doing what they're doing.'

He had ridiculed the author's suggestions for managing the disease. Paul insisted that people needed to exercise self-control. He said he felt he had wasted time reading this book. I thought that was an ironic comment, coming from one who arrives at every Reading Club meeting smelling of a secret cigar which he has just smoked. It is well known that Paul is a heavy smoker, even his fingers are stained.

Titus was the most critical. He dismissed the suggestion that addictive disease is inherited. He claimed, in his superior medical voice, that there was no evidence for that.

'It's not even an accepted medical term,' he said.

He laughed at the proposition that people can be addicted to a host of substances including drugs and food, and also to activities such as exercise, shopping and sex. Titus seemed particularly antagonistic towards the suggestion of an addiction to sex. So strong was his condemnation that I wondered if secretly he had an addiction, which he kept hidden. No-one liked my book.

My cousin, the taxi driver's wife, also had something to say about the book. Not that my choice had anything to do with her, I never liked her. She used to visit my mother regularly and I had the impression that I was talked about a lot. She is such a gossip. It was unfortunate that she and Bob lost their picture framing business and that he had to take up driving the taxi while she became a cleaner. It was my mother's suggestion that she cleaned my shop. I have always been careful what I say to her, preferring to keep our conversation at a superficial level – the weather, the family and local items of news. I avoid talking about my personal business and especially the Reading Club because I have the idea that Bob would like to become a member.

When my cousin saw me reading the book about addiction she

told me that her husband thought it a poor choice because it was not a novel. She did not agree with him; in her view it was about time that certain people in my club faced up to their addictions. I was shocked by this remark. She continued by saying that Piet was addicted to cannabis, while Titus, Joost, Huub, Paul, Hans and Milo, all had sexual perversions of various types. I told her that I did not want to hear any gossip.

'Please yourself!' she said, shrugging her shoulders.

No-one in the club liked my book. Not that other people's choices are so great. There are times when I am really surprised by what we read. Consequently, when it comes to choosing the book for the following meetings, nobody looks in my direction. Even when I tentatively suggest a book, everyone ignores me. Titus even talks over me when I say something. He can be so bloody rude. He thinks that he is above the rest of us and he is a Protestant. I can't understand why he agreed to the priest's visit. I would never have asked a priest to come to talk to us.

Now I am sitting at this table that is heavy with history and I am endeavouring to compose something according to the priest's direction. Nothing is coming to mind that is worth writing about. This is such a chore.

Maybe I should sit somewhere else because I imagine I can hear my father moaning and drumming his fingers on this table, as it is getting near to the time of his first drink. Even if it were quiet, I am not sure that I would be inspired here. Perhaps I should find somewhere other than at my mother's old table. I notice that I am sitting where he sat. I can feel the indentations where he used to bang the ends of his knife and fork hard against the wood and shout to my mother in his mad voice. The dark wine-stain circles and the stale smell of alcohol linger in the grain of the wood.

'I want a drink, I want a drink!' he would shout.

His drinking began at about 10.30 in the morning with just two beers. Any objections to this early start were met with protests and abuse.

'You're always nagging me; nag, nag, nag.'

The repetition of this word could last for a minute, even two.

He sounded like a damaged record. Defeated by his words my mother withdrew to another room.

At midday, she arranged the table for lunch. He sat down at his place and saw immediately that she had not put out any glasses.

'I need a drink,' he said in a shrill voice.

'Would you like some water?' she said, pretending not to know what he really wanted.

'Bollocks! Water is for washing, not for drinking,' he retorted, trotting out one of his well-worn sayings. She knew them all and was weary of their repetition. They were now the mainstay of their conversations. Impatient for his next alcoholic fix, he picked up his knife and fork and began to tap the ends on the table in time to the chant of, 'I want a drink, I want a drink, I want a drink.'

He was aggressive towards her in front of the family and visitors. She found it embarrassing to watch the expressions on other people's faces, as he became more and more drunk. Mostly she felt relieved when he fell asleep at the table; then she could escort him upstairs to an early bed. Only then could she try to explain his behaviour to the shocked observers.

'I want a drink, I want a drink!' The volume of the chanting would reach such a pitch that she was sure that the near neighbours could hear him. Eventually she gave up being concerned about what anyone thought. The drumming on the table was so loud that it felt as if he was banging against the inside of her head. She screwed up her face and hunched her shoulders against the noise.

'There's no wine,' she said in a vain attempt to deter him from drinking.

'Bollocks, there is. I brought some home from the shop yesterday and you've hidden it.'

'No, you drank it all last night, before you became unconscious.'

'No, I didn't drink it all. There were ten bottles, ten green bottles.'

Then he started to sing a song, which he had learnt from a British soldier in the war.

'Ten green bottles hanging on the wall,
Ten green bottles hanging on the wall,
And if one green bottle should accidentally fall,
There'll be nine green bottles hanging on the wall.
Nine green bottles hanging on the wall.
Nine green...'

'Alright, alright!' she said, knowing that he could go on repeating this tune for much longer than she could stand to hear it. She gave in – anything for a quiet life. She retrieved the cupboard keys from her pocket and dangled them in front of him. In his sober life, as a younger man, he would have embraced her hand and kissed it gently. Now he snatched the keys from her fingers and in doing so broke one of her fingernails. My mother always had good hands. She studied the damaged nail and then watched as he unlocked the store cupboard.

'Some bottles are missing!' he said on his return to his seat at the table. 'What have you done with them? I pay the rent in this house, so I'll do what I like under my own roof. Yak, yak, yak – that's all you do; no wonder I want a drink. Your nagging is killing me.'

This comment was accompanied by a gesture in which he held up his hand in front of her face and tapped his straight fingers on his thumb so that his hand looked like a little nagging mouth. She found the gesture humiliating.

'You're killing yourself with your drinking.'

'Bollocks,' he said, as he poured himself a glass of white wine, gulped it down in one swallow, wiped his mouth on his sleeve and then belched.

How she detested that swear word.

'I'm not the only one who is saying this,' she continued. 'Our children, our friends, the pastor, even your son-in-law says you're killing yourself. He should know; he's a doctor.'

He swore again. 'They've all got more bottles of drink in their homes than we have. That's bollocks.'

'You have the bottles, not me,' she said, 'remember I don't drink.'

'So what?'

'Do you want something to eat?' she said, changing the subject.

Why did she bother to argue with him? She had realised a long time ago that alcohol had damaged his capacity to think, to engage in simple, pleasant conversations. His intelligence only worked to articulate the denial of his alcoholism.

'Of course,' he said. 'The way to a man's heart is through his stomach.'

She thought for a moment about how they used to have such easy access to each other's hearts. Before the twins died, he had been a romantic man. When they were first married he cherished and supported her, and in that relationship she blossomed. Now that part of him was gone, dead!

She set the plate in front of him. He began ramming the food into his mouth. These days he ate very quickly and in the process did not always completely close his mouth. In between his lips, she glimpsed the food being mixed with saliva. Sometimes tiny pieces escaped onto the table or down his shirt. She could hear the noise of him chewing and it made her feel sick and not inclined to eat her own meal. No wonder she was losing weight. She placed her cutlery down on her plate, to indicate she had finished eating.

'Don't you want the rest of that?' he said grinning like an evil jester.

He did not wait for her to answer but pulled the plate towards him and proceeded to ram her leftovers into his mouth. To remain at the table and listen to him eating was making her feel faint. If she got up before he had completed his meal, he would accuse her of bad manners, using one of his reprimanding regional accents. When she first heard his imitations, she thought they were amusing. Now, having experienced them a hundred times, she was tired and angry with his behaviour. She left the table on the pretext that someone was at their front door.

'You're hearing things woman, there's no-one about,' he said in his version of a North Brabant accent.

Then returning to his cool voice he said, 'You're just making up another excuse to leave me? Well go ahead. There're plenty of others queuing up to take your place.'

That remark wounded her. All the hundreds of times when he hurt her, she never left him. She hid his drunkenness from others; their friends and their relatives. She made excuses for him; tolerated his unkindness and the constant smell of stale alcohol around him. She endeavoured to protect him from himself and tried everything to stop him from drinking. She wept for him, for them and for herself. Now she was empty of ideas about what to do – but she was still with him, holding onto the memory of how he once was. It was a struggle which tested her faith and her capacity to survive.

It was 1.30pm when he left the table. He had finished two beers and a bottle of wine. He settled himself in his usual chair and within a few minutes he was snoring. My mother cleared the table, realising that she had a couple of hours of peace while he slept. She knew that when he woke he would be reaching for an aperitif. The second bout of drinking commenced several hours before the evening meal. By 7.30, he was asleep and she alone again.

Gradually he drank more and ate less. His weight dropped until he was several kilos lighter than my mother. Eventually he stopped eating and just drank milk, coffee and cheap wine. The man she once knew had completely disappeared. I tried to help him; to help them both, but he refused to stop drinking and I got angry at his lack of self-control. I thought if I ignored him then he would come to his senses, cease drinking, and try to contact me. My mother said my decision of non-contact did not seem to affect him. He didn't ask about me. Apparently he told the neighbours and my cousin, who visited regularly, that I had a mental problem. When I phoned, he couldn't be bothered to speak to me. His daily routine got narrower and narrower. When he died, I had not seen him for two years. After that, I felt guilty that I had left my mother alone to cope with him. At the time, I was sure that he would want to call on me, especially nearing the end of his life. My mother said that he just wanted to be drunk. As I was angry with him, she remained quietly angry with me.

I do not know if he could have followed the advice in the book which I recommended to the Reading Club. Perhaps it might have given us a way of coping with his alcoholic dementia and his early death.

After he died, my mother moved to a small flat. The large family table did not fit into her new place. She spoke to my wife directly and asked if we would like to have the table. My wife agreed, thinking that I would take pleasure in it. My mother offered to have the tabletop repaired, the dents filled and the surface renewed. My wife had said, without consulting me, that we would take the table just as it was. Mostly I enjoyed having it in our house – it was ideal for seating large numbers of the family and friends. As a workplace, it was great; the laptop was parked there permanently, on it the children did their homework and that's where my wife read the paper every day. However, it was always too big for the room. When my mother died we decided to move it back to the shop again. Now I am sitting here. When I feel the hollows, a number of unhappy memories and the sound of my father's drunken voice are released. It is as if, by rubbing them, a genie appears bringing with it the picture of him banging the table in his alcoholic madness.

After Bert had written the dialogue between his mother and his father, he quietly wept. For years the memory of it had been replaying itself in his mind's eye. Now it had been archived in his journal, his tears released themselves and rolled down his cheeks. Something inside which had maintained and sustained his guilt was now out there, written in his own words. He had carried his parents' pain and blaming for too long. His father had died and his sisters had gone years before.

He reminded himself of his wife and children – a lively, noisy, untidy assortment of busy people with curious minds and open hearts. Sometimes he found their activities, their conversations and their music too much and he longed for a quiet space in their house. His wife was a primary school teacher. She was a vivid person and it made little difference to the volume of her voice, whether she was talking to a class of nine-year-olds, or when she was chatting to adults. He knew that some teachers were like that! He wondered how together they had produced this free-spirited, happy bunch of children, when as a child he had absorbed the sadness and quietness of his parents.

Bert blew his nose, wiped his face and felt better. In his pocket he fingered his father's old penknife. He often did this; feeling the surface warm from resting against his thigh. It was kept sharp and used every day in the shop. He opened the narrow blade, which squeaked as he carved on his mother's table 'Death has taken them away for eternity'.

The shop bell tinkled. Bert wiped his face and gave his nose another blow to clear his head. It was the doctor's wife again.

'I am sorry to disturb you, but I need another sherry glass.'

'Has my cousin been breaking your things again?'

'No, my husband said that we have been one glass short. He broke one last year. I didn't notice.'

'How's your husband getting on with our writing project?'

'I had forgotten that you are a member of his club. I don't mean it's *his* club.'

'I know what you mean. Has he produced some good stuff?'

'He's worked every day. But please don't tell anyone else. I think some of it's boring.'

'I promise I won't tell.'

'Some of it's quite explicit and therefore he can't use it. Some of it refers to your cousin. I won't say any more. So much to choose from, I don't know what he will select. He's enjoyed it.'

'That's good.'

'But I wonder if it has been worth all the time he has given to it.'

'I'm sure it has.'

'I asked him what had been the point. He said he had learnt something about himself. What have you written about?'

'Probably not so much as your husband. I've written about the reactions to a book I recommended to the club.'

'Was that the one about addiction? I don't think my husband liked it.'

'No-one did. But I've also written about the people who have sat around our family table.'

'What a clever idea. Titus should have done something like that instead of the heavy stuff he insisted on writing. Where's this table?'

'Come and see. It's in the back of the shop.'

The doctor's wife followed Bert to the back room. He ran his hand over the surface of the table and he said, 'There's a lot of history in this wood.'

'Yes,' she replied as she caught his hand in hers. She held it for a moment. 'You've been crying.'

'Yes, I was writing about my childhood and my parents – a mixture of great sadness and then realising what a fortunate man I am.'

'I don't think you're the only one who has shed a tear over this writing.'

Bert lifted her hand to his lips and kissed it gently.

'Thank you for understanding,' he said, as he carefully replaced her hand on the table.

'Shall I find you another sherry glass? Or would you like a glass of sherry? I have some which is almost fifty years old which I have been saving for a special occasion.'

'Another time, perhaps. I'll take one sherry glass. I will look forward to reading your piece about the table in the Anniversary Book.'

The non-existent journal of Piet van Rijn

Piet was a qualified sociologist. This lovable, likeable, naïve, forgetful, unreliable dreamer with an unself-conscious charm, had been in several jobs since gaining his degree, but never stayed long in any of them. Declaring himself to be a utopian socialist, he claimed that people could live harmoniously in groups, sharing their achievements, happiness and responsibilities. It was as if Piet had grown up not hearing an important code about Dutch behaviour, which said, 'Behave normally, that's mad enough.' His friends generously reframed his eccentricities into a unique brand of normality, but most acquaintances, although they liked Piet, privately thought that he was slightly crazy.

Piet ran the *Kringloopwinkel,* which was along the dyke road. He liked the principle of the shop, but he was not so keen on the everyday details of running it. For this he relied on his part-time assistant who, from inside her glass-walled office, could see to all parts of the ex-flower warehouse. On a long table once used for sorting freshly picked roses, she scanned the donated goods before deciding on their destinations. In an old tin cupboard, she locked away the valuables: cash, papers and worthful items. She kept the key in the pocket of her brown foreman's apron which she wore every day. The volunteer staff mumbled about her mistrust of them. Piet laughed when one of the helpers found the courage to tell him that his salaried assistant was earning some extra euros by selling items for her own profit.

'She's an honest woman; I couldn't run the business without her.'

Certainly the last part of the statement was true. Piet was unaware that the total amount of donated goods shipped abroad was minimal. He was not interested to know that it was more economic to sell locally and send some euros or dollars to needy people. He relied on his assistant to do everything, except remove the mice and rats which were poisoned by the vermin controllers. Piet was fascinated by their dead bodies and examined them carefully before he placed them gently in the incinerator. He enjoyed talking to the customers. One of his hobbies was painting and he had negotiated with the board of the *Kringloopwinkel* that he could use one of the large rooms at the back of the warehouse as a studio. When not chatting to customers, Piet preferred painting or sketching the view across the fields or along the river. His assistant seemed very happy with this arrangement. Piet rarely asked her about the business side of their work, but every day before they left he would wish her a pleasant evening with her family and tell her she was doing a fine job. Why should she change this arrangement?

Both Piet and his wife had previously been married. She owned an old narrow house near the cathedral, which she had bought with her first husband, who had died in 1985. As a single parent with four children to care for, she decided to convert the front room of the ground floor into an antiques shop and take two of the rooms on the first floor to be let out for 'bed and breakfast'. In that way she could work and be at home for her children. She and Piet met at a crafts fair, where she was running an antiques stall and he had a small exhibition of his paintings. The slim artist was captivated by the big woman.

'*Mevrouw,*' he said when he first spoke to her, 'I hope you won't be embarrassed when I say you have the most beautiful complexion I have ever seen.'

She smiled and blushed.

'And now you have that high colour in your cheeks, you look exquisite, an artist's delight to paint.'

How could she not be flattered? Her late husband had not been so charming.

'Your eyes are warm, your blonde hair shines. What a radiant smile.'

'Stop your nonsense.'

'How many times have you had your portrait painted?'

'Never. I don't want my portrait painted. Even if I could afford to pay you, I wouldn't want it done.'

'I am not asking to be paid. You have a beautiful body.'

'You mean I'm fat.'

'No, not fat. Plump is a better word. I love plump women. They are so generous... with their smiles.'

'Do you always talk like this?'

'Only when I fall in love.'

She laughed. 'Could you talk normally to me?'

'Certainly, but I still think you are beautiful.'

Piet continued with his compliments. She couldn't help liking him. When she invited him to her home, she saw how friendly he was towards her children. He made them laugh and treated them with the same amount of affection as he gave to his own sons. She liked the way he was willing to help her with small tasks about the house. They shared a love of talking, walking and looking at fine things. She found him a pleasing companion and a kind lover. He never seemed to get upset by anything and his appreciation for the simple things in life delighted her. Their courtship lasted one year before they married.

Their friendship continued even when the romance of their relationship had dulled. Piet seemed to spend more and more time painting at the back of the storehouse, leaving his wife to run two businesses, care for their home, her children and pay the majority of the bills. Mostly she was uncomplaining about this lop-sided arrangement, because what Piet lacked in his material contributions to their shared household, he made up for in his pleasant, loving attitude towards her. She felt understood and appreciated by her unusual husband and she valued the care and attention he gave to her children. For example, he never complained when she went away for a few days visiting relatives. How many other husbands would have been so tolerant? Even when she criticised him for spending too much time painting and too little time helping her, he said he understood how she felt and this disarmed her and she lost her anger. Mostly she encouraged him in his painting and took an interest in his membership of the Reading Club. She had read 'Priests Dying' as Piet had talked with enthusiasm about Father Antonius, his ex-teacher. As a result they spent a lot of time comparing their different experiences of education. The book gave her a new perspective on her husband and she concluded that he had had a tough childhood, which still influenced his life today. Having considered his formative years, Piet decided that he now felt positive about his time at the seminary and would not have wished for an alternative.

Piet liked the principle of the Reading Club. He enjoyed meeting the others once a month and listening to their contrasting views. However, he had always been a slow and a reluctant reader and often he did not finish or sometimes even start the monthly book. He was very pleased that the club had agreed to his suggestion of inviting Father Antonius to the anniversary meeting. He thought the priest's idea of asking the members to each keep a journal was inspiring, but as yet he had not written anything himself. He considered the task frequently and he recalled his first day at the seminary several times after telling the taxi driver about it. But as yet, he had nothing on paper. The taxi driver wrote a piece about a dog and gave it to Piet as an example of what could be written in a journal. Piet's wife suggested that he write about his painting. Although he agreed that was an excellent idea, he never took the opportunity to write something.

However, he did manage to forward the finished pieces from the other members to Father Antonius by the required date, and he was involved in the negotiation of the funding and the printing of the Anniversary Book.

The Journal of Milo Jansen

Hanging on the dark red wall facing the front door of Milo's house was a large portrait of a veiled Muslim woman. On an old Turkish table, below the picture, lived a pile of Catholic magazines, an Arabic brass tray for keys, a pair of his wife's trainers, a damaged umbrella and an altar candle, four-fifths spent. The day's post, as usual, was dropped on top of the Bible and the ash from last night's incense stick had left grey streaks on the side of Milo's well-worn guitar case.

Apart from having a Master's degree in anthropology, Milo Jansen was a gifted musician and linguist. The guitar, flute and violin were his preferred instruments, but he could also produce music from a piano and an organ. His seven year posting at the Dutch Embassy in Egypt had left him with sympathy and understanding for the *allochtonen*, the non-European foreigners who live in his town. For the last ten years, the Catholic Diocese had employed him as a social and research worker. He designed and organised projects which were used by both religious and political leaders as the bases for their policies. He received a Queen's medal for his pioneering work on integration. For several years, he had been active in the Turkish community, assisting people with official business and letter writing. In his spare time, he gave free music lessons to a Turkish boy, the son of Tarik the grocer, and to two little Chinese girls whose family owned the Yellow Dragon Restaurant in the *Waterstraat*. People from different communities revered him and they showed him their respect by always calling him *Meneer* Milo.

Milo had attended the seminary school where Father Antonius was a teacher. At the age of twelve he was devoted to the idea of becoming a priest. He was bitterly disappointed when, two years later, the principal dismissed him on the pretext that he was not clever enough to be a student or a priest. This experience stayed with him all his life and left him with an ambiguous relationship with the Catholic Church. Later Milo developed his own mission statement in which he believed that God's work was best undertaken not in churches but in the streets, on terraces, in homes and places where people worked. He preferred worshipping in simple ways; through private prayer and by helping others. The pomp and rituals of the Church did not appeal to him. In his view, the attitude of all clergy was arrogant. He believed that unless the Catholic Church changed its ways of working with believers, it would soon make itself redundant. He prophesised that the future for religious people – not just Christians – was in working together to save the planet. Respecting others was the key to success. Hallelujah!

Milo was frequently overwhelmed by his love for others. He wanted to serve and support the underprivileged, the distressed, the unhappy, the abused, and the foreigners in his community. Many people knew that he was an empathetic listener and in this capacity he had helped others through their difficult times. He was the unqualified therapist, mentor and spiritual guide to the taxi driver and his wife when they were struggling to adjust to the loss of their business. He encouraged them to find dignity in their new life. The taxi driver told Milo how some of his passengers humiliated him. The taxi driver's wife confided that she was shocked by the private lives of some of her clients.

People in receipt of Milo's kindness often endowed him with saint-like virtues. Others, misinterpreting his overtly caring attitude, misunderstood his compelling beliefs and experienced him as an overbearing preacher. Some called him 'a goat's-woollen-sock-type'; someone with a lot of self-pity and moral arrogance. After all, the Dutch do not like extravagant, self-promoting individuals and they do not like to be told what to believe.

Although he occasionally irritated certain members of the Reading Club, most experienced in him an innate softness. Whereas some members could use their words like rapiers, Milo never did. When hearing harsh words, he expressed his unhappiness. He tried to make his protests gentle. Yes, he complained about there being far too much sex in modern literature, but he always endeavoured to say that quietly.

'Those things are private and should remain so.'

Beyond his lean body with its mop of wiry hair, he had a charisma which appealed to most of the men in the club, but there was about him an air of sensuality, which some of the wives found uncomfortable. Bert's wife had complained to her husband.

'I was on the terrace with Sonja today when that Milo from your Reading Club came and sat at our table.'

'That was nice for you,' Bert said, looking at his wife as she unpacked the shopping.

'He sat so close to me. He's creepy.'

'He's a pleasant chap.'

'I'm not the only one who is not too keen on him.'

'He's harmless. You don't have to worry.'

'I wouldn't like to be alone with him.'

'He's probably more frightened of you.'

'What exactly does he do?'

'He works for the Church. I expect he thought that you needed some guidance to get back on the right path to God. Did you tell him that you don't believe any more?'

'That's none of his business.'

'We're all sinners according to Milo.'

'Why do you have people like that in your club?'

'We like him and he makes interesting comments if he reads the books.'

'Doesn't he always do that?'

'Not always,' said Bert, remembering that he always finished the books, even if it meant reading to the end of a ghastly book or staying up late the night before the Reading Club meeting. He would never not read a book.

'Who else doesn't finish the books?'

'Piet. But whereas Piet tries to cover up and makes an excuse, Milo is always open, giving reasons, such as, he has been busy giving guitar lessons and preparing his students for a music competition.'

'And you believe him?'

'Why not? Sometimes he's busy with his community work – or he has been six times to The Hague with different Turkish people.'

'The members of your Reading Club are a strange lot.'

Milo had enjoyed Antonius's book. He believed that there was a parallel between their lives. Both men had struggled with aspects of Church life, whilst retaining a belief in God. Each had encountered injustice and abuse. They had endured a lifelong struggle. Milo saw Antonius as a kindred spirit, a 'Brother in Christ', and was looking forward to meeting him again. He felt inspired to write because he had plenty of thoughts and feelings. Yes, some of these tempted and unsettled him, but he would be honest and explore them. The prospect of reflection made him feel hopeful and joyful. 'Praise the Lord,' he said and began to scribble in his notebook.

1

Lord, thank you for sunny days.

Saturday, the sun is shining; it is a good time for me to be on the *café terrace* with my flute, moving between the tables, while playing tunes, raising my hat and smiling at people. Sometimes my friend Michael who plays the accordion joins me. A few people like to give us money in return for our music. We thank them and say that we will donate it to one of our local charities. We weave in between the tables being careful not to obstruct the young waiters and waitresses in their fawn, outsized shirts, long aprons, black trousers, their 'Can I help you?' smiles and their money purses bulging with notes, small change and tips. They glide like skaters between the chairs with shoulder high trays of cups, glasses and plates. The owner of the café tends to stay in the background, straight faced, looking more like a farm worker than a clever businessman. Everyone knows the weather will be good when he orders the waiters to put out lots of tables and chairs, which temporarily extend the café area into the Town Square. Additional furniture is brought up from storage through a trap door on the forecourt of the café via an automated platform. At night all the outside furniture is returned to the cellar. Sometimes the young waitresses do this job, while the owner stands in the shadows watching them.

2

Lord, thank you for my music.

For the past few years the Mayor has ask us to play our music for special celebrations in town, such as *Santa Claus*, the Lent Carnival or during the weekend of the Art Exhibitions. Michael and I have a lot of fun. We have a large repertoire. I only have to play a few notes and he immediately recognises the melody and joins in.

3

Lord, I hope there will be music in Heaven.

Or is it silent there? Will I have my old guitar with me? My hands, will they be able to play and will I have a shoulder on which to hang my instruments? Will I even have a body? I wonder what sort of music is permitted there. I cannot imagine a life without music. Will there be other musicians to play with? Are there any sounds in heaven? Is that where I am going when I die?

4

Lord, thank you for my wife.

Myriam smiled when I shared my thoughts with her. She is not musical and she does not believe in the afterlife. She loves silence and she frowned when I told her that I would leave the world before her. She has heard me say this before. I said that I had a premonition that I would be betrayed by people whom I consider to be my friends. When I most need their support, they will turn against me.

'Before the cockerel crows three times?' she asked.

But I knew she was teasing me, because then she told me not to be so morbid. She knows that I can get preoccupied by what she calls my religious obsessions. She said that I should stop tormenting myself and remember all the people I had helped. She reminded me of the integration project, which I recently completed, and the praise I received from a government minister. In her opinion I have still got some important work to do in the community.

5

Lord, thank you for my mission.

Even when Michael is not with me, I go to the Town Square on Saturdays. Sometimes I play one of my instruments, other times I sit at a table and have a drink with some friends. Frequently one of the men from the Reading Club arrives there with his wife and they sit for a while in the sunshine. My wife doesn't like to do that. She says that the coffee is too expensive on the café terrace and that she will get a drink after she has finished giving a Dutch lesson to a Muslim friend. I think it is a good place to be; just in front of the Saturday market. Many people know me and raise their hands in greeting. I enjoy entertaining them with my music. I see them smile; some even look embarrassed when I play a tune just for them. Most people there would not understand that I consider these Saturday mornings on the terrace to be part of my Christian mission. I am modest about that. Mostly I talk and listen. When it is appropriate, I give away some small cards, which have a picture of a saint on one side and a prayer on the other.

The following Saturday, Titus and his wife were having some drinks on the café terrace in town.

'Quick, look the other way. Pretend you haven't seen him.'

'Who are you talking about, Titus?'

'There's Milo with his bloody guitar.'

'Why don't you want him to see you?'

'God! Now he's waving. Pretend you haven't seen him.'

'I can't be so rude. Anyway he's a member of your club.'

'That doesn't mean I want to see him at other times.'

'I thought he was your friend.'

'My friend? Never! He'll start his preaching and if you're unlucky he'll give you a religious card.'

'I thought you liked him.'

'Not outside of the club.' Titus stood up.

'Where are you going?'

'I have to go to the pharmacy. I'll see you at home. You can listen to his playing and enjoy his preaching. I'm off.'

Titus picked up his shopping from the café seat and called out to Milo who was approaching the table, 'Got to rush, stay and have a coffee with my wife.'

'The Lord be with you on this sunny day,' Milo said as he waved a blessing at Titus.

6

Lord, forgive them.

I went to a seminary. Father Antonius taught me history. It was very strange to read his book. I remember those days at the school very well. He may be a wise and gentle old priest now, but then he was a sharp and easily angered young teacher. My mother was asked to take me away from the seminary. The principal told her that I could not cope with the school life. That was a lie, because I remember receiving only praise for my work. I was very upset and confused at the time. Fortunately I went to another school and eventually to university. I think that was a better outcome for me than becoming a priest. These days I consider that I am undertaking God's work through my various projects. It is not necessary to be ordained or to take certain vows in order to work in the Lord's name.

7

Lord, help me to love my neighbour.

My favourite saying from the Bible is 'love thy neighbour'. I have always tried to do this. I feel upset when I hear Catholics expressing their dislike of Protestants. When Christians describe all Muslims negatively, I feel outraged. We should respect differences, celebrate one another. Women too should be given their rightful places in all societies. My wife and I agree about this. She organises assertiveness training courses for her female colleagues and in her spare time she teaches Dutch to some Muslim women in our town. One way in which I demonstrate my love for my neighbours is by being on the terrace, meeting and greeting as many people as I can. Not that any of the Turks ever sit there. The men prefer to meet in the coffee bar of HEMA, the largest shop in town. Their wives never meet each other in public places.

8

Lord, help me to be respectful.

Some women are cautious about me. I do not understand this because I only want to be friendly and supportive. Being a sensitive man, I soon become aware if someone does not like me or misunderstands my motives. My wife told me that sometimes I sit too close to certain women and that could give the impression that I am flirting. When I heard this, I became upset because I am careful to treat all women respectfully.

9

Lord, help me with my mission.

There is too much mention of sex in our society. People talk freely about something which should be private between a man and a woman. Often at the Reading Club, someone will suggest a book which has unnecessarily explicit details. I don't like to read or see such information. I have often protested, but no-one wants to listen. One of the women I counselled told me that her husband spends hours looking at pornography on the internet and that she felt rejected by him. There are several women in our town who are overtly sexual in the way they dress and behave. I feel uncomfortable and embarrassed by them. Venus Bazelman is the worst, although she sometimes makes me laugh.

Gerrit, our town vagrant, was involved in a motorcycle accident, which left him with brain damage. As a result, he has an aggressive attitude towards women, especially his mother. He says she is a whore. Since his accident, he has left his home and sleeps outside in the porch of the post office. He carries all his possessions and a crate of lager cans in a shopping trolley, which he trundles everywhere he goes. Some people are frightened of him, others ridicule him. I talk to him whenever I see him; he likes to hear me play football songs on my flute.

10
Lord, help me to rise up early.

Sometimes when I am not too busy with my projects, I find it difficult to get up in the mornings. It is easy to turn over and return to that place between waking and sleeping. My wife leaves home at 6.00am to go to the Yellow Tulip Hotel for a swim, before she starts work there at 7.30am. She retires early to bed; sometimes three or four hours before me. So as not to disturb me in the mornings, she sleeps on a mattress on her study floor. We have slept apart for a few years. At first, I missed her closeness.

11
Lord, help me to resist temptation.

I am sometimes plagued by fantasies in which there are women who want to undress me. I feel naked and vulnerable. They mock me, my body, my manhood, and I feel abused and judged. For most of the time, I endeavour to rationalise these experiences and convince myself that I am being tested to see how I can resist temptation. There is one recurring dream, which I find very disturbing. In it, I am Saint Joseph and two nearly-naked angels visit me. One is the taxi driver's wife whose colossal breasts hang heavily from her shoulders. They sway like gigantic pendulums as she flies in the air above me. Whichever way she travels her breasts fall towards earth, like a pair of inflated plumb lines. Her overt sexiness arouses me and I feel sick. The other one is a more delicate angel; that is Titus's wife. I sat with her on the terrace the other day. She is tall and slim like a willow cane. In my fantasy she is wearing a long robe, through which I can see her naked body. Her breasts are small like young fruit, but she is very sensual. These angels, who come too near, are arousing me. I want to be free of these fantasies, but the more I repel them, the more they penetrate my waking hours. There is too much reference to sex in our society. I am sure that is why I get these disturbing daydreams.

Milo felt justified in writing about a childhood memory; Father Antonius did that in his book and several of the members announced that they were writing about their schooldays. He could vividly recall the incident around his dismissal from the minor seminary. Over the years several abuses occurred there and he was ready to expose the Church. Whilst he wanted to create a well wrought piece of literature for the Anniversary Book, he also had a strong desire to describe the injustice which he had experienced as a boy. When he had completed his story, he felt lighter about the subject. He showed it to his wife; in her view he had written a very clear account of the event. It began, 'Lord, help me to understand and to forgive'. The episode was typed and sent to Father Antonius several weeks before the deadline for entries.

Milo kept secret his regular conversations with the taxi driver and his wife. 'Our counselling sessions', he called them; 'our confessions', was how the couple described them to each other. Not that he had ever received any training to become a counsellor, but he was confident that his love of people and his trust in God would be sufficient background to help his clients. The relationship between the three had started shortly after the taxi driver's business finished and had continued every month since.

At first Milo talked to the couple together. While one of them spoke, the other would listen. This was Milo's version of couple counselling and the three agreed it worked well. Occasionally he would see one of them alone; either because of their different work routines or because one of them wanted to talk about something very private.

Earlier that day, the taxi driver's wife had phoned Milo. 'I've just made some of your favourite cookies. Would you like to come by for a coffee tonight? Bob will be out driving.'

Milo had agreed. 'I can stay a short while.'

After some ample refreshments, the light chatting became more serious.

'I want to give up my cleaning job. I'm fed up with the work and the people.'

'Really?' Milo said.

'I don't like the way I'm treated.'

'What's happened?'

'It's the way they behave. They pretend they're so respectable and they're rubbish.'

Milo could have guessed that the cookies were bait. She really wanted to talk to him about something important and she did not want to do this in front of her husband. In the past, he had heard a lot about the various members of the Reading Club from both the taxi driver and his wife. Last week she told him about the fifty euros which Paul Bazelman had given to her. At the end of their session, Milo had suggested they prayed for Paul and his wife. Reluctantly she had bowed her head.

Mostly he regarded what the couple said to be exaggerated gossip and he encouraged them not to spread rumours. He always treated whatever they told him as confidential.

'Something special you want to talk about?'

'I'm worried that Bob still wants to join the Reading Club. They're not nice people. I know you're a member. You're different from the rest. Bob's so sensitive. They'll hurt him. Can't you stop him?'

'No-one's proposed him yet.'

'Piet said he had proposed Bob, twice!'

'Perhaps I was away when that happened.'

'He'd be devastated if he knew. I told him Piet's a liar. What if someone else proposes him?'

'That could happen. Bob knows all of the other members.'

'If he's proposed, will you vote against him?'

'During the next few meetings they'll be too busy with their writing to discuss new members.'

Milo had always avoided discussions about the driver's membership of the Reading Club. He did not want to be drawn into talking about that now. 'I must go,' he said, 'thanks for the cookies.'

'What, no prayer?'

Usually, after a counselling session, Milo invited the couple to join with him in saying a prayer. He would ask God to help them through their difficult times, forgive their sins and pray that all three would be helped to resist temptation. At this point, the taxi driver's wife always wondered what temptations Milo wanted to resist. In her eyes he was the perfect man. She wished that her Bob possessed Milo's strength and conviction. Imagine being married to a man with a Queen's medal, a man who did so much good, a man who could stand up to the members of the Reading Club, instead of peering shyly at them through a window.

Sometimes Milo asked them to pray for the people they had talked about. The taxi driver was always prepared to do this for members of the Reading Club. He wanted to see them as basically good men, despite their few imperfections. He would often add a small request to speed up his membership. His wife, however, was reluctant to add her amen. She would bow her head out of respect for Milo, but asking forgiveness for these guys was out of the question. She had her own suggestion for the 'Almighty' and it was not a very gracious one.

'Sorry, no time for a prayer. We'll do it next time. God bless,' Milo said as he left.

CHAPTER 5

Discussing the Anniversary Book

A few weeks before the final date for submissions, Dr. Thomas van Aken had received several pieces of writing, which he had edited and returned to the authors for approval; all except one, which he kept back. Everyone agreed with his amendments. He forwarded the copies to his brother Antonius for his inspection, before they met at Sint Jan's Abbey to make initial plans for the Anniversary Book.

Thomas had retired a few years ago from his executive literary position, but whenever he was confronted with any form of writing, he automatically donned his editor's hat, switched on his internal scanner and sharpened his critical pencil. Antonius had witnessed this every time they discussed a piece of writing, whether it was during the gestation period of 'Priests Dying' – what a painful pregnancy that turned out to be – or when they were looking at the submissions to their writing project, which was now in its third year. Whenever his brother's 'internal editor' was switched on, Antonius received a small lecture, which he had heard in different guises many times before.

'As you know,' Thomas began, 'I've long held the belief that some good writing remains unpublished. It is hidden in the form of letters, notes and email messages, which are only ever read by the recipients or, in the case of journals and diaries, by their writers.'

'You told me you read that in that American book about editing. Who wrote it?'

'Betsy Lerner. Please don't interrupt.'

Holding the pages of the Anniversary Book together, Thomas tapped the ends on the table several times and continued. 'Our writing project is designed to give those secret writers an opportunity to have their work published.'

'Spare me your usual lecture,' said Antonius, pretending to plead.

'Certainly not, I need to remind you,' said Thomas. He put down the pages, then raised himself up in his chair and looked at his brother. 'As an editor I've always been hoping to chance upon an eloquent, elegant, well-crafted piece of prose or poetry; a fine specimen of literary writing.'

Antonius sighed, 'You must have said that every time we've reviewed any writing project material.'

Thomas ignored the comment. 'When you told me about the background of this Reading Club and some of the novels which they'd read, I felt optimistic that we'd be sent some literary gems; perhaps a fine autobiographical piece or an original, illuminating, insightful reflection. Perhaps something will turn up before the last submission day.'

'I think there're some good pieces,' said Antonius cheerfully.

Thomas stood up and walked around the small room in the abbey where confrères could entertain their guests. He looked out of the window onto a cobbled courtyard, which was overseen by a life-sized, sad-faced Christ, hanging on a thin cross. Thomas hated that Christian symbol. He wondered again why his brother had chosen such an awful way of life. He continued:

'Apart from a few snippets, the contributions are disappointing. These fellows have not used the opportunities we've given them. No-one has been brave enough to reveal something important about himself; for example, no-one has mentioned his childhood, a loved one, a lost one.'

Antonius interrupted, 'You're wrong. Paul Bazelman writes about his dead mother, and Titus Dekker tells about his father. And of course Milo has described that incident.'

'Correction,' said Thomas sharply, 'Paul doesn't write about his mother, but about the contents of her trinket box. I wonder if he followed the suggestions for keeping a journal. If so, he could surely have found something more significant to write about. Do these guys lead such uninteresting lives?'

'I think his descriptions are very poignant. It made me think about what will be left when I die,' Antonius said.

'Don't be so morbid. And you're wrong about what Titus wrote. He described his coat of many colours, which was made from his father's old clothes. Apart from the details of some of the dead man's things, there's nothing about the man himself.'

Antonius shifted in his chair. Was this going to be a difficult meeting?

Thomas continued, 'Animals feature a lot in the writing: a bulldog, a damselfly, a toad, even a group of animals discussing the book, 'Animal Farm'. One could form the impression that these fellows are veterinary surgeons or zoologists.'

'Perhaps their stories are metaphorical?' said Antonius.

'If they are, they're disguising their experiences so carefully that no-one else could grasp the underlying meanings.'

'How do you know?' Antonius asked, but was ignored. Thomas glanced up at the crucifix again.

'The books they've read have failed to inform their writing. There's nothing truly autobiographical, no reflection on a life or a death, nothing romantic, no hint of a philosophical idea; religious or political beliefs. It's all superficial. Hans van den Elsen jokes about the club members, makes out they're animals.'

'That's funny,' Antonius grinned.

'It tried to be. Why didn't he give a straightforward account of what happens between the members at their meetings? He's probably an astute observer – yet we were deprived of any intelligent commentary.'

Antonius chuckled. 'I could imagine them all as different animals arriving at their club. Arrogant Pig with a book under each trotter – Intelligent Crow explaining 'Animal Farm' – Pompous Peacock with his vibrating feathers. Critical Toad could have been a description of you, Thomas.'

Thomas ignored his brother. Changing the subject, he continued, 'I had to work very hard to make the stories readable.'

'You've done a great job, Thomas,' said Antonius with a smile, as he remembered the other animals in the long poem called 'The Dutch Barn Reading Club'.

'Joost Kuijpers, the professional artist, failed to tell us about his techniques and inspirations,' Thomas continued.

'But he described how portrait painters flatter their subjects.'

'Most people are aware of that. He didn't tell us how he painted.'

'He wrote about the portrait of a woman.'

'Yes. He included a picture of her. I thought she looked a bit strange. I wanted to know more about how he works.'

'Yes I agree,' Antonius said, 'I wanted to read more about the man himself. I once saw some of his landscapes at an exhibition – variations on the theme of the industrial greenhouse.'

Thomas replied immediately, 'Why didn't he express his anger about what has happened to our pastures, which are covered with glass factories and our meadow flowers which are disappearing?'

'Hans van den Elsen wrote about the greenhouses,' said Antonius.

'Yes, but he didn't become angry about their by-products, such as the light pollution and the excessive carbon dioxide. He stated that the greenhouses are a great asset to our economy.'

'You have sufficient anger for everyone. We didn't suggest that these fellows write academic essays. I think you're very hard on them,' Antonius replied. 'You've read so much mediocre writing from professional writers that it's deadened your appreciation of what amateurs can do.'

Thomas sat down with a bump on the well-polished visitor's

chair and finished his cold coffee, and then he ran both hands across his shaved head.

'Listen Thomas,' said Antonius, 'these may be mature men, successful in their own professions, but that doesn't mean this was an easy task for them. You'll never find that great piece of literature you're always searching for; that's like looking for a Beethoven concerto in the pop section of a music shop. These are amateurs. You're being unfair.'

'Unfair, fair! Why do you always have to assess everything via your fairness filter?'

'My dear brother, you've always been a hard man,' Antonius said.

'My hardness, as you call it, means that people are clear about my professional opinion. I will not say something is good if I think it can be improved. I do not collude with those writers who want me to heap praise upon their shoulders, when I don't consider their work praiseworthy.'

'There's no need to shout.' Antonius remembered some of his brother's harsh comments about the first chapter of 'Priests Dying'.

Thomas continued, 'Have you already forgotten that it was through my so-called hardness, that the idea for your book was conceived? And later, with that same hardness, I transformed your writing from being a recital of nonsense, written in a long-winded style, into a sensitive, intelligent, unique autobiography, which became a best-seller.'

'I've always given you full credit for that. I know that you made a fine book out of my muddled words.' Antonius resisted the urge to reach out and touch his brother's hand.

'Don't tell me that editors are unsuccessful writers or poets, looking for their own dreams in the creation of others.'

'I've never said that to you; I never would,' said Antonius, 'I saw what you did to my work, yours is a much underrated profession. I know that the published writers get all the glory and the editor barely gets a mention. Thomas, why are you so angry? Your sharp wit has disappeared and in its place you are wielding a verbal axe.'

Thomas recognised this aspect of his personality. He had been told before that he was hard. Yes, that was one way of describing his honesty and directness. Previous staff and other editors had experienced the sharpness of his comments, but he was consistent, fair and honest; some thanked him for those qualities. He realised that his brother – this kind, sympathetic, understanding priest, gifted teacher, patient journal writer and loyal member of a Religious Order, which had abused and undervalued him – was a better person than he could ever be. However, Thomas was aware of a fault line in these strata of fine qualities, which was hidden beneath his brother's saintly exterior. It was his irrational, unpredictable temper. He had experienced it several times and was frequently wounded by what his brother said. Thomas blamed the Church for what he described as a punishing formation. He believed that when Antonius felt under pressure, it was as if his tiny curtained boyhood cell was being invaded. No-one was allowed in and when people came too close he defended himself with words as sharp as knives.

When Thomas visited the abbey they did not go to his brother's room; instead, they met in the bleak oak-lined visitor's room, which was next-door to what was grandly called the Chapel of Rest. This was a plain room with dark panelling, just like the one they were in. It was where the dead confrères waited, still and cold in their coffins, for their funeral and burial services. Apparently that same morning, the body of senile Father Theo, aged 96, had rested there, prior to his last journey. On the brothers' arrival at the visitor's room, one of the women from the kitchen had brought them each a piece of left-over funeral cake (which Thomas complained always tasted liked sweet foam rubber) to have with their coffee.

Thomas rebuffed the accusation that his sharp wit had disappeared. He noticed immediately that the texture of his brother's skin had become waxy and he appeared to have shrunk a little.

He said, 'It's you, you're softer than usual. You're finding everything of a low standard acceptable.' Thomas looked up again at the crucifix on the wall.

'What does it matter if these men have not achieved the standard you expect?' Antonius said.

'Of course it matters, this is what the whole project has been about. I encouraged you to be open and honest in 'Priests Dying'. The result was personal writing which the readers liked,' said Thomas tapping his fingers on the table.

Antonius felt a sharp pain in his abdomen. 'Let's not argue; life's too short.'

'I've always been angry, that's how I've got things done,' Thomas said.

'I know, but you're more so today.'

'No I'm not. It's you. You're the one who's different. Is there something you're not telling me?' said Thomas, looking at his brother.

'You'd like me to say I've found a girlfriend at last.' Antonius wondered why he had said that.

'Don't try to joke; I gave up hope a long time ago that you'd experience the torments and ravages of falling in love. And don't give me that shit about loving God – you know that I think it's nonsense.'

'Please don't swear... I wouldn't dare bring God into our conversations,' said Antonius with a small grin.

'You don't have to; he's sitting on your shoulder every time we meet.'

Antonius had lost his anger towards his brother's attitude a long time ago. Thomas's persistent rational approach to life once aggravated him; now he only felt sadness that his brother had no alternative way of experiencing the world.

'Be serious for a moment,' said Thomas more quietly. 'Is there something you're not telling me?'

Antonius sighed, 'I'm nearly eighty. I repeat myself in writing and in speaking. I forget things. I can't remember when I get to a place why I've gone there. I think it's called senility. I'm taking after our grandmother. My bowels continue to dictate my life.

Apart from that, I'm fine. When there are any changes, you'll be the first to know. Shall we continue?'

Thomas sighed, and said, 'By adding, subtracting and replacing a few words, whilst not doing anything to change the meaning, I think I've improved every piece of writing. All the writers have approved my suggestions.'

'I think you've done a wonderful job. Did you notice how many anonymous contributions there were? I'm not sure that we should have given them this option.'

'I don't agree,' said Thomas. 'It has allowed a few the freedom to write something which they might not have otherwise done, had they written under their own names. What's more, they will have some fun guessing who wrote what. I like the idea, and since we said they could have that option, we can hardly withdraw it now.'

Finally, they arrived at Milo's account of his dismissal from the abbey. Thomas had read it several times, but held back on editing. He guessed that Antonius would feel uneasy about what had been written. He was mindful of the statement which they agreed a few years ago and which appeared on the website along with the writing instructions. It read:

'Writing which refers to people or institutions in a way which we consider insulting, offensive or damaging will not be published'.

The brothers had agreed to include this caveat after they received a story which included an allegation of abuse against a priest. At the time, Thomas argued that this restriction would inhibit writers. He reminded Antonius that he wrote freely in his autobiography.

'We don't want to make this project into a repository for complaints and allegations of abuse against the Church; there are appropriate places for that information,' Antonius had said. 'While I think it is important that past and present grievances are dealt with openly and fairly, we risk becoming involved in serious, time consuming issues, if we encourage disclosures which then require investigation. It is complicated enough having to deal with difficult information; if we then print it, we risk destroying our project. Once we are told about a sensitive issue, we have to pass it on to the civil authorities. The days when the Church kept quiet about abuse are over. Thank goodness.'

'I'm pleased that at last your Church is taking some responsibility for its past atrocities, but I don't feel I have a duty to pass on information which is sent to me in trust,' Thomas said.

'Not even a moral duty?' Antonius asked, knowing these words would irritate his brother.

As an atheist, Thomas had always been keen to demonstrate that it was not necessary to believe in God in order to be a moral person.

Thomas ignored his brother's remark and asked, 'What shall we do about Milo's story? I don't think you will want to print it in the Anniversary Book.'

'Probably not. It could be damaging, but also something happened much later which Milo obviously did not know about. This is a difficult decision. Let me read it again before I decide.'

Milo had written:

The abbey bell had just struck 10.00pm, the lights were out and it was quiet, but not silent in our chilly dormitory. A thin cloud of blue tobacco smoke lingered over my cell, temporarily masking the resident odours of boys' urine and abbey cleaning fluid. Brother Petrus, our night-time guardian, had finished smoking his pipe and was asleep in his ancient folding bed in the nearby stairwell. He had removed both of his hearing aids for the night and his slow audible breathing, and occasional other noises, told those who were still awake that he was very much asleep. Most of the sixty boys in their cubicles were also deep in slumber; some in silence, others making their own night-time sounds.

I was finding it difficult to sleep, my feet were cold and my mind was alert. I fumbled under my pillow to find my torch. We

220

were allowed to have torches, but only so that we could see to use the pots beneath our beds. Reading or writing by torch light was not permitted. Undertaking schoolwork in the dormitory was forbidden, as it had to be completed in the study hall. Boys were not permitted in each other's cells. This had been impressed on parents when they first brought their sons to the seminary, and regularly said to us. Brother Petrus's main function at night was to ensure that we adhered to the night-time rules. I had never been into another boy's cell and never had anyone visit mine. However, it was obvious that some boys took the risk, that without his hearing aids, the old brother would not be aware of their movements and whispers when they visited their friends. Those still awake could hear the floorboards creaking when someone left his bed and crept along the passageway to enter another cell.

Since I could hear that Brother Petrus was asleep, I took the chance and switched on my torch beneath my bedclothes and I shone it on a small card, bearing the face of Saint Joseph on one side and information about him in Spanish on the reverse. This was not really such a risk, because I knew I would be able to hear if Petrus was 'on guard' by the noises from his ancient bed as he got out of it. Although reading at night was considered to be breaking the rules, I did not consider it a sin because I was talking to a saint. I decided when I first came to the school, nearly two years ago, that I would not take this activity to confession.

As I lay there looking at the holy face and silently and humbly asking him if he would do something about my cold feet, I became aware that two of my fellow seminarians were whispering together in the cell next to mine. I have always had very good hearing, so it was possible to tune into what they were saying. Even though they were talking very quietly, I knew who they were and that they were talking about the extra Latin lessons which Father Xavier was giving them.

Anton Sitsen, who was the visitor, was asking Martin Brinkhoff, the cell's resident, what he did in these extra lessons. At this point I was curious because my Latin was not especially good and I wondered why I had not been chosen for extra lessons. At first, I was jealous of these two boys for the additional attention that they were receiving. But then I heard Martin reply that the priest often touched him in places he did not like. I was shocked. He also said he was too frightened to tell anyone.

The two boys stopped talking, probably because Brother Petrus had ceased snoring and his bed was creaking, which signalled he was getting up. Then, making a sound like a cart horse relieving itself on the hard stable floor, Petrus peed into his pot, sighed and replaced it back in its storage space, then got back into his bed. The boys said no more and I heard the visitor move the curtain and creep back to his own cell.

By then I was wide awake and trying to visualise what happened in the extra Latin lessons. I thought about what Martin said about being touched in places he didn't like. What did he mean? I thought of some places where I would not like to be touched by Father Xavier and decided the worst place would be on my 'special member'. I touched myself there and tried to imagine how it would feel to have someone else's fingers around my genitals. That did not really work, because it just felt nice to touch myself, although I knew it was considered a sin and that we were expected to confess our sins. Was that where Martin was touched? Could it be that Father Xavier was the one committing the sin? Surely, I thought, priests do not do sins. I became confused, reached into my pyjamas, and touched myself again for comfort.

At 7.15 the next morning, I was in the confessional box. A priest sat at the other side of the screen and I began by saying that I had sinned because I listened to a private conversation about Father Xavier. I repeated Martin's words about being touched. I made the mistake of explaining that I wondered what would be the worst place for me in that sense. Then I confessed that I had touched my 'private parts' to see how it felt. There was a long silence from the other side of the screen. I could not tell whether the father was angry or shocked. After what seemed to be like several minutes silence, the priest told me to say three 'Holy Marys'. He also told me not to repeat my story to anyone and in future sleep with my hands above the sheets.

Two days later, I was summoned to the Principal's study. To my surprise my mother was there, dressed in black. Her hat was tilted too much to one side and in her hand she was holding a screwed-up handkerchief. At first I thought she had come to bring me some bad news about a member of my family. Had someone died? Looking straight ahead and slightly upwards, the Principal said that my mother would be taking me home, because I did not have the qualities required for study. He highlighted my Latin and added that he did not think that I had the capacity to keep the priestly vows of chastity, poverty, obedience and stability. He added that he was sure that I could find other ways of serving God. He said that he would pray for my family and me. Having made the sign of the cross in the air, he ushered us out of his room.

I looked at my mother, but she did not meet my gaze. She gave me a suitcase and told me to collect my things from the cell while she waited. I told her that I did not understand why this had happened, but she ignored me and repeated her instructions. I walked out of the school and across the playground to the residential building, up the stairs and into the dormitory, to my cell, which had been my bedroom for the past two years. In my mind, I was going over what the Principal had said and wondered what he had meant by my Latin and the priestly vows, which he said I would not be able to keep. I wondered how he could tell.

In the dormitory, Brother Petrus was going about his usual business of sweeping the floors and emptying the chamber pots. He did not see me as I entered my cubicle, opened the cupboard, removed my clothes and treasures, and put them into the case. I retrieved my torch and picture of St Joseph from underneath my pillow. After closing the case, I took a final look at the familiar bed, chair and cupboard. I would never return.

Brother Petrus was in the corridor and he asked me why I was not in school and what was in my case. I told him that I was leaving and when he asked why, tears filled my eyes; a sorrow pierced my heart, as the reality of my dismissal registered. Holding my hands up to my face, uncontrollable sobs came from me. Then I felt his embrace. He pulled me towards him and held me against his huge, firm, round belly. This was the first time that a confrère had reached out to comfort me. He patted my back gently and told me that there were other good schools to go to and other jobs, which were better than being a priest. Then, as if realising he was on the verge of breaking a rule himself, he held my upper arms and moved me away from his belly, so that there was a distance between us. After a final tap on my head, he told me that Saint Joseph would be my guide and I would have a good life. He said good bye, lifted up the bucket of pee, turned around and disappeared into a cell.

My mother's brother had a car and he was waiting in the school car park to drive us the forty kilometres home. I was given one of my father's clean white handkerchiefs and told to wipe my face and stop crying. No-one said anything to me on the journey and I was too frightened to talk in front of my uncle. I spent two days helping in the house, trying to get my mother's attention and my father's approval. On the morning of the third day, my mother told me that I would be going to live with my grandparents during the week, because there was a good school near their house. She packed up a case for me and my uncle drove me to the village where my grandparents lived. I went to the nearby school, where I did well with my lessons. After graduating from school, I went onto university and studied anthropology. My mother died when I was thirty. Had I remained at the seminary, I would have been ordained and helping in a parish by that time. Later, my mother's brother told me that the Principal of the seminary asked my mother not to repeat to me what he had said to her. The reason for my exclusion was that I had invented a story to disgrace a priest and two of my fellow students. The reputation of the Order was paramount. I was very angry and felt that I had been unjustly treated.

Both the brothers reread Milo's story and agreed it was a tragic tale, which had been well written. Thomas agreed that it was too explicit for the Anniversary Book. Antonius explained that allegations about this incident were later investigated. Apparently the two boys had made up the story about being touched by the priest, to tease their class mates. This whole business was a great embarrassment to the abbey school. Antonius agreed that the episode must have been devastating for Milo and others like him who experienced serious consequences because of what they overheard. The Principal at the time had handled the situation badly by assuming that Milo invented his story, and he failed to talk to the two boys who had caused the trouble. Incomplete records were kept, so it was unclear to the investigators which boys had been unjustly dismissed. Milo never received an apology from the school. During the investigation, Father Xavier was transferred to another abbey where, after a few weeks, he died of a heart attack. One year later he was officially exonerated.

Antonius said that he would write a letter to Milo, since he considered it would be inappropriate to convey their decision via email. As he did not have his address, he sent the letter in a sealed envelope to Piet van Rijn, asking him to forward it. Piet was informed by letter that they were not going to use Milo's story and that they had suggested that he submit something else.

There was still a little time left for Milo to write something else and for Thomas to receive a fine literary piece of his dreams, from someone in the Reading Club.

Piet was surprised to receive the letters from Father Antonius. As he was in the middle of painting the scene at the back of the warehouse, he put both of them in the tray containing a heap of unanswered correspondence. He would deal with them later.

CHAPTER 6

Meeting of the Reading Club

Tonight's meeting was in the back of Bert's *Wijnwinkel*. The members gathered around the great oak table where Bert had sat to do his writing. In the centre were two empty port bottles and a large platter containing the remains of a fine selection of cheese. They had been discussing a book by a Dutch writer, which was recommended by Paul Bazelman. He preferred serious literature and considered himself a fine critic. Opinions varied as to its merits; some described it as heavy reading and at times difficult to follow, while others enjoyed the book and found it thought provoking. An interesting discussion followed about what makes a best-seller. They agreed the arrangements for the next meeting. Huub looked at his watch and Titus took that as a sign that the meeting should close.

'Have we finished?' Titus asked, and everyone nodded. 'Thanks Bert, for your hospitality. Exquisite port!'

Piet raised his hand. 'This is a reminder, Gentlemen, about the Anniversary Book. I know many of you have already sent off your work and it has been edited. For those who haven't, I am reminding you that all entries must be sent to Thomas, our editor, by next Monday. If you want me to post your work, I need to have it by Thursday.'

Piet spoke with some authority. No-one would have guessed that he had not yet written anything himself. He had made a few attempts. His wife offered to help him. The taxi driver gave him a piece of his own writing as a suggestion. But as yet, Piet had done nothing. Nothing! He had just a day to produce something. The letters from Father Antonius were still in his correspondence tray.

'Piet, it was a good idea of yours to invite Father Antonius to our Anniversary meeting. I have enjoyed following his suggestion to keep a journal. He's got me writing,' Paul said.

'Written something good for the book?' Huub asked.

'I'll let others be the judge of that. I've learnt a lot. I feel like a new person,' Paul said.

'Are you going to tell us what you've written?' Titus asked.

'I don't know what the rest of you did, but a lot of my stuff's private,' Paul said.

'Tell us your secrets,' said Hans, biting on the side of his finger. Perhaps he was remembering seeing Paul in Venus's black silk. 'Have you discovered another side of yourself?'

'I see now why the journals are private. It was like getting a load off my mind, I've lightened my soul,' Paul smiled.

'My God, Paul, that sounds as if you took yourself to confession. Antonius will be very proud of you.'

'Yes, that's what it was like, confession,' Paul agreed.

'Has Venus noticed the change?'

'Certainly. We've been to Paris to celebrate. Ask no more!'

Everyone laughed, apart from Hans who continued to nibble at the edge of his nail.

'I cried at some things I wrote,' Bert said, and several of the men looked at him with surprise. They were unaccustomed to the wine merchant being so open. 'I felt relieved after I had finished writing.'

'What did you write about?'

'This table,' Bert said as he stroked the section in front of him, 'and the people who've sat round it.'

Everyone looked down at the table; some felt the top, others ran their hands along the side.

'There's some writing here,' Huub said, bending over to look along the side of the table, 'I can't make out what it says.'

'There're lots of names and initials, especially underneath. They're difficult to see in this light.'

Then Huub said, 'I wrote about some personal things.'

'A love story, is it Huub?' Hans joked.

'You think I don't know about love? Just wait and see.'

'What about you, Hans?'

'I've written about all of you. The story of the Reading Club; with a difference.'

'Nothing personal?' someone asked.

Hans became serious. 'Yes,' he said, 'I wrote a lot, but I'm not including that in the book. Yes, personal stuff. I can't say I felt better; it just worked as a distraction during some difficult times.'

'Did you cry?' Huub asked.

'In a way.'

'Milo, can we expect a prayer or two from you?'

'No, I have written about an experience I had when I was at the seminary.'

'Nothing else?' Piet asked.

'I think that's plenty. It's a long story.'

'I thought you'd write about your favourite saint. What's his name?' Titus asked.

'Or even give us a little sermon,' Paul said.

Milo looked serious. Paul had overstepped the mark, even if he was joking.

'So we are all better men now we have made our confessions and shed some tears,' Milo said with a certain edge to his voice.

'Not a better person. I think I understand myself more.' Joost stroked his moustache. Was he remembering his unhappy days in the Protestant school?

'I definitely feel a better person,' Paul said with confidence.

'We can look forward to a less critical, kinder, more generous, open and understanding Paul Bazelman, can we?' Milo said.

'Yes, I think so,' Paul said with hesitation, 'what are you implying?'

'Let's wait and see how this improvement will show itself.' Milo folded his arms, suggesting that he knew something more than he was saying.

'Show itself? It's already shown itself. I've just told you.'

'In actions and attitudes? That's what I'm talking about,' Milo said.

'Don't be so pompous, Milo. I've just told you I found the writing very helpful. Maybe it didn't work like that for you. Perhaps you think you can't get any better.'

Titus looked uncomfortable at the last comment. This conversation was getting out of hand. It was time to finish the meeting. In two months' time it was their tenth anniversary gathering and already he had planned how he would organise the evening. He did not want any disputes. Having submitted his contribution, he now wondered if it would be good enough for the booklet. It was hardly the description of a life-changing event. There was not time to do anything else now. It was too late. What he had written would have to do. He wondered what had happened to Paul. What could have changed his life, and would they notice, because he seemed just the same as usual. 'Let's finish now,' Titus said. 'Remember that the brothers only want your final pieces, not all your journal writing.'

'Thank God for that!' someone sighed.

After the meeting, Titus and Joost walked home together.

'What was Milo talking about?' Titus asked.

'God knows.'

'Did you feel different after the journal writing?'

'Not exactly.' Joost was about to say more, but Titus interrupted him:

'I worked bloody hard, writing each day. I followed the instructions and suggestions. Yes, I think I'm a better person now. I think I understand myself better. I've never been to confession. But all that writing, I suppose it was a bit like that.'

Joost had stopped to look in the window of a small art gallery. He was always keen to see what other artists in his town were producing. 'Yes, probably,' he said.

As the two men lingered by the gallery window, Piet joined them. 'Good meeting?' he said.

'What was Milo going on about?' Titus asked.

'He's upset because the brothers have rejected his piece of writing,' Piet said.

'What?'

'It named names.'

'How do you know?'

'They told me. He was asked to write something else,' Piet said with a small measure of stolen authority.

Titus and Joost looked at each other in disbelief, and then they looked at Piet.

'What did he write about?' Joost asked.

'When he was thrown out of the seminary. Something to do with abuse. Antonius was his teacher.'

'That would have been embarrassing for the priest – and us! Imagine insulting a special guest in that way. The man's a fool. Thank God they refused it.'

As if keen to change the subject in case he got in a muddle with the facts of his story, Piet asked, 'I didn't see your work. What did you send in, Joost?'

'A piece about a portrait,' Joost said, feeling thankful that he had not chosen anything which might have been rejected.

'And you, Titus?'

'The coat my mother made.'

'Sounds good.'

'You Piet. What did you write about? '

'I'm still deciding.' Without shaking hands, Piet turned away from them and crossed the road where the taxi was waiting.

'He's leaving it a bit late.'

'Do you think he's written anything?'

'Who knows?'

Joost and Titus continued along the *Waterstraat* and stopped on the corner.

'I like the Reading Club. Even when Milo goes on a bit, Huub moans and Hans jokes too much, I still enjoy being with those fellows. It's special.'

'Yes,' said Joost as he reached out and shook Titus's hand.

'Tot ziens (see you).'

CHAPTER 7

Bad News

A few days after his visit to the specialist, Antonius wrote:

This is the first time I have felt like writing since I received the results of the tests on my irritable bowels, two days ago. The doctor told me that my condition was serious and inoperable. I did not anticipate my reaction. This is not what I planned.

During my years of administering to the sick and dying, I had ample opportunity to observe others facing death. Many are numbed by bad news given by a doctor. It is usually a temporary feeling, which is replaced by one or a mixture of the following: a determination to prove the physician is wrong; a fear that a painful death will follow; an anger that the world will go on without them; a feeling of being cheated; a regret at things which have been done and not done; or a decision to die with dignity even though it has eluded them in life. Initially, very few rejoice at the thought of meeting their Maker. This sometimes comes later, especially with very old folk who are weary of living. Becoming accustomed to the bad news may take a while. Some decide that they want to ensure their financial affairs are in order, including arranging for their loved ones to be cared for. Others want to throw away things that will be of no use to inheritors or dispose of private letters or mementoes which they would not like anyone to see, even after their death.

Mention God and the Last Rites too soon and some people will be angry. At such times a few lose their faith, while others find theirs. I have seen many different attitudes. Consequently, I have had plenty of opportunities to choose how I wanted to behave, if ever I was given fatal news. My plan was to be discreet, careful and calm. I would look forward to the next life and appreciate the one that was ending.

How arrogant it was to think I would automatically assume these feelings. I did not manage any of the reactions which I planned. Although I behaved in a calm way on the telephone to my brother, that was an act, a thin façade, concealing strong feelings of anger and fear of being alone. I felt bitter. I had no wife, no children, no partner, nor any relations to be with me for support when hearing the prognosis. No-one was there to share this burden, not even the Church; after all I have done for her. I could die tomorrow and my fellow confrères would hardly be affected by my death.

Antonius telephoned his brother:

'You are phoning at a very inconvenient time. It's the middle of the News.'

'Sorry, I have some news of my own.'

'Can't it wait?'

'I want to tell you now. You will soon be able to burn those exercise books containing my journals.'

No-one else would have understood what that message meant, but Thomas did. He knew that Antonius was referring to a conversation which they had several years ago. Thomas had asked his brother why he was keeping all his old journals, which he had written since he was twelve. Thomas said that when Antonius was dead the journals would probably be burnt and that it would be better to use them as a basis for a book about his life. Thomas knew exactly what the message meant.

'What's wrong with you?'

'I really am a priest dying.'

'What's wrong?'

'A large tumour in my colon.'

'For Christ's sake brother, leave that bloody abbey and come home.'

'Please don't blaspheme. The abbey is my home.'

'You know what I mean. Come to my home. We'll look after you.'

'Thanks for the offer. The abbey cares quite well for its dying priests.'

'Don't talk like that. We'll get a second opinion.'

'I've already had one. I've promised to talk at that tenth anniversary.'

'Don't be a bloody martyr.'

'It's my training.'

'Don't be so bloody obstinate. I want to come and see you.'

'You're not usually in a rush to see me.'

'You've not always been an easy man to visit.'

'So why do you want to come now?'

'You're my brother, for Christ's sake.'

'I don't like swearing.'

'God, you're such a bloody hypocrite!'

'Don't swear!'

Thomas slammed down the phone.

Once it is known that a priest is dying, he is moved, along with his possessions, to the nursing wing of the abbey, to stay with the other ailing old boys. There the rooms are small and usually not large enough to comfortably accommodate all that the sick confrères have accumulated during their lives. Possessions are squeezed into the room by double parking books and treasures and by stacking them from floor to ceiling in a way which makes most of their stuff inaccessible. Things which cannot be shelved or stacked are stored away in cardboard boxes which sit in the basement, gathering dust until their owner dies. Then a relative or one of the confrères sorts through the possessions for anything worth keeping. Superfluous books are auctioned, letters or journals of relevance are added to personal files in the abbey archives and the rest is tossed away.

Frequently the occupants of the sick-rooms require space-taking medical equipment to sustain their lives. Consequently, these rooms can become cluttered. Some take on the appearance of second-hand book or junk shops or over-full and disorganised storage containers. On entering such rooms, it is sometimes difficult to locate the occupants in between their redundant treasures and medical paraphernalia. The inmates ironically call this place 'death row'. Antonius wrote:

I do not want to end my days in 'Death Row'. Nor do I want one of the confrères to look through my few personal possessions and decide what to keep and what to throw away. I will do that myself. This morning I found a number of letters from Wilhelmina, which I had tucked between the pages of my journal from 1990. I will have to decide what to do about this correspondence.

Some confrères had special friends, with whom they shared private relationships. These were quite different from those which existed between the inhabitants of the abbey and unlike the bond which these men had with their relatives. These special friendships, apart from generating a feeling of affection which had been discouraged from the age of twelve, also provided a kind of status for these confrères who lacked the material trappings against which ordinary men are often measured. Amongst these humble fellows, there was a little harmless boasting. Many received visitors – family, friends from religious organisations, ex-pupils and former parishioners. However, there was another group which did not make an appearance; they were alluded to by the subtle use of the first person plural pronoun. When talking about a holiday experience, instead of saying, 'I toured the island on a hired bike', the 'I' would be replaced by 'we', suggesting a holiday companion or even a private friend. A few referred to their escorts by name. It was rumoured that several had imaginary holiday chums. It was not so much stepping over the boundaries of their vows, but more giving them a gentle nudge. The close friend would have to be an unnamed female; no-one would want to give the impression that they had homosexual tendencies – they wanted to be seen as heterosexual celibates.

Antonius had a female friend but he neither told anyone nor gave a hint that she existed. In that way he was a private man. He had heard the gossip about others who had dropped hints that they had companions, but he did not like that. Not even Thomas knew about Wilhelmina, who had been on holiday with her husband Frank when they first met Antonius in 1982. His friendship with the couple had grown and for the following five years he holidayed with them by renting the cottage next to theirs. This arrangement gave each person both privacy and freedom. They could go off in threes, in twos, or be alone. Sometimes Wilhelmina and Antonius walked the beach while Frank cooked a meal. It was an easy relationship and Antonius enjoyed their discussions in which he felt safe to express his views away from the ears of the abbey or the opinions of his atheist brother. He selected a notebook in which he had written the following account:

This evening Frank and I talked while Wilhelmina did the washing-up. I offered several times to help, but she refused. I noticed that Frank never volunteered to help his wife, nor did he speak to her or seek her opinion once she had started her knitting.

Frank began, 'I think it was in the sixties that I realised that I wasn't a Christian. I was a Catholic, yes, because I'd been baptised, we'd been married and we went regularly to Mass, but inside me there was nothing connected to God.'

The regular tapping of the metal needles continued. The knitter did not look up and it was if the clicking gave a message that the she did not want to be involved in this conversation. I glanced at Wilhelmina with her agile fingers, but she did not look at me.

Frank went on, 'I was more interested in looking after my family, children, parents, in-laws, developing my business and improving my house and garden, than in going to church.'

I appreciated Frank's openness, and I wished that there was some way of involving Wilhelmina in this discussion, but the tapping of her knitting-needles deterred me from trying to include her. I didn't really want to be talking about faith, I was on holiday, but I responded to please Frank.

'I think there's a difference between Christianity and the Church,' I said, aware that I could make this into a lecture or a sermon, if I was not careful. I had witnessed some of my confrères doing this in social situations and I had felt embarrassment on their behalf. I glanced at Wilhelmina; a long glance.

'What do you mean?' Frank asked.

'This is only my view, not the view of the Church. Christianity to me is about my internal relationship with Christ. The Church is the result of 2000 years of interpretations and interferences, the misunderstanding of men believing they understood that relationship – of men taking a God-like stance, thinking they knew what God wanted, when in my opinion that will always be a mystery.'

'How can you remain a priest if you don't believe in your Church?' Frank asked.

The clicking of the needles continued. Wilhelmina had beautiful hands. Occasionally there would be a pause when she came to the end of a row, she reversed the knitting and went back the other way. I wondered what she was thinking. Could she block out this conversation and have her own separate thoughts or was she listening and later would have a conversation with Frank in the privacy of their bedroom?

'I have struggled with that question for many years,' I said. 'Eventually I borrowed some ideas from a Danish philosopher, *Sören Kierkegaard.*

'Never heard of him,' Frank said.

'He believed that man is part of the natural world, but he has an inner relationship with God which sets him apart from other living things. This inner world is not explainable.'

Frank was obviously not satisfied. 'Why shouldn't the inner world be scientifically explainable?' he said, shifting his position in the old sofa where he always sat.

'I believe it's unexplainable,' I said, wondering whether Wilhelmina had her own thoughts about this subject.

'Surely it's better to know as much as we can?'

'There are lots of things in our lives which are unknown. The future's unknown,' I said.

'I don't think so. We can predict things, measure them. Lots of things are designed and work on predictions,' Frank said. For a moment Wilhelmina glanced at him, as if that statement had a special meaning for them.

'We live our lives forwards but only understand them backwards,' I said.

'That sounds very philosophical.'

'We live our lives in relation to God and God is unknown, unknowable.' This time Wilhelmina glanced at me. I sensed her disapproval. Maybe I was sounding too much the priest. I wondered what she really thought about me.

Frank continued, 'Surely this is just avoiding the issue...when you apply reason to the question of God's existence, there're no satisfactory answers.'

'I believe there are no universal answers,' I said. This reminded me of the conversations I had with my brother when he ridiculed my ideas and asked me why I remained a priest.

'So how do you know what the truth is?' Frank said.

Did I imagine it or had the speed of the knitting increased? Was the clicking expressing an anxiety about the path of this discussion?

I said, 'That's the oldest question. For me it's been important to find a truth which is true for me, a truth which I'm willing to live and die for.'

'Antonius, that sounds very grand, even arrogant. How can you live with your conscience and still remain in a Catholic institution?'

At this question, Wilhelmina put down her knitting on the table and went into the kitchen. I could hear her opening the fridge door and shutting cupboards. She made a lot of noise, but Frank seemed not to notice. I wondered if I had said something to upset her. For some reason I felt nervous. I was suddenly aware of this social situation and its significance to me. I realised the closeness which I felt towards these people, or was it just for one of them? It was unsettling, so I took refuge in my priest's position and continued to talk in a manner which was verging on preaching.

'Opinions aren't so important as how you live by them. The human condition is such that none of us can achieve the ideal moral life. It's unobtainable. We're not perfect and I agree with the Church that we're all sinners.' I must have sounded pompous. That was not my usual way.

'I always get angry when someone accuses me of being a sinner,' Frank said, undeterred by my unnecessarily authoritative manner.

However, I knew Wilhelmina had recognised my clumsy arrogance. There was silence in the kitchen and I wondered was she about to re-enter the room and express a point of view? But she did not return.

'I think we all need help to become ideal. I think it's God who can help us, others look to the Church,' I said looking towards the kitchen.

'What about Christ?' Frank said.

As I had feared, this debate had grown more like a lecture. I regretted this, although I had answered Frank's questions honestly. But what was Wilhelmina doing there in silence in the kitchen? I turned the question back on Frank, 'What do you think about Jesus?'

'I've always found him very frightening, a rather unnatural child, and a very sad person,' he said.

'Would either of you like a drink?' said the voice in the kitchen. The question appeared to interrupt Frank's concentration.

'Antonius?' he said, as if reissuing his wife's question.

'No thanks,' I said.

'A coffee,' called Frank in response to his wife's offer.

'Not just before you sleep, have a tea,' said the voice in the kitchen.

'I'll be going to bed now,' I said, realising that without saying more than a few words, Wilhelmina had terminated our discussion and indicated that the evening was over.

Frank died in 1987 and Antonius became a good support to Wilhelmina through his visits and by his letters. The following year she asked Antonius whether he would like to continue their usual holiday arrangements by renting adjoining cottages on an island off Dutch the north-west coast. After a couple of years she suggested that it would be cheaper if they shared a two bedroom cottage. Antonius agreed but set out his routine and need for privacy. Prior to one of their holidays, he had been working hard to finish writing a brochure about the history of the Abbey School. He had little notice for this commission and it coincided with the end of the school term. The combination of different pressures overflowed into the holiday, and for a small reason Antonius became very angry with Wilhelmina. She had withdrawn to her room and the next day she left, leaving a letter expressing her horror at his attitude.

Now, eighteen years later, he held that letter in his hand; it was wedged between the pages in his journal and creaked when he opened it. When he read the first line, the whole scene came back to him. In her anger, she said that if others experienced his vitriolic outbursts, as she had, then she wondered why he had been allowed to remain in the abbey, to work at the school and in his different parishes. She described his angry words as being unchristian. Finally, the most painful thing was when she said that she now understood why various abbots treated him unkindly. She thought that they were weary of his uncontrollable anger. At that time, he wondered how she could not see what she had done to him. He thought he had told her that sometimes he became upset. Whilst he regretted some of the things he had said, he had not apologised as he held her responsible for triggering his feelings.

He knew he alarmed people. Having experienced this side of him, some folks never forgave him or trusted him again. However, Wilhelmina recovered from her anger and their friendship continued. She was encouraging when he was writing his book and understanding when Thomas wielded his sharp, critical editor's voice. During the years, Antonius wrote several entries about Wilhelmina.

She is a quiet woman by nature. Perhaps she has always been so from childhood or maybe it is the result of living with a very interesting, but talkative husband. It is peaceful to be with her. When there are silences, she does not rush to fill them with unnecessary words. Nor does she ask me many questions about my life, faith and family; but I feel free to talk about these things with her. I enjoyed cycling on the island; the scenery is wonderful. I do not cook at the abbey, so it was a pleasure to do this for us. Wilhelmina is a pleasant companion. Perhaps, had I married, I would have wanted a wife like her.

At the end of a holiday:

A week is long enough. I became irritated by her long silences and I do not like the smell of her perfume. Frank was a good holiday companion, I miss him.

Further in his journal was a postcard from Wilhelmina, displaying a view from the top of the Rockefeller building in New York. It had arrived in an envelope so that no one else could read it. Antonius put all her correspondence together in a pile, and considered what to do. Then he wrote a letter:

Dear Wilhelmina,
    I received bad news from the consultant: my condition is beyond repair. He did not give me much time to repent all my sins, say my goodbyes, and there will be no more book talks after the next one. My brother wants me to stay with him and to seek another opinion about my condition. I don't want to do either. My time has come. I have made my final arrangements. I hope the Bishop will grant my request to be buried at my former Dutch abbey. I would prefer if you did not attend. I would like our private friendship to go with me to my grave. It was a pleasure to know you and Frank. God bless you. Warmest regards, A.

Antonius borrowed the abbey shredder. In his hands he held the bundle containing all of Wilhelmina's letters, notes and postcards. They represented the nearest he had ever been to a relationship with a woman; perhaps to any person. A special feeling settled itself around his heart. He had experienced this a few times before when he was close to Wilhelmina, when he received her letters and sometimes when he spoke to her on the telephone. In the past he had pushed that sensation away, believing it was forbidden in priesthood. Now he let it linger and grow within him. It expanded and moved up around his throat. It was a pleasant sensation, a caring, loving feeling of friendship. Or was he fooling himself? Perhaps it was love and desire he was savouring. Could he have been a good husband and father? Was it a sin to be considering that now? Now, when he had perhaps a little time left? He wondered what it would be like to die in her arms, or should he be resigned to end in Death Row? He wanted to be strong but as he changed her correspondence into thin wavy strips for recycling, a tear ran down his cheek. Just one postcard remained. He liked this picture of their Dutch island and did not want to destroy it – not yet.

Many times he had joked with his brother about burning his journals after his death. Now he was not so sure if he wanted this for his archives. Secretly he hoped that Thomas would read them. He would leave a key and a note so that they could be deciphered. Then he realised that if Thomas looked at them he would discover his private friendship with Wilhelmina, which he had carefully kept from him. He considered whether his holiday companion would like to have his journals in which she and her husband were mentioned. But then he remembered that not everything which he had written was kind; so he disregarded that idea. He did not know what to do, so he did nothing. Waiting until he came back from his last talk was probably the best thing to do.

CHAPTER 8

The journey from Belgium to The Netherlands

From his seat in the Belgian abbey's entrance hall, Father Antonius had a clear view of the drive. Just outside the front door was a huge, ancient, deciduous magnolia tree. In spring, it had been laden with elongated cone shaped flower buds made of layers of pink-white silk petals curled on top of each other like slivers of praying palms. As these delicate parcels opened, each flower adopted its own oriental pose. After the blooms finished, new buds unfolded to create a canopy of dark green oval leaves, which served either as a sunshade or as an umbrella for visitors waiting at the abbey door. Today it was raining and the leaves were shining. Antonius wondered if he would see next year's flowers or even the fall of the yellowed leaves in the autumn.

Today was the Reading Club's tenth anniversary meeting. In the half hour he had been sitting in the entrance hall, he had been to the lavatory twice. The medicine to stop his diarrhoea was taking a long time to work. In the previous week, he had argued with his brother who said that he should not bother about giving the talk to the Reading Club. Thomas had slammed down the phone. Antonius hated to feel controlled and invaded by anyone; especially his brother.

He ran his hand through his abundance of grey, wavy hair and across his forehead, which was slightly damp, and he looked again for the promised car, which should collect him. Tomorrow he would phone Thomas to tell him about the anniversary meeting and ask him not to be so concerned. He checked to see that he had everything for his stay in The Netherlands, including the boxes containing two hundred copies of the Anniversary Book. This was to be his last book talk. He did not want to break his promise to the Reading Club. Had this been a less important appointment, he would have cancelled. He felt weak.

The taxi arrived on time and the driver came into the entrance hall. 'I'm looking for a Father Antonius,' he said.

'I am he.'

'I'm looking for a priest.' The taxi driver looked puzzled.

'Were you expecting me to be wearing my robe?'

The driver hesitated, 'Yes…I am pleased to meet you Father,' he said, with a slight bow.

In response, Antonius stretched out his warm, sweaty, slightly trembling hand. His face creased up into what might have looked like a smile of confidence, but it wasn't. He felt nervous about getting to the destination and he hoped that he had sufficient energy to give his talk.

'I might need to stop on the journey to use the lavatory,' he said.

'That will not be a problem, Father, we can stop as many times as you like. It's a long time before the Reading Club meeting this evening.'

As Antonius sat in the passenger seat next to the driver, he became aware of the pristine condition of the car's interior and of the pleasant smell in its atmosphere.

'Is this your car?' he asked, wondering how much such a luxurious vehicle would cost.

'No, Father, it belongs to the taxi company.'

'Is it new?'

'No, it's five years old,' the driver said.

'It's in good condition.'

'Thank you Father, I like to keep things clean.'

It seemed to Antonius that the driver had placed an emphasis on the word clean. Was that because he thought this passenger, with his unpredictable bowels, might soil the cab's interior? Had someone told him that the abbey nurse had issued a supply of incontinence pads to this recently diagnosed dying priest? Was it obvious that he had an embarrassing addition to his undergarments?

The driver started the car and they began their journey.

'How long have you been working as a driver?' Antonius asked.

'Part-time for six years, and full-time for the last two.'

'What did you do before?'

'I owned a picture gallery and framing shop, but the business went down; we were forced to close.'

'Sorry about that.' Antonius studied the driver's profile. He had the appearance of an intelligent fellow; very smartly dressed. Why was he driving a cab?

'People don't buy many pictures these days. Young folk with all the money like the minimalist look. You know, bleak rooms, uncomfortable furniture, no unnecessary things like pictures. The last picture I framed was for the doctor in the Reading Club – a print of Henri Fuseli's, 'The Nightmare'. A Gothic artist – it didn't really fit in his house.'

The priest glanced sideways at the driver and noticed how the flesh of his neck folded over the top of his white shirt collar.

'I don't know the picture,' Antonius said, 'although I am familiar with the work of the Gothic artist, William Blake. I find him sinister. Why didn't it fit in the doctor's house?'

'The doctor lives in one of the oldest and largest houses in our town – he bought it in the 1970s and got a government grant for renovation. My wife helps with the housework. People say that the doctor used the grant to start his art collection – must be worth a fortune. Every wall has at least one old painting on it.'

'What about your picture?'

'Fuseli's print doesn't fit in with all those originals. Framing that print led to some friction between the doctor and my wife.'

Antonius felt some abdominal twinges. He hoped that talking might help to take his mind off his grumbling digestive system.

'Why was that?' he said, pushing his lower arm against his abdomen in an attempt to curb the pain.

'Don't want to give you a bad impression of the doctor. You'll be meeting him this evening; and the others.'

Antonius looked out of the window at the cars and lorries on the motorway and he thought about the gossip he had heard over the years, both inside and outside of the abbey. Mostly people did not consider the impact of what they passed on to others.

'Thanks for your concern,' he said, 'but I'll judge the doctor when I meet him later. What about the picture?'

The driver continued, 'When we realised we would lose our business we needed to find other ways of earning our living. Luckily I could extend my driving work but my wife, who knows a lot about art, had only her shop and picture framing skills.'

'That's happening a lot these days. Even people with excellent references can't find work,' Antonius added.

'Eventually she went to work at the doctor's house helping with the cleaning. She does this for a number of people. She rarely saw the doctor. He was in his surgery or working in his study which she was never asked to clean. When he came out of this room he locked it – never greeted her. The doctor's wife asked if we could frame a picture for her husband.'

Antonius thought it rather unfriendly of the doctor not to greet the taxi driver's wife.

The driver swung out to overtake a huge lorry, and then continued:

'As my shop was closed I asked a friend if I could use his equipment to frame the picture. He didn't charge me, but the materials were expensive. I didn't ask the doctor to pay me for the work I did. It took me several hours.'

'Did he like it?'

'Yes. Told my wife he'd seen the original painting at an exhibition in London. Then he gave a fancy story about the artist having a real nightmare after eating some under-cooked pork. Said he'd treated many patients for digestive problems. Made it sound like a medical picture. Father! That was rubbish! That wasn't why he liked the picture.'

Antonius turned slightly to face the driver and noticed his large sausage fingers gripping the wheel. On his ring finger was a plain gold band, tourniquet tight. 'Why not?'

'It's one of those porn pictures. Old fashioned, but pornographic.'

'Oh dear!' said Antonius.

'My wife knows about art; those Gothic artists, including Fuseli. In their day, these paintings were popular – suggestive, you know! Erotic and sinister. Shall I tell you about the picture?'

Antonius had not expected to receive a lecture on erotic art. 'Please do,' he said.

'The 'Nightmare' shows a woman in a see-through gown on a bed. She's been tied up. She's either dead, asleep or – excuse me Father – she's waiting for it, with her eyes closed.'

'Waiting for what?'

'Sex.'

Antonius was surprised, then amused that the driver was speaking to him freely. Mostly people censor their social conversation when talking to a priest. However, he was wondering just how explicit the driver was going to be.

The driver continued. 'The lower part of her body's on a bed – the upper part hangs over the end. On top of her is a small deformed man. You can guess what he's just done.'

'It sounds like a strange picture!' said Antonius.

'Behind this scene is a horse with its mouth slightly open and its eyes bulging. Who knows what it's doing there?'

'And that's pornographic?'

'You'd need to see it to understand.'

'I'm impressed,' Antonius said. Then, as if to correct himself, he added, 'I'm surprised at how much detail you remember.' The priest wondered if the driver had a strong liking for the picture, but he was careful not to say that. Instead he continued, not quite truthfully,

'I have the impression that you don't like this painting.'

'No, I don't. There's too much of that sort of thing in our society.'

'Did you frame the picture?' Antonius asked, wondering if picture framers ever refused to frame offensive pictures.

'Yes, I did,' said the driver in an angry manner, as if he had been forced by the doctor to undertake the commission. 'My wife delivered it to the doctor's house. He was there. He unwrapped the painting and asked her what she thought of it.'

'And?'

'She said she found it sinister and over-sexualised. Told him about Gothic artists and their erotic pictures. She noticed the doctor was glancing down at her bosom. Not the first time this has happened. She's well built, you know. Men often stare at her breasts; she says that most don't know they're doing it. She had expected the respectable doctor to be more careful where he set his eyes.'

Antonius shifted in his seat and his eyebrows went up a little. He sometimes noticed women's breasts.

The driver continued, 'He was surprised that my wife knew so much. Then she asked him where he would hang it. According to her, there was not a free wall in the house. He invited her to his office – a dirty place.'

'Sounds like it could've done with some of her thorough cleaning,' Antonius said.

'Dirty in the other way too! The doctor pointed to an empty space on the wall. Asked my wife to hold the picture there, so he could judge the right position. She did, turned her head to one side so he could have a good view of the picture on the wall. Then she saw this book.'

'Which book?'

'Pornography in the 20th Century'. She read some other titles.

Each one was a dirty book: erotica, pornography, all types of perverted sex.'

'That must have been quite a shock!'

'She was horrified – didn't want to be in the doctor's study – but didn't know how to get out. He asked her to adjust the position of the picture – took his time looking for a pencil. Her arms began to ache. She told the doctor to hurry. She was about to drop the picture.'

'I know that can be very tiring,' said Antonius, focussing on the aching arms and ignoring the pornographic books. He was attempting to sound interested, even though his gut was giving him sharp pain.

The driver continued, 'He came up behind my wife, put his hand underneath her arm and touched her breast, before marking the wall with his pencil.'

'Oh dear, how unfortunate,' Antonius said, as he fought against an urge to laugh.

'She screamed. Doctor apologised, said that he had touched her by mistake. He had hurried – knew her arms were aching – said he'd tried to get to the wall quickly. She thought he had touched her deliberately. It was all too much.'

For a moment, Antonius's pain was overridden by his imagination, which quickly created a comic scene of a tiny, tiny doctor trying to find a gap between this woman's enormous free floating breast and her flabby upper arm. Antonius sucked in the sides of his cheeks, like a schoolboy stifling an illicit giggle.

'Was it an accident?' he said, squeezing away the amusement from his mind.

'Probably. But she was distressed when she came home. She cried. Said she wouldn't go back to work there again – wanted me to tell the doctor's wife what had happened. We talked it over – decided not to make any decisions – not before we'd discussed it with a friend – our spiritual mentor. Our counsellor, I suppose you'd call him.'

'Your priest?' Antonius asked.

'No, he's not exactly our priest.' The driver continued, 'How could she prove it wasn't an accident? What would be gained by me or my wife saying anything to the doctor or his wife? I said that she didn't have to continue working there, if she didn't want to. But, if she decided to leave, she'd have to give *Mevrouw* Dekker a reason.'

'Not necessarily,' said Antonius, his curiosity acting as a light anaesthetic to his pain. 'What did she do?'

'The doctor's wife phoned us; said her husband had told her about the misunderstanding. She wanted my wife to know how sorry she was – they sent her some flowers – hoped my wife wouldn't stop helping them. My wife always liked the doctor's wife. She said she would continue working for her. She hasn't seen the doctor again.'

'Quite a story,' said the priest.

'So, that's our respectable doctor for you, with his erotic picture, his dirty books and an inclination to touch women's breasts.'

Antonius felt pain and rumblings in his lower bowel. 'May I ask you to stop at the next lavatory?' he said.

The driver pulled into a service station. There he went into the restaurant, while Antonius hurried to the toilets. Downstairs, across a shiny marble floor, was a thin, pale-faced concierge waiting with her hand outstretched for a tip. The priest took out 20 euro cents from his purse and found the nearest cubicle.

They continued their journey. The scenery was varied: young forests of oak, silver birch, ash and brambles emerging from carpets of heather; then small towns shielded from traffic noise by elaborate, graffiti-covered screens. An occasional restored windmill contrasted with the high speed train track, which followed the motorway for many kilometres. Antonius noticed the wetness of his country, with its rivers, canals, ditches and flood plains in abundance. He could see the lowness of these lands by the vastness of the skies.

'I enjoyed your book,' the driver said, 'I re-read it recently. You said that you'd kept a journal since you were twelve.'

'Yes, I was grateful that my grandmother suggested that I wrote regularly. Without that, I wouldn't have coped with the seminary or being away from home. Writing was like talking to her.'

'You had some difficult times in the seminary?'

'Yes. I was unprepared. The other boys always knew they would be priests. My elder brother was the one who was chosen, not me. I was jealous of the attention he received. Unfortunately, he drowned, one month before he was due to go to the seminary. A year later, I had taken his place. For many years I thought that my parents blamed me for his accident.'

'I remember finding that chapter about your brother very sad,' said the driver.

'At first, I left that part out of the book, but Thomas, my brother and editor, said that the readers would like to know why I had been sent to a seminary.'

'Did you feel guilty about your brother's death?'

'I did. On the day of the accident, my brother had persuaded me away from my book to play a game with him. We were taking it in turns to hide and then to see how quickly one could be found by the other. He went off to hide.'

'You don't see the children today playing that game.'

'I grew tired of the game and went back to my book. Two hours later my mother asked me where my brother was. I didn't know. She went looking for him. Half an hour later, she had found him face down in an irrigation ditch.'

'Drowned?'

'The water was completely covered with pondweed; apparently, it looked like a green path. She pulled his body out of the water and tried to revive him, but he was dead. The green weed clung to his hair and his clothes. She carried him home and laid him on the table. She wept and then shouted that I should have kept with him.'

'That must have been a great trauma for you,' the driver said.

'For all of us. Even now when I am anxious, I can see my

brother's body covered with that green pondweed; he's dead on the kitchen table, in a puddle of ditch water. He was buried in the cemetery near the church, in a special section reserved for children. Our priest spoke to me after the funeral. He said it was my duty to take my brother's place in the seminary the next year, when I would be twelve.'

'Did you want to go?'

'No. He told me that all Catholic families should have a priest son. I felt punished for not looking after my brother. But I made myself believe that there would be some good things in becoming a priest.'

'It was good that your grandmother suggested a journal,' the driver said.

'She was a clever woman; a French Protestant. I was her favourite. She told me I was intelligent. My parents never said that; they didn't want me to get grand ideas. She warned me that intelligent people were often feared; sometimes treated badly. When my brother died, she was very sad. She knew that I would take his place at the seminary. She gave me some notebooks in which to keep a journal.'

'I was surprised that you were allowed to do that,' the driver said.

'I never asked permission, my grandmother said it was alright to write privately. I hid my notebooks.'

'Where?'

'In a shoe box; thirty small notebooks just fitted inside. I kept my writing small; I wrote a lot on each page.'

'Then your brother gave you the idea of the book.'

'Yes. Once he came to my room in the Dutch abbey. He noticed the boxes of journals on top of my cupboard. He asked me why I was keeping them. He said when I was dead, no-one would want to read them; very likely they would be burned.'

'That was a bit harsh.'

'He can be, still is. I'd never considered this question before. I was shocked. He suggested that I use the journals as a basis for a book about the life of a priest. He called it my final labour of love for the Church. My brother is a retired editor and declares he's an atheist; says he feels neither love nor respect for the Church. You're not a Catholic?'

'No Father, my wife and I are Protestants.'

Antonius continued, 'I've spoken to many lapsed Catholics, including those who no longer believe in God. Few are able to entirely let go of their religion. Beneath my brother's bluntness, I recognised that his connection with the Church had survived. He was serious; he said he would help me by editing what I wrote. It was his idea that through my personal accounts, the Church could learn about itself – where it had gone wrong and how it was still making mistakes.'

'Why would he bother helping you if he didn't still have some feeling for the Church?'

'Exactly my thoughts. I think it showed that he was still connected with the Church.' Antonius continued, 'I had not read my old journals for years. But when I did, memories returned of students, priests, pupils, various congregations and different abbots. It took me days to read every notebook. I felt pleased that I had written regularly and freely about my experiences. My brother was right – my writing did reveal a history of issues, wider than my narrow life. For example, in reading my own story, I understood why there are now few priests in our Order.'

'What did your Church think about your writing?'

Antonius looked out of the window. The clouds were piling up in the sky. He noticed a mosque in a nearby town and thought about how angry he had been with the Church when he had received his recent diagnosis. He had decided he would carry on his life as normal, although he was beginning to wonder what that meant, since life could no longer be the same. He appreciated that he could chat to the taxi driver because he could never do that with Thomas, who was always so intense when they spoke.

'I don't think that some in my community liked the details,' Antonius replied. 'My brother gave me some guidance. He said I should be bold and selective. Avoid being long-winded and include personal details. Fortunately, I had learnt to use a computer! I sent him a few ideas and my first chapter. He was so ruthless with his editing that I was nearly deterred from writing the rest of the book. I was angry at his suggestions. How dare he rewrite my history? But with his guidance, I persevered and completed the book in twelve months.'

'That was quick?'

'It took another six months to refine it. Thomas made it more acceptable for what he called, the 'general reader'.'

'The general reader?'

'I mean the majority of ordinary folks, rather than specialists in religious life and history.'

'Like me and my wife?'

'I sought agreement from my abbot to have it published. I don't think he liked some of what I had written. A month later, I was transferred to the Belgian abbey. My new abbot was not so worried about the contents of my book and gave his permission for its publication. My brother found a company willing to publish. Many people have written to me saying that my book has helped them to understand the influence that the Church has had on their lives. I have received letters from Catholics and Protestants.'

The driver shifted in his seat. They had been travelling for two hours and he was beginning to feel hungry. 'And now you're famous!' he said.

'I wouldn't say that. I've been asked to give a number of talks about my book. I don't enjoy these sessions; they're a bit too public for me. I get nervous. A few years ago, we started this writing project; getting people to keep journals.'

'My wife keeps a diary, that's like a journal, maybe she could write a book.'

'Quite possibly.' Antonius had heard this type of comment before. He thought it was likely that many people believe that they have a book within them. He continued:

'Since we have introduced this format, the talks have gone better. On the university website is a set of instructions for writing. Participants choose one or two pieces from their journals to develop; we print these in a small book to commemorate my talk. My brother edits the work and takes responsibility for the production. That's the '2005 Writing Project'. Erasmus University is our main sponsor.' Antonius felt a spasm just below his diaphragm. 'Can you stop at the next lay-by? I need to use the lavatory,' he said.

The driver turned into a service station. The priest did not want to eat anything. After visiting the toilet he felt weak, so he sat outside on a bench while the driver had a snack. He now had a pain running down the lower part of his back. Soon the driver returned, the two men got into the car and they rejoined the motorway.

'Are you alright, Father?'

'I'm fine. Please continue the conversation. It's helping to pass the time.'

The driver hesitated, and then continued, 'You were talking about your brother's suggestions for writing.'

'For the Reading Club, I sent them to Piet van Rijn and he circulated them to the others.'

'I know about the task,' the driver said.

'Are you a member of that club? Sorry, then I have misunderstood your position. I do apologise.'

'No, I'm not, not yet. Piet made an application for me to join the club – it wasn't successful. They rejected me – not good enough. If I'd been accepted, I'd be feeling good – less of a failure. Piet said that he'd try again after tonight's meeting. He thinks one of the members might be leaving.'

'I hope you are successful this time. May I ask you why your business failed?' Antonius said.

'A combination of things. Apart from framing, I sold pictures and small frames; ornaments for the home. Customers stopped buying these things. What a loss when we had to close! My shop was elegant; designed the interior myself – it was wide and long – the floor was covered in pale wood – there were many lights, in the ceiling, on the sidewalls – very elegant and yet cosy. The shop was taken over by an insurance company – the inside redesigned, the wood flooring covered by a carpet with the company logo. My workshop was converted into a kitchen, a manager's office and two cloakrooms. The new occupiers took over our backyard – my wife's plants, table and chairs were dumped.'

Antonius had heard a few sad stories about lost businesses. 'That must have been very hard for you both,' he said.

'I made nice frames in my workshop. Not many people realise what skill is required. Everything has to be precise – no room for error. My speciality was mounting and framing pictures – the sort that people bring back from their holidays, rolled up in tubes.'

Antonius said, 'My sister brought a painting home from the Dominican Republic and the framing cost twice as much as the picture.'

'Easily! The materials are expensive and it takes a long time. As you said, the price of the framing could be twice or three times as much as the cost of the picture. The doctor's print had cost about €14 and he had to pay treble that for the materials alone.'

'You must have felt very bad when your business closed.'

'It was a sad day when we emptied the shop. A framing company from Den Bosch took away some of my stock – they only paid me €200 for materials which had cost me over €1000. Two men from a shop clearance company removed most of what was left. They levered up the counter, splitting some of the flooring; took the shelves, the unsold ornaments and pictures; disconnected the light fittings; then gave me €300 for stock which had cost several thousand guilders.'

'Awful.'

'The shop looked dreadful – I was stressed – in a state of shock – I had to get away – left my wife and her cousin to clear up the rest. The next day the insurance company builders began work on the conversion.'

'Tough. Your wife's a strong woman,' Antonius said.

'She is… I used to have nightmares – people queuing to get into the shop. In my dream, my wife had opened a small coffee counter in the front window. Some tables and chairs were outside, creating a nice terrace. The doctor was a waiter, taking orders and serving coffee and apple cake to members of the Reading Club. I was at the rear of the shop handing customers brown paper packages containing their purchases. The shop was buzzing with conversation like the *Café Terrace* in the Town Square on a Friday evening. No reason to close down.'

'Dreams can be cruel,' Antonius said.

'This one was. It always ended in the same way. A great noise came in the distance. Before my wife and customers could get out of the shop, a bulldozer from the insurance company rumbled up the street, through the shop window and crushed every one. I tried to save her but I was helpless; swimming in slow motion. Next to me the doctor was laughing.'

'A recurring dream?'

'I had it many times. Eventually it passed.'

'Did you get any help?'

'Not with the debt. That took a long time to clear. Milo Jansen supported us in other ways. He's a member of the Reading Club.'

Antonius recalled Milo's essay. 'Yes,' he said, 'I know the name, I've corresponded with him. How did you meet him?'

'I was outside his house. Could see into the neighbour's living-room. On the wall was a large canvas, which I had mounted and framed when I had my shop. It triggered a vivid memory of the day my shop was cleared. I was shaking. Felt cold and naked. Milo saw me – asked if I was all right – can't remember what I said – he invited me into his house – made me a coffee and asked why I was shivering. Told him about my recurring dream and memories of the shop.'

'That was thoughtful of Milo,' Antonius said.

'Yes. He explained that I was having a reaction to a trauma – apparently it's not uncommon. People have dreams – he called my frequent memories, flashbacks. He said that I should try talking about what happened, it would calm my thoughts and convert them into memories. Working for the Catholic Diocese, he was used to talking to people who have problems. He visited us regularly. The wife and I took it in turns to talk to him about the loss of our business. It helped. Slowly we moved on from our trauma and started a new life. We're very grateful to Milo for supporting us. He's our friend.'

'He sounds like a good man.'

'Yes, he is. Unfortunately there're people who misunderstand him. He works hard to support the immigrants in our town. Does a lot of good in his free time. Not many people know that he's got a Queen's medal for his community work. My wife overheard one of her women employers describing Milo like a cockerel in a pen of hens. I don't understand why some people say such spiteful things. Do you Father?'

'People like to gossip. Tell me how you know about my suggestion for the Reading Club?'

'From Piet van Rijn. I know him quite well. Take him often to the meetings in my cab. You can't help liking him – even when he's drunk. Not that I approve of drinking. My wife and I don't drink. Couldn't afford to lose my licence. We can have a good time without alcohol. Do you like a drink Father?'

'A few years ago I enjoyed a drink, but since my digestive problems, I have to be careful,' Antonius said.

The driver continued, 'Piet told me about the journals. I know that he recently sent you the story about General De Gaulle, the bulldog. I wrote that.'

'Really? I'm sorry, I didn't know it was your story. It had Piet's name on it,' Antonius said.

'I don't mind. I enjoyed writing about that dog – it belongs to a neighbour. Before the creature was the subject of my story, I hated it. Now I smile when I see it waddling along the road, with his owner several paces behind. But I still object to the way many people allow their dogs to foul the pavements and the grass.'

'So that piece about General de Gaulle is your creation?'

'I haven't seen what he sent you, but yes, it was my idea.'

'But I've credited that to Piet,' Antonius said.

The taxi driver grinned and said, 'Good, I am delighted – at last, I've gained entrance into the Reading Club, without anyone of those respectable fellows knowing.' He chuckled, 'Don't say anything to the members or Piet. Wait till I tell my wife!'

'Alright,' said Antonius, who felt relieved not to have to find a way of acknowledging the driver's contribution, without disgracing Piet or reprinting the booklets.

'I've brought extra copies with me; I'll make sure you get one.'

'I look forward to seeing my story in print – as well as the other contributions.'

'Some members sent in more than one piece of writing. It's a good book, we were careful not to include anything which we thought unsuitable.'

'Something unsuitable? I'm not surprised,' the driver said.

'What do you mean?'

'Never mind. Just something I heard. Probably not true. Many have worked hard at their writing,' the driver said.

'How do you know?'

'It's a small community, people talk to one another about such things – especially the wives. My wife heard that some of the members found the task extremely difficult; even those who write regularly in their jobs.'

'Do you know any of the other Reading Club members?'

'I know all of them.'

'What are they like?'

'They're all respectable fellows,' said the driver.

'Really?'

'No. Not completely.'

'Oh, really. What do you mean?'

'Take Joost Kuijpers. A miserable-looking fellow – very thin and round-shouldered – never seen him looking smart. Unfriendly, rarely returns a smile or greeting. Used to come into my shop to buy art materials. Tells people that he lectures at the college of art – doesn't work there any more. Goes to Amsterdam – got a second studio there. Makes a good deal of black money painting pictures of prostitutes and the like.'

Antonius was shocked, but did not respond. He remembered Joost's description of a portrait of a young woman and wondered if she was a prostitute.

'Bert de Lange – another misery – owns a posh wine and spirits shop near the river. He's related to my wife who cleans his shop once a week. She was very close to Bert's mother – thought her son was an unkind man. Piet van Rijn says you can always buy a good bottle for a special occasion at Bert's shop. Never gives a discount – not to his friends, not to his family. My wife and I don't drink. Did I tell you that already?'

'Yes you did.'

'I've seen enough drunken people – we made a good decision not to take alcohol. A pity that Bert's father drank so much – he was an alcoholic. Family tried to hide it. In the end, Bert gave up trying to help his father, who died of a diseased liver and alcoholic dementia. Bert will be bringing a few bottles of very good champagne to the meeting. Do you like champagne, Father?'

'As I told you, I have to be careful these days. Could you please stop at the next lavatory, because I think that my stomach is upset again.'

The taxi driver stopped the car outside the motorway restaurant and Antonius was pleased that the lavatories were near to the entrance. His face was pale as he got back into the car and lowered himself slowly into the passenger seat.

The driver continued with his knowledge of the Reading Club members. 'Then we have Paul Bazelman. My wife cleans his house. Thinks he has feminine tendencies, if you know what I mean. He inspects schools – makes sure they are using their funds properly. His wife is different – she paints her toenails black – very chatty and not very discreet about her phone calls. My wife thinks that she's a flirt.'

'Oh!' Antonius said, wondering how much more information he would hear.

The driver continued, 'Venus Bazelman told my wife that her husband found writing his journal very difficult – she opened his computer and read what he had written – she didn't tell my wife the content. Anyway, my wife is very careful not to repeat what she hears and sees at work.'

'You seem to know a lot about these people.'

'Then there's Hans van den Elsen – a management consultant, whatever that means? Has an office at home, but travels a lot. His wife runs an antiques shop in town. Nice woman. There's a rumour – I don't take any notice of rumours – that he's more than friendly with Venus Bazelman.'

'I'm always cautious about rumours,' said Antonius, not being completely truthful.

'The only single man in the group is Huub Schevers. Sold the cleaning business which his uncle left him and opened an antiques shop near to the museum. At one time my wife worked for him – she didn't like him very much – said he was a bit creepy. You know what I mean. Most people say he is gay – I'm not bothered what he is. He collects erotic objects. My wife doesn't approve of that sort of thing.'

'I understand', said Antonius, wondering what the taxi driver meant. He remembered a rather long-winded piece of Huub's writing about the damselflies, which, even after Thomas's careful editing, had remained a lengthy story.

'Then there's Milo Jansen. Already told you about him. He's not always popular with the other members of the club. I think because he's very negative about some of the books which are chosen – too much sex in them. Believe me, Father, he's a good man.'

'I'm pleased to hear that.'

Antonius felt very tired from his pain and from the conversation. He did wonder why the taxi driver wanted to join the Reading Club when he was critical about most of its members, but he decided against asking him.

'If you don't mind, I think that I'd like to sleep for a while. I feel quite exhausted from all the stops we've made.'

'You alright, Father?'

'No, I feel dreadful. I have a sharp pain in my abdomen. Maybe, if I can sleep, I'll be well enough for tonight's meeting.'

'If you're ill, I'll drive you to the nearest hospital. Your health is more important than the Reading Club. I can always deliver the books to the club tonight if necessary.'

'That won't be necessary'

'We're very near your old abbey; do you want me to make a detour so that you can see it again?'

Antonius repeated, 'That won't be necessary.'

Father Antonius closed his eyes. He became aware of the noise of the traffic, and thought about his former Dutch abbey. He was still waiting to hear if his request to be buried there had been granted. He visualised the graveyard adjoining the abbey: a large square of land bounded by a natural hedge of hollies and horse chestnut trees and its two black, iron gates giving a wide entrance to a large, flat lawn on which identical small, grey gravestones stand upright. As if carved by the same stonemason, each simple cross bears the monastic name and surname, and the date of birth and death of the confrère who is buried there. Grass cutting is easy here as there are no lumps, bumps, or tiny walls to negotiate. Only a large bin for dead flowers has to be moved when the grass is cut. Antonius had always liked the simplicity and the equality of it. It is a peaceful place, not ornate or untidy like some graveyards where he conducted services.

The funerals of confrères are usually well attended. Sometimes there are more people in attendance than at the Sunday services. Everyone from the abbey and many from the local community will be present, whether they knew or liked the deceased. This is the custom. Even if the person has not lived there for many years, the church will be quite full. After a burial, coffee and funeral cake is served for everyone in the great refectory. Antonius imagined his brother and his family attending his funeral, looking pale in their black clothes. Their confusion at being in an alien place, bombarded by beliefs with which they do not agree, might be mistaken by others for grief. Thomas would be his usual grumpy self and not shy to announce that a priest's life is a wasted life. He will no doubt refuse to participate in the custom of throwing soil on top of the deceased's coffin – Antonius's coffin.

The driver glanced at the priest and saw that he was asleep.

CHAPTER 9

Delivering the Books

After a few kilometres, Father Antonius became delirious; he started to moan and clutch his belly. The taxi driver took him immediately to the nearest hospital. There the priest's condition was assessed as serious and he was admitted as an emergency. Antonius was put into a bed and connected up to a life support machine. Although confused and in a lot of pain, he told the driver to leave him and deliver the anniversary books to the doctor's house.

'I'll be alright here. They'll phone my brother and the abbey. Someone will be here soon. You were right to bring me to the hospital. Thank you.'

The driver reluctantly agreed to leave. It was still the rush hour and only fifteen minutes before the start of the Reading Club meeting. It took him twenty minutes to reach his flat; another twenty to shower and remove the hospital smell from his hair and clothes. He put on a crisp white shirt and his other suit, which had been airing by a window. Several glasses of cold water cooled his feelings and dispersed the sensation of nausea which had been pummelling his stomach. He was concerned.

Should he have left Antonius alone in the hospital? The priest had insisted. But now there was an extra sensation within his system. Was it nervousness or excitement? He was going to deliver the anniversary books, to enter and address the club on behalf of their special guest.

Meanwhile the members began to gather in Titus's main room, which was decorated with small flags and garlands of balloons. Book covers had been copied, cut into triangles and fixed to a string. The result was some colourful bunting which was draped around the room at eye level. Titus had devoted several shelves in this room to storing the Reading Club's books. On the inside cover of each volume was written the date on which he read the book and the date of the club's discussion. In addition, there was a notebook for recording members' comments and the average score awarded to each book.

Bert de Lange arrived early with three bottles of champagne chilled to the correct temperature, four bottles each of white and red wine, together with a box of glasses which he used for his wine tasting evenings. Titus had ordered several plates of Dutch delicacies from a local chef; these were sitting together with the drinks on the large side cupboard. In front of each place at the grand table was a list of all the books which had been read during the past ten years, together with their scores.

Within five minutes everyone was there – apart from Milo. They were all wearing bow ties and dinner jackets of varying styles. It did not matter that some were a bit tight or that one or two of the trouser bottoms were unfashionably flared. Their choice to give the celebration a formal flavour was a good one. On their arrival, Titus's wife, who was wearing a long black dress for the occasion, told every man how handsome he looked. She ushered them into the spacious front room where Bert presented a glass of champagne and Titus welcomed them with a warm handshake and an offer of some food. All were enchanted and amused by the flag decorations. The champagne was quickly absorbed into their blood streams and the level of laughter and camaraderie swelled.

'Piet, have you heard from the priest?' Titus asked.

'I am sure they will be here in a moment, the driver's very reliable,' Piet said, attempting to reassure the host who was beginning to look anxious.

As the big Lexus parked outside of the doctor's house, Bob van Dillen, the driver, realised that he was about to make his debut into the Reading Club. It was not quite how he had visualised his entrance; but that did not matter – it was a beginning. First, he came with an important message from Father Antonius, which he had rehearsed and modified over twenty times on his journey here. This, together with the anniversary books in which was printed his story about General De Gaulle, would afford him an impressive introduction. The priest insisted that he took a copy, which he left in his flat for his wife to read. Inwardly Bob smiled.

Titus's wife showed him into the main room. Seven members of the Club sat around the huge table. The driver could see and smell that they had been drinking. The room had the atmosphere of a party. An infusion of alcohol and the smell of small Dutch doughnuts were in the air. He put the box of books carefully on the antique table and everyone stopped talking and looked at him. Addressing the members, as if he were the personal secretary for Father Antonius, he conveyed the news about the hospitalisation of their special guest. There were some groans and concerns about the health of the priest. The driver reassured the meeting that the hospital would be contacting the Belgian abbey and the priest's brother. There was nothing more that could be done. The priest had sent his best wishes. Titus stood up, shook the driver's hand, thanked him for his care of the priest, opened the box of books and handed one to Bob. Now he had two copies.

The driver was ushered out of the room; there was a sad pause. The excitement and anticipation had gone. What an anti-climax!

Then Piet, assuming some authority and pretending to have knowledge of the priest's intentions, spoke up, 'Father Antonius would want us to have a good time. I suggest we distribute the books, drink to his speedy recovery and enjoy what has been written.'

The printing of the books had been partly sponsored by *Boeken Boeken,* the shop in the *Waterstraat.* Its owners' policy was to support local writers. Only recently, they made a special window display of one of the doctor's books and five years ago they printed a collection of Joost's industrial landscapes. The Anniversary Book carried an acknowledgement to the shop for its support in the printing and for supplying the books for the Reading Club during the last ten years. Joost created the book's cover and illustrations.

Thomas van Aken, Antonius's brother, had successfully applied for additional grants towards the cost of printing. The members had chosen to have top quality paper. Their book had developed into an expensive project. In other situations they would have preferred a cheaper option – not to spill money. But after an evening discussing whether to have the cheap copy of lesser quality and no illustrations or to go for the best, they had chosen the best. Each person had agreed to buy several copies in order to cover the costs. Of course, one or two moaned, but several were pleased to order four and five copies and Titus wanted ten. *Boeken Boeken* ordered one hundred copies, which they would sell for €8 each. The manager planned to send complimentary copies to the local libraries and to all the members of the local council. After all, the shop's name was on the first page.

The book was 22 cm wide by 20 cm deep and had a shining, stiff, coloured cover. The finest quality paper had been used. It felt substantial and refined; it smelt of newness and promise; it looked classical, elegant, even beautiful. This was their book. Pride and the feeling of brotherhood overwhelmed them, their usual Dutch restraint went gliding out of the window, and they became stupefied, as if the sail of a windmill had struck their heads. Assisted by champagne, the members began to read their book. Some flicked through the pages hoping to chance on their work. The more methodical ones began at the front with the introduction, followed by the contents page and read though from cover to cover. There was a lot of laughter and noises of approval, some back slapping and congratulations. Various guesses and accusations as to who had written the anonymous contributions shot back and forth across the table. For some, this was the first time they had seen their work in print and they felt proud. Compliments flowed and the writers glowed.

THE READING CLUB ANNIVERSARY BOOK
1997-2007

CHAPTER 10

INTRODUCTION

To celebrate the 10th anniversary of the Reading Club, its members have created this collection of short stories and reflections. Their inspiration came from two sources. First, they read the book, 'Priests Dying' by Father Antonius van Aken; an autobiography based on his journals 1940-2003. Secondly, they participated in the '2005 Writing Project'. The members were encouraged to keep private journals in which they wrote regularly during an eight week period. There were no restrictions on content; everyone was free to choose any subject, although we did offer some suggestions. After the writing period, we asked the members to reread their journals, select one or two of their ideas or themes and from these develop stories, poems, descriptions or reflections. To follow are the results of their endeavours.

The Reading Club would like to acknowledge the help of their local bookshop *Boeken Boeken* for its contribution towards this publication and for supplying the club's books during the last ten years.

My brother and I would like to thank Erasmus University and 'The New Writers' Foundation' for supporting the '2005 Writing Project'. Finally, we would like to congratulate the members of the Reading Club for their participation. We wish them a happy anniversary and hope that they will continue to read and write with pleasure.

Thomas van Aken, Editor

CONTENTS

Caveat Lector[1]

It is well known that authors of novels and poets find much inspiration from their own life experiences – from places they have been to and people they have met. In the pages of their notebooks and the vaults of their memories they stock-pile potential writing material – a station waiting-room, a musical instrument, a recurring dream, a newspaper headline, an insect in a pond, a furtive glance, a chance remark, a penetrating voice, a crooked nose, a sharp smell, a subtle flirtation. Even a word written backwards can provide the starting point for a story; for example the word lezen can be reversed to become nezel; a good name for a metaphorical damsel. Sometimes these impressions form the starting points for characters and plots. Once embraced and developed by the writer, the original detail – the person, or the scene – loses its significance and ceases to be real. Through the author's skill and imagination, a new character or setting evolves which is often believable, but not true.

The sophisticated reader understands this process and does not look for a biography of himself in what has been written. Instead he realises that while his hat, his hair, his manners, his dreams, his talents, even his wife have been used as a starting point, beyond that there is no likeness intended or to be found. The original speck disappears as a more flamboyant, extravagant, exaggerated, ridiculous, outrageous person takes his place; because it is in reading about such larger than life characters that readers take their pleasures.

[1] Reader beware!

Sometimes people want to find themselves in stories and are disappointed when they are absent. Others look for small parts and are pleased or conversely angered when they think they have been featured. It could be that you were neither my inspiration, nor my starting point, nor the beginning of the person you think to recognise. But does it really matter how the character or the plot were conceived, when the end result is a wonderful story?

Anonymous

Early Morning Writing

I am awake. It is 5.00am and it feels like the middle of the night. Maybe it was the sound of the newspaper coming through the door or the noise of a flower lorry travelling along my street and bumping over the speed humps, which disturbed me. Heavy vehicles are only supposed to use this road between 10.00am and 4.00pm, but many ignore the regulations and there is no-one to police the movement of this transport. I have a full bladder and I need to have a pee. Perhaps I have been woken by the host of writing ideas which are lining themselves up in my mind. They are elusive and I don't want to lose them; I must get up and write them down now.

I should rise quietly. My wife is snoring gently beside me and I do not want to wake her. She will complain if I tell her I am going downstairs to do some writing. I want to get to the computer before the queue of ideas breaks up and marches out of my memory. I need to rise slowly these days, otherwise I become dizzy. My legs always feel heavy in the mornings. My circulation is sluggish and it does not immediately beat into action. It is dark. If I switch on the light, it will wake my wife. Our bedroom is at the top of the house; I have to grope my way down to the floor below, holding onto the banister firmly, otherwise I could fall. The painted stair-treads are potentially slippery beneath my bare feet. Once I tumbled; it was very frightening. In a few years, this house may be too much for us – too big, too steep. We will have to look for a place which is all on one level.

Safely on the second floor, I seek my way in the dark to the bathroom; I shut the door, switch on the light and squint in its brightness. Having emptied my bladder, I glance in the mirror at the grey, lined, just-out-of-bed face with its night time stubble. My hair is untidy and sticks up. My wife says that I look like my Uncle Ernest in the mornings – hardly a compliment because he was a very scruffy man. He is dead now.

My God, I am looking old! My eyes are blood-shot, my teeth are scummy brown and my mouth has the flavour of a drain. Should I clean my teeth? No. I had better list those ideas before I do anything else. I shuffle from the bathroom to my study and open the computer, resisting the temptation to see if there are any email messages – it's only 5 o'clock! Why does it take such a long time before the journal file is ready? I read the previous entry and correct a few errors. I should resist the temptation to do that when I have new ideas waiting to be listed.

I begin. I tap at the keys without looking up. 'Tuesdat' appears on the screen. My unwashed sleepy fingers have pressed a 't' instead of a 'y'. After correcting the mistake, I pause and think. I am aware that the warmth which I brought with me from my bed has dissipated; I feel chilled. There is a draft coming in through the study window. My mouth is lined with a foul-tasting slime; I should have cleaned my teeth. My legs feel heavy and my feet are as cold as a marble cheese counter. I look down at my ankles with their thread veins, like crimson coral. My wife says these uncomfortable blemishes are caused by sitting too long at my desk. Now we walk each day to improve my circulation; I do not believe that this exercise helps.

During the last few days, I have been thinking a lot about writing. This is not the only early morning when I have woken up with ideas for my journal, but this is the first time I have got up and come directly to the computer to write them down. Now I am here and ready to write.

I am ready!

Where are they? Where are those ideas?

What has happened to that line which was knocking on my mind, shouting to be set free, demanding to be recorded? There were so many of them up there in bed; down here I can't remember one. I have forgotten what it was that I wanted to write. My feet and back are cold and my mind is blank. Now what shall I do? Return to bed and try to warm my feet against my wife without waking her or go downstairs, have a coffee and read the paper? Will I ever remember what they were?

For certain, I will NOT be doing this again. No more early morning writing for me!

Anonymous

Cycle Ride into Town

Cycling into town usually takes ten minutes; I can do it with my eyes closed. Today I'll keep my eyes open and linger along the way. First stop will be in the narrow road leading to the dyke. It cuts straight between two vast areas of commercial greenhouses, which have spoilt the view and flattened our meadow flowers, but earned millions of euros for the economy.

Skeleton staff, rarely seen, run these efficient glass factories where machines, not people, plant the seedlings flown in from Kenya in trays. Inside these see-through palaces, air, water, temperature and humidity are automatically controlled. Neither pests, bacteria, viruses, strong winds, nor frost threaten these plants. Their growing medium is soft, nutritious, weed-free and sterile. Day and night, these unnatural plants enjoy constant light at optimum intensity. They know no seasons. Growers, eager to extend the shelf life of their produce, have eliminated imperfections. The result is that the roses have lost their perfume and the tomatoes have no flavour.

Planting and picking is a continuous process. Every day, lorries take boxes of cloned flowers to florists and same-sized vegetables to supermarkets in north-west Europe. Successful? Certainly. Note the export figures; see the growers' grand houses.

Now, up a slight incline to get to the new dyke road – no more than fifty metres – I'm puffed out! Onto a flat road again, that's better.

Between the dyke and the river is an artificial meadow; a long hollow created to contain floodwaters. When the river rises, its water spills over the banks into this shallow area, where temporary lakes are formed for opportunistic winged visitors; hundreds of water fowl. Today on the gentle sloping sides of the meadow, sheep are nibbling the grass; yellow labels in their ears and green circles on their backs advertising that they've been serviced by a ram or inseminated via a human hand. I'm stopping to watch some geese grazing. There's a brightly coloured cock pheasant, cautiously nodding and stepping between the nettles.

Beyond the green margin of the flood meadow is the great river, a commercial waterway, carrying goods west to Rotterdam, east to Germany. I'm leaving my bike on the dyke road to walk down the slope and across the meadow to the water's edge. The currents are strong here; they snake across and beneath the grey, frosted-glass surface. It's dangerous! This river is for experienced navigators only.

Look east and west at any time of day and you'll see a few smug, squat, self-sufficient tug boats. They'll be chugging and pushing before them large low-in-the-water barges, sometimes as many as six, in two rows of three. Each barge can carry forty, sixty, maybe eighty containers. Well laden, with much of their cargo below water level, the barges ride so deep that the river spills over their side decks. The tugs are the strong boys, panting and puffing their staccato breaths, exhaling whiffs of diesel fumes. Their relentless tut-tut-tutting can be heard from the dyke road. Each tug has a radar navigation system gyrating behind its bridge, making night-time travelling a safe option. Stalwart, reliable, steady, unsinkable, these are the container trucks of the river; slipping through the water, churning up the foam.

There's one with a grubby Dutch flag flapping at right-angles in the stern, catching exhaust fumes from the engine. The captain's car and bicycle are on the top deck, the curtains are closed in the sleeping cabins and the galley has its door open to reveal a fat chef working.

Belgian Carmen is close behind, followed by German Titan with its maze of metal pipes, like external grey intestines, exposed upon the deck. Within a few minutes they've disappeared. Around the bend in the river is coming the next convoy – tut-tut-tutting!

Back to the dyke road. I need to cycle a bit faster to overtake four elderly cyclists, affectionately known as members of the Dutch grey-wave; riding on their upright bikes and pedalling in slow motion. I'm not old enough to join that group; not yet! Next, a solitary skater gliding on rollerblades, bent forward from the waist, hands held behind her back, her auburn hair waving like the flames of a beacon. Don't I know her? Surely, that's our local magistrate.

It's busy on the dyke road today. Here comes a professional group of cyclists pedalling in unison, quickly and quietly. Seven young men and one young woman, all with tight bums and thick muscular thighs; each wearing yellow and black close-fitting Lycra suits and sleek, grooved helmets; they have just overtaken me in a sigh.

In the distance, I can hear the sad clanging of the cathedral bell; it's another funeral.

I've stopped to watch a circular cloud of starlings bouncing about in the sky and to listen to some invisible busy birds twittering amongst the shrubs, trees and reeds. A black cormorant is circling overhead. Now he has started his descent. Feet in front, he skids along the water before coming to a stop. Landing safely accomplished, he joins the rest of the gang who are parked up around the water's edge. Some are standing statuesque on land, like men in black balaclavas and long, black raincoats; others are waiting on redundant poles which are the remains of an ancient jetty. Many of the birds are holding out their wings as if they are nailed to miniature crosses and looking like an unfortunate band of black-robed martyrs. I wonder about the function of this position. Is it restful? Surely their wings must ache after a while. Is it to cool their bodies after flight or to ventilate their feathers? Or what? Ignoring the need for evolutionary logic, the answer is obvious. The cormorants' position is designed to be a constant reminder of The Crucifixion – they are living black crucifixes!

One of my favourite birds is the heron. There's one standing motionless, guarding his strip of water. Canada geese are fun, plump-bellied like a gaggle of corpulent cardinals they waddle and graze between the meadow plants.

That's a treat! A stork is gliding above me, lazy on a mild thermal. In the next village, there's a large colony. They nest on poles and chimneys and are well fed; over-fed by the human inhabitants. So comfortable are their lives that some of these birds resist their natural instinct to migrate, to travel south for the winter months. They stay, to be looked after by humans.

Look out! An uncertain ewe is on the path. 'Move your arse, you stupid animal. Can't you see me, don't you hear my bell?'

To avoid a collision I dismount. I'll wait for the silly animal to move out of my way. After going this way, then that, she finally decides to move off the cycle path. A herd of cattle are standing shin-deep at the river's edge. They look like an idyllic scene from an old painting by a Dutch master.

Onward! Pedalling slowly, I pass a line of ancient willows, cropped and stunted. Some are leaning off centre, on-guard like a band of drunken soldiers with curled up hedgehogs for hats. Sometimes when the river is high, these trees have their lower trunks in the water; but not today.

I'm nearly at the town. There's a small harbour here, where old and new boats are moored. The road slopes and I cycle fast while passing the nineteenth-century ferry house where once passengers waited to be taken by boat to the other side of the river.

Here I go! Through the fifteenth century brick porch, the entrance to the old city. To one side we have the fine wine and spirits shop belonging to Bert de Lange and to the other is the elegant antique shop belonging to my wife. Next-door is Harry's cycle shop. He's a helpful and friendly man. I like Harry! I've bought all the family bicycles from him. He's also sold me several onderbroeken; you know, those awful tight-fitting undergarments with a great padding between the legs; they're supposed to stop the discomfort caused when layers of material are squashed and rubbed between the saddle and one's nether regions. My wife won't thank me for telling you that she has purchased several of these unflattering items in an attempt to have an easy ride!

Just a little further to go; 200 meters the wrong way down a one-way street. I love the way these old houses look as if they are leaning on each other for support. They've been carefully renovated: bricks repaired and pointed and woodwork restored and painted to a high gloss finish. Only colours from a limited range are permitted on these houses: beiges, light browns, creams, and what the Americans call 'Charleston Black'. Around The Square and in the adjoining streets, many of the old houses have been converted into shops. I'd like to live inside the old city wall, but it's so expensive here.

Finally, I've arrived in the inner city. It's taken me an hour.

This morning twenty tables with their chairs have been set out on the terrace in front of the café in the Town Square. Now I've parked my bicycle and I'm looking for somewhere to sit. I can see a few customers I know. I won't join them. Today I prefer to sit by myself. I want to write about my journey; I need to have something for my journal.

Look at those gabled houses opposite. It's hard to believe that some of them date from the sixteenth century. A few still have redundant external pulleys on their top floors. These were once used for hoisting large objects up to different levels and in through the removable windows, because traditional Dutch staircases were always steep and narrow. There's the tobacconist's shop on the corner; I don't go there any more. I gave up smoking many years ago. Is that building sloping off-centre more than usual? The one next to it has a commemorative plaque bearing the name of a famous family. Who were they? Can't remember. I'll look later. Then there is another elegant, three-storied house. The ground floor is used by the optician. Next-door is my bank.

I'm ready for a coffee. This table is wobbly. Before the waiter puts the cup down, I'll ram a beer mat between the cobblestones and the table leg. Where's my notebook? Which pocket did I put it in? Found it. I'm ready to do some writing. There's Joost Kuijpers in his paint-splattered jeans and T-shirt crossing the Square. I expect he's going to the supermarket. As usual he's in a trance. No, he's seen me, and I receive a wave.

There's a classic picture: an elderly Protestant woman, wearing a cautious, long, grey skirt and high-collared grey blouse. She is wheeling her black oma-fiets (grandmother's bicycle) across the Square in front of the café. She has her shopping in a willow basket. Her long, grey hair is twisted tightly into a knot and fastened at the nape of her neck. She looks pale and serious. Her beauty regime of carbolic soap, water and no make-up has given her a translucent complexion. On Sunday, she'll probably wear a black hat, a black dress and walk with her sombre-clad husband to their local church.

I inhale a whiff of smoke from a nearby cigar. Its owner and his wife are sitting together, but apart, at the same table. Staring in different directions; have they nothing more left to say to each other? Perhaps they are stuck in a marriage with nowhere else to go.

Delicious! I'm sipping my double espresso. I love its bitterness; I hate the brown dishwater which the English call coffee. I feel 'at home' in these familiar surroundings. The young waiter leaning on the beer pump at the counter is watching me. Perhaps he is wondering what I am writing.

Hans van den Elsen

Father Joseph and Father Mimo

Two priests, vowed to a life of celibacy, were making a pilgrimage to the shrine of Our Lady of Fatima. They came to a wide river where they met a beautiful young woman who wanted to get across to the other side but feared that if she tried she might be swept away by the strong current. The elder of the two, Father Joseph, offered to carry the young woman on his back and take her across the river. The younger, Father Mimo, was surprised, even dismayed by the offer, but followed as his confrère waded through the water with the woman's arms around his neck, her body pressing against his back and her legs being held by his arms. It was a treacherous venture and once or twice the old priest stumbled on the rocky bottom of the riverbed. Having reached the other side, Father Joseph set the young woman down. She thanked him and the two fathers went on their way. Father Mimo was obviously disturbed by what his colleague had done in being so close to a woman, feeling her body, touching her legs. After they had walked five kilometres, he turned to his companion and said:

'Joseph, how could you pick up that woman and carry her across the river?'

The old priest looked coolly at his companion and said, 'Unlike you, Father Mimo, I put her down an hour ago!'

Anonymous

General De Gaulle

My neighbour, Herbert, has a French bulldog which I call 'General De Gaulle'. The creature is overweight and stiff, either through lack of exercise or through arthritis. His daily public appearance lasts about fifteen minutes, when he waddles with stiff hips, and probably painful paws, on his daily lavatory excursion. Every morning at about 8.30, Herbert puts on a heavy jacket, as if he is planning a long walk, ever optimistic that the General will join him. The man leads the way and the dog walks at a discreet distance behind his owner. It is as if neither wants to be seen walking with the other. My neighbour looks as if he would like to disown this non-dog-like creature. Whatever happened to his dream of a strong, virile companion running after a ball and able to walk long distances?

De Gaulle moves like an old man who has been sitting in his favourite chair behind the geraniums for too long. This little outing helps neither his mobility nor his disposition. The dog walks fifteen metres to the end of the street; another eight metres take him across the main road and onto the roadside verge. Due to recent excavations, the turf has been removed, leaving De Gaulle with plenty of freshly-dug muddy soil for his ablutions. He sniffs around to identify his favoured spot and takes up a position to do his business. Unfortunately, lack of exercise has caused the General to become a little stubborn in his motions. During this public performance, his owner remains a good five metres away, looking more as if he were waiting for a bus than waiting for his dog to crap.

De Gaulle then moves onto lavatory site number two and there defecates with a lot of effort. Herbert, who was obviously watching out of the corner of his eye, probably recognises that the beast has ended its daily ablutions and he tentatively starts to walk up the gravel path towards the park where, incidentally, there is a very smart hedge-enclosed grassy area specifically for doggy poos! It is just fifty metres away from the General's favoured roadside stop. What's more, our local authority has recently provided bins which dispense brown plastic bags especially designed for owners to pick up the warm droppings of their canine companions.

Herbert, who has newly converted to safeguarding the environment – he does his bit to save energy and recycle rubbish – feels not inclined to avail himself of this innovation. He leaves the General's 'messages' to be collected by the 'pooper scooper', a small tractor which arrives weekly to clear away the animal debris.

De Gaulle is not fooled by his owner walking in the direction of the public dog lavatory. Now that he has opened his bowels, no purpose would be served by him going any further up the path. He turns around and waddles at a slightly faster pace in the direction of his home. Is it the call of his comfortable basket, the promise of a pleasant meal or a lighter feeling around his rear end which speeds up his return home with his master obediently following him?

Piet van Rijn

A Coat of Many Colours

After my father died, my mother made a jacket for me using small pieces of fabric from his suits, shirts and ties. I think of it as my coat of many colours. In total she used over 200 sections of cloth. Each one was cut out to form a perfect square or rectangle, and then hemmed by hand, before being machined together. Sitting at her sewing machine nearly all day, it had taken her three weeks to make. The patches are mainly dark colours: browns, greens, greys, and blues. They blend together comfortably. The jacket is edged in black silk made from a shirt which my brother brought back from Italy for the old man. The garment was never worn and it remained at the bottom of a pile of clothes, still in its original cellophane bag, until my mother used it for this jacket. She cut the shirt into diagonal strips to make a binding, which goes around all of the edges. The jacket is kimono style. It wraps over in the front, unisex style, left or right. Originally, it had a silk belt but I have replaced that with a rope tie.

My coat of many colours hangs behind the door of my study. Sometimes I wear it when I have been sitting at my desk for a long while and I feel cold. I like to look at the different shapes and recognise some of my father's old garments and the remnants of a duvet cover which we had in our house in the 1960s. When he died, I felt too distressed to handle any of his possessions. Later I told my mother to dispose of his clothes. Thankfully, she ignored my advice. Instead, several months later, she removed a selection of my father's jackets, trousers, shirts and ties which were still in his wardrobe. Using a large pair of dressmaker's scissors, she cut pieces from several garments. I thought cutting up his clothes and making a jacket would be a great emotional experience for her, but she remained with dry eyes throughout.

I love this old jacket. My wife says it is becoming dirty and I should get it cleaned. I am reluctant; some of the pieces are delicate and could be damaged. The smell of the coat, the smell of my father, might be lost.

I like to touch the squares cut from his old grey suit, which he wore every day towards the end of his life. They remind me of the way he sat in his favourite chair reading the paper, smoking a cigar and drinking his coffee. There are three squares from the pinstriped suit, which he had when he was the head teacher of the local primary school. On both sleeves there are some pieces from the dark blue suit which he bought for my sister's wedding. My mother had chosen the material which, my father said, irritated his skin. Apparently, after the wedding, he refused to wear the trousers again.

The material from one of his favourite shirts is there too – the one with the unfashionably large collar. On one pocket is a section of a tie, which his niece gave to him. It shows herons in flight. My cousin thought my father would like it because he enjoyed watching these birds on his bike rides along the dyke. On the other pocket is a figure of a woman – a 1940s pin-up – a piece from an old tie which a British soldier had presented to him at the end of the war. He never liked it and it remained forgotten at the back of his wardrobe.

I often wear the jacket when searching for a solution or seeking new ideas. I think of what my father might have suggested to me. At other times, I wear it just to feel comfortable and to marvel at my mother's creativity and her great ability to recycle materials. Sometimes I pull the rope belt tight around my waist and drift away into my private world.

Since my mother's death two years ago, there has been a box of her clothes in our attic. My wife has been telling me to take it to the recycling bins outside the swimming pool or to Piet's Kringloopwinkel. I am not ready to do that; not just yet. I wish my mother had taught me how to sew, so that I could make a patchwork garment out of her old clothes

Titus Dekker

The Story of Nezel, the damselfly who did not want to mate

Having grown tired of chasing and devouring small water creatures in order to satisfy its insatiable appetite, the damselfly followed the instinct to move into the next phase of life. It climbed out from the pond and attached itself with insect 'super-glue' to a reed, where it sheathed its body in a delicate nymph case. There it remained for several weeks, looking dead. However, inside a great transformation was occurring. The insect was redesigning itself from a water-based, squashable, segmented nymph with two simple eyes and gills like paddles for breathing and propulsion into a grown-up, air breathing insect with a brand new streamlined, three sectioned, hard cased body with two sets of aerodynamically efficient wings, massive eyes and a sexual identity. This was Nezel. She was a female with all the right bits and pieces to be a prolific egg layer.

Whilst inside her little changing-room she heard other damselflies talking. They were discussing the previous stages in their lives and agreeing that they had now reached the climax. This phase would be short but exciting. They would mate and produce the next generation. One male said he had already coupled with a female. He kept hold of her until the eggs (he called them his eggs) were safely deposited on the underside of a lily leaf. Since then he had eaten a good feed of gnats. Now he was ready to find his next mate. Nezel was horrified at what she heard. She wanted neither a short life span, nor a mate. Is this all there is in life: eating and procreating?

With that uninspiring thought, her nymph case split and her new body came out into the world; crumpled, wet, but perfectly formed. Her wings were creased and not fully extended. A transparent liquid began to pulse through her lace-like veins. Slowly, by hydraulic pressure, her wings expanded. Excess moisture evaporated and her body became firmer and took on the colour of her species.

When they are dried out, most damselflies fly away from the water and concentrate on becoming sexually mature by eating and frequently shedding their skins, before returning to a pond or stream for mating. Nezel did not fancy doing that. She was not hungry and felt drawn in another direction, which took her first along a stream where she saw both dragonflies and damselflies mating. She was horrified to see how in both species the male grabs the female around the neck or head. Often he remains in that position even when she is laying her eggs. Nezel thought that practice was barbaric.

Then her travels brought her to a small pond. There were no damselflies to be seen, but near to the pond was a huge creature. He was waving his arms in order to deflect an attack of gnats, which were biting him. Nezel flew through the swarm, catching some of the little biters in the small net apparatus beneath her mouth and frightening away the rest. She perched on a reed and settled in the sun, aware that the large animal was watching her, but she was not afraid. The animal was a man; a famous artist who had been successful with his pop-art pictures in the 1960s. Although they now fetched good prices, they belonged to other people and he no longer profited from them. Nobody seemed to want his recent creations. He had lost his flair and inspiration.

Nezel made this pond her home. The artist became intrigued by the damselfly. He made sketches of her body and her antics. He took photographs with his high-powered lens camera. Tentatively he began to paint. First, he produced very realistic pictures of his pond with Nezel perched on a bent reed. Then he became more creative and adventurous, reproducing sections of her body, magnifying them, and creating patterns inspired by her details. He observed her from every angle. Even the most abstract of his pictures contained some reference to Nezel. She became his inspiration, his trademark, and very soon people were pleased to buy his work – even before the oil paint was completely dry.

Nezel stayed around the pond. There was plenty to eat and at no time was she aware of eggs developing inside her. One misguided male had clasped her around the neck; she was not interested and he let go. The artist became an expert on damselflies and dragonflies. He learned that adults of Nezel's species do not over-winter. His damselfly would die at the end of the summer. He could not face the prospect of finding her dead body floating in his pond. Before the end of her season, he left for South America.

Through his painting, he had earned more money than he could use. Most of it he gave to a small village in Brazil, which needed irrigation and water purification equipment. The gift transformed the life of the villagers who were thrilled when their benefactor visited them to see for himself the improvements. Thanks to his donations, their crops thrived and the giant dragonflies, which had disappeared, returned and had begun to lay their eggs in the mud at the base of the village's pineapple plants. He took many pictures and drew and painted this species. However, even the most exotic dragonfly could not replace the inspiration which Nezel had been to him. He had many images of her, both from his artwork and in his mind. He hoped they would remain sufficient inspiration for him to continue his painting when he returned home from his tour in the spring.

The artist knew that the damselfly eggs, which are laid late in the previous season, hatch in the following June. Within a week, the nymphs would be propelling themselves through the pond chasing food. They would shed their skins several times before they were big enough to emerge from the water and fix themselves to reeds and make their cases, in which the miracle of metamorphosis would rework their bodies.

However, before any of the nymphs in his pond had emerged from the water, a fully grown damselfly appeared and perched on the reed where Nezel usually sat. She had exactly the same marking. When she flew, she swooped and dived in a familiar way. She did not fly away when the artist came near to her. He was convinced that this was Nezel. She had over-wintered to continue being his inspiration. Much to his delight, the artist went on to paint this special damselfly at his pond for many years. Through the sale of his pictures, he was able to help more villages in different parts of the world.

Perhaps Nezel defied her genetic instructions and lived on beyond her season to discover, in becoming the inspiration to an artist and great benefactor, that there was more to life than eating and procreation.

Huub Schevers

My Mother's Possessions

I have two things which once belonged to my mother: a box of trinkets and a photograph album.

I had looked at the contents of the box once, shortly after my mother's death. The sadness of her departure was too sharp for me to appreciate just what my sisters had selected for me as my inheritance. Now I am opening the box again. My first impression is the smell of old, sticky, unloved things. The sour perfume pricks the back of my nose and will probably stay there for the remainder of the day. Inside there is one piece of jewellery, a small gold cross which I never saw my mother wearing. I think she owned several crucifixes. She was a religious woman. Next, a jagged-edged picture of a wedding group and a sepia snap of a young man in priest's clothes. Some old coins and a small suede pouch of buttons are tucked in a corner. Last is a small leather case containing a stiff, silk, black handkerchief, home to a tiny tooth and a lock of hair. I feel sad, not at the death of my mother, that is fading, but by what remains of her in these few possessions. To have nothing would be better than this collection of useless trinkets.

The second item of my heritage is this old photograph album; it smells musty. As I pick it up, I feel a film of greasy dirt on its cover. I flick through the black pages. Many of the old photographs have been removed. One remaining snap is of me at a birthday party. Someone has cut out my face, so that my headless body remains. I feel upset. Who did that? The culprit was in a vicious mood, because the angles of the cut are jagged and hurried, as if done in a temper. The cutting instrument has damaged the page underneath. Fortunately, there are some pictures of me with my parents. There is one of my first day at school. It was taken in front of the old abbey building, there is a horse and cart in the background and a very young looking Father Antonius is standing beside me in the foreground.

Paul Bazelman

Love Smoking

I relinquished my single self, my free spirit, my creative soul, my sensuality, my sexual freedom, my unique spirituality, my risk taker's instinct, my familiar habits, my comfortable ways of living and my indoor smoking. I let go of some good friends and said goodbye to a lot of fun.

I traded that in for love and for living together.

I compromised in order to get along. I heard the directives, the embargoes, the orders, the protocols, the no-go areas and the forbidden fruits. You implied that this was the way I should demonstrate my love. I complied, extinguished the flame of my passion, and put out my fags.

I was the flexible one who made all the adjustments. By the tone of your voice and the expressions of your face, I learnt what was in order and what was out of order. You had the jurisdiction, the sovereignty. In agreeing to your terms, I sold my soul to the devil, hid my cigars – and all for love.

I was tolerant, open-minded and easygoing; but that was not enough for you. Living as a couple, loving as a couple required certain rules, your rules. In that way I have become a passive companion, having opted for a quiet existence of domestic obedience. I have traded a bright life for predictable monotony, which you persisted was healthy.

From the first day as a couple, you insisted that there should be no smoking in the house or by the garden door. No smoking near an open window or standing on the front step in my morning gown. No throwing the cigar ends behind the lavender bush or over the hedge into the street. No smoking near you when out walking or in a restaurant. No smoking in other people's houses, even when everyone else is. No leaving cigars and lighter on tables or shelves. No asking you to buy me cigars when you are shopping or to bring some from the airport. No kissing after I have just smoked, unless I wash my hands, clean my teeth and use a mouthwash. Yes. No smoking!

Like my cigars, my burning desires have been stubbed out, extinguished and in their place is dull, predictable life.

Anonymous

The Dutch Barn Reading Club

Guess what the beasts are discussing tonight?
Yes. 'Animal Farm', in Dutch translation.
Kuke-le-ku!
In English for the brighter creatures.
Cock-a-doodle-do!
And as for clever clogs Pig, the book's proposer,
he's read it in both languages, twice over.

Ram is tonight's host; the venue is the old Dutch barn.
One of his ewes has arranged refreshments.
First to arrive is Pig walking on two legs,
with his English copy under one trotter
and the Dutch translation under the other.
Peacock and his good friend Crow follow,
they fly in together, having shared a library copy
and discussed their views.
Predictable, critical croaking Toad is next.
Then secretive Rat who is pleased to escape his sewer
and become a respectable animal for an evening.
Always late is adorable Cuckoo who has the unfortunate habit of
using the nests and stories of other birds.
Finally Cockerel, who is equally as proud and
beautiful as Peacock, arrives to contribute his missionary call using
his uncertain poetry:
Kuke-le-ku.
I-am-warning-you.
Cock-a-doodle-do[2].

[2] Cock-a-doodle-do is the English version of *Kuke-le-kuke,* a cock crowing

Reading books on a certain private subject,
is-not-good-to-do!

The animals sit in a circle, cackling, crowing, croaking,
and bleating, about what has been happening on the farm.
When Peacock, the self-appointed leader
(no other creature wants to be in charge)
stands up, opens his fan and switches on his vibrating feathers,
the others know that it is time to cease their inconsequential chatter,
and proceed with the real business of the evening:
Reviewing 'Animal Farm'.

First to honk – sorry I mean squeak – no sorry –
I think you would prefer me to say speak – is Pig,
the book's proposer who obviously likes the book's content,
primarily as it reinforces the commonly held belief that
Pigs are extremely smart!

Next is dark, sleek, modest, black Crow,
a member of the most intelligent species of birds,
succinct and insightful in his analysis.
He informs the others that this is not a story about the supremacy of
pigs, but a metaphor, describing the consequences
of the Russian Revolution.

The royal family was deposed,
Communism replaced the Tsars and the proletariat became
equal – at least at first.

Iridescent Peacock, bright and articulate, continues
his deeper analysis, in a rather lengthy explanation;
prior to which he opens his fan in preparation for his deliverance
and then closes it during his final paragraph.
Then Ram, who rarely grasps the nuances of well

crafted prose or the underlying meaning of anything... says
he likes the way the animals flocked together to help each other.
However he did not care for the ending,
when the pigs moved into the farmhouse,
because they are such messy creatures.
He suggests that sheep would have been a better choice
because they have fine woollen coats.

Toad puffs himself up, inflates his amphibian lungs,
blinks his bulbous eyes and croaks his usual
two-toned, caustic commentary - they've heard it all before!
His predictable censure, his disparaging disapproval
and red-pen assassination,
this time of Pig's recommended book.
The porker squeaks and shrugs his bacon shoulders
as if to say he does not care a ham for Toad's opinion.

Artful Rat has accessed a copy of the book by travelling
along a sewer pipe beneath the Waterstraat and entering
the bookshop via a disused mouse hole.
For several nights he had popped into
Boeken Boeken, to have a read.
He thinks it a sad story of an unnecessary struggle by
a group of large and foolish animals to take over a farm from humans.
As a member of a high class group of vermin,
he says that it is possible to utilise every aspect of
human corruption and abuse
and still lead an easy life.
Provided that one is discreet, practically invisible,
one could live within a few metres of humans
and they would never know.
Successful? Certainly!
Just look at our population.
We breed like humans!

When all of the animals have expressed their opinions,
there follows a cacophony of animal noises,
screeching and squeaking in 'fifty different sharps and flats'.
When Peacock opens his fan, the caterwauling ceases.
Each animal is directed to award the book a score.
From Toad comes the lowly 3, while Pig gives the maximum 10.
Crow calculates and records an average of 6.5
for 'Animal Farm'.

Ram, more famous for following than leading, surprises all of the animals by being the only one to make a suggestion for the next month's book. He says he is tired of reading English novels and wants to propose one written by a fellow citizen; actually, it is a female writer, a ewe, Buttercup Schaap – whose book is called 'The Vegetable Way'. It is an autobiography, a popular genre amongst the group, of a sheep, who lived a long, happy life on a farm where they had ceased growing animals and started growing vegetables.

Kuke-le-ku.
I'm tired of lamb stew.
Cock-a-doodle-do.
Vegetables are good for you.

The animals conclude their evening by singing the club song to the tune of Wilhelmus (the Dutch national anthem) and afterwards they fly, run, amble, hop and some walk home on two legs.

Written by Mol (Mole)

Hans van den Elsen

The Common Toad

Hiding, hoping that he won't be discovered, squashed between the flower pots, concertinaed into the smallest space, his bent back legs folded tight; the toad sits - solitary, motionless, and afraid. His brown, lumpy skin is the colour of earth; his warts like mini boils are designed to be his camouflage. But I've seen him and his grey and white underside. Neither his reputation nor his two glands, which produce a foul tasting and irritating secretion, will afford protection for him at this moment. He thinks he is hidden; but he is exposed. How could any female find this unfortunate amphibian handsome? His broad, flat, fat body, short toes, webbed hind feet, together with his shining snout, orange and black eyes with horizontal pupils make him more suitable for a witches' brew, rather than the apple of a princess's eye. Looking at his shape I can see he is an old one, perhaps in his last season. Maybe he is already impotent. Or can he manage to copulate one more time? The spring in his step has worn away. He has lost the elastic in his vital parts. Most likely, he will die of fright in his hiding place, rather than leap away to safety.

He is hoping that the footsteps, my footsteps, have not seen him. Partly hidden under the incinerator with his Mona Lisa smile, he is breathing hard. His eyes like beads show the fear he feels. He has the appearance of a slimy creature. But that's an illusion; he is cold and dry with an unfortunate reputation. Now he is vulnerable. How easy it would be to crush him with just one step. I could shatter his bones, squash his flesh and ruin his name. Like a man caught without his trousers, he stays motionless, hoping that nobody will see him. But I have caught more than his reflection. How could I expose this little helpless creature? Unkindly I have penetrated his territory. I'll just pass by and pretend that I have not seen him there. He probably wishes that he could retreat to his winter hibernation, his hole in the ground; but there is no way of finding the earth in this paved garden. He is trapped. When I am gone he can only crawl away. I expect he wishes he had slept the summer through and missed out this time completely – toads can do this.

Once he was a virile beast with a great capacity to mate. Amongst his species the male is smaller than the female. I guess that makes it easier for him to sit on her back and there, without tenderness, to ambush his mate, take her from behind and copulate. In his vice-like hold he takes his Venus and she succumbs in order to get the mating over as quickly as possible. In his birthing pond, the next generation is spawned and he becomes sexually redundant for another year. It might have been his last shot.

A male toad rampant with a season's sperm can become confused when offered a stick or a finger. He will wrap himself around either and it takes some time for him to discover that he is not grasping a female. Some never do. Another phenomenon is a group of male toads all clinging together in a sort of group orgy; it is not all 'straight' in the amphibian kingdom. Males have a special call if they wish to be released from a perversion of other male toads. The females are silent. What's more, toads are sit-and-wait predators with long, sticky tongues attached to the front of their mouths; ideal for catching insects, larvae and slugs. But I don't think this male will be catching any flies. He is more concerned not to be seen. All toads regularly shed and often eat their skins. Is that like eating your own words? Thousands of kilos of toads are squashed every year on the roads. I will not add one more to that pile. I am trespassing in his garden. I will pretend that I have not seen him.

Rat Face

The Feminine Portrait

Portraits and landscapes are painted in different languages. I consider the latter to be my mother tongue, but occasionally, for business purposes, I go abroad and have to deal in the foreign principles of portrait painting. Like most portrait painters before me, I set out to flatter and please my commissioner - after all, he or she is paying the bill. I know the end result has to be unrealistically attractive. I will do my best to suggest and even enhance the sitter's good qualities, whilst underplaying those not so attractive features.

In a landscape picture I make stationary anything which is moving. With people, it is different, faces are changing all the time and their bodies are rarely motionless. The challenge is to capture the essence of a thousand facial movements and the flavour of the person in one snapshot pose. When first meeting new subjects, I sometimes feel a bit unsure about how I will paint them. It is important that I get to know people and observe their expressions as they reveal themselves to me in our conversations. Mostly I warm to my subjects after we have talked. It helps me paint if I like the sitters or admire some of their features. I find out about their lives and see if they can tell me something about themselves, which they would like me to convey in their portraits, including any requests they have for the setting. Usually, after I have had a conversation with a sitter, that person appears entirely different, often more attractive or softer or kinder than in my first impression.

I was asked to paint a portrait of a person who wanted to look very feminine. That was an unusual request, which challenged my capacity to analyse that quality and convey its essence on canvas.

The sitter chose to wear a long, black, silk dress for her portrait. The bodice was tight and the skirt fell into soft folds from her hips to the floor. It was a beautiful garment and fitted her rather square body very well. The dress had long sleeves, emphasising her angular shoulders, which she hunched when she talked and pretended to flirt with me. She had long arms and rather large hands with bright red nails like talons. The dress had a split down one side and her right leg was visible up to the thigh. She wore high boots made of shiny leather, which I thought emphasised her rather large feet. Her hair was a mass of blonde, shiny curls. Her make-up was heavy; bright red lips, thick dark lashes and a blusher, which drew attention to her high cheekbones.

Even though I asked her to remain still, every now and then she insisted on pushing out her lips, as if getting ready to give some imaginary suitor a kiss. She filled the studio with her expensive perfume, which lingered long after she left. In our conversation prior to the painting, she said that she had always wanted to look very feminine but, because of her height and shape, that was impossible. She asked if I thought I could make a beautiful portrait, even though she realised that she could never be a gorgeous woman. So, working from several photographs I modified and softened some of her features in the same way that portrait artists have done for hundreds of years and I gave her a soft smile. The end result was a flattering likeness. When she saw herself in my picture, she said that I had done exactly what she wanted.

Joost Kuijpers

The Old Table

Dear Great Table,

You have been in my family for more than one hundred years; filling various rooms in different homes and, leaving no space for much else. On you, shopping has been unpacked, food prepared and meals eaten. Newspapers, books and letters have been read. Accounts, homework and greetings cards were smartly dispatched. Adults have leant on you, children sat beside you and babies were laid sleeping upon you. Sewing machines have made clothes and typewriters tapped messages on top of you. Once, a motorbike engine was dismantled on your surface. At your side grazed knees were washed, splinters removed and once an injured crow was given first aid. Money has been counted, spent and lent and coins tossed. Cats sharpened their claws on your legs. Once our Dutch Barge dog jumped up on you and stole a steak from a shopping bag. Turkeys have been plucked on your top. Fine wines, vintage ports and mature whiskeys poured, spilt and stained your deck. A thousand cups of coffee made temporary warm circles on your surface.

Generations have sat around you through sad, happy and ordinary times. Anniversaries, successes and births were celebrated and disasters, losses and deaths have been mourned alongside you. People have shed tears, shared secrets and negotiated deals next to you. My father wrote his Will, Simone felt her first pain of labour and Ome

Willem died, sitting up close to you. Between your legs little children played and made imaginary hiding places with their friends; lovers carved their names in your secret places.

You have been taken for granted, abused, stood upon, pounded, misused and undervalued. We complain that you are too large, too heavy and too old – yet we utilize every one of your square centimetres, by placing hats, coats, shoes, computers, toys, bottle openers and umpteen wine glasses on your great surface. You stood firm when thumped by a drunken attack and you absorbed a wife's tears and witnessed her loneliness when the man she once loved departed and a ghost took his place.

Tell me Great Table, which artisan made you, cut and planed you, fixed your top to your legs with wooden pegs? Who scrubbed you, raked out your grain and dug stale food from your ridges with a pin or a nail file? Who else has fallen asleep, resting his head on you? How many games of cards have been played on your deck and who won when toy armies waged war upon you? What family secrets have you kept to yourself? If only you could tell me.

Bert de Lange

The Glass Waiting-Room

I am Mehmet, the cleaner; the old Turk, they call me. People here think I don't understand Dutch. Many behave as if I am invisible. Humiliating? Yes, it was at first, but now I am used to it. In Turkey, I was a respected teacher of several eastern languages; in the Netherlands I am a cleaner. The work is tedious. I never liked filthy things. But here I am, dealing in dirt all the time. I clean the train station, the Adult Day Centre and the offices of St. Mary's Foundation. Most people in these places ignore me. A consequence is that I hear them talking about other people. Gossip they call it. May Allah forgive them. I could write a book about all I see and hear, but no-one will believe it.

The meeting of the three most talked about people in our town took place the other day. It was 10.00 in the morning and I was cleaning the waiting room on the south platform. The railway line is high and the waiting-rooms are up four flights of stairs from street level. The architect used a lot of glass throughout the building. You get good views of the countryside and you can see who is arriving at the station.

From the waiting-room, I spotted the English woman at the ticket machine below. It is surprising how many so-called intelligent people have difficulty with this apparatus. The English woman made several attempts to buy a ticket; even from above I could see her face red. Eventually the ticket appeared. Then she ran up the four flights of stairs to the platform. She moved quickly for a woman of her age. What is her age? Opinions vary – somewhere between forty and sixty. By the last flight she slowed down, and then she stopped for a moment to hold onto the handrail. I could see her breathing hard. By the time she reached the platform the train was just moving off. She watched it for a moment then went at ease into the waiting room. She would have to wait half an hour for the next one.

I am sure the English woman does not realise how often she features in gossip. People talk about what she wears, they criticise her grey hair. They say that she and her Dutch writer husband have a troubled marriage. I think people find her intriguing; even a bit mysterious. They do not talk to her, but about her. Luuk, the pastor, has even written about her in his private book. I read a few lines from it when I was cleaning his office. His notebook was open on his desk. He wrote some things about the English woman that would be considered a sin in my religion. No man of my faith would admit to having daydreams about a woman other than his wife. I had read it before I realised what he had written – may Allah forgive me.

There are metal seats along two sides of the waiting-room. Most people sit down and pick up one of the free Metro papers to read. The English woman remained standing, looking out of the window. Was she just staring into space or was she looking at the huge Dutch sky, the great brown river winding its way to Rotterdam from Germany, busy with slow moving cargo barges, or at the windmills? I like those windmills. These days they are turned by electricity. Maybe, like me, she is still amazed by the hundreds of bicycles which are parked every day at the station. We all have bicycles in the Netherlands, even us foreigners. The English woman looks quite at ease on hers.

I have to confess I was curious to know what she was doing on the north side of the line. She usually travels in the other direction to Eindhoven, where she works in an English School. With my cleaning trolley I made my way to the corridor outside the glass waiting-room. She seemed to be sorting through her pockets. As I pushed my broom along the floor, I could see that she was counting some notes. I did not recognise them; perhaps it was English currency. Then she studied her passport for a while before replacing it in her pocket. I did wonder if she was going to England, but she had no luggage.

Then bad luck happened because Gerrit arrived at the station, pulling his usual crate of lagers on top of a shopping trolley. He always uses the lift to the platform. It stinks of stale urine and flat lager. Like a tomcat, he marks his territory by peeing in the lift and scattering his empty beer cans. When I first started cleaning here, I felt sick at this smell and tried to get rid of it. Now I don't bother. I often see Gerrit at the Adult Day Centre. He is the town's vagrant who sleeps rough in the porch of the Post Office. He travels up and down to the next station without a ticket. They say his mind was damaged after an accident. I do not think he has ever been violent but I know he can be frightening. Sometimes he shouts, especially at the women.

As soon as he saw the English woman through the window of the waiting-room he began to moan at me in Dutch, as if it was my fault that she was in there.

'What's that woman doing in my waiting-room? Everyone knows that I like to have the place to myself. Mother is a whore. I want the whole world to know that God will punish her and all the other whores. This English woman is a whore too. The people at the Day Centre talk about her. She's married to that writer man. He's crazy. But they don't send him to be with us.'

Gerrit opened the waiting room door and pushed in his shopping trolley. The English woman turned to him and smiled. Gerrit continued to moan.

'How dare she smile at me? I wish she would piss off.'

I have heard that the English woman does not speak Dutch. But she seemed to understand the message and she came out into the corridor and to my surprise she began to talk to me. She asked me if

I spoke English. I nodded. She asked me if I was married. I told her that my wife had died ten years ago. May Allah give rest to her soul. She asked me if I thought it was wrong for a husband to insult his wife. Then she wanted to know if there were some things that I would not have tolerated from my wife. She gave me no room to answer her questions although I was prepared to do that; I have quite clear ideas on the subject. Instead, she continued talking. I was amazed at how open she was, to me, a stranger. She said she was leaving her Dutch husband. She was tired of arguments and insults. The final wound had been inflicted on her that morning when her husband said she was crazy – as crazy as Luuk, the pastor and as mad as Gerrit, the vagrant. She was returning to England. She had some money and her passport.

To my surprise the English woman returned to the waiting-room and, ignoring Gerrit, she continued to look out of the window. I went on with my sweeping then I noticed Luuk arriving at the station. Gerrit had seen him also.

'Is that Luuk I see parking his bike below? He's got that bloody flute. He plays it everywhere. I don't want to talk to him because he starts his preaching – he thinks I don't know God, but I do.'

The three most talked about people in town were now there together in the waiting-room. Luuk lifted his hat in greeting and then got out his flute and began to play a Dutch tune. This seemed to quieten Gerrit who drank one of his lagers almost in one swallow; then he tossed the can in the corner of the waiting-room. Luuk turned to the English woman and played an English song, which is sung at football matches. He smiled at her, and then asked if she was travelling to Utrecht. She nodded.

The train was approaching the platform. Gerrit moved his trolley out of the waiting-room. Luuk lifted his hat in an exaggerated gesture, indicating to the English woman that the train was in the station. Up until this moment I thought, even hoped, that she was going to change her mind about leaving the country. In my opinion, wives should stay with their husbands. But she followed Luuk and got into the train. Automatically the doors began to close. Then she held her hand against the door, it stopped moving, the safety mechanism caused it to open again and she got off the train.

The doors closed again and the train started. I got a small look at Luuk's surprised face. The English woman walked back into the waiting-room. There she picked up Gerrit's discarded lager can and put it into my big bag of rubbish.

'How could I explain to people why I was leaving?' she said, as if I had asked her a question. I wanted to reply, but the words would not come to my mouth. Several times I appealed to Allah to give me some wisdom to impart to the English woman, but nothing came forward onto my lips.

Huub Schevers

CHAPTER 11

The Anniversary Meeting

It was in the midst of a lot of merriment and bonhomie that Milo arrived with his guitar, 45 minutes late. It had been agreed that as part of the celebrations, he should provide the music for a small sing-along. He had produced some song sheets. There were good songsters in the group, but also one or two who did not enjoy community singing. Huub always maintained that Milo's guitar, like Paul's singing, was out of tune.

Titus greeted Milo and explained about the absence of Father Antonius. He said that the taxi driver had delivered the booklets, which people were now reading. Milo was given a glass of champagne and a copy of the Anniversary Book. He was then directed to a seat between Joost and Bert. Both said hello, then turned their backs on him and continued their interrupted conversations with others. In that moment Milo felt resentment for the group. They were ignoring him. He had rushed away from a Turkish family who revered him. After giving a music lesson to their son, the grateful family had insisted that he took a coffee and a piece of sweet Arabic cake. He knew it would be impolite to refuse. This had made him late.

He quickly decided that he did not agree with the members' decision to continue with the celebration without Father Antonius. It was disrespectful. They should have waited for his recovery. He felt harassed. He had rushed to get here and they could not even be bothered to wait for him before distributing the books, drinking too much champagne and eating most of the food.

It had been past 7.00pm when Milo had returned home from the Turkish family. Only then had he remembered the club's decision that they should wear dinner jackets and bow ties for this auspicious occasion. He raced upstairs and located his suit, which he had not worn for a year. It had fallen from its hanger and lay at the bottom of his wardrobe. Then he searched for a proper white shirt. He did not have one, so he retrieved a creased black shirt from the bottom of the dirty linen box. The iron seemed to take ages to heat before he could press the shirt, including the underarms, which emitted a strong smell of several days of body odour. There was not a suitable bow tie amongst the few he owned. From his son's wardrobe he pulled out a bright red one, without noticing the grease stain in the fabric. Later in the evening Huub, charged with several glasses of champagne and white wine, loudly drew attention to the spot.

Milo sipped the champagne; it had a sour taste. Looking at the Anniversary Book, he decided that the front cover was insignificant. He was not going to like it, just because it was obvious that everyone else did. Did he want to read this book? Not particularly. He finished the champagne and then Titus brought him a plate of hors d'oeuvres. Lamely he flicked through the book; the paper and the format were attractive and he could not deny that he liked the illustrations. He recognised the artwork of Joost. Turning to the index, he looked for his contribution. There was no mention of it. Did he put his name to his writing? He could not remember. Maybe his work was under one of the anonymous pieces. He decided not to panic but to take his time and to read all the contributions until he came to his own. Titus offered him another glass of champagne. This one tasted more pleasant.

Once or twice in the reading of the book, he shook his head, as if disagreeing or disliking what had been written. He sighed audibly at the story about Father Joseph and Father Mimo. In the last entry, 'The Glass Waiting Room', he decided that he recognised himself immediately in the character of Luuk with the flute. More importantly, it was clear that his piece – his masterpiece – about a very significant experience, his dismissal from the abbey school, had not been included. He called over to Piet who was sitting at the opposite end of the table.

'Where's my piece of writing?' Milo said, endeavouring to speak above the noise of the others.

Piet cupped his ear, suggesting that he could not hear Milo. Then he shrugged his shoulders as if to apologise, smiled and then looked away. However, Titus had heard Milo's question and decided to avert any disputes by calling the meeting to order. In the absence of the priest, he had devised a programme. When the members were quiet, he spoke:

'Now that we've all had a chance to read our book, I think we should proceed with the evening's business. I suggest we start by giving our impressions about our book and then we could share our experiences of keeping a journal and say if we think it has added to our understanding of Father Antonius's work.'

Fully charged by two glasses of champagne, Milo's anger shot into his words. In his view the time for gentleness had passed. His campaign against certain negative aspects of the club needed a different approach. He rose to his feet.

'I'd like to say a few things. First, I want to know why the account of my boyhood experiences, which I submitted in good time, hasn't been included in this book. Secondly, since I've been ridiculed in the story about the glass waiting room and the absurd joke about the two priests, I want all these books withdrawn. I've a right to do this. I wasn't asked if I minded being used as a character in some of these stories.'

The first to reply was Piet. 'I'm very sorry that you're upset. Father Antonius sent you a letter explaining why your story wouldn't be used.'

'I did not receive any letter. To where did he send it? How did he know my address?'

'He sent it to me in a sealed envelope. I did not read it but sent it on to you,' Piet said.

'I never got the letter. Are you sure it's not still sitting amongst that pile of correspondence on your desk?'

'No, I definitely sent it,' Piet said.

'I'll come back to that.'

Then turning to Huub, the author of 'The Glass Waiting-Room', Milo said:

'I think you should have shown me your story first before you submitted it. How would you like to be ridiculed in the way you've done to me? What's more, you have shown Gerrit in a bad light and you haven't even bothered to change his name. It is obvious that the English woman is based on Paul's wife and I am sure he feels embarrassed about that. You have humiliated our Muslim brothers and sisters. You have ridiculed their serious efforts of integrating in our society and minimized their contribution to our local community by mentioning only a simple station cleaner. I wonder why it is that the world considers The Netherlands as a tolerant country. They should listen to some of you complaining about the Muslims who live in our town. I feel ashamed of your attitude. On the subject of faith, all of you were quick to ascertain each other's backgrounds – Protestant or Catholic, you wanted to know. Yet there is not any mention of the Christian faith in any of these stories. Ever since joining this club I've seen it as my role to remind you of your Christian beliefs in the choice of books and your comments about them. And by the way, Huub, the Turks don't keep referring to Allah in the way you suggest.'

Huub replied, 'Milo, I wasn't writing about you. I saw Gerrit at the station and from that I made up a story. The starting point for the English woman was someone I met in Majorca twenty years ago. You're not the only musician in the world. I have great respect for the Turk who cleans the station. I often talk to him, his wife works for me. In their country they were both teachers.

Remember, I ran a cleaning company and for years I was a cleaner myself. At heart I'm still a cleaner. In my mind I had the Turk as the hero of the story. Didn't you read Caveat Lector in the Anniversary Book?' And becoming sharp, Huub said, 'I had expected you to be a more sophisticated reader. What exactly in the story offends you so much?'

Milo ignored the question, turned away from Huub and back towards Piet.

'I want to know why my story wasn't used. Compared with some of the nonsense that has been printed in this book, mine is a very good piece.'

'I think you need to speak to Father Antonius about that.'

'I can't because he's not here,' Milo shouted.

'This is not something to discuss now.'

'That's your opinion. I want to tell my so-called friends my story.'

'Not now, Milo,' Piet said.

'Will they be shocked? Do you know the reason why my story wasn't printed?' Milo asked.

'I don't know the details. They were contained in the letter which was sent to you.'

'Which I did not receive,' Milo repeated.

'All right, which you didn't receive. Apparently, in your story you made reference to a number of people; the editors decided this could be construed as offensive and inaccurate. You were asked to submit something else.'

'Really, I thought you didn't know the details of the letter which was sent to me,' said Milo raising his voice. 'It was offensive for me to mention the names of two of my school mates from fifty years ago, but not offensive for me to be ridiculed in a story?'

'I did not edit the Anniversary Book. We all agreed from the outset that this would be left to Father Antonius and his brother. They've had a lot of experience in these matters. I'm sure that they were only doing it to protect you. I'm sorry that your letter went astray.'

'In the absence of the written story, I will tell you all what happened to me when I was at the seminary where Father Antonius was a teacher.'

'Not now, Milo. It's not appropriate,' Piet pleaded.

'It's much more appropriate than what some of you have written.'

Titus rose to his feet. 'Calm down, Milo. Maybe you could give us all a copy at the next meeting; we can decide if we think the brothers made the right decision not to print it.'

'Oh no! You're not fobbing me off like that. I've read what all of you have written, now you can hear my contribution. Sit down and shut up!'

Titus looked astonished and sat down and Joost said, 'I hope you're not going to ruin our evening.'

Milo ignored him, realising that not one of them would have the courage to leave the room or to physically restrain him. He sat down, drank the rest of his neighbour's champagne and began his story.

'This is what happened to me when I was twelve...'

Milo knew his story by heart. He even got a few laughs about the brother peeing in the pot. However, nobody laughed during the remainder of his tale. When he had finished, the group was numb. Some looked angry, perhaps because Milo had criticised the contents of the book and had spoilt the atmosphere of their party. There was a long silence as if each man was considering his response; but no-one had the courage to give his opinion. Perhaps some agreed that the story should have been printed; others may have felt a great deal of sympathy for Milo; it could even be that someone had experienced abuse himself – but no-one spoke.

At last Titus said, 'You shouldn't have told us that. The editors were quite right not to include it in our book. Now you have burdened us with your story.'

'Have I made you feel uncomfortable? Good! At least I've been honest in my story; I haven't hidden anything. Not like the rest of you hiding your secrets.'

Huub interrupted, 'Now sit down and shut up, Milo. Haven't you said enough already to ruin our evening?'

But Milo was undeterred, 'You, so called respectable gentlemen. It's about time you all woke to what's happening in the real world. This Anniversary Book is pathetic – stories about dogs, tables, flies, and toads. Toads!' As he repeated the last word, he turned around to face Paul. 'I note that in one of the stories, the female toad is called Venus. That's an unusual name for a toad and an unusual name for a Dutch woman to have. I don't know anybody else in our town whose name is Venus, apart from your wife. Did you notice that, Paul? Did you wonder why someone had used your wife's name in a story? Did you wonder whether he was really describing a toad or was it another animal?'

Paul shrugged his shoulders, but no-one understood from the gesture if he had seen the connection.

'Did you spot that the writer didn't have the courage to sign his own name? He called himself 'Rat Face'. Perhaps you saw that there was a rat in another piece of writing. I'll leave you to figure out that mystery for yourself.'

Milo turned his back on Paul and addressed the rest of the group.

'This is just one example of how these fables are façades. Just like the façade of your respectability. Consider those secret activities, which are not so respectable; all those things which you think are private. You're wrong, they're not. I know that most of you are involved in some form of perverted activity. I have warned you often enough in the club, but you have ridiculed me.'

Hans said in a serious voice, 'I don't think you should say any more.'

'Why not? Afraid of what I might reveal about you? I've plenty more to say. Did you know that one of your members has a collection of pornographic books and pictures in a private room in his house, that another does business with transvestites and prostitutes, a third collects erotic objects, another is an adulterer and one person has a penchant for dressing up in his wife's underwear? That leaves two. There is one amongst you, a so-called Christian man, who abandoned his parents when they needed him most.'

Then Milo, looking fierce, slowly turned to face the last member of the group.

'Finally I come to you, Piet – likeable, unreliable – rarely do you complete the club's books. The story of the bulldog is not yours. Bob, the taxi driver wrote it. Tomorrow you'll return to work and find my letter from Father Antonius at the bottom of a large pile of correspondence. You're a cheat and a liar.'

Everyone looked uncomfortable. It was as if Milo held them by their pubic hairs. They were his prisoners. He knew that not one would dare to speak for fear that he would elaborate still further details of their secrets. Now it was time to remind them of his mission.

'I've tried to help you consider some of the real issues in our local community; you wouldn't listen. I suggested that we invited people from different backgrounds to join us. I put forward the Muslim banker who works in Den Bosch; you rejected him. Then you refused to accept the Muslim doctor who has a practice in Dordrecht.'

Huub reacted. 'We turned them down because we already had eight members.'

'What's the difference between eight, nine or ten members? Your houses can all manage a group that size. You said no to Bob van Dillen, the taxi driver. He's an avid, intelligent reader, but you decided that he didn't fit with your out-dated classification of respectability.'

'Milo, he was never properly proposed and, when he was mentioned in passing, you were critical about him,' Paul protested.

'I certainly wasn't. Yet another lie against me.'

Several people looked in the direction of Titus as if hoping he would take control of this situation. He was usually in charge for most of their evenings and they were in his house, but he was staring straight ahead.

'The truth is that you think these men were not good enough,' Milo said. 'I think they were too good for this club.'

He pushed his chair back and stood up. 'I'll not be returning for further meetings. You can find someone else, someone respectable to fill my place.'

Milo paused. Was he hoping for a response? No-one spoke or even looked at him. He departed, leaving his guitar in its case on the side cupboard.

The room was silent. After a few moments, Titus tried to encourage people to return to the programme, but it was difficult. They tried unsuccessfully to regain the high spirits of the evening. Bert plied them with more wine but that seemed to intensify their low mood. They decided that they would finish the meeting early. It was impossible to tell what anyone was thinking; everyone looked sad and stunned.

Piet, embarrassed and upset, stood up and left the room. He went into the hall and opened the front door to see if the taxi driver had arrived early to collect him. The limo was not there. As he shut the front door, the wife of Titus came into the hall. It was the second time she had heard the front door opening and closing. She was still wearing her long black dress but now she had an old cardigan draped around her shoulders. Instead of her best shoes she had put on some scruffy yellow house shoes and a pair of socks. Piet glanced down at her feet.

'I've been reading and I got cold', she said, as if Piet was asking for an explanation of her strange apparel. 'Is everything alright?' she asked.

'I was looking to see if my taxi had arrived.'

'Has the meeting finished?'

'Yes.'

'That's early,' she said. 'I thought the celebrations would go on all night.'

'No.'

'Did I hear some shouting?' she said.

'A few people got upset.'

'I hope that didn't spoil the evening. Titus was looking forward to this so much. He enjoyed preparing the room and he wrote a lot in his journal. He wouldn't tell me which piece he had submitted. He said I should have to wait until the book was launched. I am looking forward to reading what he wrote. I asked him not to write anything about me.'

'Yes,' Piet replied as if he had not heard what she had just said.

'How many pieces of your writing are in the book?'

'Mm.' Piet hesitated. He debated whether to say none, one or several. If he said the latter, he could claim that he had created some of the stories written anonymously. But was it worth telling more lies because, within a short time, Titus would be giving her his version of the evening? The magic of the anniversary had been lost. The book had shrivelled and the knot in the celebration balloon had been undone; the air had escaped in a loud fart and only a spent latex skin, looking like a fragile distended stomach, remained. The disasters of the evening were pressing on Piet's shoulders and the contents of his stomach were preparing themselves for expulsion.

'Excuse me. I feel ill,' he said.

Titus's wife gestured towards the cloakroom across the hall. Inside Piet was sick. Everything had been too much to digest. He washed his face and hands thoroughly and looked at his reflection in the mirror – blood-shoot eyes, drops of water on his hair and down the front of his shirt. In the distance he heard a loud bang. He wondered why anyone would be making such a noise at this time of the night. He could hear voices. Were they laughing? What exactly were they doing? It sounded as if something was being smashed.

He brought both hands up over his mouth and let out a long sigh. 'What have I done?' he said, talking to his reflection in the mirror. 'Yep, I read Milo's letter but I thought I'd sealed it up again and sent it to him. Didn't I? Not sure now. How did Milo know that the taxi driver had written the story of 'General De Gaulle'? How did Milo know about the others? Who told him that one of the members has a collection of pornographic books and pictures in a private room in his house? I wonder who that is. Is that really true? He said another does business with transvestites and prostitutes; perhaps Bert sells them wine. Huub is probably the one who collects erotic objects. I don't know who the adulterer could be, but I can imagine Titus dressing up in his wife's underwear. I have no idea which one abandoned his parents when they needed him most. I don't believe any of it.' Piet splashed his face with water again.

The doctor's wife returned to the party room – no-one was there. Perhaps Titus had taken them all into the conservatory for a last drink. She started to clear away the debris when she too heard a loud noise, like a car knocking into another one. She looked out of the window. The street was empty. She continued gathering the glasses. Someone had left a copy of the Anniversary Book. She opened it and got as far as the index when there was another loud noise. She turned her head in the direction of the sound. Perhaps Piet had fallen down in the cloakroom or broken its large mirror. She left the party room and walked into the hall. Outside the lavatory door she called to Piet:

'Everything all right?'

'I'll be out in a moment.'

She walked towards the back of the house, looking into all the rooms on either side of the hall. Nothing had fallen down which could have made that noise. Then there was a third crash, which seemed to come from the kitchen. She walked to the door, tried the handle, but it was locked.

'Are you in there, Titus?'

'We won't be long.'

'What are you doing?' She turned the door handle again. She could hear voices and jangling noises. 'Open this door!' There was a pause, a few more unusual noises, then Titus turned the key and opened the door. Around her kitchen table stood the remaining members of the Reading Club each holding a glass. Milo's guitar case was in the middle of them.

'Why did you lock the door?'

'A mistake. I'm slightly intoxicated.'

'What's Milo's case doing there?'

'He left it behind. We want Piet to return it. Where is he?'

'Throwing up in the lavatory.'

'He's had too much,' Huub said with a short laugh. The doctor's wife shot him a glance and he became serious again.

'What's been going on here?' She could feel a dubious energy in the atmosphere and she was sure there were fine particles of dust floating in the air. She could smell something had been happening...but what?

'I'll tell you later.'

She looked at Bert and remembered the time in his wine shop when they had stood beside his great table. He had kissed her hand. She had thought about that for days afterwards. Surely, he would tell her what had been going on while the kitchen door had been locked. Her eyes sought for an explanation, but he shrugged his shoulders slightly, as if to say, don't ask me.

Titus gestured towards the door. 'The gentlemen are just leaving.' Some put their glasses on the table and others finished their drinks. One by one, they made their way into the hall. That left the two of them in the kitchen, 'You go to bed,' Titus said to his wife, 'I'll clear up later.'

'No need, Mieke's coming tomorrow. She'll do it.'

In the hall, the remaining club members said thank you and goodbye to the doctor's wife. No-one gave her kisses. She shut the door and went upstairs.

When Piet came out of the cloakroom, Titus was standing in the hall holding Milo's guitar case.

'What was all that banging?' Piet asked.

'Nothing. It was coming from the neighbour's house.'

'I would complain if my neighbour made such a noise at this time of night.'

'It's alright; it won't happen again. Is the taxi driver taking you home?'

'Yes, I was looking to see if he'd arrived.'

'Can you ask him to deliver this to Milo?' Titus asked.

'Certainly,' said Piet, taking the guitar case.

'I've put a copy of the booklet inside.'

Piet went to open the case.

Titus stopped him. 'Don't open it; I had a job to shut it with the book inside.'

CHAPTER 12

One End

The taxi driver collected Piet from the doctor's house and was very interested to know how the evening had gone. Piet spun an answer which was fairly neutral.

'I liked seeing my story about General De Gaulle in print. I noticed that you didn't change anything I had written,' said the taxi driver.

Piet lied, 'I told the club that you had written the story.'

He wanted to avoid a conversation about the evening's events. 'Could you deliver Milo's guitar?' he said, lifting the instrument a few centimetres off his lap to indicate what he meant.

'That's not like Milo to leave his instrument behind.'

'No, it isn't,' Piet said.

'I've never told you this before, but Milo helped me and my wife through a very difficult time. I was traumatised when my shop closed. Had dreams and flash backs. Thought I was going mad. Milo supported me and guided me through this and back onto the road and into this taxi. My wife's never enjoyed her work; she's often troubled by what she sees and hears. Milo counselled us. He's a good listener. Nothing we couldn't tell him. Call him 'our father confessor'. Not to his face, of course, he'd be embarrassed. You know, he's a modest man; a good man.'

Piet was tempted to say that Milo had been one of those who had objected to the driver becoming a member of the Reading Club, but he thought that there had been enough revelations for one evening.

'Want me to collect you, third Thursday of next month for the Reading Club Meeting?' the driver said, hoping that Piet would remember his promise to apply again for his membership. Bob assumed that now the club knew he was the author of 'General De Gaulle' they would welcome his attendance.

'No,' said Piet, whose thoughts were on the events of the evening. He realised that much of what he had told the taxi driver during these journeys to and from the Reading Club venues had been repeated, with some additions, to Milo. He also worked out that the driver and his wife in their counselling sessions had passed on information about everyone in the Club. How else would Milo have known about everyone's secrets? And were they true?

'Is the Reading Club stopping now it's ten years old?' the driver joked.

'No, but we might be doing things differently in future. We haven't decided yet. I'll let you know if I require a lift. Thanks for delivering the guitar.'

Bob parked the limo, picked up Milo's guitar and knocked on the front door. Milo answered and gestured for him to enter. But the driver remained on the door step and handed over the case. Immediately Milo felt that it was heavier than usual.

'There's a book inside. It's got my piece in it, about the bulldog,' the driver said proudly.

'How was Antonius when you left him?' Milo asked.

'Bad.'

'Will he survive?'

'Don't know.'

'I really wanted to see him tonight,' Milo said, 'that man is an inspiration. I wanted to tell him that his book has given me courage to continue with my mission. No matter how many times I am tested, I'll never be crushed.'

'That's positive,' Bob said, wondering why Milo had used the word 'crushed'. He knew Milo was not always popular with some people, but who would want to crush him? Bob did not know how to further respond, he was unaccustomed to his counsellor talking about his own feelings in this way. 'I've got to go now,' he said.

'Won't you come in for a while? Milo asked. For once he wanted to talk and to have someone listen to him. 'Let me make you a coffee.' He longed to tell Bob what had happened in the club, to describe how he had been ridiculed in two stories, to express how he felt when he realised that his account had not been printed.

'I haven't really got the time', Bob said.

'Only for ten minutes.' He had never pleaded with the driver before, but he wanted to explain why he had persisted until the club heard about his dismissal. He wanted to describe how he had alarmed them all by telling that he knew about their secrets. Finally he wanted to justify why he had said farewell to the club.

'Sorry, I can't stop,' Bob said, and turned away from the man who had spent hours listening to him and his wife, who had been there when they both cried and felt wretched about themselves. Milo had been kind and sympathetic. He had encouraged them to feel positive about themselves and to be careful in their dealings with others. He had prayed for them and with them. Now when he wanted a little bit of understanding for himself, Bob denied him; three times.

'Are you sure? I want to talk to you.'

'Can't stop. Have a client waiting.'

Milo closed his front door, put the case on the table and opened it. Inside was a pristine copy of the Reading Club Anniversary Book, uncomfortably nestling on the debris of his shattered guitar. His prized possession was no longer a musical instrument, but a tangle of loose strings and jagged splinters – like a mangled heron kicked to death by cruelty, crushed and then jammed into an unlikely coffin, too small to take its rearranged carcass.

CHAPTER 13

The Other End

On the 11th of August 2008, Thomas sat at his brother's desk in the Belgian monastery and studied the picture postcard of a small Dutch island where Antonius had spent his holidays for the last ten years. Thomas had never been there himself, preferring something a bit more cultural, rather than windy beaches and cold bike rides. The message on the back read:

'Don't worry, I will not embarrass you by attending your final service. Thank you for showing me that a good friendship is as precious as a Catholic marriage. With love W'

Thomas had not the energy to think about the meaning of the message or the sender of this card. He opened the NRC, his preferred national newspaper, and wondered whether he should have written something. He knew the editor personally; he would have surely given him some space. Thomas thought about his brother, beginning with their recent meeting in which they discussed the Tenth Anniversary Book. Then he recalled previous arguments and disagreements about their writing projects.

Usually Thomas was irritated by his brother's willingness to accept inferior, juvenile, silly written contributions. There was a lot he did not like about Jean-Pierre (he did not always use his monastic name). He had mostly disliked his brother's quiet belief, his stubbornness not to be persuaded by the geological evidence about the age of the world or by the conclusions of Charles Darwin concerning evolution; surely that would be sufficient proof for the simplest of men. But no, Antonius had held fast to his belief that God was the Creator of the world. Antonius did not mind that Thomas was outraged by the cruelty of the God of the Old Testament and appalled by the atrocities carried out by various Churches in the name of the Almighty.

'Yes,' he had said, 'we haven't always got it right.'

Antonius had smiled when Thomas complained about the Church's view about contraception, abortion, euthanasia and the exclusion of women from the main roles. The priest would say he was aware of all of these things and then add:

'But the Church is more than the sum of its histories.'

Thomas remembered their battle when Antonius was writing his book. Helping his brother achieve a best selling autobiography was like extracting a reluctant bad tooth which had been set in a stone gum. There was a lot of shouting, resistance and pain for both the patient and the dentist.

Thomas lingered for a moment in his thoughts about his brother's book. The end result had probably been his finest achievement as an editor. He had transformed a priest's journals – disjointed, long-winded, repetitious meanderings of an intelligent child (in his opinion priests never grow up), a child whose mind had been narrowed by a peculiar formation. He had changed it into something that many people wanted to read. There, in his brother's stories, both men and women found themselves, their beliefs, their troubles, their inner thoughts. The disclosure of some of Antonius's reflections nearly resulted in him being excommunicated. The Church was not quite brave enough to do that. Forty, even twenty years ago, there would have been no compunction in expelling the wayward priest.

Thankfully, he was simply moved out of the country to a monastery whose abbot was more progressive and less threatened by the pen of an intelligent priest. Writing his book was surely Antonius's greatest labour of love. Thomas hoped his brother's confrères would some day be insightful enough to recognise this achievement. They should! Antonius had prophesied the decay of the Dutch Catholic Church, should it choose to remain unchanged. He predicted that the 'grey wave' which filled the pews, along with the ageing confrères who occupied the choir stalls of his former abbey church, would die out; become extinct. Where were all the youngsters, children and babies; the next generation to be the congregation of Mother Church? In 'Priests Dying' Antonius had challenged the old ways. He had beseeched his Order, 'Think about the future before all your priests are dying!'

Angry with his brother – yes – angry with himself – yes; Thomas bloody was! In addition, there was another feeling that had been with him for two days. It seemed to occupy his whole body; it lay particularly heavy in his chest area and filled his head, pressed against his eyes. It had replaced his appetite and had kicked him in his gut. His energy had gone, his sharpness had retreated. Something hard had left him, and a vulnerable tenderness had taken its place. His voice had adopted a new quality and the world was different. His usual vocabulary was absent. In fact there were no words yet given to describe how he felt at this moment about his brother. In the past, things had been different; they played by the rules of their upbringing, and their unacknowledged bond was parked somewhere outside of conscious awareness. Now that bond felt a hundred times stronger and was sitting centre stage. It had seemed to Thomas superficial, inadequate, inappropriate and far too personal to attempt to set down or speak out this overwhelming presence, which was pressing to spill over the top and out of him. To say he loved his brother was completely inadequate. But, if only he had said that; just once.

As he had turned to page 17 of the newspaper, he read the

name 'Otto Spoorenberg'. This was occupying most of the 24 different-sized boxes, each edged with a thick black line. The largest one contained words of praise and of missing him, from Otto's wife, children and grandchildren; a small poem had been included. A famous cheese company was well represented. There were messages of condolence from directors, managers, union representatives and ex-colleagues; each in their own box and every one commenting in a different way about Otto's fine qualities and long service between 1950 and 1995. In addition, there were messages of condolence from his Rotary Club where he had been president; from his Golf Club where he had been captain and from his Wednesday billiard pals with whom he enjoyed some good times. The neighbours in the cul de sac where he and his family lived for the past 25 years, paid for a small box and a few lines. In total the family, friends and colleagues of 78 year old Otto had purchased twelve boxes in which to say their farewells.

'God! Why am I reading about Otto Spoorenberg?' Thomas said to himself.

In the bottom right hand corner of the page, beneath a discrete tribute to André Henkel, G.P. was the smallest black edged box. Thomas took a deep breath and a swig of whisky and read the only published tribute to his brother.

There were no words of warmth, no expressions of missing, and no recognition of a life dedicated to God and Antonius's religious Order. Absent were tributes to his long teaching career, his pastoral work, his parish work, his leadership of a well established

> *We belong to mother earth*
> *But death comes to us all.*
> *We are born unequal*
> *But we die all the same.*
>
> **Fr. Dr. Antonius van Aken**
> 1928-2008
> Ordained priest 1952
> Teacher 1958-88
> Transferred 1999 to
> Sint Jan's Abdij
> La Rochelle, Belgium,
>
> *May our brother be granted*
> *eternal peace*
>
> 9th of August 2008

historical society or his various published articles. There was no mention of his book – his best selling book, which had touched the hearts and minds of both Catholic and non-Catholic readers.

Perhaps another whisky would stop the world from appearing like a shivering old movie, a view through a dirty window or a reflection in a distant mirror. Another swig might stop sounds from being too loud and voices saying irrelevant things. Another drop might rearrange his organs, stop his head from pounding and return his spirit to how it once was. With his appetite gone, food tasted revolting – Thomas felt sick. God! He craved for an anaesthetic, something to sooth his feelings. Another glass of whiskey; it smelt like vomit; he drank it anyway. It soaked his tongue, washed through his mouth and awoke the back of his throat. The alcoholic vapours went up his nose and there they bumped into another smell, which had been up there for a few days. It was the smell of old peoples' homes, geriatric wards, crematoria, dead men's clothes. It was acting as a filter, a gatekeeper. No sensation passed into his interior without diffusing with or rebounding against this smell. It had penetrated his skin, got up his nose and changed his insides. It had altered his impressions of his outer world. It was the smell of death; his brother's death.

For the layout of the announcement, the Belgian abbot Dr. Anselm van de Vijver (or more likely his assistant), had chosen the standard format, which had probably been used many times before in commemorating Antonius's predecessors. To those familiar with the meaning of certain phrases used by the Church on such occasions, it would have been clear that in the word 'transferred', disgrace was implied. Thomas knew that it meant that Antonius's Dutch abbey had not approved of his book. It had upset his abbot and the diocesan bishop and both dignitaries wanted to be rid of the author. Putting Antonius in a remote Belgian monastery to care for its archives was their best way to deal with the old but recalcitrant priest.

When the Belgian undertakers had sought approval to bring the body of Antonius to the Chapel of Rest in the Dutch abbey, they were denied. When Thomas in his turn contacted the Dutch abbot to explain that his brother had wished to be buried there, he was denied. Even when the abbot was reminded that Antonius had lived in the abbey for fifty years, that he had been a loyal priest who had given all the proceeds from his best selling book for the restoration fund, the request to be buried in his favourite cemetery was denied. In total three times.

On 12th August 2008, Antonius van Aken was laid to rest in the grave yard attached to Sint Jan's Abdij, La Rochelle, Belgium.

Epilogue

Thomas had asked his family not to attend the funeral because he wanted to be alone. After the non-inspirational service in the Belgian Abbey Church, he had stood nearby as six confrères lowered the coffin on strong ropes and he watched while the mourners each dropped a handful of soil into the grave. He refused to do that himself because he loathed the hollow sound of the earth landing.

The burial party left for the Abbey refectory for the customary funeral cake, black coffee and inconsequential conversation. But Thomas lingered a while by the open grave. For a last time he peered down at the coffin, which now had an uneven layer of soil scattered over its top, and for a moment he thought about Antonius's body trapped inside the wooden box. Looking up to the monastery he noticed that the last mourners had gone inside, just a few smokers stood by the front door. No, he did not want to join them. This place was not where Antonius had wanted to be buried.

Bending down he picked up the floral tribute, which he had brought with him that morning. The perfume of the roses cleared his head a little. He turned away from the grave and, still holding the flowers, walked towards the car park where he carefully placed them on his back seat. As he opened his driver's door, a woman in the car next to his got out of hers. She was also holding a bunch of roses.

'Can you tell me if there are any mourners still in the grave yard?'

'No. I'm the last. I've just buried my brother.'

'Are you Thomas?' she said tentatively.

'Yes. Do I know you?'

'No. My husband and I were friends of your brother. We used to take our holidays with him. I'm Wilhelmina Claveaux.'

'W?' Thomas asked.

'How did you know?'

'I'm guessing. I found a postcard from you amongst my brother's letters.'

'He asked me not to come to his funeral. Aren't you going to join the other mourners in the Abbey?' Wilhelmina looked towards the abbey.

'No. I can't stand any more of this ritual. I'm taking my flowers to the grave yard in the Dutch Abbey where Antonius wanted to be buried.' Thomas pointed to the tribute in the back seat of his car.

'Will you take mine too?' She held out her flowers for Thomas to take.

'Come with me.'

'Yes, I would like to do that. I'll follow you.'

By mid afternoon, the couple were near to the Dutch monastery. They stopped in a layby where Wilhelmina went into a wood and returned with two branches. Then, using Thomas's penknife, she cut them to size and bound them together in the form of a cross. Later, in the abbey cemetery, they located the next empty burial plot, where Antonius's grave should have been. Thomas hammered the rustic cross into the ground with the back of his shoe. Wilhelmina placed her unmarked flowers in front of it. Crossing out his original message on the card attached to the roses, Thomas wrote:

338

May your spirit stay here for ever.
Love, Thomas.

Bending down he carefully placed his flowers next to those of
his companion. A tear moved slowly down his cheek. Wilhelmina
took his hand in hers and Thomas looked down at the make shift
cross and smiled.

Acknowledgements

My husband Jean, writer of seven non-fiction books, inspired and encouraged me to create this novel. I used stories from his life as the starting points for different characters and various settings in my book. Having read and re-read its drafts he must surely know the contents by heart; yet his interest has never faltered.

The account of the relationship between wheelchair-bound Salvador and Joost, his art teacher, was inspired by my friends at Waveney Sailability who have shown me that a disability does not have to be a barrier to sailing through life.

I created the story about Bert's father as a way of explaining the deaths of two friends who were heavy drinkers; one had Korsakoff's disease, the other one's mind and vital organs were poisoned by alcohol. Reading 'No Big Deal' by John Coats and speaking to my friend Daniel Farnham from the 'East Coast Recovery Project' in Lowestoft, enabled me to change my mind about my friends' deaths. It was more helpful, although still sad, to believe their demise was the result of their addictive illnesses, and not their selfish behaviour. I am grateful that John allowed me to use his book as the basis for the one which Bert recommended to the Reading Club. Thank you also to my friend Carole Creed who shared with me her experiences of caring for her late husband James. Her story was the inspiration for the dialogue between the parents of Bert de Lange.

The following people have read different drafts of my manuscript and offered suggestions and encouragement. I am grateful to Jan Hart, Liz Kent, Meg Edgar, Evert Jan Smeenk MA and Ton Hilte MD. A reader from Hilary Johnson's Agency provided me with some professional comments; her feedback was critical, but proved to be useful in the final draft. Thanks also to the staff at Matador who have carefully guided me through the process of self-publishing. Peter Venrooy, a Dutch artist, created the illustrations and Corey Mateer designed the book cover and my website **www.patricia-vanstratum.co.uk.** Rebecca Moore has been my research assistant.

Some special people; priests, ex-seminary boys, members of a number of reading clubs, authors and strangers I met, all unknowingly provided me with starting points for the fictional characters which I have enjoyed writing about. Thank you all. With words which Huub wrote in the Anniversary book, I conclude my thanks:

'Sometimes people want to find themselves in stories and are disappointed when they are absent. Others look for small parts and are pleased or conversely angered when they think they have been featured. It could be that you were neither my inspiration, nor my starting point, nor the beginning of the person you think to recognise. But does it really matter how the character or the plot were conceived, when the end result is a wonderful story?'